THE
DEAD
BETRAY
NONE

A VISCOUNT WARE MYSTERY

J. L. BUCK

KENMORE, WA

CAMEL PRESS

A Camel Press book published by Epicenter Press

Epicenter Press
6524 NE 181st St.
Suite 2
Kenmore, WA 98028

For more information go to:
www.Camelpress.com
www.Coffeetownpress.com
www.Epicenterpress.com

Author's website: janetlbuck.com

Design by Rudy Ramos

The Dead Betray None
2022 © J. L. Buck

ISBN: 9781942078906 (trade paper)
ISBN: 9781942078913 (ebook)

Printed in the United States of America

Dedication:

To Jeanette, the sister I never had

Chapter One

The thundering hooves of swiftly moving horses echoed through the dense fog. Lucien Grey, Viscount Ware, feathered his pair of blood bays around the sharp curve, the curricle's wheels slipping a brief moment on the wet road. The encroaching trees opened onto a broad misty park, revealing the familiar Doric columns of Baron Sherbourne's yellow-and-gray sandstone manor. Despite the dismal morning, the estate held good memories for Lucien, and a fleeting smile crossed his lips.

Easing the bays to the left toward the stable yard, he brought the light carriage to a halt, and his groom, Finn, slipped off the back to run to the horses' heads. The high bred team danced in place, snorting at the abrupt end to the journey, their hot breath forming tiny clouds in the icy air.

Lucien leapt to the ground, his top boots squishing the sodden maple leaves blown over the cobblestones. He tossed the reins to Finn. "Be good to them. They earned it."

"Aye, m'lord." The small man, somewhere in his thirties, but not much over five feet tall nor eight stone, gave his master a toothy grin and flipped a shock of reddish-brown hair out of his eyes. "Sev'teen mile in a' hour an' a bit more. They be getting oats an' barley for sure."

Lucien nodded casual approval and yanked off his leather driving gloves, using them to brush at the dried road dirt on his multi-caped greatcoat. A burst of rain and sleet from the same storm that must have blown through the baron's estate had caught him on the Great North Road from London.

With a final slap of the gloves, he abandoned the futile effort to make himself presentable and strode toward the country house, his lean, muscled frame moving with the ease of a man used to action. A twinge of disquiet returned a frown to his face, and his eyes narrowed. Four years of clandestine missions in the glittering courts and ballrooms of the Continent—their elegant setting no less deadly than the wretched battlefields—had taught him to trust his instincts, and something was off the mark about this assignment. A part of him had known it since Lord Rothe's man came pounding on his door before dawn.

Lucien's nostrils flared in the cool breeze. Why was *he* sent to investigate a country housebreaking? Rothe had failed to tell him something about the theft, something vital that had captured Whitehall's rapt attention. Lucien had sensed an undertone of anxiety in the habitually composed Marquess of Rothe, the man in charge of the Crown's secret spies.

What the devil had Prinny's War Office gotten him into this time?

Only one way to find out.

Sweeping back his disordered black hair that defied his valet's best attempts to tame it, Lucien cut through the edge of the sculptured gardens. He raised a hand to acknowledge the long-time gardener putting a final prune on the hedges and covering the more delicate ones with burlap, and he noted the faded colors, the leafless branches. The unusual mild weather was at an end. The storm had left behind a nipping cold, a harbinger that winter's harshness was fast upon them.

Sherbourne Manor's side door opened, and Andrew Sherbourne, the baron's auburn-haired second son, stepped out, very much the country gentleman in a brown coat and tan breeches. His lanky form closely matched the viscount's six feet height, and their eyes met in a level look.

"Well, Sherry. Did you arrange this theft just to ruin my evening?"

Sherbourne's hazel eyes lit with humor. "Who was it this time? Miss Haverton, or the Widow Stine?"

"Bite your tongue, my friend. Would you have me besmirch a lady's reputation by answering such an impertinent question?" Banter was easy between them, an upshot of a friendship formed as boys at Eton, fourteen years ago.

"*Pardon me.*" Sherry's playful drawl was more befitting a gentleman of the dandy set than the serious world he and Lucien shared. His voice returned to normal. "Whatever your plans were, I am not at all sorry to see you. Indeed, a most welcome sight." He gripped Lucien's hand a moment and fell into step. "You are earlier than I dared hope. Skefton has been an insufferable carper." He cocked his head, belatedly taking in Lucien's disheveled appearance. "I say, is that mud on your coat? Did you get doused by the squall that passed through here?"

"Not long. Only this confounded fog the last eight miles, albeit the wind cut through me like a knife." Once the storm swept past, a mile or two at their spanking pace had sloughed off the rain and sleet, and the roads had remained reasonably firm due to the long, dry autumn. It was slush thrown by the horses' hooves and the wind that had coated him with dirt and debris.

"The gales rattled the upstairs windows," Sherry allowed, pulling the garden door open. "And brought in colder weather. The ground was covered with frost early this morning." He gave Lucien a shrewd look. "I doubt the storm slowed those bays of yours."

"A sure wager. Not more than a misstep or two." Lucien cut off a satisfied laugh as they entered the manor, their booted footsteps on the dark polished wood of the hallway announcing their presence. He took in the fashionable furnishings and the Persian rugs in the drawing room across from them...and grimaced at the silence. He had expected voices and activity, the usual sounds associated with a houseful of guests. "Where is everyone?" he asked with misgiving. He turned and stared at his friend. "No, Sherry. The three or four coaches I met on the road...do not tell me they were coming from here."

Guilt suffused Sherbourne's face, but he held his answer when the butler appeared. Lucien dispensed with his gloves, beaver hat, and greatcoat, revealing a spotless dark blue Weston coat and fawn-colored breeches.

"I confess they were," Sherry said as the butler departed. "A sorry business, I own, but I could not hold them, could I? Not without explaining yesterday's theft was more than a simple pilfer of baubles. But Rothe would have my head if the truth got out." He waved a hand in exasperation. "I doubt if anything short of violence would have delayed them after the constables came blustering about last evening. It only took the magistrate threatening to call in Bow Street's thief-takers for our guests to show their heels this morning. I wager half of them had not risen so early since infancy."

"He did alert the runners," Lucien said, "but due to the stolen packet, the Crown interceded and sent me instead…putting you at my disposal, I might add. You could have asked for the assignment yourself."

Sherry snorted. "Rothe would have refused. With my family involved, it would be awkward to be in charge. Besides, something tells me this problem may require two of us. Partners once again." He lay a companionable hand on Lucien's shoulder with a lazy grin. "In truth, I would rather have you reporting to his lordship than me."

"Acting the skulker, eh? As it happens, I'm not opposed to a little action. I have felt rather flat of late."

"A sad consequence of war, I think, this constant restlessness we feel." Sherry exhaled a quiet breath and shot a glance at Lucien. "Do you regret refusing Rothe's request to infiltrate the revolutionaries?"

Lucien snorted. "Lord, no. I will not spy on countrymen, no matter how loud and out-spoken they may be."

For four years, Lucien and Sherbourne had served as intelligence officers in England's longstanding dispute with France that began in 1793 with the execution of the French aristocracy and erupted into open warfare after a declaration of war in 1803. Upon their return to England two years ago, Whitehall had quietly recruited the pair to fight against the French threat within England's borders.

A few months ago, Lord Rothe had attempted to extend that secret agreement to include civil unrest, and the two men had turned him down.

"It would feel…I suppose, disloyal," Lucien continued, "to turn around and use the skills gained defending England against our fellow citizens. And I can't deny some of the dissidents' complaints have merit." He gave a careless shrug. "Since we are no longer on official status in the Crown's army, I am content to leave that duty to others who must accept orders or are less particular in their choices. Why do you ask? Have you misgivings?"

"Not a bit. But Rothe was not best pleased. He has kept us cooling our heels for weeks at a stretch, and the inaction has chafed."

"I think he is over it," Lucien mused, as he reflected on his recent conversation with the marquess. "He was not annoyed today. Not with us, that is. Let us make the best of this assignment—although the urgency to recover this packet escapes me—and perhaps he shall find more frequent and challenging uses for our time. By the by, he issued two orders that should aid us. The constables will be dealing only with the village and its occupants, leaving the Quality house guests to our tender mercies. And a unit of soldiers is already out scouring the countryside for the thieves."

"Helpful, indeed. We shall need them all. The thieving scoundrels have had ample time to scatter—going on twenty hours." Sherry shook his head. "I bungled it. I didn't realized how serious it was at first when only a couple of things had been reported missing. We didn't notify authorities or begin a search for two or three hours, and by that time it was dark—"

"This happened during the day?" Lucien asked in surprise.

"Yes, we had all bundled up midday and gone to visit some local ruins, even ate over there. It was cool, but not bad. In any event, it was after dinner last night when people began packing for home before we realized how much jewelry and other property was taken from our house guests. Even then, I wasn't too concerned until Colonel Skefton admitted a war packet was missing from his bedchamber. And that confession didn't come until *after* the constables had come and gone. I'm sure he would have kept it secret, if he thought he could."

"A touchy conversation, no doubt."

"Exactly so." Sherry gave a gruff laugh.

Lucien shot his partner a look. "What is going on, Sherry? The way Rothe and now Col. Skefton are acting, this has to be more than an ordinary packet on troop movements." The message received by the intelligence unit at Whitehall had merely said an intercepted French communiqué in Skefton's hands had in turn been stolen by a house thief. Not a word about the contents. Nothing to warrant the tension lines around Lord Rothe's eyes.

"I wish I knew. Col. Skefton has been evasive over details, but he is nervous, even fidgety, not half as composed as he pretends. And…he attempted to leave before you arrived."

Lucien's steps faltered. "The devil he did."

"Oh, yes. I had to step between him and the door. I reminded him Rothe would be sending someone who would need his report, and he still argued. But…well, I insisted."

"So, where was he going?"

"London, he claimed. Honestly, Lucien, he was acting so odd I was uncertain what he intended. Since that conversation, he hasn't spoken to me."

"Bloody cox-comb."

"He is that, if not more."

Lucien heard the suspicion in Sherry's voice. "You fear he is holding something back?"

"Maybe, but how would I know?" Sherry gave a self-conscious shake of his head. "Oh, I suppose not. I simply dislike the man."

"Yes, well, it might interest you that he has misplayed his hand this time. When I left London, the Home Secretary, the War Office, and Rothe were more than put out by the lack of information. I would swear they know or suspect what was in the packet—and were very keen for confirmation."

"I didn't know anything else to report," Sherry protested.

"Never fear, my friend. Rothe knew the fault lay with Skefton.

The colonel's career would have been better served if he had put his arrogance aside for once."

"Not him. He refused to reveal anything," Sherry said with disgust. "But I agree the packet is something special. Skefton is in a stew over its loss."

Lucien frowned. The colonel's behavior confirmed there was something he and Sherbourne did not yet know. "As well he should be. Even he must blanch at the prospect of facing an irate Lord Rothe, a man not to be taken lightly. Prinny chose well to put the marquess in charge of his private spies."

"That's true," Sherry muttered. "And yet I think Skefton's distress goes beyond that."

As did Lucien...and Skefton was going to tell him what it was.

"So, my friend..." He gave his partner a sardonic look. "Since Skefton is less than forthcoming, and you allowed the witnesses and thieves to gallop away, what do you expect of me?" His tone was teasing, but he was frustrated and cross...not with Sherry, God no, but with Rothe for keeping too many secrets, with himself for arriving too late—and with the members of the ton who considered themselves too superior to deal with the constabulary or Bow Street runners.

As most house parties ended on Sunday, Lucien had known time was short to catch witnesses before they dispersed. He had chafed at the official indecision at the War Office that delayed him and at the constant interruptions that prevented a private moment with Rothe that might have yielded greater information. Two hours later, he could wait no longer. Once on the road, he had pushed his horses in hopes polite society was still abed in the country. His haste—and the stress on his high bred team—had been for nothing.

Sherry's chuckle broke into his thoughts.

"Why, Lucien, I am surprised you need ask of our expectations," his partner quipped. "We depend on you to catch these lawbreakers and recover the stolen belongings...by this evening, if you would not mind." When the viscount failed to reply in kind, Sherry dropped the flippant tone. "I wrote down names and asked a few questions last night. And I compiled a list of missing items, but it may be incomplete. Every one of the bedchambers showed signs of the thieves' search—open cupboards and drawers, clothing tossed about—yet only half the guests reported losses." He shrugged. "I'm not sure how to explain it. They may not have yet missed anything, or they chose not to tell me, for whatever reason."

"Trifling losses, perhaps? A matter of privacy? I doubt it matters." Lucien thought about the scene Sherbourne had painted. "A very bold thief, who made no attempt to conceal his activity. It suggests a hasty, random search for anything of value he could find."

"An attempt to mislead us?" Sherry lowered his voice. "Considering the stolen packet, isn't it probable the culprit was an agent of Napoleon rather than a common thief?"

"But why would an agent waste time ransacking the other rooms? A big risk with little to gain."

"The way I figure it is a French agent or agents followed the packet to the house but knew nothing of Colonel Skefton or where it might be hidden. Hence the rushed and untidy search." Sherry gestured down the hallway. "At any event, we can make sense of it later. It is past time to rescue my father. He has been closeted alone with Skefton for nearly an hour."

Lucien glanced at his mud-streaked boots, scarcely fit for a house call, and released an audible sigh. "No help for it." He turned a right corner onto the connecting hall without pause, for he knew the manor well. Several pleasant holidays from Eton and Oxford had been spent in this household. "Anything special about this weekend house party?"

Sherry shrugged. "It was Mother's idea, but Father has never turned down an opportunity to hunt. She planned a quiet gathering of old friends, but the Selkirks asked to bring their daughter Emily and two female friends visiting from London. Then Miss Hodges-Jones had her great niece visiting. Naturally, mother had to even the numbers with younger gentlemen. That is when I was summoned, and so the party grew, but still small by most standards. The only thing…well, the guest list could be troublesome. Other than locals, the rest were from London and associated with the House of Lords, the Home Office, or Foreign Office, in one way or another."

"Not unexpected considering your father's political connections, but it raises the concern—whether likely or not— that if the French had help with the packet's recovery, it could have been someone close to the government. Rothe is aware."

" Is Skefton under scrutiny? Or that secretary of his?"

"Both. Until we know more, everyone at the manor yesterday is a suspect." Realizing how awkward this was for Sherry, Lucien turned the conversation to less delicate details. "Exactly how many guests is your idea of a small gathering?"

"A mere fifteen. All of them out of reach now, except the colonel and the neighbors. Oh, I forgot Miss Hodges-Jones and her niece. They're still upstairs."

"How many extra servants did guests bring?"

"Two grooms, one abigail, and the colonel's secretary who is also his valet. It made housing and seating him awkward, I can tell you. The other guests shared our regular staff of fourteen and the five villagers hired for the party."

Lucien made a dissatisfied sound in the back of his throat. As many as two dozen witnesses had scattered—to London, to the village, to their own estates. It would mean a slow start to the investigation. Despite this daunting thought, when they reached the study door, he straightened his cravat, brushed back his hair once again, and strode into the room.

The baron and Colonel Skefton both rose. The graying military man, well into his fifties with a weathered face and rigid stance, remained standing beside his chair. Baron Sherbourne— an older, slightly stocky but distinguished version of his son— came forward, smiling and extending a hand to Lucien with a firm grip.

"By Jove, Ware. I lament the circumstances that brought you here, but I am gratified to see you. How is your father? I have not spoken with the earl in a year or more."

"He is well, sir. I am delighted to find you looking the same and will inform him you inquired." Lucien turned to the colonel to cut off further discussion of his father. The baron knew the circumstances of Lucien's family life and still held out hope that father and son would reconcile. "Colonel Skefton."

"Viscount." The colonel's brief bow was stiff.

Lucien had little more than a passing acquaintance with the stiff-necked military man, but Skefton's opposition to the Crown's use of the aristocracy in intelligence efforts was widely known. Despite Sherry and Lucien's four years of service—as well as those by other members of the haute ton—Skefton continued to insist they were ill-suited and under-trained for such missions. It had to make the colonel's current situation most embarrassing. Lucien might have felt compassion if not for the arrogant scowl on Skefton's face.

Lucien returned his attention to Baron Sherbourne. "I beg pardon for coming to you in all my dirt, sir, but I understood the theft of the French document was of some urgency."

"And discretion, surely," the colonel snapped, stepping forward with his chin jutted. "I intend no offense to the baron, but you and I should be discussing this in private."

"I disagree." Lucien spoke before their host could politely acquiesce. "Given his knowledge of his guests, the servants, and recent events, I welcome the baron's insight. Our goal is a swift recovery of the packet, and that does not require a public discussion of its sensitive contents."

Skefton's mouth compressed in a thin line, and Lucien stiffened. He was in no mood for the colonel's supercilious behavior or needless resistance and allowed his face to show it. To his surprise, Skefton acquiesced.

"Very well, my lord," the colonel said, lifting his nose just enough to be noticeable. "I assume you carry the proper authorization?"

"Skefton!" Sherry glared at him.

Lucien's smile froze, his cold, clear voice very much that of the earl's son. "To be sure, Colonel." He ignored Sherry's indignation and quelled his own reaction to the insult. He slid a hand into his waistcoat pocket and brought out Rothe's letter vouching that the viscount represented the Crown in this matter. The letter of authority was intended to put local constables and magistrates at ease, not to verify his status to known associates. Skefton was being churlish.

The colonel perused the single page in silence. When he folded it and attempted to put it in his own pocket, Lucien held out his hand. "If you please, sir. We would not want to lose anything else, would we?"

Skefton flushed, and Lucien tucked the letter away. Without a doubt, Skefton was ill at ease being questioned by someone half his age who not only outranked him socially but was privy to more of the monarchy's secrets than the colonel knew existed. Skefton was assigned to the Alien Office, the publicly-acknowledged intelligence unit inside the War Office and was not one of Prinny's handpicked spies. Lucien suspected it rankled.

Baron Sherbourne cleared his throat and held up a decanter of dark amber liquid from the sideboard. "The hour is a bit early, but I, for one, could use a drink. And you had a long ride, Ware. A spot of brandy?"

"With pleasure." Lucien approached his host, and his smile returned. "My throat is rather parched, sir."

Tension in the room eased a degree or two.

When the men were seated with glasses of the baron's very respectable, if not entirely legal, French brandy, Lucien listened to the events of the last two days. Except for a question now and then, he didn't interrupt until they were finished.

Setting down his empty glass, he rose, paced across the room, thinking over all he'd heard, and stopped to lean a shoulder against the marble fireplace mantel.

"So, as I understand it," he said reviewing the facts aloud, "our soldiers shot a French courier on English soil, found the packet, and knowing Colonel Skefton was visiting Sherbourne Manor, they brought it to him early yesterday morning." He shifted his gaze to the colonel. "And you hid it among your belongings with the intent of delivering it to Rothe *after* the house party was over."

"The delay was not for my convenience," Skefton said, perceiving the note of censure. "Waiting to leave with the other guests—when we might draw less attention—was a reasonable strategy, I thought."

Lucien bit back a retort. Skefton's attitude confirmed he had considered the communiqué's content was highly sensitive. Delaying its transfer to a superior violated standard protocol, a critical mistake and a needless risk that backfired. But it was not Lucien's place to pass out reprimands. The marquess would see to it.

"If I may continue," Lucien said. "Yesterday afternoon—while the weather was better than today, I presume—a pleasure trip to nearby ruins was attended by all the guests, except Miss Hodges-Jones, who was ill, and involved most of the servants in transporting guests and food back and forth. During this outing, a thief or thieves entered Sherbourne Manor unobserved and made off with a variety of items easy to carry. Money, jewelry, a watch, dueling pistols, some scarves, and the French packet. Anything I missed?"

"That's about it," Sherry said.

"Ah, the two small paintings from the hall were taken," his father added.

Lucien's interest sparked. "Valuable?"

"Not much. I believe, my wife simply admired them."

"What about other rooms? Paintings, silver, gold? Any of that missing?"

The baron shook his head. "Not even disturbed."

"So straight upstairs to the bedchambers and straight out again," Lucien muttered. "Done in haste but with a plan, I fancy."

"Thank God no one was harmed," the baron said. "Imagine what might have happened if anyone had come back early and interrupted them." He looked at Lucien. "Now that you know about the outing, surely that removes household members and guests from suspicion."

"Of direct participation, yes. All but Miss Hodges-Jones."

"What? Marjorie is no thief." The baron's voice raised. "The woman is more than seventy years old, and my wife has known her for fifty of those. She would have gone home yesterday except she awoke too ill to get out of bed. And she slept all afternoon."

"How can you be certain?" Lucien could not resist asking. The old woman was undoubtedly innocent, but the fact that the baron felt he had to give such a spirited defense was amusing.

Even Sherry hid a smile, but he intervened to explain. "Miss Hodges-Jones's niece gave her a healthy dose of laudanum before we left."

"Quite so, but go on, Ware, ask her your questions, if you must," the baron groused.

Knowing the elder Sherbourne was venting his offense at any suspicion of those under his roof, Lucien responded affably, "I will do that, sir. And her young relative. Who else would have been around the manor during the afternoon?"

The baron's indignant air turned thoughtful. "Some kitchen and scullery staff, I suppose. A maid or two. The stable boys were back and forth. Maybe others."

"I asked around," Sherry said. "They'll all be available at your convenience."

Lucien nodded approval. "You *have* been busy."

"This is nonsense," the colonel interjected, as though goaded beyond reason by the conversation. "Why are you talking about old ladies and servants? We all know this was the work of French agents."

"*I* don't know that." Lucien eyed him. "It is one possibility, and perhaps the best, but we cannot afford to overlook others."

"To some extent I'm inclined to agree with the colonel," Baron Sherbourne said. "It was an outsider. Had to be. He must have watched the house waiting for just such an opportunity." He sighed heavily. "Our servants would *not* do this. Most have worked here for years. We have trusted them with our lives and our children's lives."

Lucien was sympathetic and refrained from pointing out that times of political unrest often tested old loyalties. Not to mention how the long years of war had resulted in rampant poverty, and petty crime rates had risen as the poor became desperate just to survive. A few quid might well have convinced someone to tip off a thief or gang of thieves to a house party of presumably wealthy Londoners. The war packet may have been no more than an unexpected windfall.

Unless Skefton's theory was correct... What if the courier wasn't traveling alone? Under those circumstances, his French compatriots may have tracked the packet and recovered it.

Lucien ran a hand over the back of his neck. One thing he was sure of, strangers had not been watching the house for days without the servants or someone from the village noticing. The timing of the theft was more suggestive that the intruders—thieves or spies— had information about the trip to the ruins from someone in the Sherbourne household.

He straightened from the mantel. "We have work ahead of us. Let us begin at the colonel's bedchamber. I am interested in where the packet was kept. A quick look at the other guestrooms would also not be amiss. Shall we say interviews with the servants in forty-five minutes?"

The baron nodded. "I shall let the butler know. He will have the staff and library ready for you upon your return."

Chapter Two

Lucien, Sherry, and the colonel walked three abreast as they climbed the broad central staircase in silence. On the first floor landing, large windows at the rear overlooked the formal gardens; on the front they provided an unfettered view of the entrance park. Identical connecting halls from each side maintained the manor's symmetrical style, providing access to the east and west wings of guest bedchambers. The formal staircase continued to sweep upward to the ballroom on the second floor. An unobtrusive door on the rear northeast corner opened into the narrow servants' stairs leading upward to the attic and female servants' quarters on the third floor, and it went down all the way to the kitchen, cellars, and lodgings for the men in service.

Skefton gestured toward the east wing. "This way." He took the lead, stopped at the second door on the left, and hesitated before reluctantly stepping aside to allow the viscount to enter first. "It is rather disordered," he said. "We did a thorough search before concluding the packet was gone."

More frantic than thorough, Lucien decided. He stepped around displaced furniture and piles of belongings, closed the hallway door with a firm shove, and turned to confront Skefton. "Is this private enough for you? Tell us exactly what we're looking for. What the devil makes this packet so bloody important?"

Skefton threw a look at Sherry, and Lucien forestalled him with a warning. "Don't say it. You saw Rothe's orders. Andrew Sherbourne is as much a part of this as you are. More from now on."

The veins in Skefton's neck tightened. "I would prefer to keep tighter security, but so be it. The communiqué looks ordinary

15

enough, like any other letter, folded and sealed with red wax but with no direction or name on the outside. When unfolded, the reverse side is filled with columns of numbers, French words, letters, and symbols." He paused. "I believe it to be Napoleon's new cipher."

Lucien stared at him speechless. *You bloody, blundering fool.*

After two centuries of using the same ciphers for war communications—which were easy to decode—the French had switched to a stronger code last spring. To Prinny's delight, George Scovell, a code breaker for General Wellington, had broken it in two days. Then, a month or two ago, Napoleon's code makers had turned the spy world upside down by replacing the broken code with the Grande Chiffre, an encryption so complex no one knew where to start unraveling it. Documents under the old ciphers became obsolete, and the latest French communiqués remained inviolate despite long hours and sleepless nights by the War Office's best code breakers.

The viscount found his voice with a surge of anger. "You are just now telling us? My God, sir! You should have taken it straight to Rothe the moment it came into your possession. You cannot be blind to its importance."

"Certainly I am not," Skefton snarled, his face growing crimson. "I also knew the French would do anything to get it back, and two hours to London is a long, dangerous ride if you're being hunted. I had hoped to hide unnoticed among the other carriages leaving today."

"Well, you failed…sir. We could have protected it, if you'd told us." Sherry's gaze swung to the viscount. "Confound it, Lucien. I should have kept everyone here in the event they knew… something."

"How? At the point of a pistol?"

"I might have done it, if I had known."

"Good lord, Sherry. A fine ruckus that would have caused. In any event, we must get word of the cipher to Rothe as swiftly as possible, confirming what I'm certain he already suspects."

"I would be in London talking to him by now," Skefton said with a contemptuous jerk of his chin, "if *he* had not forced me to stay."

"You should have told me everything," Sherry retorted.

"Let it go, gentlemen. It's done." Lucien swallowed his own anger to keep from taking a swing at Skefton and turned to survey the room. "Show me where the packet was kept."

Skefton pointed to a sturdy armoire pulled away from the wall. "Behind there in a locked writing box. It couldn't be seen or reached when the furniture was in place."

Not an obvious hiding place. A painstaking search must have taken place, but more so than other rooms? Had they known what they were looking for? And who was likely to have it?

Lucien pictured an image from his childhood—his stepmother's small, wooden travel desk with its slanted top, a piece delicate enough to carry away or break open. The lock on it would only keep out someone who respected privacy. "Was the box metal or wood?"

"Rosewood." At Sherry's strangled sound disparaging the wood's popular use for fragile, decorative pieces, Skefton growled, "I didn't have anything else more sturdy with me. I was not expecting a courier."

"So what happened to the box? Did the thieves break it open?"

"It was taken."

Lucien lifted a brow. "That is curious. It would have been easier to slip the letter into a coat pocket."

"Or grab the courier's leather bag," Skefton conceded. "The soldiers found the bag tied around the Frenchie's neck with the letter inside. I put the code back in the bag before placing it in the box. I cannot explain why they took my desk, but it's obvious the thieves knew the code was in there. A spy in the house, I'd say. Mark my words, one of Baron Sherbourne's servants supports the Frogs."

Sherry ignored Skefton's accusation. "Could be they were frightened by somebody returning to the house, grabbed the desk, and took off."

Lucien gave him a startled look. "Yes, another plausible explanation." The thieves might even have snatched the attractive box to sell, not knowing what was inside.

He turned away, cutting off further speculation. They had already said more than they should in front of Skefton. With England's security at risk, Lucien didn't trust anyone who knew the cipher was in England, especially not the colonel or his secretary. Skefton was acting guilty and defensive. In an effort to redeem himself, mightn't he go haring off on any wild theory, evidence notwithstanding? Lucien wanted the culpable person condemned by facts, not just someone chosen at random to relieve the colonel's embarrassment—or hide his own treasonous acts.

Lucien kept his expression blank. "Your man is free to pack, Colonel. Lord Rothe will be eager to talk with you. Please convey to him that I shall report in person or by messenger no later than tomorrow night."

Skefton frowned as though he objected to carrying Lucien's message, then must have thought better of it. "Yes, well, I had hoped I could report this would be swiftly resolved. Such does not appear likely as you are determined to pursue these *other* possibilities. I shall leave within the half hour."

"A list of the houseguests will be ready for you to take to the marquess," Sherry said. "Maybe the War Office will find something in their backgrounds that will point us in the right direction."

"I would not count on it," the colonel muttered. He hurried toward the door.

"Oh, Colonel," Lucien said, "When your valet has a moment, I need to delay you long enough to question him." He turned away, rather pleased this time by Skefton's scowl.

• • •

Lucien kept the tour of the bedchambers as brief as possible. Underneath the evidence of a hasty search, a musty odor in several rooms and lack of care among dressing items gave him unwanted insight to how some of the Quality would live without their personal servants.

As they neared the far end of the west wing, Lucien knocked on the door of Miss Hodges-Jones's room. A young miss with an ashen face, big eyes, and nervous hands opened it a few inches, informed them she was the lady's great-niece, Georgina St. Clair, and that her aunt was indisposed. "She is ill and resting. You will have to come back later."

"Perhaps you could step into the hall, and we could speak with you without waking her," Lucien suggested.

"Oh, no, not without Auntie. You shall have to wait."

Lucien placed his hand on the door when the girl attempted to close it and frowned. She acted rather fearful. Was it maiden sensibility when faced by two unknown gentlemen, or did she have something to hide? Given her age and station in life, he could scarce believe it had anything to do with the theft.

"Just a couple of questions about the thefts," Lucien coaxed.

"I was not here. We were all at the ruins," the young woman insisted. "Well, not Auntie, but she was asleep, and no one came into the room."

"How do you know?" Sherry asked.

"Nothing was taken or even moved out of place. I must go now."

Lucien's frown deepened, but he let her shut the door this time. Had the thieves by-passed this room because they'd been warned the aunt was there? Or had they looked in—maybe even stepped inside—seen her sleeping, and moved on? Why not search it anyway? What could an old lady do to stop them… unless they knew she would recognize them—and they had no stomach for killing her. His brows lifted at the possibility. Despite Miss St. Clair's ready denials, her aunt could have been half-awake to see or hear something. Lucien would be back to ask.

Sherry gestured toward the opposite hallway. "The younger men are always lodged in the east wing. We need to hurry along, it is close to time for the interviews."

Lucien nodded. "Lead on." He turned his head as the sounds of a carriage-and-four rose from the courtyard. "Were you expecting additional company?"

"Good God, I hope not. I'd guess one of the neighbors wants to hear all about the thievery. Small villages live on gossip, you know."

Lucien's eyes glinted with humor as he thought of the many *on-dits* shared with him by Sophia, the Widow Stine. "As do cities and the haute ton."

"Well, yes, I suppose that is true," Sherry acknowledged. "At all events, Father will take care of it."

But minutes later as they exited the last of the bedchambers, the voices of Lady Sherbourne and an unfamiliar female reached them from the vicinity of the main stairs. On their way down to the library, Lucien and Sherry met the ladies on the landing. The baroness introduced a fashionable, fair-haired young woman with astute blue eyes as Lady Anne Ashburn, daughter of the Earl of Chadley, and another great-niece of the ill woman Lucien had yet to meet.

"I have not laid eyes on you in…it must be ten years," Sherry said, bowing over Lady Anne's hand in obvious admiration. "I recall a skinny girl with freckles visiting Miss Hodges-Jones, not the vision you have become. Are you in society now? I have not seen you in London's ballrooms."

She laughed with ease, a rather lyrical sound. "I do socialize, but family circumstances have kept me in the country." Her smile faded. "I do not wish to offend, gentlemen. It is a pleasure to see you again, Lord Sherbourne, and to meet you, Lord Ware," her frank glance encompassed them both, "but I am anxious to see my aunt. It is not like her to be so dreadfully ill."

"An understandable concern, my lady. We shall not keep you," Lucien said with a polite nod.

"Until dinner then," Sherry added. "I hope you find your aunt much improved."

"That would be wonderful, indeed, but I do not plan to stay for dinner. If the doctor allows, I shall have Aunt Meg in her own bed at home by nightfall."

"You cannot leave yet," Lucien said. "Not until we speak with your aunt and cousin." When her eyes snapped to his in astonishment, he realized how bluntly he'd spoken. "Pardon my hasty words, Lady Anne, but I truly must talk with them."

"Whatever about?"

Her tone held a sharp edge now, and Lucien sighed. This was all he needed to complete a frustrating morning. It was his own fault for allowing his irritation over other things to surface, but that only increased his discomfort.

"We had a housebreaking yesterday," Sherry began.

"Several thefts, in fact," Lucien said. "Everyone is being questioned."

"Questioned?" Lady Anne stared at him. "You make it sound like an interrogation. Are you suggesting my elderly aunt is a thief? Or perhaps my cousin who is barely out of the schoolroom?"

The baroness hastily intervened. "Oh, no, Lady Anne, I am certain they mean no such thing."

"I should hope not." Lady Anne kept her eyes on Lucien.

"Standard protocol," Sherry agreed, throwing Lucien a pleading look, as though wondering how the conversation had taken such a sour turn.

Lucien gave her a disarming smile, hoping to smooth over his *faux pas*. "We are merely gathering information from guests and staff to understand what happened. We can discuss this again... after you have spoken with your aunt and the doctor. We will, of course, abide by his medical advice."

"An excellent plan, my lord." Her tone was acerbic. Raising her chin, a sure sign she did not find his smile as appealing as other ladies had in the past, she gave the briefest nod. "I must see to my great-aunt now."

The baroness frowned at both men and urged Lady Anne toward her aunt's bedchamber.

"Rather outspoken," Lucien remarked when the ladies were out of hearing. "It may explain why beauty and title have still left her unwed into her twenties."

"Rather a severe judgment, Lucien. After all, she has been hidden away in the country." Sherry's mouth twitched in amusement. "You may be losing your famous charm, my friend. As a child, Lady Anne spoke her mind, but she and her family were never high in the instep."

Lucien brushed it off with a short laugh. What Lady Anne thought was the least of his concerns. "On to the interviews, Sherry. With luck, one of your servants knows something that will make it unnecessary to bother the ladies again."

Chapter Three

Lady Anne pressed her lips together, silently fuming as she and the baroness approached Miss Hodges-Jones's bedchamber. His arrogant, inconsiderate lordship would *not* be bothering Aunt Meg. Not unless her aunt was feeling much, much improved—and chose to receive him. How could he suggest a seventy-year-old woman or her young cousin would have any knowledge of such a crime?

Lady Sherbourne eyed her with understanding. "Men can be very singled minded, do you not agree?"

"Oh, my lady, I am so sorry." Anne was instantly contrite. Her last few days had left her out of sorts. A lengthy trip with numerous delays—a thrown wheel, a lame horse, the storm—and then arriving to the alarming news her favorite, if only surviving, great-aunt was ill, so ill she could not be moved and, according to her aunt's butler, might even be dying. Lady Sherbourne had done her best to reassure her that was not so, but Anne's anxiety had not settled. And then she'd run into *him*. She took a steadying breath and gave a rueful smile. "I should not have spoken with such heat. My mother would be embarrassed for me. But is he always so...so intense?"

The baroness's eyes rounded, then she smiled. "Lucien, you mean. Not always. He is usually quite delightful and was the sweetest boy. But the war changes a man." A hint of worry crossed her face. "It changed them both. I shall leave you now. I believe Miss St. Clair is already with her. If not, your cousin's room is next door. Please let us know if you need anything."

Ah, yes, Georgina. Anne had forgotten her cousin was there. She felt a twitch of curiosity. What had brought the frivolous girl to such a staid party? But that was a question for later. "What does the doctor say about my aunt's condition? Can she go home today?"

23

"He has not yet seen her. She insisted that he not be called yesterday, and considering her mild complaints—an uneasy stomach, a dull headache—I agreed to wait. She was tired and declared all she needed was a good night's rest. I hoped so too, but when I saw how mopey she was this morning…well, at her age, one cannot be too careful. I sent for Mr. Galpin and expect him any moment. Meanwhile, I shall have a room readied for you."

"Thank you. You are very gracious to offer shelter to an uninvited guest, but with all that is happening, you scarcely need extra company, and my aunt will do better at home. I hope to depart by midafternoon."

"Please don't hurry away on our account, my dear. You are most welcome to stay. At least wait to make your decision until the doctor has examined her." At Anne's acquiescence, the baroness turned and descended the broad staircase, her gown brushing against the steps.

Anne tapped on the bedchamber door. "Aunt Meg, it's Anne." She tapped again.

A muffled voice responded this time. Anne turned the brass doorknob and stepped inside, swiftly hiding her alarm upon seeing her aunt's pasty complexion and the morose expression on Georgina's face. Aunt Meg was holding the back of one hand against her forehead, but her eyes were closed.

Oh, my goodness—was Auntie's health worse than anyone realized? Was she indeed in a bad way?

Managing a smile, Anne hurried to her bedside. "How worried I was when I heard you were ill, but I see Georgina is keeping you company. Why, you shall mend in no time."

The old woman's eyes fluttered open. Before she could speak, Georgina sprang to her feet. "Annie! Oh, thank God." The young woman with fetching dusky ringlets and cornflower blue eyes clutched at Anne's arm. "I thought it was those dreadful men again. I am *so* glad you are here."

"Has his lordship been bothering you?" Anne frowned, throwing her cousin a pointed look of inquiry, but she bent over the bed when her elderly relative murmured something. She took her great-aunt's hand, patting the soft, wrinkled skin. "What is it, Auntie? I am right here."

"My darling Anne," the old woman said, sounding stronger this time and lifting her head off the pillow. "You need not have come—"

"Of course I came," Anne said. "But you must not bestir yourself. Save your strength for our journey. I came to take you home as soon as the doctor allows." She was heartened to see a spark of approval flicker across her aunt's face.

"It would be nice to be home, but I feel very foolish, child. There is nothing wrong with me that hot soup, tea, and a little rest will not cure. How inconvenient you had to make this journey. What a botheration I am."

"Nonsense. Had you forgotten I was arriving at your home yesterday for a visit? It was only a short drive here this morning. I brought the large carriage and two strong footmen. We shall have you home in style by nightfall." If they could escape the clutches of Lord Ware, she added to herself, picturing the viscount's unyielding expression and those serious gray eyes that allowed no opposition. A sudden thought furrowed her brow. Why was a London lord inquiring into a country theft like he was in charge? Where was the village constable?

A loud rap on the door announced the arrival of Mr. Galpin, a middle-aged surgeon with a fading hairline and slightly sunken cheeks. His self-assured laugh and confiding manner set her mind at ease that her aunt was in good hands, and Anne complied without protest when he shooed her and Georgina out of the room.

Anne paused with one hand on the door and asked him, "Will she be able to go home today? I have a carriage waiting—"

"If you allow me to examine her, I'll tell you soon enough," he said, the twinkle in his eyes belying the gruffness of his words. He turned back to his patient. "Now, Miss Hodges-Jones, what seems to be the trouble?"

Anne and Georgina waited impatiently next door. Georgina paced the bedchamber, twisting her lace handkerchief into knots, and Anne studied her with a frown. She was rather surprised to see her heretofore self-absorbed cousin so upset over someone else's well-being.

"Will she be all right?" Georgina blurted. "I was all at sixes and sevens, never having taken care of a sick room before."

"I know you were a great comfort. And now that the doctor is here, he will know just what to do." Anne put an arm around the girl's shoulders. "Come, sit down, and tell me what has transpired. When did she take ill?"

As they sat close together on the edge of the bed and discussed their aunt's illness, Georgina relaxed, and they shared a quiet laugh over Aunt Meg's determination to keep playing Whist late Friday night until she won.

"There you are," Anne said. "Auntie has simply done too much. She refuses to accept it is that time in life when she should slow down just a trifle. I daresay this is one of those passing ailments."

"I hope so." But Georgina's troubled expression returned, her gaze fixed on her lap. She sighed repeatedly, which Anne interpreted as her cousin wanted to tell her something but was holding back. She waited.

When Georgina decided to speak, her voice was unsteady, halting. "Um, I am afraid it was more than the card game. Or even the late hours. She has been, well, worried, and I guess it is my fault."

"Why? What have you not told me?"

Georgina raised rounded eyes, studied Anne with a frown, and then dropped her gaze again without saying a word.

Anne stifled an impatient sigh. Despite the four-year difference in age and the width of two country shires that separated their homes, they wrote each month or two and visited when they could. Georgina often shared her troubles with Anne as she might with an older sister, and Anne was fully aware of the girl's faults. As Georgina's parents had no other children, they had indulged her to the point she was rather spoiled, impulsive, and often thoughtless.

By nature, Georgina had a very good heart, but it got her into scrapes more often than not, such as her *rescue* of an eight-year-old waif from the Leicester city streets and taking him home with her. The child's prostitute mother reported a kidnapping, embarrassing Georgina's family, and after the constables returned the boy to his mother, her father's valet discovered an expensive pair of cuff links and a gold watch were missing.

Anne had held out hope that her cousin's recent engagement to Lord John Bennington—an event highly approved by her family— would mature her, but by all accounts, it had not. The girl's present demeanor was a guilty look Anne had seen before.

"Georgina," she repeated, softening her voice to conceal her rising apprehension. "What is amiss?"

"Everything." Tears welled-over and trickled down her face. "I have ruined it all."

For one brief moment, Anne cringed at the thought Georgina might be involved in the house thefts. Some kind of strange, childish folly. How would they ever explain it to Lord Ware? Then she realized how absurd she was being and took a quiet breath. "It cannot be as bad as you imagine. Why not tell me whatever is worrying you? Maybe I can help."

Georgina's lengthy sigh was soulful. "No one can help." But she began to talk, mostly about her engagement to Lord John. "Everyone was so thrilled. His wealth, his title. No one cared what I wanted."

"But he is young and handsome. I thought you *wished* to marry him. You wrote to me in such happy words."

"I do. I mean, I did. Oh, it is so complicated. He has these beautiful brown eyes that make one feel *so very* special." Georgina hugged herself, her eyes closed, and then they popped open, and she straightened. "But Freddie and I love each other. It was decided years ago. And, well, he recently reminded me."

Anne began to grasp the problem. "By Freddie, you mean the local vicar's son near your home?"

"Yes." Georgina turned to her with a smile. "So, you recall my speaking of him. He is such immense fun. In fact, he is *perfect*."

"Then you should not have accepted Lord John's offer."

"Please, do not scold me, Anne. I truly, truly did not intend to cause trouble."

"But why did you agree to the engagement, um, the second engagement?"

"Lord John was so sweet, so romantic, when he came to ask." Her cousin sighed dreamily. "And the beautiful flowers. I did not think about Freddie until it was too late."

"Oh, Georgina, you can be such a goose." Anne saw the martial light in Georgina's eyes and cut off any further hint of scolding. "What does all this have to do with Aunt Meg?"

"My parents refused to accept my devotion to Freddie. They sent me to Auntie until I forget Freddie or until the wedding to Lord John. But how am I supposed to forget him when there is so little to do at Auntie's house?" she cried. "An occasional country dance but never a ball. No outings to the bookstore. Not even someone to join me in a ride."

"And you got bored."

"Well, it was bound to happen, was it not? And then..." She stopped, as though about to say more than she intended.

"What is it? Have you done something else?"

Georgina looked away. "No. Nothing to speak of. Auntie just worries so much."

Anne watched Georgina's averted face. No question the girl was hiding something. Anne might have pursued it further, but a rap on the door claimed her attention. She opened it to find Mr. Galpin. He was smiling.

"Nothing to worry about," he assured her. "A touch of dyspepsia. It has sapped her strength, but she should rally by mid week."

A mild stomach ailment. "Oh, thank you, doctor." Anne's thoughts flew to plans for getting her aunt home and into her own comfy bed. "How soon may she travel?"

"Whenever she feels up to it."

Anne stepped into the hall to go to her aunt's room and arrange things, but the doctor's next words stopped her. "As I think on it, the drive to her home in a heavy carriage would take over an hour, would it not? Maybe tomorrow would be best. This damp weather is not good for her, and skies may clear by morning. And she can use the extra rest. She is fatigued, and before she attempts the move, I should see her again. Just to confirm her mild cough does not worsen overnight. Meanwhile, a little fennel tea as often as she will take it should bring her spirits back sooner than later."

Recalling her aunt's exhausted face, Anne accepted the delay with good grace. If one more night would make Aunt Meg stronger, it was worth the wait.

"I am grateful, doctor. You have eased my fears. We shall look forward to your visit in the morning."

"Bright and early," he warned. "I have other rounds to make."

After Galpin left, Anne ordered the prescribed tea, notified Lady Sherbourne she would be delighted to accept her offer of lodging for the night, and she and Georgina returned to the sickroom. Aunt Meg was awake and already looking better. Getting a professional opinion that nothing was seriously wrong had a powerful recuperative effect.

"Auntie, such good news."

"I admit he relieved my mind. Come, sit and talk with me." Aunt Meg patted on the bed beside her.

They were making plans for tomorrow's journey when a maid arrived with the fennel tea. She set down the tray. "Lord Ware asked me to inquire when he might speak with you and Miss Georgina."

"To us?" Miss Hodges-Jones asked, surprised. "I wonder why."

Drat the man. He must have waylaid Galpin on the doctor's way out. Anne bit back a sharp retort and explained that Lords Ware and Sherbourne were questioning everyone regarding Saturday's housebreaking. "I cannot imagine why they have involved themselves or what they hope to learn from you," she said. "You need not oblige, Aunt Meg."

"Oh, no, I wish to help...if I can."

"Are you sure? It seems most unnecessary."

"It's all right, Anne." Miss Hodges-Jones gave her a questioning look before nodding at the maid. "Tell Lord Ware I shall be happy to receive him in half an hour."

"Very good, ma'am." The maid curtseyed and took her leave.

"I doubt if I know anything useful." Aunt Meg looked apologetic. Her gaze shot to Georgina's face. "Have you spoken with him?"

"I did not know what to say, so I thought it best to wait for you."

"Very good. Yes, indeed. But you needn't worry. Tell him the truth, everything you know about these criminals."

Georgina acted confused. "But, Auntie, I know nothing about them."

"Precisely."

Anne had watched the exchange in silence since Georgina's odd comment about not knowing what to say. Aunt Meg too chose her words with care, almost as though they shared some secret. But what nonsense. Surely she imagined it.

Aunt Meg raised her hands in a flutter, smoothing the covers around her. "Find my best robe, and help me get presentable. I refuse to greet the gentlemen with my person in disarray."

"Oh, yes, of course," Anne said with a sniff. "We mustn't do anything to offend Lord Ware."

Her aunt looked up with a reproving frown. "Why Anne, whatever is wrong? You appear to have taken a dislike to the viscount. It is unlike you. Have you had an unfortunate encounter with him in the past?"

"No, I met him just minutes ago, but…" She went on to explain their brief meeting. The incident sounded trivial in the retelling. When her aunt arched a bemused brow, Anne regretted having said anything.

• • •

Anne watched the interview of her aunt and cousin from the back of the room. So far the gentlemen were on their best behavior. The viscount was gentle, respectful, in questioning her aunt, his smile softening the high, aristocratic cheek bones, adding warmth to his gray eyes. Sherbourne, she was happy to see, was still the amiable person she had known in childhood, and neither lord raised an objection to Anne remaining in the room.

Aunt Meg had answered their questions without hesitation... and most of those asked of Georgina; what odd behavior. Her cousin's subdued silence added to Anne's uneasy curiosity.

"I wish I *had* seen or heard the scoundrels," her aunt declared. "I do not take laudanum as a rule, and it put me right out. I cringe to think they might have come in while I was sleeping, but our jewelry was safe in a box under my bed. I assume the thieves had the decency not to disturb an old lady."

"Good Lord," Anne murmured, thinking how tragic it might have been if the housebreakers had chosen differently. Her poor auntie had been at their mercy.

Lord Ware shot a glance at Anne, his eyes revealing he shared her thoughts.

"One would hope." The viscount stood. "Thank you, Miss Hodges-Jones. I believe we have taken up enough of your time. I wish you a speedy recovery. Ladies, have a pleasant day."

When Sherbourne had also taken his leave, Anne closed the door behind them and returned to the bedside.

Aunt Meg leaned against the pillows, exhaling a deep breath. "I rather like your Lord Ware, Anne. A delightful and most attractive young man but with an air of mystery about him. I'd say there is more to him than he wants the world to see."

Auntie might be right, Anne mused. Mayhap she had misjudged the viscount and mistaken his character after all.

Georgina scowled. "Well, I don't like him. He appeared to doubt every word I said."

"Hush, child. You imagine things. It is over now."

Anne heard the subtle warning and gave her aunt a sharp look. There was that hint of a shared secret again. Georgina could certainly be a chatterbox, but what had Aunt Meg been afraid her cousin might say?

Chapter Four

Lucien sighed wearily and pushed back his chair, relieved the two hours of servant interviews were over. He flexed his shoulder muscles and glanced at Sherry lounging at the end of the cherrywood library table, then rose and crossed the room. The wind was whipping the tree branches outside the window, creating a tap, tap, tap, and he watched for several seconds before turning to his partner, "Well, what do you think?"

"I would stake my best horse that none of them is our thief."

"Thieves, you mean," Lucien said. "It took more than one given the short time they were in the house. But I get your point," he added with a quick grin. "You don't want me nabbing the cook or the old nanny."

"The cook, God no. We would starve without her, but now that you mention the nanny…" Sherry scratched his chin. "The thought has some appeal. Nanny was dreadfully quick with the switch. However, holding her at fault for this could be difficult. She left our employ a dozen years ago—saying she was needed to care for a sick relative, but I am certain my sister succeeded in driving her away."

Lucien chuckled. "That bad, huh?"

"Are you referring to Nanny or my sister?"

Considering how toplofty Camilla had gotten after marrying a duke's son, and what a vengeful child she had been, it was a good question. "I value my skin enough not to answer that," Lucien said. "But back to the interviews…We've established a time period when the theft occurred, and all of your staff are accounted for during that half hour between three o'clock, when the guests left for the ruins, and three-thirty, when many of the servants returned after delivering the food. Oh, I suppose one of them could still be involved by tipping off the thieves, but no one we interviewed said or did anything to make me suspect them." He returned to drop into his chair and stretch out his long legs. "The precise timing bothers me. I believe these thieves have done it before—a well-trained gang, in fact—and yet no one has reported strangers in the neighborhood."

"We have yet to ask in the village."

A tap on the door heralded the baron's return. "Any progress?" His voice held a hint of underlying tension.

Lucien looked up. "We narrowed the time of the theft, three to three-thirty—when all but a sparse few of your staff were away from the house."

"Capital news." The baron's relief was palpable. "As expected. So what happens now?"

"We keep asking questions. Are you certain none of the guests slipped away from the *al fresco*?"

"I cannot vouch for each one, but a rider or carriage leaving would have been noticed, as would anyone absent long enough to walk here and back." Baron Sherbourne settled into a wingback chair. "None of our staff saw anything?"

Sherry shook his head. "Perhaps the constables will have better luck. Villagers would notice strangers in the vicinity."

The baron perked up. "You have concluded it was strangers, Frenchmen mayhap?"

"Not entirely," Lucien corrected. "Whether the intruders were French agents or common thieves, they may have been tipped off by locals or someone at the manor. So, for now, let us talk about your guests."

Baron Sherbourne frowned, but he settled in for a pain-staking review of each visitor, who had stayed where, and what, if anything, they had reported stolen. Lucien had a particular interest in those lodged closest to Skefton who might have woken when the soldiers brought the packet and overheard what was said or suspected its contents had value. Such a person would have had ample time—several hours—to alert thieves or French spies on the outside. But his theory became less promising when Sherry pointed out the bedchamber of secretary/valet Horace Sims—already an obvious suspect—had been on Skefton's right and Retired Gen. Miles Whipple—a staunch supporter of the monarchy—on the left.

"What about others on that wing? Lord Braden across the hall, and the younger men, Ramsey and Voss?"

The baron shrugged. "I know nothing of the two young bucks, except Voss is a prime shot on the hunt field and my daughter suggested their names as eligible guests. Lord Braden, on the other hand, is an old friend and member of the House of Lords. I cannot fancy him engaged in criminal or treasonous activity." He frowned, shaking his head. "The same is not true for his wife, however. Perhaps I am too unkind, but she is forever running up gambling debts and keeps the tongues wagging with her indiscreet behavior."

"Flirtations or affairs?" Lucien asked.

The elder Sherbourne hesitated. "I cannot say for certain."

"We shall find out. A potential suspect, I'd say," Lucien reflected. "Her lifestyle could make her susceptible to either bribery or blackmail. Was she accompanied by an abigail?"

Sherry nodded. "Sally Wey. Questioning her might be useful. Servants know all our secrets."

"As you say." Lucien drummed his fingers on the table. "But overall, this is an unlikely group of lawbreakers."

The baron gave a snort of laughter. "Pardon us for not having more disreputable guests."

Lucien smiled, but he was more frustrated than amused.

"We still have Ramsey and Voss," Sherry said. "I dined with them at my sister's London house a few months ago when she was matchmaking for some society miss. I assume she considers them good ton, but both are rather reckless and quick to take up any dare. I heard Voss has a ladybird in keeping."

"Hardly worthy of gossip for a bachelor," the baron remarked.

"Ramsey's dueling pistols were stolen," Lucien said, reading Sherry's list of lost property. "Strange he brought them to a house party. I should like to know why. And what about Emily Selkirk's London friends?"

"The ladies? Not suspects surely!" Sherry protested. "I have danced with both. You have too, I'm sure. Just a pair of pretty misses."

"Pretty misses cannot be spies? Come, Sherry." Lucien's voice was casual, but for a moment Lisette's face flashed through his head, bringing back a misty dawn in Paris, a betrayal that haunted him still.

"But these are *English* females."

Lucien threw his partner an exasperated look. Sherry's protest jarred. He should know better.

• • •

The small village of Calney, with fewer than three dozen cottages, appeared sleepy that midafternoon. A handful of larger cottages with smoke drifting from their chimneys, a small church built in the 1500s, a shack for the single unpaid constable, and a public tavern lined the main road. According to Sherry, the pub house also served as the post office and bakery, and every Wednesday morning, Mrs. Lytle sold her delectable rabbit pies there.

A public green of four trees—now barren of leaves—and two benches sat at one end of the village to provide relief on hot summer days. Lucien watched as three young boys, oblivious of the damp, chilly air, threw sticks for a brown spotted dog to chase. The only other visible activity was two women bargaining with a traveling peddler for chapbooks, the popular, inexpensive books of folded paper.

Smiling at the quiet scene, Lucien reflected it was good he had left his city-born groom at the manor. Calney would have fed Finn's firm belief that nothing happened outside London.

At Sherry's direction, he halted the team in front of the constable's shack, a weathered shed not much larger than a foaling stall. There was no sign to identify its use. "How would one know this belongs to the constabulary?"

"It's a *small* village. And as a rule, he can be found at home. Not much serious crime in Calney."

The boys broke off playing with the dog and ran to Lucien's side. The oldest, a dark-eyed child of about ten, asked, "Need help with yer horses, mister?"

Lucien looked the boys over as though considering. "What are your names, lads?"

"Harry, sir," the oldest replied. He jerked his head toward the younger ones. "Me brothers, Bo and Sam."

"I am Viscount Ware." Lucien held out the reins and a coin. "Now, Harry, I'm right fond of these horses. There is another coin for you and your brothers when I return, if you take good care of my team and walk them while we conduct our business. I won't be long, but I don't want them to get cold just standing about."

"Yes, sir. Take as long as ye likes."

Lucien smiled at Harry's enthusiasm, and he watched them lead the horses away before he followed Sherry into the tiny office. It held a single cabinet and three-foot desk with its wood chair. Two more wood chairs—for the extra constables currently in the village, no doubt—left no more than room to turn around. Not surprising, the shed was empty.

"I would *like* to say Constable Wainwright is working the case, not taking a nap somewhere," Sherry said dryly. "Shall we track him down?"

"A note should be sufficient for now, reminding him to interview the servants hired for the party. If he has failed to do so, it should spur some action. We can stop in the morning to see what's been learned."

Once the note was left, a brisk, two-minute walk brought them to the vicar's cottage where they spoke with Gilbert Mannering and his wife, Patience. The pleasant, mid-thirties couple chatted without reserve, but they were as bewildered by the theft as everyone else. When the wife was called away by a crying infant, Lucien and Sherry took their leave. The vicar walked them to the door. Spotting the chapbook peddler at the neighbor's, he remarked that a few other regular hawkers came through the village selling their wares—grain, dried beans and peas, household goods, clothing— and tinkers wandered in offering to mend pots or knives, but he hadn't heard of anyone asking unusual questions or behaving out of the ordinary. "No one who looked like the criminal type," Mannering added.

As they collected the curricle and horses a few minutes later, Lucien was still musing over the vicar's last remark. "Unfortunately, culprits are not always accommodating enough to look like criminals."

Sherry shrugged. "But wouldn't it be nice?"

Chapter Five

Jeremy, Marquess of Rothe, shifted as though his desk chair was uncomfortable, but it wasn't the true cause of his restlessness. Impatiently pinching the bridge of his nose, he listened to the ordinary sounds of his secretary and clerks working in the outer office of his Whitehall offices—the chatter, the banging of file drawers. His staff had come in on a Sunday afternoon, perhaps to impress him, but they should have spent the day with family. God knows it would have been his first choice. Most Sundays he reserved for church and family. *Not today.*

He rose and went to the window, his sharp gaze taking in the small courtyard in front and the connected Horse Guards' building on the far side. Where was Skefton? Why had he not yet presented a report?

Not that he begrudged the passing hours—Oh, devil it. Lord Rothe gave an irritated jerk of the head. He certainly *did* resent it. Of course Ware needed time to question the colonel, but Rothe loathed being kept in the dark. And for that he had the colonel to blame. As far as he could deduce from Sherbourne's brief note, the entire disaster could have been avoided if Skefton had not dawdled around, giving a thief time to intervene. He clenched his empty fingers that should be holding the code key right this minute.

Rothe tilted his head at the sound of footsteps in the hall, the clipped stride of a military man. *About time.* He returned to sit at his desk and picked up a written report as the knock came on his door.

"Enter," he ordered. He kept his eyes lowered to the document, appearing engrossed, even after Skefton stood before him.

"Sir?" the colonel said after a moment.

Rothe took his time before lifting his gaze. "Close the door, Colonel." He returned to perusing his reports until the door was shut and Skefton was again before him. He did not invite the colonel to sit but gave him a cool look. "Have you recovered the packet?"

"No, my lord. I came directly here."

"Have you discovered who took it or where to begin looking?"

"The French, sir." Skefton spoke with conviction. "I believe they recovered it, but Ware is…" Skefton paused, indicating he wanted to say more, his tone critical.

Rothe felt his anger rise but kept his voice level. "Yes, do go on."

"Very well, sir. Ware was still at the manor when I left, interviewing houseguests and servants. None of whom were present when the theft occurred."

"Where were they?"

Skefton told him about the Saturday *al fresco*. As though encouraged by Rothe's silence, his manner grew ever more disparaging as he related his conversations with Ware and Sherbourne and why he felt they were mishandling the situation. "They are wasting good time, sir, allowing the Frogs to get away."

Despite his disgust, Lord Rothe held his countenance. The colonel's blatant prejudice against the aristocracy was clouding his judgment. With such a bias, it was a wonder he accepted orders from Rothe or even the Prince Regent.

"Yes, yes. I understand you would approach it in a different manner. All that is duly noted," Rothe interrupted, "but tell me how the communiqué was lost."

And so Skefton finally came to the crux of the story: the dawn visit from the soldiers, his examination of the packet and realization of what it must be, and his decision to hide it in his room until Sunday.

"You did what?" Rothe reared from his chair, slapping his hands on the desk, and leaned across, glaring at Skefton. "I knew there was a delay, some kind of mare's nest…but you *decided* to wait? Hell and damnation, Colonel, what is wrong with you? Any schoolboy would know better. That cipher could have been the deciding factor in this bloody conflict with Napoleon. Your blunder may have cost English lives."

Realizing his voice had risen to a shout, Rothe cut himself off. He stared down at his desk until he had gained control and then dropped back into his chair. When he looked up again, the colonel stood at rigid attention, his eyes on the wall or windows behind Rothe. His expression was stony, and Rothe felt the man's unspoken rage.

What the devil did *he* have to be angry about? Rothe clenched his jaw and fought against a return of his own fury. When he could, he spoke in a monotone. "Anything else to report?"

"No, sir."

"Then get out." Rothe waved an abrupt, dismissive hand toward the door. "Return to the Horse Guards. I shall not need your services again."

Skefton's gaze snapped to Rothe's face. "But it was not my fault…" When Rothe's expression gave him no indication of softening, the colonel abandoned his protest. "Yes, sir." He turned and yanked open the door.

Rothe noted the deafening silence from the outer office. His outburst had carried to his staff—not that he cared. Perhaps they'd leave him alone until he had mastered his temper. He bent over his papers again to further discourage interruptions. When Skefton slammed the outer office door, Rothe tightened his lips. If he'd had even the smallest thought of forgiving the colonel, that sound had destroyed it.

He had finished reading two reports from the front lines before his long-time secretary, Benjamin Sloane, ventured into the room. Excellent timing, Rothe thought, as he had at last recovered his normal composure.

He looked up. "Yes, Sloane. Did you lose a throw of the dice?"

A hesitation, then a doubtful, "Sir?"

A smile tugged at the corners of Rothe's mouth. "How was it decided you should approach me first?"

"It was thought I was the least likely to be discharged." Sloane displayed no emotion other than a brief flicker in his eyes. "Is there anything I can do for you, my lord?"

Rothe's smile broadened. "They were right, you know. I could not do my job without you. But no, Benjamin, there is nothing I need at the moment. Go home to your family, and tell the others to do the same. I have no need for any of them and shan't be much longer myself."

"Very good. I shall see you in the morning, sir."

Their eyes met in a brief flash of understanding. After twenty years working together, the marquess doubted if Sloane could do much that would get him dismissed. "Until tomorrow."

Once Sloane left, Rothe rested his elbows on the desk and steepled his fingers. He strove to put aside his irritation with Skefton and dispassionately analyze the man's behavior. What an egregious lack of judgment. Was the colonel so incompetent? Had he fooled his superior officers all these years, or had they granted him promotions just to move him out of their command? Shameful, if that was the case, but not unheard of.

Or, heaven forbid, had the colonel abandoned his country? Was the housebreaking nothing but a trick, a calculated deception to hide the fact Skefton himself had given the cipher over to the French?

Rothe tapped his forefingers together, and after some consideration, he shook his head. In all truth, Skefton's betrayal was unlikely...even unthinkable. Rothe knew the family—the father, the grandfather, honorable and steadfast. Surely this was the rushed decision of an aging officer losing his grasp on command in a rapidly changing military. Arrogance and wounded pride were behind this, not disloyalty. Rothe straightened, having reached an acceptable conclusion.

He picked up the last of the urgent paperwork, finished reading a report from Vienna, wrote two brief messages for dispatch in the morning, and put everything away. Once the documents were stacked in desk drawers or in the security box in his wall cabinet, he locked them all and dropped the key in his pocket.

Since a light was still burning in the outer office, he put out his candle wall sconces—creating a brief but strong scent of melted wax and smoke—and pulled the office door closed behind him. He stopped and frowned at the two men still at their desks. Why were Coatley and Hatcher still here? Did his clerks habitually ignore his orders—or Sloane's—and he had failed to notice? He took a deep breath, owning he was out of sorts and not yet rid of the encounter with Skefton.

"Gentlemen, why have you not gone home?"

He heard little of their explanations of unfinished tasks. He just wanted the office cleared so he could lock the door. "It does not matter," he conceded, "but go now. Next time, you should follow Mr. Sloane's directions."

The clerks moved with haste, sending an occasional uneasy glance his way, as they tidied their desks and scurried out the door. He waited until he heard their footsteps on the stairs, put out the wall candles, and crossed the room to snag the last lantern. He trotted down the stairs to the first floor, his boots clicking loudly. Each step punctuated his dissatisfaction…with Skefton, with his staff, and even himself. He had been proud of running a secure and ordered office, yet recent events indicated that might not be the case.

Still, he felt he could rely on Ware and Sherbourne. Their skills and loyalty had been proven time after time. If the cipher could be recovered—if it hadn't been destroyed or smuggled back to France—they would find it. He stopped at the bottom of the stairs, blew out the lantern, and turned up his collar as he stepped into the cold night, hoping he was right.

• • •

Sherbourne Manor was quiet that Sunday evening. The only house guests, Miss Hodges-Jones and her nieces, had taken a tray in the elderly woman's bedchamber, and Lucien enjoyed a private meal with Sherry and his parents. After sharing a bottle of port and a few hands of cards, Lucien and Sherry retired for an early night.

They were on their way to the Selkirks' country home by mid-morning on Monday. The day had dawned clear and cool, decent traveling weather, and despite their timely rising, they had missed Miss Hodges-Jones's departure by more than an hour. Lucien suspected the managing older niece was responsible for the hasty exit. Since it didn't matter in the least to his inquiry, he turned his thoughts to the day ahead. He hoped to have answers or at least a plan of action to present to Rothe by the end of the day.

"That is Selkirk Hall." Sherry pointed through the bare branches of a large oak tree off to the right side of the road.

Easing up on the reins, Lucien took a quick glance at the sprawling, gray stone structure. "Quite a rambling house."

"Owned by the Selkirk family for three hundred years. Half a dozen generations have made changes and added new rooms, resulting in a comfortable hodge-podge."

"I don't recall hearing much about the family when we were lads."

Sherry shrugged. "They have no sons, just Cousin Edward, Selkirk's heir. I was invited on his summer visits, but otherwise I had no reason to be there except when collecting my sister. Camie and Emily Selkirk were great friends, and as the older brother it was my duty to fetch her home."

Lucien flicked a glance at his friend, an older brother, yes, but not the eldest, not Sherbourne's heir. Sherry rarely mentioned his half-brother, Graham, but over the years, Lucien had gleaned parts of the story. At nineteen, Silas Sherbourne had been away fighting in the East India conflicts when his young wife died in childbirth. His first-born son was raised by her family in his absence. Over the years, Graham visited Sherbourne Manor infrequently and had never been part of Sherry or his sister Camilla's lives. Still a bachelor at thirty-eight, Graham now lived in London, heir to a country estate he barely knew, a home that Sherry loved but would never own. But that was none of Lucien's business, and Sherry never complained.

The viscount reined in the bays as the Selkirks' groom ran out to meet them.

They were expected, and the butler showed them into the drawing room where the family had gathered. Sir Cedric, a balding man in his fifties, came forward and introduced Lucien to his petite wife Harriet, a pleasant woman whose dark hair was showing streaks of gray, and to their attractive daughter Emily. At Sherry's broad hint, Lucien took the parents aside while Sherry sat down with the daughter. Lucien smiled at his friend's maneuvering. Emily was a vibrant young woman with rich brown curls and green eyes that sparkled when she laughed. He'd be surprised if Sherry remembered to ask her anything about the house party.

Lucien began his own conversation with polite formalities, and right away Sir Cedric asked after his father. Lucien suppressed a sigh. He had not known they were acquainted.

"Only met him once," Sir Cedric explained. "We had a pleasant conversation two years ago at a London dinner party. I found him quite knowledgeable on the farming of barley."

While Selkirk acted surprised by that, Lucien was not. Salcott had always been an attentive steward of his estates. Indeed, he was attentive to every portion of his life, except his only son and heir. Lucien was relieved when his host turned the conversation.

"Just what is going on, Lord Ware?" Sir Cedric's gaze was direct. "No one sends an earl's son down from London to inquire about a petty housebreaking." His voice carried, and Sherry's conversation with Emily halted. The room waited for Lucien's response.

He gave a rueful smile. "I shall not insult you by denying it, sir. Nor can I give you the full explanation you want. Suffice it to say, the Crown has a security interest in Saturday's thievery, and I would be grateful for whatever you can tell me."

Sir Cedric's jaw tightened, but he nodded. "The war, eh? Espionage, perhaps? No, no, I understand you cannot tell us, and I can accept that. How can my wife and I be of help?"

Sherry resumed his tete-a-tete with Emily, while Lucien inquired about strangers in the area, suspicious activities, or odd occurrences. At first, they could think of nothing until Sir Cedric suddenly held up a finger. "That brawl. Not here, but over in Shelby, a forty minute ride. A bunch of young rascals from out-of-town tore up the tavern."

"When was this?"

Sir Cedric looked at his wife. "I told you about it the day Jed told me. When was that?"

"Let me see...two weeks ago, I believe," she said, thoughtfully. "Yes, that's right. It was the day I had a letter from Julia Warburton's mother saying she would be here for the house party."

Two weeks was a long time for a gang of thieves to hang around the area, but the incident was worth pursuing. He would see what local constables could tell him.

"Is it important?" Lady Selkirk asked.

"Hard to say, but we'll find out. Any other thoughts?"

The couple shook their heads, and Selkirk added, "Calney is a quiet village."

"Is that not part of its charm?" Lucien agreed. "What can you tell me about Emily's London friends who attended the house party?"

"Julia and Helen?" Lady Selkirk smiled. "Lovely young women with little interest in anything except fashion, gossip, and eligible gentlemen. They both had jewelry stolen, pretty pieces but of little value."

While she went on to list the young women's lineages and social connections, Lucien sat politely, waiting for her to finish. She came to an abrupt halt with a smile as though suspecting his interest had wandered. "Listen to me go on. One more thing—if this is about the war as my husband suggested...then you may rest easy. If Julia or Helen gave it a thought, they would be loyal to the Crown... and our troops. You know how ladies admire a soldier in uniform. And, of course, Julia has a brother in one of the Hussar units."

"Excellent point, my lady. You have great insight." He glanced across the room to see if Sherry was finished and found him deep in conversation with Emily, their heads close together. The occasional light laughter suggested a flirtation. So that's the way the wind blows, Lucien speculated. If Sherry had his eye on someone in his own social class, he might be serious this time.

Lucien returned his attention to Emily's parents, brought the interview to a close, and stood. "Sherry, are you ready? The village constables will be waiting for us."

"Yes, you're right. We should go." Sherry said his goodbyes to Miss Emily, leaning forward to whisper in her ear. She blushed.

Lucien hid a smile. Beyond doubt, something was happening between those two.

• • •

As Lucien's curricle entered Calney at a slow trot only minutes later, the door of the constabulary hut flew open and a young constable ran toward them.

"Is that Wainwright?" Lucien asked.

"No, but this fellow was at the manor Saturday night," Sherry said. "His name escapes me."

"I dare say he has been watching for us." Lucien halted his horses and stepped down.

The constable was already talking in a loud, excited voice. "My lords, there has been a *development*." He paused, full of the importance of it, awaiting affirmation.

"Yes, my good man," Lucien obliged. "What is it?"

But the constable turned in obvious annoyance as Harry ran up and eagerly interrupted, "My lord?"

"Not now, Harry." The constable frowned and reached out to push him aside.

Lucien stopped him by handing the boy the reins. "Ah, Harry, my lad. Right on time. I will settle up with you later." With a quick nod, Harry led the team to the side of the road. Lucien lifted a brow at the constable. "Now, sir, may we hear your tidings?"

"Uh, yes, of course. Tim Barrow, the blacksmith's son...he is one of them thieves! The magistrate has gone to the smithery to take him up."

"Not alone," Sherry protested. "The magistrate is, uh, rather old—"

"Oh, no, sir. The other constables be there too."

"Then let us make haste to join them," Lucien urged, impatient to know what was happening. Waiting for the constable to piece out the story, bit by bit, could take all day.

They crossed the road, cut behind the tavern, and came out on a rutted path. The cottages were smaller and older on this row. As they turned toward the far end, Lucien caught the distinctive odor of burning charcoal and heated metal. A horse neighed somewhere ahead.

As they walked, Constable Jem Liffey introduced himself and then rushed into speech as though determined to impart the rest of the story before they heard it from someone else. He kept up a constant chatter to the effect that a village maid hired for the house party had told young Barrow of the Saturday afternoon trip to the ruins. "She knowed he was up to no good, and he weren't doin' it alone."

At this point, they arrived at the blacksmith's shop. An elderly, rather frail-looking man Lucien presumed was the magistrate and two constables confronted a brawny man wearing a thick apron smudged by coal dust and flying sparks over his heavy coat—the alleged culprit's father, no doubt.

At their approach, the constable that Sherry whispered was Wainwright turned with a scowl. "The lad took off. Got clean away right after the thievin'."

Lucien nodded to acknowledge what he'd said and turned to address the blacksmith. "I assume you are Mr. Barrow. I am Viscount Ware—"

"I'm Barrow, all right," the man cut in gruffly. "And I know who you be, yer lordship, and why yer here. Whole village knows."

"Then perhaps you would be good enough to tell us where we may find your son."

"London. I tol' these gents. Got 'isself work there."

"What kind of work?"

"Din't say. 'Cept a London nob promised 'im a bag o' coin."

"And you didn't ask what he had to do to earn it?" Sherry asked.

The blacksmith shrugged his well-muscled shoulders. "Don't think Tim knew."

The Barrow family appeared to share a regrettable lack of curiosity. "Did he mention the nob's name?" Lucien probed. "Or where he'd be staying?"

Barrow shook his head. "E'll send word." His brow dipped. "The constables say 'e done stole from the big house. That be true?"

"We're not certain. I would like to hear what your son has to say. If he gets in touch—"

"*When* he does, I'll be sendin' word to ye." The work horse tethered beside the forge stamped an impatient hoof, and Barrow picked up his hammer and tongs. "If ye don't mind, work's awaitin'."

"One more question…where did Tim hear about this work?"

"O'er a tankard, I reck'on. 'E said somethin' about a friend named Billy." Barrow shook his head. "Don't know 'im meself."

"Appreciate your time. We'll let you know if we learn anything of Tim."

The big man's gaze softened for a moment. "Right. I be obliged if ye would, 'm'lord." He turned away, his interest again on the horse's set of new shoes.

While Lucien and Sherry walked back to the main road with the local authorities, Constable Wainwright filled some gaps in the story.

"Young Molly Belcher worked at the manor last week. I meant to talk with her this morning, but before I got there, her pa brung her to me. Said she had some 'fessin' up to do. And 'deed she did. She let the Barrow lad and his friends into the manor. They wanted blunt to get to London, so I reckon ye'll find the lot of them in town by now."

"That explains a lot," Sherry said.

"Hmm, yes." Lucien wondered how much more Molly knew about Tim's plans. "Where does the girl live?"

"Three houses from the vicar. You want me to go with you to question her again?" Wainwright asked.

"Not at all necessary. You have done excellent work, and we need not take up more of your day." He smiled and offered Wainwright two coins. "I cannot stay to join you, but I would be honored to buy all of you a round of ale."

"Right kindly of you, sir." Not waiting for further encouragement, the constables and the magistrate took the coins and disappeared into the tavern, laughing and slapping one another on the back.

Lucien approached Harry, still watching over the curricle. "Walk the horses down around the corner, off the main road, and wait there for us. It'll be a few more minutes."

"Sure nuff." The lad's eyes lit with mischief. "But they won't be leavin' the tavern anytime soon to see nothin'."

"Go on with you," Lucien said, amused by the lad's impertinence. He nodded at Sherbourne, and they returned to the dirt path behind the main cottages.

"You think this girl will talk better without them?" Sherry asked.

"Do you doubt it? Half a dozen men standing around would shake any young chit's confidence."

The Belchers' two-room thatched cottage was easy to find. Mr. Belcher bade them enter, his expression stern, as he directed them to the kitchen table where a rosy-cheeked girl of fifteen or sixteen was already sitting. She glanced up with a shy smile as though welcoming their intrusion, and Lucien suspected she had been receiving a lecture from her father. While Lucien and Sherry pulled up chairs across from Molly, the girl's father remained standing near the stove, and her mother quietly disappeared into the back room.

Lucien kept his voice gentle. "We haven't come to cause you more trouble, Molly. I have a few questions, but first, would you repeat what you told Constable Wainwright?"

"I don't 'member what all I said, but it were my fault." She hung her head, staring at her lap. "Papa says so."

Lucien glanced at her father's stoic face. "Fathers always want their children to do the right thing. Perhaps this would go better if you just answer my questions. I understand Tim Barrow is a friend of yours. Have you known him long?"

"Always. We grew up together." Her head came up, and she blushed. "If you mean acourtin', more'n a year. But I guess it's over now. He be diff'rent after Billy come along."

"Who is Billy? Another friend?"

She shook her head. "No friend of mine. Billy Tate. Tim met him during a kick up at the Blue Fox. Over in Shelby. Two, three weeks past."

"Tell us about Billy…and his friends," Lucien said, remembering Sir Cedric Selkirk's mention of a brawl and that several ruffians had been involved.

"Only seen him twice. Older, maybe eighteen, lots of red hair. Thinks he be somthin', he does. He, uh, showed Tim a bag full of coins and said he got 'em working for a fancy lord in London. Them shiny things took hold a Tim's head. He couldna think of nothin' else. It weren't long before he said he and Billy and Billy's friends was goin' to London. I was mighty cross fer him wantin' to run off and leave me behind."

"And after that?"

"I didna see him fer days till I took work up at the manor. Then here he come, actin' all sweet, promisin' he'd come back from London and get me once he was settled. I didna think anything amiss when he asked about them lords 'n' ladies." She shrugged. "I thought he wanted to sweeten up with me, but he dint."

"Why do you say that?"

She gave a resigned sigh. "Because…well, one night he showed up and told me to leave work early on Saturday, before eventide."

Lucien's interest spiked. "What day did he tell you this?"

Her forehead puckered in thought. "Mayhap Wednesday or Thursday."

"Are you certain it was not late Friday or early on Saturday?"

"No, 'twas before I burnt ma's bread Thursday night."

Lucien exchanged a weighty look with Sherry. The theft had been planned before the French packet was intercepted or came into Skefton's hands. Turning the information over in his head, he attempted to reconcile it with everything else they knew…or thought they knew. Common thieves. It had always been a possibility, but an unlikely one. So where did that leave them?

"Did I say somethin' wrong?" Molly asked looking worried.

"No. Just unexpected," Lucien reassured her. "You are doing fine, Molly. Did he say why you should leave early?"

"Not at first, but I kept after him till he confessed he and his friends was goin' to rob their rooms while ever'body was at dinner." She looked up. "I said not to do it, that it weren't right, and it were dangerous. Really I did, but he dint listen to me."

"You shoulda told me," her father grumbled, unable to stay silent any longer. "I woulda put a stop to it."

"I'da got Tim in trouble."

Mr. Belcher shook his head and gave a loud snort. "So now yer both in a hobble."

Molly's lips firmed, and Lucien moved on to the next question before father and daughter got caught up in a row. "Since the theft occurred in the afternoon, not during dinner, do you know what changed their plans?"

"Well, uh, me, I guess. Come Saturday morning, I heard everybody was goin' to them ruins. If the house be empty, I reckoned it'd be safer for Tim, so I slipped out and told him." She sat back and sighed as though relieved to have it over, but her father gave her a hard look.

"Tell his lordship what else you done, Molly."

"I was gonna." She frowned and lifted her chin. "I…I let them in the back door."

Now we were getting somewhere. "How many? Who were they?"

"Five countin' Tim. Four of 'em had scarves tied over their lower faces like they was on the high toby, but I dint know who they was. Billy weren't there."

Interesting. Was he the gang leader, directing things but playing it safe? "What happened then?"

"I showed them the servants' stairs, and that was all. Oh, I said to keep away from Miss Hodges-Jones's room 'cause she was old and sick." Molly twisted her fingers together in her lap and peeped up at Lucien. "I know I shouldna helped them, but, well…if they was goin' to do it, weren't it better that no one be around to get hurt?"

"Been better if you'd tol' your papa 'fore it happened," her father said, getting in the last word.

Chapter Six

Lucien and Finn were on the road to London within the hour. The spirited bays were fresh, and the miles slid swiftly past. At this pace he'd make it to Whitehall before government offices closed, and he was eager to share his latest information with Lord Rothe.

What irony, he mused, that the highly prized cipher had fallen into the hands of common thieves. How did that affect the chances of recovery? He just wasn't sure.

Sherry had remained in the country to oversee the local searches and interview the owner of the tavern in Shelby. Lucien was counting on him to come up with descriptions of the gang members. Without those details or some other clue to their identity, any pursuit of the thieves into London's underworld was no better than folly.

Lucien flicked the reins to swerve around a rough patch of ruts and shot a quick glance at Finn. The small man was hunched into his coat with the sniffles, convinced the country air had given him a nasty cold. Lucien shook his head, settled back into a steady pace, and returned to his own thoughts.

How did the London nob figure into it? Was he the master criminal behind one of London's lawless organizations that ruled the rookeries and dark alleys of the eastside? Or something simpler—a pawnbroker or fence of stolen goods, a gentlemen down on his luck who hoped to avoid debtors prison or pay off a blackmailer by partnering with thieves?

What did any of those possibilities mean for the fate of the cipher? Would the thieves, or whomever they reported to, recognize what they had or toss it away as worthless? Even more troubling, had the thieves known about the packet all along? The criminal world had its own spies, and the cipher would be worth a high price on the black market. If the thieves had planned to intercept the courier and witnessed the soldiers get to him first, they might well have followed the packet to Sherbourne Manor. And what would they do now? Was it destined for a secret auction—or did they already have a buyer?

Lucien's curricle crested a steep hill, and he spotted several carriages clustered below, including a mail coach. He slowed his team to a walk, assessing the situation. A collision blocked the road, backing up equipage from both directions.

"Want me to get down and take a look?" Finn asked.

"No. Stay with the horses." Lucien handed him the reins. "I'll find out how bad it is and see what can be done."

Although no one was injured in the accident, the phaeton involved suffered two broken wheels, not fixable without expert help. The other vehicle, a farm cart, was upended and one of the horses had broken free. When Lucien arrived, the horse had been caught, someone had sent for a blacksmith, and the phaeton's occupants had been offered seats in a waiting coach to get them out of the cold. Beyond that, on-lookers appeared uncertain what to do next. Lucien and another gentleman organized the men to clear the roadway by turning the farm cart upright and pulling the disabled phaeton off to the side.

Due to the mishap, the hour was later than Lucien had hoped when the bays' hooves crossed the various cobblestone, wood, and dirt streets of London. He drove straight to the War Office. Despite the late hour, Rothe would be waiting.

He turned onto Whitehall and stopped at the imposing stone structure with two wings and a center archway, covered by a cupola and clock tower, that led into St. James Park. A courtyard in front of the archway separated the two wings. The Horse Guards were quartered in the north wing, War offices and other administrative offices in the south.

"I cannot say whether this will take minutes or hours, Finn. If I have not returned within the half hour, take the bays home. And get the cook to give you something for that cold. I'll walk or take a hackney."

"A hackney, my lord?"

Lucien's lips twitched. "Disgraceful, I know, but I doubt if one short ride in a hired conveyance will damage my reputation beyond recovery."

He left Finn still frowning his disapproval and entered the building, taking the stairs to the second floor where Rothe had his offices. Although housed within the official section of War Offices, the marquess reported directly to the Prince Regent and had his own set of rooms. The Secretary of War and Rothe cooperated and shared intelligence, but sharing often came *after* missions were completed—except in critical situations—such as the missing key to Napoleon's latest code.

Thus, Rothe's was not the only office active this late in the evening. Lucien noticed lanterns in most of the first floor rooms, and he passed lads carrying messages in and out of the building. As Lucien crossed through Rothe's outer office, two clerks and three under ministers were clustered around a desk piled with reports. They glanced up and eyed him with blatant speculation.

Rothe's private office door stood open, and the marquess sat at a desk of gleaming dark mahogany, its surface nearly obscured by scattered documents. Lucien tapped on the doorframe, and Rothe rose with uncommon haste, an expectant look on his thin, well-bred features. As was his custom, Rothe's lean figure was attired in an elegant gray coat, matching pantaloons, and a silver and black waistcoat. He would have looked distinguished even without the silver streaks in his dark hair. "What news, Ware?"

"Something unexpected." Lucien pulled off his hat and greatcoat as he advanced across the room. "It appears the theft involved—"

"Wait one moment," Rothe interrupted, looking over Lucien's shoulder. "Curious ears."

Lucien turned and caught a glimpse of the two clerks, Joshia Hatcher and Adam Coatley, retreating from the doorway. Shaking his head, he crossed the room and shut the door before returning to Rothe and continuing his report. "The cipher was stolen by a gang of common thieves, one lad local to Calney, the rest may be London-based. Even more surprising…this housebreaking was set up at least a day or two before our soldiers captured the packet."

"Good Lord." Rothe's brows lowered as he took in the implications and sank into his desk chair. "They stole the cipher *by accident*?"

Lucien shrugged. "It looks that way, sir. But why was a London gang even in the area of Sherbourne Manor? Could they have been sent to watch for the cipher? Or was it fate that landed it at a home they intended to plunder? I just don't know."

"Do sit, Ware." Rothe waved an impatient hand. "I want to hear everything."

Lucien went over Molly's interview and other pieces of evidence more than once until Rothe was finally satisfied. In the two hour process, they discussed every possibility, no matter how remote, of who had the cipher now.

"Too many threads come back to London's elite circles and potentially into the government," Rothe said. "If the thieves knew about the Grande Chiffre—either before or after they took it—who told them? It isn't as though it was common knowledge. So, do we have a traitor somewhere? I have to assume so and keep the details of our search as secret as possible." He sighed, rubbing the bridge of his nose. "The Prince Regent will have to be told and one or two others. I'll be as vague as possible, but we cannot keep the facts to ourselves for long."

Lucien shared Rothe's concerns. Prinny was not known for his discretion, nor was his circle of friends, an influential but indulgent group, and one of their main vices was gossip.

"It cannot be helped," Rothe said. "Follow up as we discussed—young Barrow, Billy Tate, pawnshops—" He cut himself off and shook his head. "Devil it, I do not need to tell you what to do. Carry on, and report when you have something I need to know. Let me worry about the rest. I shall discreetly ask Bow Street to watch for Barrow and Tate, and I'll talk with the War Secretary. Perhaps someone will know of organized gangs roaming the countryside or highwaymen active in the Calney area."

"What about the nob involved?"

"*If* there is one." A grim smile creased Lord Rothe's face. "Social gossip may help us there. These little secrets do tend to get out. I will ask around."

Lucien got to his feet, picking up his hat and greatcoat. "So shall I."

"Work with haste and as little fuss as possible. If we could recover the key without the French knowing we have it… By Jove, Ware, think of the intelligence we could forward to our generals. It might shortened this damnable war."

"None too soon," Lucien said. "By the by, I noticed the code-breakers were working late tonight." His tone invited Rothe to explain.

"Their decision, not mine. Word of the key being in England has given them hope. Skefton said it had columns, not a wheel, and they seized upon that as a place to start. Not enough, I fear, but I would not gainsay them."

Lucien slipped on his greatcoat. "Sherbourne should have news soon if anything else is happening in the Calney area, including French activity. By now, Napoleon's staff knows they are missing a courier. They're bound to have someone trailing the cipher too…if they haven't already recovered it."

"That would be unacceptable," Rothe said bitterly.

"My lord?"

"Letting the key slip through our fingers would be the biggest bungle of the war."

When Lucien stepped out of Rothe's office, the same two inquisitive clerks and under-minister Storr scattered to their desks. Storr glanced at Lucien and then looked away. Had they been eavesdropping again, or just gossiping when they should be working?

Lurking outside Rothe's door was unprofessional. Their avid interest in the cipher was understandable, but these men were paid to respect secrecy. He was tempted to report the incident to Rothe.

Lucien put on his hat and gloves while he debated. *Devil take it.* He was seeing trouble everywhere. No one deserved to lose his job and reputation over a minor lapse of curiosity. He gave each man a warning scowl and walked out, headed for the stairs. He'd take a much harsher view if it happened again.

Exiting the building with a frown still on his face, Lucien hailed a hackney, slumped against the carriage's worn seat, and closed his eyes. His Hays Mews townhouse near Berkeley Square was not that far, and he would have walked but for the bitter cold and a nagging ache in his temples. Rothe's frustration had added to his own. The prospects of recovering the code key were daunting, and the marquess was hoping for—no, counting on—a miracle. Lucien was not certain he could deliver one.

The hackney jolted to a stop. As Lucien stepped down, he noted that Hughes had lit the lantern at the top of the wrought iron arch over the walkway, illuminating the two front steps, the cream-colored side pilasters, and the overhead fanlight framing the dark blue door.

Discarding any thought of going out for the evening, he handed his coat, hat, and gloves to Hughes and bespoke a hot meal. After picking at his food, he retired to the library with a glass of brandy, dropping into his favorite leather chair next to the fire. He rubbed his right temple and pondered his schedule for tomorrow. Where did he start?

His valet woke him at midnight and suggested he'd be more comfortable in bed. Lucien had dozed off before forming any kind of plan or even finishing his brandy. He nodded at Talbot and left his glass sitting on the side table.

• • •

Morning brought a clear head and fresh perspective. After a substantial repast, Lucien charged his footman Robert with a particular errand and called for his grays—his favorite team to get around town—and the phaeton. The somewhat larger carriage with its raisable "head" should offer some protection from the bitter wind. He arrived at Mrs. Sophia Stine's residence by ten thirty, a most unfashionable hour.

Sherry was behind the times in assuming Lucien had a romantic relationship with the raven-haired widow. They had once shared a torrid *affaire*—eleven passionate, gratifying months—but when Sophy made it plain she wished to marry again, and Lucien realized he saw no long-term future for them, they mutually agreed to back off. That was more than a year ago. They had made the difficult transition to friends—not that he wasn't tempted now and then, and he had seen *that* look in her eyes, but they had persevered with the friendship.

And friends could be called upon for assistance. Sophy was highly social and privy to most every *on-dit* in town. If anyone could help him sort out the house party guests and any nob who might resort to thievery to solve his financial problems, it was the Widow Stine.

Entrusting the grays to Finn, Lucien bounded up the front steps. The butler raised a brow at the viscount's early, unexpected arrival. "Madame is not receiving yet, my lord."

Lucien grinned and handed him his hat and coat. "Don't bother to announce me. Sophy," he shouted up the stairs, "are you decent?"

"Lucien!" a laughing voice called back. "Do come up, darling. Nothing is showing that you have not seen before. Where have you been these past ages?"

He entered her bedchamber to find the lady sitting at her dressing table, wrapped in an oriental, red and black silk robe. Her lady's maid Maria was doing her hair. "You are up early," he remarked. "I was afraid I would find you still in bed."

"Afraid or hopeful?" she asked with a coquettish smile.

Lucien chuckled. "Perhaps a little of both."

"Well, you are sadly out of luck. I am being taken for a drive through Hyde Park in an hour or so."

"A new beau?"

"I have not decided." She moved a long, black curl off her shoulder and studied the effect in the looking glass.

His smile broadened. "Well, bundle up, my love. It is quite crisp this morning."

Maria finished with her mistress's hair, and Sophy turned to eye him. "Why are you here at this dreadful hour, Lucien?" She gave an exaggerated sigh. "I can tell it is not for my delightful company. You have that resolute look about you."

He arched a brow. "Do I? You wound me. I always enjoy your company." He paused before adding, "But I confess you do know me well. I have come to ask a favor."

Surprise flashed across her face. "Truly? Since I am certain I will grant it, shall I regret it afterwards?"

"I hope not. To be more precise, I am in need of information, a bit of gossip."

Her expression lit up. "Oh, excellent. I feared it was something serious, and now I confess to being intrigued. Maria, leave that task for later, please, and come back to help me dress in half an hour." Sophy stood and linked her arm with Lucien's, drawing him toward the chairs by the marble fireplace. Maria closed the door on her way out.

"Are you just going to quiz me, or might I know what this is about?" Sophy looked up at him with speculation as he seated her.

The warmth of the fire felt good after his chilly ride, and he turned to warm his hands for a moment before turning back to her. His lips curved upward. He'd expected her to wheedle him for the full story behind his request, and since she could not be much help without knowing it, he gave a succinct summary. "Thieves broke into a country house on Saturday while family, guests, and most of the servants were on an outing. Among the property taken was a document of great value to the Crown. It is not clear whether the thieves knew what they were taking or merely admired the decorative travel desk in which it was hidden. Whoever took it, for whatever reason, recovery is imperative."

"Oh, my. And you've been given the task?"

"Yes, but I wasn't finished with my tale. One of the thieves, a village lad, claimed they were working for a *London nob*."

Sophy's green eyes widened. "One of us? How delightfully vulgar. The boy must be made to reveal this person's name at once."

"An excellent thought, my dear, except he took off. To London with the rest of the gang, we presume, and as you know, this is a big town. The odds of locating one young lad without some direction are not to my liking. The nob might be an easier do…yet I find myself at a standstill. Where to start? He—or she—could be one of the houseguests, and they are under scrutiny, but of equal possibility, if not greater interest at this point, are lords or ladies driven by reasons yet unknown."

"Yes, I see. Young gentlemen are not above going off on a mad lark, often inspired by a wager," she offered.

"I shall look at the betting books and ask around the clubs, but I'm doubtful that's the answer. The theft appeared well planned and executed. Professionals, I suspect. Hired by someone with a desperate need for funds—gambling debts, poor investments." He hesitated and then told her the rest. "Considering the document taken, one of Prinny's enemies may be involved, someone sympathetic to the revolutionaries…or, heaven forbid, to the French."

"The French?" She eyed him. "So, that is why *you* are investigating. Is this document truly that important?"

When he murmured, "Even more," she sighed.

"Let us hope it is not already in the hands of enemies." Sophy paused in thought. "If the nob needed money, would he gain enough from one house theft to pay his way out of serious trouble? Ladies do not take expensive jewelry to a stay in the country."

"I had not considered that," Lucien admitted. "But that is not to say this was their only housebreaking."

"Even so…" She gave a quick shake of her dark curls. "Most of our class would not rub shoulders with common thieves merely to pay debts. Trust me, Lucien, more is at stake. Perhaps if you told me the names you have…"

"There *are* a few houseguests of whom I know little or nothing."

"Why, Lucien, aren't you the sly-boots?" Her eyes twinkled. "You truly did come to me looking for gossip about our peers and acquaintances. I should be offended you believe I trade in common tittle-tattle… although I do love a good story."

He laughed. "Never *common*, my dear."

She sniffed. "Well, who are they?"

"Lady Braden comes first to mind."

"Isabelle? At a country party?" Sophy let out a soft gurgle of surprise. "Oh, mercy. I would love to witness that. So, her husband has finally dragged her from London and its many temptations." She tapped a finger on her pursed lips. "Yes, at first blush, she does make a good suspect. Her heavy losses at the Faro tables, her romantic indiscretions. However, they are very well known…and theft? Not that it is morally implausible, but she would never think of such a scheme."

"What if someone suggested it?" Lucien asked, reluctant to give up his best suspect.

"She would laugh. Isabelle expects Lord Braden to take care of everything…and he does, paying debts and ignoring the rest. Heaven knows why. Most husbands would have exiled her to the country three years ago when she came close to ruining young Collings. No, my dear, she is too indifferent to debts and her reputation. Who else do you have?"

"Julia Warburton and Helen Arcott. They are friends of Emily Selkirk, and Lady Selkirk vouched for them."

"I'm not surprised," Sophy said. "Both are proper young ladies, nothing out of the ordinary. Julia is a sweet thing but quite featherbrained, and Helen is the opposite, far too level-headed to be in the peak of fashion."

"And Patrick Ramsey?"

"He was there? Now that is interesting. Old family. Old money. A second son with independent means and engaging manners. He is popular with the younger set but quick to take offense. Last week, he seriously wounded the Lorrington heir in a pistol duel. Over a woman, of course. The incident caused quite a stir, and the Lorrington family threatened to lay charges against Ramsey until it was certain the injured man would recover."

"That clears up one mystery," Lucien said. "A hasty retreat from London explains why he brought his dueling pistols on a country visit."

"Was George Voss with him? He was Ramsey's second."

Lucien gave a confirming nod. "Good friends, I take it. Sherbourne said Voss has an actress in keeping. Is that common knowledge?"

Sophy laughed. "Oh, yes, the Darby woman. An opera singer, and just the latest of a string of very public affairs. He is also well-breeched. A n'er-do-well man on the town. I scarcely think he would consort with thieves or spies. However, if you discover one of those two is caught up in something nefarious, so is the other."

"Noted. Meanwhile, you've left me with no suspects. Everyone else at the house party was already crossed off my list."

"Then we must think of new possibilities. I must confess, Lucien, this is most intriguing. Let me see… On the political side, nobody comes to mind who has advocated radical or reformatory ideas. But of course, they would keep such controversial views secret, would they not? Maybe so deeply hidden that Society doesn't know."

"One would try," Lucien agreed, "but secrets don't always stay secret. Otherwise, there would be nothing for the gossips. By the by, I would be remiss if I did not include the names of Colonel Philip Skefton and his secretary, Horace Simms." She looked at him sharply, and he realized his tone had given away his own antipathy.

"Never heard of Horace Simms." She gave a delicate shrug of dismissal. "The colonel makes infrequent appearances at musical soirées and dinner parties. He is quite stiff, haughty—and is widely considered a dead bore. How did he become a suspect?"

"A guest at the house party."

"Well, there you go. Since I find him tedious—and I can tell he is not in favor with you either—I nominate Colonel Skefton to be the traitorous thief," she said with a hint of laughter. "In fact, may I make suspects of all those in Society who I do not hold in high esteem?"

He quirked a brow. "We both know you will do as you please, dear lady. For purposes of *my* inquiry, however, you may only include those who associate with denizens of the underworld."

Sophy gave an unladylike snort. "If association is your criteria, I fear that would be a large group. Young gentlemen, in particular, frequent certain houses near Drury Lane and Charing Cross, among others, where they have abundant opportunity to meet all manner of lawbreakers. If you like, I shall ask around if anyone's activities have drawn particular notice of late." Her smile returned. "Being subtle, of course. I find myself quite eager to assist you by exploring the latest gossip at this evening's parties."

"Not that you need an excuse." Lucien chuckled, stood, and raised her hand, bestowing a kiss. "My gratitude, Sophy. I apologize for interrupting your toilette, but you have been helpful...and delightful company, as always. I shall take myself off before your beau discovers us and challenges me to pistols at dawn." He stepped back. "Please keep my inquiry between us. For the present, it must remain secret."

"You know I will." She stood, her gaze troubled as she reached out a hand to touch his cheek. "Desperate or driven people can be dangerous, Lucien. You must be careful. I do not have so many true friends that I can afford to lose one."

Chapter Seven

When Lucien returned to his townhouse late that morning, he found his footman and valet in his bedchamber, examining a stack of clothes set on the dressing table. Robert was laughing. The valet's expression was pained.

"Nothing to your liking, Talbot?" Lucien strode across the room wriggling out of his coat, and Talbot jumped to assist him.

"These…used tradesman garments Robert fetched are drab, inferior in quality, and I must add they have a slight *odor*, my lord."

"Only slight? They sound perfect," Lucien responded with a grin. "Will they fit?"

"Fit *you*, my lord?" Talbot gasped, stricken by the prospect.

"That is the plan."

Talbot swallowed hard at his master's odd behavior and began a grievous perusal of his choices. "This, this, not this, but this might do…and these, if you must. Where do you propose to wear them?"

"To make inquiries in St. Giles, Seven Dials, and any other place frequented by lawbreakers and cutthroats where Viscount Ware would stand out and a man of trade might not."

"You can't mean to go there alone," Robert said. "I should go with you."

"Wouldn't that defeat the purpose?" Lucien shot a quick glance at his six-foot, handsome footman. The viscount's own height was already a disadvantage, but two tall men might as well be preceded by a town crier. "How could we ever hide your pretty face?"

Even Hughes pressed his lips to cover a smile.

After a time, Lucien glanced in the full-length cheval glass and pronounced himself satisfied with the transformation to the unassuming man he saw. His hair was rumpled, his working class clothes a nondescript brown and frayed at the collar, cuffs, and elbows. And the boots? Well…Hughes cringed at the sight of them. Lucien wrinkled his nose. His valet was correct about the odor from his new attire, but stale sweat would not be noticed where he was going.

"Shall I call for your carriage, my lord?"

"No, I shall find my own way. You're excused, Robert. Thank you."

As Lucien left the house five minutes later, Finn ran up to him. "Ye can't be meanin' to take a hackney agin," he protested. He stopped to look his master up and down. "Where ye be goin' lookin' like that?"

Lucien knew his servants were often too outspoken, but living alone he had allowed it and honestly didn't mind. He eyed the smaller man and played to his groom's weakness. "I am starting the day in Seven Dials, which is no place for my horses."

"Nor ye." Finn frowned, then gave him a knowing look. "Ye be followin' the quids."

"If by that, you mean looking for the thieves' stolen goods, then yes. I assume some of them have been sold by now, and if I can discover where, I hope to find out who brought them in for sale."

"I ken ye." Finn's shoulders slumped as he turned away. "But watch yer back, m'lord."

• • •

Lucien stepped down from the hackney at the edge of St. Giles Parish. After a swift glance around, he hunched his shoulders in his worn coat and set out on foot, his head down, his gait relaxed but steady. As hoped, he aroused little interest. On the narrow streets of row houses, he only met four women hastening to market or to complete other errands in order to get home and out of the cold. Half-frozen laundry moved stiffly in the gusts of wind that did little to remove the odors of human and animal waste that wafted from the streets and refuse piles. The dense housing of the rookery, built to provide for the working class, now bulged with immigrants and those moving in from the country to find jobs. But good jobs were scarce. In order to survive, families took to menial labor or became street hawkers, costermongers, pickers, and dustmen. Others turned to thievery or worse.

He turned onto Little Earl Street, approaching Seven Dials, a seedy part of town named for the intersection of seven streets like spokes on a wheel with a sundial pillar in the center. Lucien increased his vigilance. The area had started as a respectable neighborhood in the mid-1690s but over time deteriorated as houses were subdivided into lodgings, shops, and even small factories. Every street boasted at least one tavern, and pawnshops—many owners doing double-duty as fences of stolen goods—were easy to find. Cutpurses, pickpockets, and thugs inhabited the alleys and dark corners.

Lucien's ultimate destination was the area's collection of pawnshops. Despite the biting cold, street activity was greater as he grew close to the main intersection, and he dodged and threaded his way among grubby children, scurvy dogs, a hawker shouting "Sharps and Pots," housewives, and merchants with food stands. A dozen or so of the poor and unemployed with no place to go had started a fire in the street and were huddled around it.

Keeping a hand on his pocket, and an eye on where he placed his feet on the unswept street, Lucien studied the vendors and shops for any indication they might be fencing illegal goods on the side. He stopped twice, once at a stand of trinkets and again at a likely-looking costermonger who was selling "special" items hidden behind the piles of potatoes in his cart. Neither hawker had the goods Lucien described but were willing to sell him anything they had at what they insisted was half the going price. He shook his head and asked about other possible sellers, paid each a shilling for the information, and moved on.

When the vendors along the street yielded nothing, he started his rounds of the pawnshops. At each stop, he used the same story, portraying himself as the nephew of an elderly woman cheated of most of her valuables by two young swindlers.

"I hope to retrieve a few pieces for her. Family heirlooms, largely of sentimental value," he told the pawnbrokers. Typically, they were uncooperative until he said he was offering to buy the pieces back. That always caught their attention, and they listened to Lucien's description of the five items he felt were unique enough to identify: a ruby necklace, a sapphire broach, an ornate and valuable Rousseau watch, the engraved dueling pistols, and Colonel Skefton's rosewood writing box.

By four thirty, he had examined dozens of items and been offered "good buys" to console his imaginary aunt but nothing on his list. Exiting from his latest disappointment, Lucien scowled at the dark shadows. Dusk had fallen; shops were closing. The search had taken longer than expected...and been less fruitful. Perhaps he should have brought Finn or Robert to help. He reluctantly turned toward home.

As Lucien rounded the corner of Earl Street, he spotted the three gold balls of a pawnshop and the name Pratt's in the window of a shop tucked next to The Black Hat tavern. The "Open" sign was still up. One last try.

He stepped inside, setting the bell over the door tingling. A graying man with a short beard and a few extra pounds straining the buttons on his dark-brown vest looked up from behind a glass-topped counter. Shrewd eyes scrutinized Lucien, no doubt calculating the size of his purse.

Lucien glanced around. The shop was rather small, but the owner had made good use of the space, displaying a wide variety of merchandise. Beyond the counter, shelves lined each wall, and the floor space contained neat rows of tables, large baskets, two coat trees draped with shawls and scarves, and a large umbrella stand holding an assortment of umbrellas, parasols, and ornate walking sticks.

"May I help you, sir? I was about to close, but I'm happy to show you anything of interest. We have something for everyone."

Lucien smiled affably and approached the counter, verified he was speaking with Mr. Pratt, and recited his standard story. He showed him the list of stolen items.

The old man shrugged after a quick look. "Don't recollect any of those. You can look around for yourself."

"Thank you. I believe I will." On the second rack, Lucien picked up a silk shawl that might be one of those stolen from Emily Selkirk's London friends. It had an edge of entwined blue flowers that Sherry's notes had mentioned. Lucien ran the fine silk through his fingers and regretted he had not taken the time to interview the two young women for a more detailed description. "Lovely shawl," he said.

"Came in just yesterday. Any young lady would be well pleased to receive such a gift."

"Do you recall who brought it in?"

"A lad, I believe."

"Red hair?" he asked, thinking of Billy.

"No-o." Pratt's voice was careful now. "A straw-haired country lad. Nice enough but not onto town ways if you ken what I mean."

His pulse jumped. Tim Barrow?

"Did he give a name?" Lucien no longer hid his interest.

The shopkeeper's smile faded into a look of wary resignation. "They never do, and I don't ask. They'd just fib." He sighed. "I guess you're gonna tell me this was one of your young rascals."

"He might be. You must have questioned why a country lad would come in with such a fine silk shawl. Did he sell you anything else? Perhaps items of similar or greater value?"

Pratt's face hardened. "I don't take in goods I know are stolen."

"No offense intended, sir. I am not a thief-taker from Bow Street, and I assure you I'm prepared to pay to recover my aunt's property."

The man huffed to himself. "Well, there was a watch." With obvious reluctance, Pratt opened a small drawer on the back of the counter and reached inside, pulling out a tray of watches, cuff links, stick pins, and other men's jewelry.

Lucien resisted the urge to grab Ret. Gen. Miles Whipple's distinctive Rousseau pocket watch. There was no mistaking the 1660s heirloom: a gilt brass watch in an engraved silver case carrying the watchmaker's name. The face held three dials and an aperture, showing the time, month, day, moon phase, and zodiac symbol, surrounded by elegant scrolling foliage.

He nodded and picked it up. "This is one of the pieces. The watch has been in our family for six generations. How much are you asking?" Lucien watched the man struggle between greed and honesty. He waited to see which would win.

"For you, fifty pounds."

Pratt had compromised, stating a sum above what he would have paid the thief yet far below the watch's true worth. "Twenty-five," Lucien said. "I dare say you are still making a good profit and free of unwanted notice from authorities."

Pratt nodded, knowing full well Lucien could call a constable and recover the watch without paying a quid.

"What else did the boy bring you? Do you have a Rosewood writing box?"

"Nah, he didn't offer one. Sold me a set of fancy dueling pistols, but they were engraved with a family crest, and I offered them to the owner first."

"Ramsey," Lucien said.

Pratt's eyes widened. "Yes, that's the name. How did you know?"

Lucien scrambled for a reasonable explanation. "His family are neighbors of my aunt. She wasn't the only one fleeced."

The pawnbroker accepted that. "Well, the young buck who lost the pistols was right pleased to buy them back."

Which meant he paid well, Lucien thought. "Yes, no doubt. Now, about the lad who sold these…had you seen him before? Any idea where I might find him?"

The man pulled a disinterested face. "He'd been drinkin' at the pub next door. Sly sent him to me, but I don't know anything else about him."

"And Sly is…?"

"The publican of The Black Hat tavern."

• • •

Lucien paused at the tavern door to allow his eyes to adjust to the dim interior. Unlike the elegant pubs on Fleet Street or the gentlemen's clubs of London's west side, the Black Hat's dark, rough-hewn furnishings and low-beamed ceilings were worn with age and created deep shadows, lightened by a few candles, the lanterns hanging over the bar, and the fire from a stone hearth. It smelled of stale beer and smoke.

Choosing a seat at the far end of the bar, Lucien swiveled sideways so he could see a major portion of the room and ordered a pint of ale. He nodded his thanks as a man in his early forties with long, dark brown hair tied back set down his drink. A patron addressed him as Sly, but he was in a hurry filling orders for the bar maid, and Lucien didn't attempt to engage him. Instead, he let his gaze drift around the tavern.

It was early, and the occupants appeared to be unskilled laborers on their way home or those whose day of petty thievery or begging had netted sufficient coin for a pint. Nobody fit the Barrow boy's description or that of his friend Billy. Noting how chatty the pretty barmaid was, Lucien took his tankard to a nearby table, caught her eye, and signaled for another fill.

She grabbed the empty tankard and soon returned a full one with a saucy smile. "Ye be new 'round here."

"First time. I was supposed to meet a young friend, but he's late. I don't suppose you've seen him. A fair-haired lad about eighteen. Name's Tim."

"Not t'night. Sorry."

"I hope I'm in the right place. Have you seen him before? Maybe last night? Or you might recall his friend Billy with the red hair?"

"Can't recall everybody." She flashed him stiff smile, not as friendly as before, and left.

Drat. A clumsy misstep. Did she not know Tim, or was she put off by a stranger's questions? *What now?*

He had taken his first swallow of the new pint when Sly slid onto the opposite bench. The bartender's dark eyes speared him, and his voice came out in a low growl. "I don't like strangers comin' in bothering my staff. I seen ye switch places. Thought Letty wud be an easier mark than old Sly, huh?"

"I did, yes," Lucien said, realizing all he could do was brazen it out. "I'm trying to locate a young friend."

Sly's mouth twisted warily. "Why? Despite yer togs, ye're not the kind that comes in here. What's the lad done?"

"Fallen into bad company. Thieves."

"It happens. Times are bad."

Lucien eyed the other man. "Not the petty stuff. Professional lawbreakers, cutthroats. Tim's just a country boy. They'll soon have no use for him."

Sly nodded slowly, as though considering the implications. "Why are ye tellin' me?"

"You met the lad. You sent him to Pratt last night."

The man's lips drew back in displeasure. Lucien suspected the pawnshop owner would soon be getting an earful.

"He won't survive here," Lucien persisted. "Tell me where I might find him or his friend Billy Tate."

Sly's head came up. "He be hangin' with Red Billy? Your lad come in here alone."

"Billy brought him to London."

Sly exhaled a gusty breath, stared into space, and finally said, "You best be lookin' on the docks. Anchors Down tavern. I wouldna go after dark, nor alone, if ye value yer skin. But ye best hurry. Don't tell 'em I sent ye."

When Lucien left the tavern, he was struck by how dark it was. Low-hanging clouds obscured the moon, and he could hardly make out the store fronts in the developing fog. Street lanterns were few and far between, shedding little light. Too bad the area had not progressed to the gas lighting that had recently appeared on parts of Pall Mall. As it was, he could see no more than a few feet away. If cutthroats were waiting in the shadows, he would never see them until too late. He struck off at a brisk pace, staying close to the street. The sooner he was out of St. Giles, the better.

A part of him was tempted to head straight to the docks, but without a hackney or someone to back his play, it would be a long, cold walk through undesirable and dangerous streets with little hope of success. Grudgingly, he turned west. On the first two streets, he passed several men hurrying home to dinner and a boisterous band of young rowdies who might have given him trouble if he had looked worth the effort. Once he entered the section of row houses that had been dotted with laundry earlier in the day, he had the road to himself.

Or he thought he had.

In the silence, he grew aware of footsteps behind him. The sound unmistakable and somehow furtive. He stole a glance over his shoulder. In the dim light of the solitary lantern at the last road crossing, he made out two figures ducking into a shadowed storefront. Lucien increased his pace. Perhaps they were on their own business that had nothing to do with him, but he wasn't taking any chances. Many years had passed since he first learned the scent of peril.

Moments later, the rhythm changed, the footsteps drawing closer. Lucien wasn't worried yet. He had an army knife in his right boot. What concerned him was the possibility more cutthroats had circled around to get ahead of him. He eyed the shadowed, foggy road crossing just ahead.

Changing direction without warning, Lucien cut across the street. As soon as he heard running steps behind him, he broke into a run. Rounding the first corner he came to, he slipped into a dark lane and yanked the knife from his boot. The putrid smell of rotten food, human refuse, and things he chose not to think about assailed his nostrils with rabid persistence. Rats rustled in the debris at his feet, but Lucien didn't flinch. He had played this game before. He gripped the knife, waited...and listened.

Stealthy footsteps crept nearer. Two male voices, low and cautious, whispered in a language Lucien knew well. Frenchies.

"Where did he go?"

"In there. I am sure of it."

Lucien stepped into their path, flashing the knife in their faces so they couldn't miss it, and spoke in their native tongue. "Looking for me?"

Reacting clumsily, one man swung a wooden club, missing him, while his companion scuttled backward, shouting for help. Three men sprang from the fog on the far side of the street.

Bloody hell. Lucien didn't care for the odds of one knife against five cutthroats. On the club's second swing, he slashed open the arm wielding it and kicked him in the groin. Lucien took off running again. Shouts and pounding boots chased after him. He cut to the next street, hoping to find a better place to hide or even a night watchman—not that a Charlie was likely in this part of town.

After crossing two more street corners, he was breathing hard. He couldn't keep up this pace much longer. Glancing over his shoulder, he spotted three pursuers. Someone must have stayed behind to help the wounded man. They were closing fast, but three made better odds if he was forced to stand and fight.

Spotting what he thought might serve as a hidey-hole, he darted into a narrow passage between buildings. His mistake was evident the moment figures loomed in the foggy shadows ahead of him, boxing Lucien in. He swore under his breath, sliding to a halt.

"Hey now, wot's this?"

What the devil? It was God's English, somewhat mangled. Cutpurses and thugs undoubtedly but not his French pursuers. A thought occurred that might turn this to his advantage.

"French spies!" he shouted. "Frogs! Right behind me and looking for a fight." Even ruffians and scoundrels could be loyal Englishmen.

"'S'at so? Where? We'll give it to 'em," a gruff voiced snarled.

"There, Blackie. Aye sees 'em." One of the English thugs shouted as Lucien's pursuers appeared in the dim light at the end of the alley. "Let's get 'em, me lads!"

A half dozen ruffians pushed past. Grinning at his good fortune, Lucien accepted this as the perfect time to make himself scarce. He ran in the opposite direction and kept running until his boots hit cobblestones. When he saw increasing numbers of street lanterns ahead, he slowed to a brisk walk. Once he was out of St. Giles, he hailed the first hackney he found.

Resting his head against the hard back of the coach seat, Lucien blew out a breath. That had been close and no chance meeting. Had they followed him all day? Not likely. Anyone hanging around Hays Mews would have been noticed, and after years of covert missions, he wouldn't miss a tracker for that long. They'd picked up his trail recently, but where?

Pratt's? The Black Hat? Yes, one of those or any of the other places he'd stopped to ask questions in the last half hour or so. Someone had sent word to the Frenchmen, someone looking for *him*, or for someone asking similar questions. How had they known about him?

The obvious answer was a person he'd talked to in the last few days or hours was in league with the French. He absorbed this sobering thought, and his lips curled in a grim smile. The attack proved one intriguing fact...the French didn't have the code key either.

So who the devil did?

• • •

Lucien reached home to find his townhouse lit up more than usual, including the public rooms. Did he have a visitor at this time of evening? No coach stood outside.

Hughes met him at the door, his expression set, his pose stiff, a sure sign something had roused his disapproval. "Ah, my lord. A timely arrival. A Constable Tench is waiting in the parlor."

"What does he want?"

Hughes sniffed. "He will not say, except that he wishes to speak with you."

Hence the butler's annoyance.

His curiosity piqued, Lucien took the stairs two at a time, changed clothes to something more fitting his station, and entered the parlor. "I hope I have not kept you waiting long, Constable Tench. May I offer you tea or something stronger?"

The man turned from the fire where he'd been warming himself. "No, m'lord. Thank you. We must not tarry but leave with haste."

"Must we? To where?"

"To view a body."

• • •

Since Tench had arrived on foot, Lucien took his curricle for greater ease in threading the narrow streets, with the constable beside him and Finn on behind. He begin to doubt his wisdom in not choosing the greater safety of a closed carriage when Tench directed him into Wapping and they turned toward the docks. Despite the efforts of the River Police, or in some cases because of them, the area remained lawless. Police efforts to curtail pilfering from the anchored river boats had forced much of the riffraff inland, and the adjacent area had become more violent and dangerous than ever before. Just a week ago an entire family had been brutally clubbed to death, and the vicious assailant, dubbed the Ratcliffe Highway Killer, had not yet been apprehended.

"In there, m'lord." Tench pointed toward a narrow pathway between buildings. Two constables guarded the entrance. "They're waiting for you down there."

Waiting for *him*? He pulled his horses to a stop and handed the reins to Finn. "Don't stray, lad. And stay sharp."

"Aye, m'lord. We be safe enough."

"See that you are. Come, constable, let us not keep your chaps waiting longer." He nodded at the constables standing guard and shifting from foot to foot in the cold.

The glow of lantern light through the fog revealed their destination deep in the alley. Lucien frowned, taken aback by the size of the gathering—several constables and a man he recognized as a Bow Street runner. Then he noticed the tall, slim figure off to the side. Lord Rothe. What had brought him out on a cold night?

Lucien went to him first. "My Lord, what has happened? I did not expect to find you here."

The marquess met his gaze. "I'm sorry to say it, but I believe your country lad has been found."

"Tim Barrow?" Lucien's heart sank. What rotten luck. He had hoped...well, never mind that now.

"Come. Have a look." Rothe walked briskly toward the gathering.

The crowd parted, revealing a man with a medical bag squatting beside a still figure. Lucien had never met the Barrows' boy. Could he provide a trustworthy identification from a vague description? But when the surgeon moved aside, the features of the Calney blacksmith were clearly stamped on the bloodied face of his only son. Lucien sighed at the nasty head wound—a single blow from a club or metal pipe—and the gaping slit on the lad's throat.

"Yes, I'd say that is him. The likeness to his father is strong."

Rothe nodded. "A straightforward killing. He'd done his part, and they got rid of him, just as you predicted."

"I would have preferred being wrong. They didn't waste any time. He just pawned some of the goods yesterday," Lucien turned away from the sight. "Why are all these other people here?"

"The report we received was the Ratcliffe Highway Killer had struck again."

Lucien looked up and down the alley, assessing where they were, and finally nodded. They stood between the Ratcliffe Highway and the docks, not far from the location where a linen draper, his wife, his infant child, and his apprentice had been bludgeoned to death last Saturday night, by happenstance, the same day the cipher was lost. He hadn't realized it at the time, but no wonder Whitehall had been in such disarray on Sunday morning. "You've dropped that theory, I assume."

"Yes. The surgeon says the wounds are different. More efficient, less frenzied. And none of the family had their throats cut."

"And yet everyone is still here," Lucien said.

"Curiosity, I suppose." Rothe cleared his throat. "I waited to talk with you. Barrow's death is a setback to your inquiry. Have you anything positive to report?"

"Nothing except I'm certain the French have not recovered the packet. While I was poking around Seven Dials this evening, I was set upon by Frenchmen. They weren't after my money."

"You weren't injured?"

Lucien shook his head. "No, a fortunate escape."

"No possibility of capturing them, I suppose."

"There were five, and I was alone, sir."

"Yes, of course. I shall look forward to reading your report on how it all came about." Rothe dropped into deep thought. "Walk with me." He turned away from the group and started toward the end of the alleyway where the dense fog would provide greater privacy. Lucien kept pace. "It's not just the cipher I wanted to discuss, although God knows we have to break this new code soon, but...a greater concern has surfaced. I could not speak of this at the office, because..." He turned his head toward Lucien, his features still shadowed in the dim light. "To speak bluntly...we have a traitor inside Whitehall."

A chill touched Lucien's neck. "How do you know?"

"I have suspected it for weeks. Too many leaks of information, disrupted maneuvers on the battlefield, unexplained delays in communications, but I had no proof these weren't just bad luck, fortunes of war. But this morning, I learned the soldiers sent word to me of the cipher's capture *before* it was delivered to Skefton. A message I never received."

Rothe paused to let that sink in. "The soldier who delivered it couldn't locate anyone in charge early that Saturday morning, so being exhausted and knowing it was written in code, he slipped it under my private office door, poking it out of sight. So where did it go? No one admits to seeing it."

"Not Sloane?"

"No, and I'd rather suspect myself."

Lucien had a stab of guilt, recalling his past concerns about office staff. "I should have mentioned this before. The night I returned from Sherbourne Manor, do you recall some of your staff were hanging around your office door?"

Rothe's gaze sharpened. "I do. We closed it for privacy. What are you saying?"

"When I opened the door to leave, I noticed three of them walking away. The thought crossed my mind they had been listening at the door. I dismissed it as misplaced curiosity, but now I have to wonder." He gave Rothe the names of the clerks, Joshia Hatcher and Adam Coatley, and the under-minister, Thomas Storr. "Would any of them have a key to your private office?"

Rothe gave a harsh bark of derision. "Not from me. But half of London might have. Why do you think I lock my private papers and critical documents in a metal box and hold the only key to it? As you are aware, these offices belong to the Home Office. Anyone in Whitehall or in the Prince Regent's group of confidants might have a key to our doors. A dozen individuals of whom I am aware."

"And they could have shared it with a dozen more," Lucien said thoughtfully.

"Devil take it, Ware. You are not making me feel better."

Chapter Eight

Lady Anne Ashburn lifted the quill pen from the page, rubbing at the small ink stain on her finger. Had she missed anything that would interest or amuse her mother? The letter was already long, the first since she had arrived at Aunt Meg's five days ago. She recounted her trip, her short stay at Sherbourne Manor due to Auntie's illness—she was doing much better now—the theft at the house party, how Andrew Sherbourne had grown into such a gentleman, and meeting his friend, the arrogant but handsome—if she was being truthful—Lord Ware. She had *not* mentioned her own ill manners. After all, the fault was his for being so provoking.

Anne jerked her head up when her aunt's maid burst into the room without knocking. "Good Heavens, Mary. What is it?"

"Oh, my lady, forgive me. But you must come quick. The mistress is in *such* a state, and I cannot find her smelling salts."

Anne rose, forcing herself to remain calm in the face of the maid obvious alarms. She set the pen down before she splashed ink all over. "What brought this on? Has she taken ill again?" Aunt Meg had appeared so much better. In fact, she had ventured downstairs to the drawing room the last two days.

"I don't know, m'lady. She was fine when I brought the morning tray. Now she's shaking and moaning. Best you see for yourself… and hurry. If you please," Mary added, getting hold of herself. Her eyes lifted toward the bedchambers above. "Her ladyship is mightily upset."

Anne gathered her skirts and swept up the stairs with Mary close behind. As they reached the landing, Georgina burst from Aunt Meg's bedchamber and ran down the hall away from them. She was sobbing. *What in Heaven's name?*

"Georgina?" The girl ignored her and vanished into her own bedchamber, slamming the door behind her. Dreading what she'd find, Anne hastened to her aunt's room, tapped once, and entered without waiting for a response.

Her seventy-year-old aunt sat hunched in an upholstered chair next to the window; her knitting had fallen to the floor. She clutched a letter in one trembling hand, a crushed handkerchief in the other, and moaned as Anne knelt beside her.

"Oh, Annie." Aunt Meg stared at Anne, her own face gray, appearing to have aged overnight.

"I am here, dearest." Anne took her free hand. "What is it? Are you ill?"

"No, no. Where are my smelling salts? Mary can't find them."

Anne closed her eyes and ran through the house in her mind. Sometimes her ability of total recall came in handy. Where had she seen that bottle? Ah, yes. "Her sewing basket in the parlor, Mary. Fetch them quickly please." As the maid disappeared out the door, Anne turned to her aunt again. "Tell me what I can do. What distresses you so, Auntie?"

"That foolish, foolish child." The elderly woman thrust a crumpled letter at Anne, then dropped her hands to her lap, clutching the lace handkerchief so tight her knuckles turned white. "I should have told you before, but I hoped nothing would come of it. Certainly not this...I never dreamt..." Her voice failed, and she made a strangled sound

Anne read in silence.

My darling Georgina. Anne dropped her eyes to the signature. *Frederick.* Oh, drats. Was this Freddie, the vicar's son? She read on as the young man expressed his undying admiration for Georgina in the most effusive terms reserved to poets and those suffering the pains of their first calf love. He begged his beloved to slip away and meet him.

What a botheration! How unfortunate the young man continued to pursue an affianced woman, but why did his impassioned note merit such drama from her aunt and cousin?

Before Anne could ask, Mary hurried into the room and administered the reviving remedy to her mistress. Aunt Meg drew in a ragged breath.

"Thank you, Mary," Anne said. "She will be fine now. You may go."

"Yes, my lady."

While her aunt was regaining her composure, Anne examined the letter again and turned it over. There was no seal or direction. Eyeing her aged relative to ascertain she was recovered enough to discuss this, Anne asked, "Was this delivered by hand? Is Freddie here?"

"No, no," Aunt Meg moaned. "The damage is already done. That is a copy someone has painstakingly written and sent to me in the morning mail."

"A copy? I don't understand."

Her aunt's bosom heaved as she drew in and exhaled several lengthy breaths. "I suppose I must tell you all. When Georgina came to stay with me, she promised she would cease all communication with the vicar's son. So improper for an engaged lady. Despite her promise, a letter—in fact, the original of this copy—was delivered to her the first night of the Sherbournes' house party." Aunt Meg raised the handkerchief to her lips. "She did not tell me. Not until it was too late, and the letter had been stolen in that dreadful housebreaking." She grabbed a hasty breath, her eyes welling with tears. "Now I must pay five hundred pounds, or she will be *exposed*." The word carried all the weight of standing naked before the world.

"But that is blackmail." Anne was appalled, not just by the shocking amount, but the sheer act of effrontery. "You must be mistaken."

"Well, I'm not. Here is the blackguard's note in which *the letter* was enclosed," Aunt Meg said in a querulous tone as she shoved another paper at her.

Anne read it to herself in an undertone. "Five hundred pounds brought to the library at Barbarys' Christmastide Ball, eleven o'clock, 24 December, will purchase the original letter. And my silence. In the event you fail to pay, the letter is certain to ruin Lord John's holiday." Anne looked up. "What a vile person!" The wickedest, in fact, to prey on an old lady and a child, for Georgina was no more than a willful, naive young girl.

She read it again, looking for anything that might betray the sender. "This is the writing of an educated person," she said. "Any suspicion who sent it?"

"None. None at all." The muffled words came from behind the lace cloth pressed tightly to her aunt's lips.

"Then we must think on it. Who are the Barbarys?"

Aunt Meg sniffed and lowered the handkerchief. "Old and dear friends from London. Bridget, that is Lady Barbary, and I were presented at court together many, many years ago. We were inseparable friends until she married. She still invites me to their annual ball, one of the highlights of the London winter season. I have not attended in more than a dozen years, but when I knew Georgina was coming to stay, I told them I would bring her."

"A dozen years? Then how did the blackmailer know you'd be there *this* year? Who knows of your planned visit?"

"Bridget's household, of course, but the guest list is not secret. Anyone might inquire about it, and they could tell someone else, and... Oh, dear." Aunt Meg's voice trembled. "We shall not go. We must stay away from London," She waved her hand, fluttering the crushed handkerchief like a flag of surrender. "But that will not prevent Georgina from being ruined. I cannot pay five hundred pounds, Annie. Not in two weeks time. Half that amount, maybe, but not all."

"Could we appeal to Freddie for funds? After all, we would not be in this hobble but for him."

"No help there," her aunt said, dismissing the thought out of hand. "He is but a poor, country vicar's son. No funds and apparently no sense. I first thought to apply to Georgina's father, but she cried and pleaded against it. It is true he would be furious."

"As he should."

"Well, yes, and if that was all that would happen, I would tell him, but men can be so impractical. I *know* Roger. He would feel honor-bound to speak with Lord John, and such an advantageous wedding would be off." She stopped on a sharp gasp. "What a scandal if he should cry off! The whispering, the dwindling invitations, and Georgina standing alone beside the dance floor, snubbed by partners at every ball." Aunt Meg dabbed her eyes. "The poor child is devastated and *so very, very* sorry."

"She could have been sorry a little sooner," Anne murmured. She didn't for a moment think her cousin was in love with Freddie. The way Georgina had gushed the past week over Lord John and the lavish wedding plans convinced her Freddie's appeal was the thrill of the forbidden, the romance of illicit, secret meetings. "This is what you both were hiding from Viscount Ware. I thought there was something."

Guilt flushed Auntie's face. "What else could I do? Revealing her childish mistake would not help his inquiry. The letter had no value…or so we thought. Oh, Anne, I have made a muddle of it. How do we get out of this coil?"

Anne sank into a chair. "I don't know just yet. We shall think of something."

• • •

After ordering a pot of tea and doing her best to settle her aunt's nerves, Anne went to find Georgina. The girl presented a forlorn picture, sitting in the window seat of her bedchamber, staring out at the cold wind whipping the tree branches. The last storm had stripped the trees nearly bare. In contrast to the bleak weather, the bedchamber was warm from a leaping fire in the hearth and smelled of lavender, Georgina's favorite fragrance.

The younger girl didn't react to Anne's presence until the touch on her shoulder. She looked up then, her eyes red and puffy. Anne felt a pang of sympathy. Georgina wasn't entirely at fault for being so irresponsible. Without siblings, she had been raised to believe she was the center of the entire world.

"I suppose she told you," Georgina said, her voice subdued.

"Yes."

"I warned Freddie not to write or try to see me. Truly, I did."

Anne sat beside her. "Was that before or after he came to the house party?"

Georgina looked away, returning her gaze to the gloomy scene outside the window. "Well, I told him before I left home that we should not."

"Did you make it a definite no?" Anne remained gentle but persistent.

"I have now. Auntie said I must."

"Now? Do you mean you met and talked with him at the house party?" Aunt Meg had not mentioned that.

"I had to, did I not? On that Thursday before dinner we spoke behind the stables." Georgina's eyes moistened again, and her lips quivered. "We said goodbye forever."

"Really?"Anne prodded. "Did you mean it?"

"Oh, yes. Our last meeting was beautiful and *very* tragic." The girl gave an audible sigh. "I fear he is wounded for life, and I shall love him always, Annie. I shall."

Anne suppressed equal urges to laugh and to shake some sense into her cousin—but, enough melodrama. She absently straightened the twisted cuff on her sleeve and chose her words with care. "I am quite sure you shall, first loves are never forgotten, but your decision to part was very wise for both of you."

"Then why do I feel so awful?"

Georgina looked so forlorn that Anne leaned over and hugged her. "Our emotions are often slow to accept the truth. It will get better, I promise. But for now, we must talk about this blackmail letter."

Georgina pulled back, her expression souring. "That horrid maggot pie! How dare he write to Auntie demanding money?"

"Georgina! Wherever did you learn such language?"

"Fred—I cannot remember. Surely you agree the blackmailer is a horrible, vulgar person."

"Yes, of course, I do. You said 'he'. Do you know who it is?"

"No, I don't, but no lady would do such a thing."

Not a proper lady. "I find it strange the letter was taken. Strangers would not know who Freddie was or that the letter could have any value. Did you talk about the situation to anyone at the house party?"

Georgina looked horrified, her eyes big and round. "I would never. I am not a stupid child."

Somewhat debatable given current circumstances. "Could anyone have seen you together that night?"

"We were careful. No one was anywhere near us."

Anne considered other possibilities. "What about the person who brought the note to you?"

"A maid found it at the back door, and the seal was not broken when I got it. She couldn't know what it said."

"What seal? For that matter, how did she know to bring it to you? I found no name or seal on it."

"Not on the copy. The real letter had both. Freddie was careful it would be read only by me." Georgina slumped back against the window frame. "Why are you asking all these questions? The blackmailer is one of the thieves."

"I'm not so sure. A common thief wouldn't use a Society ball for the exchange. I fear your letter has fallen into the hands of someone far more clever and devious."

Anne pressed Georgina until she was confident her cousin had told her everything that mattered. She finally rose, gave the girl an understanding hug, and left her still sitting in the window seat.

She closed the door behind her with a faint shake of her head. Despite her earlier hopes, Anne could not think of a realistic alternative to meeting the blackmailer's demands.

• • •

That evening, the three women put their heads together, discussing that to do. The lengthy and tearful conversation ended in an inevitable conclusion—a way must be found to pay the blackmailer.

Anne pressed her lips together to keep from blurting out what else was on her mind. She just couldn't distress her relatives further by raising the possibility that the blackguard might renege, refusing to return Freddie's letter, even after payment. Time enough to worry about that if it happened, but she loathed having to trust such a despicable person.

"Where do we obtain the funds?" Aunt Meg asked, her voice tight. "I am sorry, my darlings. I do not have it."

"I have ten pounds left from my allowance," Georgina said. "And papa is sending one hundred and fifty for my Christmastide ball gown. I could buy a less expensive one, and we could use the rest."

"You will contribute all of it," Anne said. "This is your responsibility, Georgina."

"But—"

"We can add new ribbons and furbelows to another of your lovely gowns, one that London society has never seen. You will be fine. I have twenty pounds I brought with me. So that brings us to one hundred eighty."

"I shall tell my man of business he *must* find the rest," Aunt Meg declared, sitting straighter now a plan was taking shape. "And I shall recover my strength to chaperone you in London, Georgina, and…and meet with the blackmailer." When Anne started to speak, her aunt shushed her. "No, Anne. Georgina cannot be allowed to face this scoundrel herself."

"Good heavens, no!" Anne could not imagine how badly that would go. "Nor do I wish you to risk your health, Auntie, in such a frightening situation. You asked for my help, and this is something I can do. I shall deliver the money."

The resulting argument was brief; even Georgina recognized it was the best of rather limited options. Before they retired for the evening, Aunt Meg wrote to the Barbarys that she would be bringing an additional guest. "At least you shall have your first

London ball," Aunt Meg said, giving Anne a tearful smile. "I am happy for that."

The idea startled Anne. She had not thought that far ahead.

Late into the night, she lay awake in bed, listening to a tree branch scrape against the house with each new gust of wind and staring at the ceiling in the dim moonlight. She had finished her letter to her parents without mentioning the blackmail. If she told them, they would be alarmed and forbid her to go to London.

And she must go. There was no one else.

As it was, her parents would be delighted she was extending her stay to include a holiday in London. Her gentle, beautiful mother—left an invalid ten years ago after barely surviving scarlet fever—had become insistent the past year that her father take Anne to London and find a sponsor to bring her into Society. Anne had never asked or even dreamed it would happen, feeling she was needed at home. But Father had hired a nurse this year that Mother had taken a great liking to, and it had made this visit possible. *And now London.*

With even a brief taste of London society a real possibility, Anne found herself excited, and she smiled in the dark...until she remembered with a jolt that she she going there to confront a blackmailer.

Chapter Nine

Lucien frowned at the hazy dawn breaking outside his study window. A spark and pop from the fireplace drew his attention, and he crossed the room to kick the chunk of hot coal back into the fire. Leaning a hand on the marble mantel, he stared into the crackling flames. His jacket, waistcoat, and cravat lay discarded across a chair, his boots dropped beside it. His shirt was untucked and hung open, the warmth of the fire brushing against his bare chest. An empty brandy glass on the table gave evidence of his earlier indulgence, but Lucien was not foxed. He had been thinking for hours.

Tim Barrow's brutal death—a life ended too young, poor lad— left a small village grieving, but it was also a serious blow to the cipher's recovery. Barrow had been their best link to the gang, but Lucien was not at a complete standstill. He had Billy Tate's name, and a confirmed connection between the gang and the London docks. Not that navigating that lawless area would be easy. Between the east end's homegrown cutthroats and French agents, this inquiry was an ever increasing challenge.

Yet none of that had kept him pacing the floor. The traitor inside Whitehall changed everything. He glanced at the empty glass and considered another drink, then rejected the thought. He would need a clear head in the days ahead.

The stolen code key could provide them pieces of Napoleon's war strategy, but it was nothing compared to the urgency of unearthing the French spy privy to all the sensitive information that went through Whitehall—England's troop movements, Wellington's plans, and a host of unrelated government secrets. And what of the danger to Cabinet members or to the palace itself?

Was anybody safe with a traitor in their midst? A lone assassin could bring the monarchy crashing down.

Picking up the fireplace tongs, Lucien retrieved another loose coal and set the tongs back in place. He rubbed his fingers against the early morning bristles on his chin. He should go to bed, but not until he made a decision. His gut reaction was to drop his present inquiry, to interrogate every person in and around Whitehall, to find the traitor and cut out his heart. But if Rothe had been looking for months without success, what could Lucien do that the marquess had not?

Devil it. His course was obvious. Follow the cipher. After all, why was it brought to England if not to use? When he found the code key, it would be in the hands of the traitor.

• • •

After the scene in the alley and his late night musings, Lucien had to dunk his head in cold water to get going by midmorning. Within the hour, he was in the docklands, dressed in clothes more fit for a laborer than an aristocrat. It was a poor disguise. Anyone taking a second look would not be fooled, but he kept his head down and avoided drawing excessive attention. Having Finn by his side in similar attire was helpful.

The streets near the river teemed with workers loading and unloading the hundreds of ships at anchor and with sailors on leave or headed back onboard. Many were already drunk or still inebriated from the night before. The strong odor of fish and sewage dumped into the water was staggering to Lucien, but those who lived and worked in the area took no notice of it. He wrapped the wool neck scarf over his nose.

By-passing the river bank drinking establishments and houses of ill-repute, they made their way toward the warehouses. Finn's cousin Ewan worked at one of them, and with any luck, he could put them onto Billy Tate.

"That be the place," Finn said, pointing toward a two-story, corner building. "I'll get 'im." He disappeared into the building, emerging two minutes later with a man taller and heavier than himself but with the same topsy-turvy red hair.

The sour look on Ewan's face was a sure sign he had no wish to be there. "Cain't help ye," he protested.

"Can't or won't?" Finn growled. "His lordship is lookin' fer bad 'uns. Thievers an' murderers."

Ewan looked away. "Ye be gettin' me in trouble, Finn. I gotta go."

"*Ewan.*" Finn's voice was low but demanding.

Lucien jiggled a few coins in his pocket. "I am willing to pay for information."

Ewan shot him a scathing look. "Keep yer money. It ain't worth me life." He dropped his voice as he turned away. "Since yer 'ere, an dint care 'bout yer own skin, ye could have a pint at Anchors Down." He walked hurriedly back into the warehouse.

"Sorry, m'lord. Thought he'd help us."

"I believe he did." Lucien had heard the tavern's name in Seven Dials and overlooked it in the wake of the attack by the Frenchmen. "I feel a great thirst coming on."

The black paint on the white-washed sign with the anchor was chipped and faded. The tavern's dark interior was similarly neglected, but even at this hour it was filled with noisy, drunken sailors and lightskirts. A fight broke out before they found a seat. The docks had become the most violent section of London, partially due to the drunken sailors, but poverty and resentment bred by the River Police's efforts against smuggling and thefts of ships' goods had festered among local residents. Life had become cheap on the docks.

Lucien stayed well away from the fracas and settled in a back corner, wary of getting caught up in the violence and exposed as an interloper. He shouldn't have brought Finn here.

But the small man acted quite in his element. His infectious grin and Irish blarney worked their magic on the barmaid, and she soon admitted she knew Billy Tate.

"You shouldna be askin' about 'im. Ain't safe," she warned in a near whisper. "But aye, Red Billy comes in 'ere time t' time."

"Today?" Lucien asked.

She glanced over her shoulder nervously and shook her head. "Too early. 'E comes late."

When a second fight erupted, Lucien decided they'd be better off to wait outside. They finished their drinks and left. Lucien was looking around for a place to keep watch on the front door when Finn tugged on his sleeve.

Two large thugs, tough-looking cutthroats with bulging upper arms, walked toward them. Locals stepped out of their way. The men had their eyes trained on Lucien.

"Get out of here, Finn. Do not argue, just go," Lucien said quietly, cutting off his groom's protest. "If you haven't heard from me by evening, tell Hughes. He'll know what to do." His butler was the one person on his staff that had direct knowledge of Lucien's work for Lord Rothe. "Go now."

Finn growled a protest deep in his throat but did as he was told.

The ruffians ignored Finn's departure. They stopped, massive arms hanging at their sides, blocking Lucien's path. The man on the left with a thin scar across his forehead said, "Mr. Cade wants to see you."

Bloody Hell. Lucien hid his surprise. Several thoughts flashed through his head as to why the man known to all of London as the Gentleman Thief wished to see him. "I don't believe I know Mr. Cade. Who is he?" he asked, just to needle them. Who didn't know the name? It figured prominently in street gossip and in the news sheets. Oddly enough, he had yet to be convicted of a crime or arrested more than once or twice. Cade was either very lucky or well-connected through his deep pocketbook.

The thugs didn't bother to answer his question beyond one of them showing the knife held in his fist. "Let's go. *My lord*," the scarred man snarled.

Lucien returned a benign smile. "Such gracious manners. By all means, let us be on our way."

Although Cade's men didn't touch him, with one on each side as they walked away from the dock area, escape was out of the question. Fortunately, Lucien wasn't thinking about escape. He looked forward to meeting the Gentleman Thief.

At the first corner, they turned away from the river, and Lucien spotted the coach with two rearing tigers emblazoned on the doors: Cade's calling card. No one knew if he was entitled to use the crest or if it was a pretension he'd adopted. The ruffians waved the carriage forward to meet them, and Lucien climbed aboard. The guards chose the opposite seat and sat in stony silence throughout the drive. Lucien paid them little mind. He was more than curious to learn Charles Cade's role in this nasty business. For there had to be a connection. Why else would his hirelings be dragging Lucien off for a chat?

Lucien reviewed what little he'd heard about Cade. He owned and operated Cade's Club, a former coffee house now one of London's notorious gentlemen's clubs. Otherwise his background was murky, compiled of rumor and innuendo. Reportedly raised on the streets of London after the death of his prostitute mother, the young street urchin known as Charlie was transported for petty theft. To where, no one knew for sure, but he returned on a privateer ship when eighteen or so to become one of the top receivers of smuggled and stolen goods over the following decade. While his predatory dealings with enemies and business rivals denied him entrance to most of Society's homes, grudging acceptance of his status as a gentleman derived from his elegant lifestyle, his wealth, and his self-proclaimed lineage.

The coach slowed and stopped. When the carriage door opened, Lucien recognized the rear entrance to Cade's Club. Even from the back, the ornate mansion was impressive, a tribute to the business acumen of a self-made man claiming to be the by-blow and last remaining descendant of landed gentry. Hence the crest displayed on his coaches.

The thugs hustled Lucien up the outside stairs to the second level and into a long hall. At the far end, they tapped on a closed door, received permission to enter, and Lucien was shoved inside.

He straightened and got his first look at Charles Cade.

Well-trimmed dark brown hair and mustache, medium height, mid-thirties, dressed in an expensive but conservative style. Indeed, he was a gentleman by appearance.

Cade lifted a brow. "Ah, you have arrived. Do come in, Viscount Ware."

Lucien stepped forward, inspecting the room—a spacious and stylish study from the Persian rugs on the floor to the polished cherrywood furniture—before returning his gaze to the man. "Charles Cade, I presume."

Cade's mouth twitched as though amused. "Just so." He glanced at his men. "Wait outside." When the door closed, he crossed to a side table and poured himself a glass of port. He didn't offer one to Lucien—setting the tone of the meeting. He gestured for the viscount to take one of the arm chairs and seated himself behind the desk. "I must say I had previously thought better of your sense of fashion."

Lucien looked down at his well-used and rather odorous second-hand attire. "Remiss of me, I know, but I had not anticipated such an urgent invitation from the Gentleman Thief."

For several ticks of the wall clock, the two men appraised one another. Lucien felt no particular alarm. Despite the gangs and far-flung criminal activities attributed to Cade, he kept his club scrupulously free of criminal conduct that might arouse the interest of authorities or the disgust of his Society clientele. His gaming tables were reputed to be among the fairest in town, his demi-monde the most discreet.

Although Cade's expression hid much of his thoughts, his pale blue-gray eyes were hard and cold. He took a sip of his port before setting it down. "Then let us get to it. You have been asking questions in parts of town that are unusual haunts for an earl's son, even one with your carefully calculated reputation."

Lucien tensed. Cade implied he knew things about Lucien's background that he should not.

"Nothing to say?" Cade asked.

"I did not perceive your observation required a response. But I do wonder why my activities are of interest to you. Unless, perhaps, you employ Billy Tate, a red-headed fellow with light fingers."

Cade shrugged. "A common name. What do you want with him?"

"He stole several items from friends of mine."

A skeptical smile. "Hardly worth such an extensive search."

"Also suspected of murder."

"Is that so? Regrettable, to be sure, but I would have thought murder was a matter for the likes of Bow Street." Cade leaned forward, his gaze meeting Lucien's. "Your presence in St. Giles and around the docks is making people…uneasy. It is bad for business." He flashed a hard smile. "Stay where you belong, Viscount, or I fear for your safety in these less civilized parts of town. I do not wish you harm…not if it can be avoided…for it would bring the authorities nosing around. I have a proposal instead. I will make the necessary inquiries, and if I come across this Billy Tate, he will be delivered to you."

What the devil was Cade about? Lucien must have touched a nerve somewhere. "I appreciate the offer, but I must do this for myself."

"For Lord Rothe," Cade corrected, leaning back in his chair with a smug look. "Surprised I am aware of the association? London is my town, viscount. Little escapes me."

"You're mistaken this time. My inquiries are on behalf of the Sherbournes, old family friends. Billy and his friends broke into their country home," Lucien said levelly. He had no intention of acknowledging his ties to the War Office. Not to this powerful and ruthless man. "A young village lad was murdered."

"Only one perspective of your inquiry, I think." Cade lifted a hand in a show of indifference. "Never mind. I have no quarrel with your activities in support of the Crown…unless they hinder mine."

"Do I detect a threat?" Lucien asked mildly.

Cade's eyes narrowed. "Think of it as a friendly warning. Accidents to a man of your station might occur if he wanders into unsettled parts of town." He rose in dismissal, his eyes on Lucien. "Have I made myself clear?"

Lucien stood. "I dare say we understand each other well enough. I shall see myself out."

"I trust our next meeting will be more congenial."

Lucien doffed his hat and opened the door. Cade's men were waiting to escort him. He turned to look over his shoulder. "A sentiment I can share. Good day, Mr. Cade."

The club owner gave a single nod and a smile that failed to reach his eyes.

• • •

Lucien stood in an alley behind Whitehall, staring at the second body he had seen in two days. He sucked in a sharp breath of cold dawn air. Not more than fifteen hours had passed since he left Cade's office. He sighed and squatted beside the still form. Limp, red hair hung around the pale face of a youth in his early twenties. His rumpled clothes bespoke London's east side. A knife protruded from his chest, soaking his brown jacket and the ground with a pool of dark blood turning into freezing slush. Lucien reached out a hand to smooth the note pinned to the dead man's chest and read the single scrawled word, "Billy."

He swore under his breath and stood. Cade had delivered Billy all right...and made certain he would never talk. Had the Gentleman Thief taken this drastic step to protect his regular illegal activities or did he have other, more sinister reasons for silencing the young man—such as impeding Lucien's hunt for the cipher? Was it possible Cade was a French agent, even the master spy in London?

A man brushed past the constables and knelt on the far side of the body. Lucien recognized the medical man from the scene of Tim Barrow's death. He wonder if the constables had called him or Rothe. After a short inspection, the doctor looked up, his dark eyes meeting Lucien's gaze. "He died within the last four hours, I'd say. Nothing else I can tell you beyond the obvious. The stab in the heart killed him."

"Thank you." Lucien turned away, allowing the small group to do what needed to be done. He was sickened by Cade's disregard for human life. Not that the club owner had done it himself. A *gentleman* would not dirty his own hands.

If Cade or his cutthroats thought that murdering Billy would stop Lucien's inquiries, they had mistaken their man. Indeed, Lucien suspected he was getting close to answers someone didn't want him to know.

• • •

Having no clear path to the thieves after Billy's death, Lucien changed his approach, moving his inquiry into the haute ton. He spent the next two days making the rounds of society functions from afternoon musical soirees to evening theatre parties, listening to the latest *on-dits*—the scandals, the gambling losses, the unfortunate family connections, diatribes against the Crown— anything that might lead to traitorous activities, the identity of the Whitehall leak, or the mysterious *nob*.

Although Cade remained under suspicion, Lucien picked up other names of interest—including Lord Fitzwilliam, a peer of the House of Lords who had recently married a French cousin, and Edward Bastian, a younger son who was floundering under gambling debts—and passed them along to Rothe. Nothing had yet provoked a deeper inquiry, and Lucien continued his rounds of engagements.

Monday morning, freezing rain lashed at the window panes, and Lucien was in no hurry to navigate the icy streets. He indulged in breakfast in his bedchamber, and midday had passed before he stood in front of his looking glass, putting the final twist on his cravat. Satisfied at last, he shrugged into a dark green coat with Talbot's assistance. He was engaged to meet Sophy and a small group of friends for a museum visit at two o'clock. The latest Egyptian exhibit was reputed to be out of the common order and not to be missed. He also hoped Sophy had learned something to assist his inquiry.

Giving his sleeve a last tug and smoothing his cuff, he paused at the sound of boots running up the stairs and exchanged a look of inquiry with Talbot. His valet shook his head.

Andrew Sherbourne strode in unannounced. "What? Still primping at this late hour?"

"Sherry! Did you just arrive in town?" Lucien grinned in welcome before looking askance at his friend's dripping, windblown hair and soaked garments. "My God, you are drenched...and a disgrace to your valet." He tossed him a towel.

"Is it that bad?" Sherry vigorously rubbed his hair, peered in the looking glass, and made a face before discarding the towel and smoothing his hair back in place. "Don't tell Francis. He might quit on me, and a good valet is hard to find. Although I am certain he suspects. He is following in the carriage, while I rode ahead."

"What possessed you to ride in this weather?" Lucien urged him toward the hallway. "Let us talk in the study. Talbot, take Sherbourne's wet things and send my regrets to Mrs. Stine. Oh, and tell her I hope to call no later than tomorrow."

"Very good, my lord." Talbot grabbed Sherry's wet outer garments and hurried down the stairs ahead of them to be met by a scowling Hughes at the bottom. The butler grabbed the outer garments, studiously ignoring the man who'd dripped all the way up the stairs.

"I could use a drink to ward off the chill," Sherry said as they made their way toward the study. He glanced sideways at Lucien. "I have good news. We captured a French agent in Calney."

Lucien paused his stride. "With the cipher?"

"No. We weren't that lucky. He came to Calney to see if the theft was a false rumor and to verify the cipher was no longer in the area." They continued to the study, where Sherry crossed to the fireplace, thrusting his hands toward the warmth of its flames. "It is bitter cold out there, and I would have waited for the freezing rain to pass, but I had to warn you. The Frenchie was one of four who came into England to retrieve the cipher. The others came to London. Days ago." Sherry turned his back to the fire and rested one arm on the mantel. "We got nothing else from him—no names or descriptions, but they're in town, hunting the code key. And you'll be in their way."

Lucien gave a nod. "I fancy they picked up a couple of friends. I ran afoul of five of them," he said, resting a hip on the corner of his desk.

Sherry's brows shot up. "What happened?"

"A dark alley in St. Giles. Clubs and knives. My skin was saved by a gang of patriotic English cutthroats."

"By Jove, my friend. You get into too much trouble without me." Lucien grinned. "Have you anything else to report?"

"Small stuff. Two bands of three or four Frenchies were chased off at attempted upcountry landings. Bold moves. They may have been bent on other mischief or back up for those already after the code key."

"All this activity proves the cipher is still in England and not yet beyond our reach," Lucien said. "Is that all?"

"Uh, well, nothing else concerning the theft." Sherry dropped into an upholstered mahogany armchair. "Am I going to get a brandy or not?"

Lucien turned away from the sideboard with two brandy glasses in his hands. "Patience, my friend." He handed a glass to Sherry before taking the opposite matching chair and eyeing his partner. "What are you taking great pains to avoid telling me?"

"Not avoid. Just working up to it. We are expected at the theatre tonight. Miss Emily Selkirk is in town for the Christmastide Ball, visiting her friends from the house party. We were chatting before she left home, and the theatre came up. I, um, said we would meet them in their box tonight."

"We? You and me?" Lucien quirked a brow. "You committed us both?" He sighed at Sherry's nod. "What production is playing?"

"Something Shakespeare."

"You hate Shakespeare." Lucien sipped his brandy. "Miss Emily must have been quite persuasive. But why must I share your misery?"

"Devil it, Ware. Quit being difficult. I need you there. You know you are going to go. Now tell me what other trouble you've gotten into…or started."

Lucien gave him a wry smile. "This may pale in light of Miss Emily's imminent appearance…" He paused, watching his friend pull at his cravat. Then his smile faded because what he had to report wasn't amusing at all. "But it affects everything else. Rothe says Whitehall has a traitor on the inside."

Sherbourne straightened with an oath. "Hell and damnation, Lucien. That is not amusing. Egad, you're serious. Does he know who it is? Oh, I suppose not, since you said *has*. What is being done?" He got up and strode to the sideboard. "I need a second shot. How about you?" He picked up the brandy bottle.

Lucien shook his head. "Not for me. Rothe is working on it and hasn't asked for help on his end. I think the best way we can help is to chase down the cipher and hope we find the spy at the same time."

He spent most of forty minutes bringing Sherry up to date on recent events—the pawnbroker, the assault in St. Giles, his meeting with Cade, and Billy's death, including the note pinned to his chest.

Sherry snorted. "Sounds like a warning—here is what you wanted, now stop nosing around or else."

"I am aware."

"Then what—" Sherry's question was interrupted by a loud rap on the study door.

"Yes?"

Finn flung the door open, an indescribable look on his face, something akin to horrified triumph. Lucien came to his feet. "What is it?"

"In spite of wot 'e said, Ewan been askin' around an' learnt t' names o' three coves Billy hung 'round with. But, demme, m'lord, they all be dead." Finn's ruddy face was pale, and his accent so pronounced it took serious concentration to understand him.

My Lord. Had Cade gone on a killing spree and done away with the entire gang? Lucien poured another glass of brandy and handed it to Finn. "Drink this, my man. Then tell me when and how they died."

His groom drank greedily, then wiped his mouth with the back of his hand. "Last week he says. Throats be slashed an' the corpses later spirited away."

Lucien frowned. They died when Billy was still alive? Had he sacrificed them to protect himself?

"French agents may have found them," Sherry said.

"Perhaps." Lucien acknowledged that was a third possibility and looked at Finn again. "Were they tortured?"

"Naw, jest kilt."

"Not the French then," Sherry said. "They would have made them talk first."

Lucien nodded. He and Sherry had seen too many corpses on the Continent after French interrogation. "I agree. This was Cade's order or Billy on his own, covering his tracks."

"And then Cade killed Billy?"

"Seems about right. After I brought up Billy's name."

"Cade is one cold-blooded devil. But why'd he do it? Protecting his criminal interests or was he after the cipher?"

"Perhaps both," Lucien mused. "I intend to find out."

"How?" Sherry grabbed his arm. "You cannot be planning to confront Cade. He has an army of cutthroats to stop you."

"He wouldn't be the first to try. Devil it, Sherry. If Cade is working for the French, what else would you have me do?"

• • •

In full gentlemen's dress with tails and top hats, Lucien and Sherry entered the new Royal Theatre by the Doric portico in Bow Street, passing the statutes of Tragedy and Comedy. Lords and ladies, and likewise mistresses, thronged the grand staircase and the anteroom to the private boxes. Inside the main theatre, the galleries of the privileged and the floor pit of tradesmen and common folk were filling rapidly.

Sherry pointed out the Warburtons' box where they were to meet the ladies on the second of the three balconies that stretched in a horseshoe from one side of the stage to the other. Upon their appearance, Miss Emily introduced Lady Julia Warburton, Miss

Helen Arcott, and two young bucks who were already dancing attendance. Lucien joined in the casual chatter until he spied Sophia Stine in a box across the theatre and excused himself, leaving Sherry and the other gentlemen to entertain the ladies.

Lucien paused at the entrance to Sophy's private box, amused by the scene. Three beaus hovered at her side, sharing *on-dits* and outrageous stories as they competed for her attention. She looked especially fetching. The shimmering silk gown matched the gleam in her green eyes, and a revealing neckline caused a twinge of regret that their affair was over. As he stepped inside, her face brightened, and she held out both hands.

"My Lord Ware, what a pleasure to see you."

He made his apologies for missing the museum visit, and the conversation remained general for some minutes. After a while, Sophy turned to Sir Stephen, the tall, fair-haired man who was her escort for the night. "Would you be a darling and get me another champagne?" Once he was on his way, she smiled coquettishly at her other admirers. "I really must have a private moment with Viscount Ware before the curtain goes up. Perhaps I shall see you again at intermission?"

The men accepted their dismissal with a show of reluctance, bowed, and withdrew. Sophy tilted her eyes up at Lucien and patted the seat beside her.

He smiled and sat. "How heartless you are to send them away."

"They shall return. After you were so cruel as to neglect me this afternoon, I wanted you to myself for a while. And…I have two names to share. You told me—rather pointedly, I might add—to be discreet, so my admirers had to go."

"So, I did. My apologies, my lady. As ever, you are the soul of discretion. When it suits you."

"Odious man."

"Saucy minx."

They smiled at one another in intimate harmony as only close friends and old lovers do.

"Let me tell you at once before someone interrupts," she said, leaning toward him. "Weatherby and Notley. As everyone knows, Lord Stephan Weatherby is a habitual drinker. He has gotten worse and has run up large debts with trades all over town after gambling deep and losing at clubs like Cade's. I know it is acceptable to most men, but he is also frequenting much worse places in Old Nichol and other godless rookeries. He acts desperate, playing for higher and higher stakes to win back his fortune, which, of course, no one ever does. The Honorable Bertram Notley is acting the bear-leader, taking him into these places. Do you know him?"

"Only by sight and reputation. Yellow-gold curls?"

"Yes, a disreputable man."

Lucien cocked his head. "In what way? I have not heard that."

"Perhaps a better word is unscrupulous." A delicate frown marred her forehead. "He preys on the weaknesses of others, and his association with Weatherby is exceedingly odd. Six months ago they were at daggers' drawn, close to a duel over a nasty remark Notley made about Weatherby's betrothed—now his former betrothed. She jilted him over the growing debts and bouts of drunkenness."

"How *do* you learn this stuff?" Lucien marveled.

The impish smile came back. "People tell me things. But wait, there is worse to be told of Lord Notley." Her face lost its humor. "Blackmail. I know one woman he treated so."

The devil he did. What kind of ramshackle scoundrel *was* Notley?

The widow's escort returned with two filled champagne glasses, ending the tete-a-tete. He shot Lucien a piercing look. Since the curtain was about to go up, Lucien took the hint and rose, kissing Sophy's hand. "Thank you," he whispered, then straightened. "It was a pleasure, Mrs. Stine. I trust you will enjoy the play."

• • •

Lucien made his way back to the Warburton's box and slipped into his seat behind the ladies just as the play opened. Sherry gave him a look of inquiry, and Lucien responded with a nod, then turned his attention to the stage. During the opening moments, the crowd was typically silent and attentive before boredom set in or gossip became more titillating, and he welcomed the quiet to consider what Sophy had said.

He pictured Weatherby's narrow, pinched face. A rather spineless fellow, actually, and he was forever foxed. Maybe not ape drunk as Sophy described, but Lucien was not surprised Weatherby had been divested of his modest inheritance by the gambling dens who preyed upon unwary young men. But would such a man have the courage, however twisted, to use thieves or espionage to recoup his fortunes? He might…if someone else arranged it.

Notley interested him. Older than Lucien—and a decade older than Weatherby—lived on the fringes of Society, and thus was not well-known. Although his features were not displeasing to the ladies, his eyes were forever calculating. Lucien had heard rumors of his rakish ways with women but nothing about blackmail. Of course, such a charge would not be bandied about without proof, and Sophy would not have repeated it—even to him—unless she was certain. Lucien's lip curled with distain. Had the man no honor?

He was going to find out. Sophy had raised a good point…it was *more* than strange that two men who'd been on the brink of a duel were now patronizing the underbelly of London…together.

Chapter Ten

Anne stifled a laugh of pure delight. She could not stop smiling as she followed Lady Barbary, Aunt Meg, and Georgina into the coach. What an amazing evening. Her first experience of the London theatres was unforgettable; she'd been charmed by Shakespeare's *As You Like It*. The crowd noise during the performance was unexpected, but the chatter hadn't prevented her from hearing the actors or from getting lost in the story.

Anne wiggled her hands into her muff and settled against the soft seat, sighing in contentment. How wonderful they'd arrived at the theatre in time to watch as thousands of elegant Londoners poured into the boxes and galleries. And, oh, the gorgeous gowns.

Andrew Sherbourne had been there, and she would have waved except he was with Lord Ware. To be truthful, the arrogant viscount had looked splendid in evening attire, his darkly handsome face and figure drawing more than one lady's attention. Too bad his character was not as attractive.

They had entered a private box with three young women, who Georgina later pointed out were acquaintances from the Sherbournes' house party. The viscount had then slipped away, and she next noticed him kissing the hand of a lovely black-haired woman in a low-cut gown of green and gold. They acted *quite* friendly, and it had crossed Anne's mind this might be his mistress. Living in the country had not kept her ignorant of the ways of London Society. She had studied the woman with a critical eye but truly could not find a single flaw. Anne had sniffed and turned away.

When she had looked at the beauty's box sometime later, Lord Ware was gone, and another man sat beside her. So, *not* the viscount's mistress. It made her think better of the woman's taste in men.

During intermission, Georgina had nudged her. "Do you think *he* is here?"

"Yes, Lord Ware came with Lord Sherbourne."

"No, silly. Not him." Georgina had dropped her voice dramatically. "The blackmailer."

"Oh, good heavens. I had not even thought of it." But Georgina's question had destroyed the magic for a moment, making her uneasy, and Anne had looked around to see if anyone was watching them. After a while, she relaxed again, impatient with herself for letting Georgina worry her. While the Barbarys were well-known, drawing their share of visitors to the box and curious or admiring glances, no one was staring with animosity. And yet, Anne wasn't so naive to think the blackmailer would give himself away so readily.

The coach lurched, jolting Anne back to their present ride home. She grabbed her hat as the wheels hit a series of deep ruts, and Georgina clutched her arm with a trill of laughter. Anne smiled to see her cousin so carefree. The girl had not mentioned Freddie in days. Indeed, her betrothed Lord John was arriving in town tomorrow, and Georgina had been shopping for a new muff and bonnet she just had to have to go driving with him in Hyde Park.

"Was it not a wonderful night?" Georgina bubbled over when the carriage steadied. "So many glorious gowns. Reds and greens, and a *divine* azure blue. I long to wear such brilliant colors."

"You will someday," Anne assured her. "But darling, you look wonderful in the pastels befitting your age."

Lady Barbary smiled her agreement. "The new hair style with your curls piled on top is very becoming, Georgina. Lord John will be enchanted."

Georgina preened, touching her hair. "Do you think so?"

Back at the house, they crowded into the entry hall while removing coats and hats. Aunt Meg's sudden shriek startled everyone, and the elderly woman clapped a hand over her mouth.

"Oh, my. I am so very sorry. I…I do not feel well. Yes, that is it. Not well at all. Anne, would you help me upstairs?"

Shocked by this abrupt illness, Anne took a firm hold on her aunt's right arm. "Indeed, Auntie. Georgina, her other arm, if you please."

Aunt Meg didn't look at all unsteady. She practically dragged Anne up the stairs before Georgina even reached them. Ann could not say what…but something was very wrong.

Over the clamor of voices from the hallway offering advice and assistance, Lady Barbary's calm tone quieted the others. "What can we do to help, Margaret? Should I call the doctor?"

Aunt Meg shook her head and continued to climb. "No, no. No need for that, Bridget. I must lie down for a while."

By now, Anne was positive her aunt wasn't ill. She acted frightened, and tension radiated from her body. Anne glanced over her shoulder at the upturned faces below. "I believe she is overly tired, Lady Barbary. Tea might be nice, if it is not too much trouble."

"No trouble at all. I shall see to it."

As they entered Aunt Meg's bedchambers, she pulled away and whirled around to face her great-nieces. "What a fuss! I am so sorry, but I was caught unaware when the footman handed me this." She opened her hand to reveal a crumpled letter. "It is too much for me to bear." She sank onto the edge of the bed, clutching her hands to her chest.

Anne unfolded the letter as Georgina impatiently angled her head to read it. Upon finishing the note, Anne flung it on the bed in disgust. "A nasty reminder…and so unnecessary. 'Do not fail your appointment at the Christmastide Ball. You know the consequences,'" she quoted.

"Horrid, horrid man!" Georgina exclaimed. "Why does he not leave us alone? He should know we have no choice but to pay." She flounced away to throw herself on the fainting couch.

Anne gave a soft groan of agreement. "I daresay he wishes to keep us fearful. But his threat is scarcely news, Auntie. Why did it overset you so greatly?"

"Another day, it might not. I...well, I heard from my man of business this morning, and ... Oh, my dears, I did not tell you earlier because I just could not ruin our evening at the theatre." She exhaled noisily. "He sent all the funds he could on such short notice. So much is invested, you know. It was only two hundred ten pounds, far short of the five hundred we need."

Anne calculated the figures in her head. "Not that short, Auntie. With the one hundred eighty we had, and the extra forty mama sent me for a hat, we have four hundred and twenty."

"You cannot give up your hat," Georgina protested. "The one at the shop was so becoming. Besides, we'd still need eighty pounds." Her voice sharpened as it hit home just how large the remaining amount was. "What can we do? If Lord John learns of Freddie's letter, he shall think me unfaithful even before we wed."

"It shall not come to that," Anne said. "I can always buy a hat. We must put our heads together and think of a way to raise the additional funds."

"I suppose we could get jobs." Georgina looked perplexed. "What could we do? I doubt I should make a very good housemaid."

Anne laughed at the absurdity. "I agree with you, but we might sell something."

"Become street vendors?" Georgina's eyes widened. "We could ask Cook to bake pies or bread to sell, but it is dreadfully cold to stand outside."

"No, dear, I did not mean that either."

"What an excellent thought, Anne. I know just what to do." Aunt Meg clenched her hand in emphasis. "We shall pawn our jewelry. My most valuable gems are at home, but I brought a silver and jade broach of my grandmother's to wear at the ball. It might bring half of what we need."

Georgina jumped to her feet. "I shall give up my sixteenth birthday necklace. I would not miss it, because Lord John gave me one that is much nicer."

Anne sighed for the hundredth time at Georgina's immaturity, knowing the greater sacrifice Aunt Meg was making, but without a better idea, they adopted their aunt's proposal. They inspected their combined jewelry collection and selected four pieces that might be sold or pawned for the great sum of eighty pounds.

A mild squabble ensued over who should visit the pawnshop. It was an unsavory business no lady should undertake, but they could not entrust it to a servant and risk setting tongues wagging. Georgina, as could be expected, was eager to go. She considered the prospect a grand adventure, but in the end, Anne was once again deemed the logical choice.

A lump formed in her throat. She could not deny the discomfort, even fright, she felt at the prospect, but she hid it from the others with a short laugh. Between a blackmailer and the pawnshops, she would have very out-of-the-common memories from her first trip to London.

"Now that we are agreed, I am off to bed," Anne said briskly. After kissing her aunt and cousin goodnight, she crossed the hall to her own bedchamber, changed into night clothes, and dismissed her maid. She sat at her dressing table, thoughtfully brushing her hair. London was living up to her expectations in so many ways. The shops, the theatre, and still to come was next week's Christmastide Ball. Her first London society ball was certain to be a glittering night.

The intervening days would be busy. They had already received more invitations to holiday social engagements than they could keep: elegant dinner parties, soirees, museum outings, and, of course, there must be shopping trips. Their ready funds might be depleted, but purchases could be financed by trade accounts. If she was careful, her generous allowance would cover her debts in the next quarter.

She sighed and pressed her lips together. She *would not* allow a despicable blackmailer to ruin everything. The jewelry must be sold right away. As soon as the onerous task was behind them, they would be free to throw themselves into the gaiety of the season. For a few days she and Georgina could dance and laugh under Auntie's indulgent gaze as though they had not a care in the world.

• • •

The following afternoon, Anne slipped out the back door of the Barbary Mansion. Anxious not to be seen, she hurried through the streets of Mayfair on her way to a Drury Lane pawnshop. Since she couldn't waste their meager coins on a hackney nor explain her need of a carriage to their hosts, she walked the entire way. She had put on her oldest, least fashionable day dress, an old coat she and Georgina had found in the attic, and a large bonnet to conceal her face. Despite this modest attire, a woman alone drew too many glances, and the sight of the pawnshop's golden balls brought a rush of relief.

A bell announced her entrance, and Anne stopped just inside, surprised and intrigued by the display before her. She had never been in such a shop with so many kinds of items from clothes to vases to silverware piled on every table and shelf. After a moment, she wrapped her confidence around her and approached the bearded man behind the counter.

"Good afternoon, sir."

"Welcome, miss. What may I do for you?"

"I have a few pieces of jewelry to sell." When she and Aunt Meg had talked it over, they decided a pawnbroker would offer more for an outright sale. Besides, they would not have the funds to redeem any pawned property before their London visit was over.

She opened her reticule, pulled out the silk scarf in which she had wrapped the selected pieces, and spread it open on the counter. The gems sparkled. They looked so lovely that perhaps she wouldn't have to sell them all to obtain the necessary funds.

The shopkeeper picked up each one and inspected it. "I will give you forty pounds for the lot."

Anne pushed back a rush of dismay. She had seen enough bargaining in the country markets to hope this was a beginning offer. She arched a brow. "Surely you jest, sir. The broach alone with its jade stones is worth twice that."

"When new, maybe," he conceded. "It's out of fashion now. I could be stuck with it for months or years." He studied her face. "Overrun your allowance, have you?"

"A little." She managed a smile. The man was impertinent, but she dare not antagonize him into withdrawing his offer altogether. She did *not* want to seek out another pawnshop. "Such a small thing at the time, but now…well, sir, I really must have a good deal more than you have offered."

The man rubbed his chin. "Mayhap I could go fifty."

"But sir! I cannot take a pence less than ninety."

They haggled for several minutes. He went to sixty. She dropped to eighty-five, he went to sixty-five. Anne started to fold her silk scarf as though to leave.

He sighed. "Final offer. Seventy."

"Eighty."

He pulled at his beard. "The very best I can do is seventy-two. Sorry, miss."

Fustian! The scoundrel was not the slightest bit sorry. She debated walking out, but there was no guarantee she would find a better offer…and maybe less. If she accepted, they'd be eight pounds short. So close. Surely the blackmailer would be satisfied.

He'd simply have to be. Anne nodded. "I will take it."

She stepped out of the shop two minutes later, the money tucked in her bag. A frown wrinkled her brow but she raised her chin. Too late for regrets. She glanced up and down the street to make sure no one of her acquaintance had ventured into this rather questionable part of town and took off at a brisk walk, eager to leave the unpleasant task behind.

Chapter Eleven

Several minutes earlier, Sherry and Lucien had strolled down Drury Lane in hopes of gathering greater information on Weatherby and Notley.

"Upon my word, Lucien!" Sherry exclaimed before lowering his voice. "Is that not Lady Anne?"

Still mulling over their meager results so far that day, Lucien struggled to recall who Lady Anne was before bringing to mind the attractive but prickly Anne Ashburn from Sherbourne's house party. He followed Sherry's gaze across the lane and recognized the fair-haired woman hurrying along the opposite side of the street. What the devil was she doing here? Drury Lane was no fit place for an earl's daughter—one without a maid or other escort.

"Indeed, it is." Lucien stepped into a shadowed doorway to watch her progress unobserved.

"Not safe for a lady," Sherry said, echoing Lucien's thoughts as he joined him. "Should we do something?"

"Like what?" Lucien shrugged. "I doubt if she would appreciate our interference. Considering her attire, I would say she is hoping to avoid notice."

She stopped, staring at a shop window and entered the pawnshop.

"Egad, that *is* a surprise," Sherry remarked. "Dealing with a ferret? I thought her family was deep in the pockets."

"By all accounts, they are. But anyone can get into dun territory. You know how easy it is to run through an allowance." Lucien gave him a teasing smile. Sherry was frequently in need of a small loan to get him through to the next quarter.

"I always repay you."

"Did I suggest otherwise? But Lady Anne may not have an accommodating friend."

As the minutes passed while they continued to watch, a troublesome thought occurred to Lucien. What if she was disposing of property taken from the house party? Would it not explain the younger cousin's nervous behavior when they tried to question her?

Sherry cleared his throat. "Uh, Lucien, I hate to mention this, but could the old lady have faked her illness? Maybe she and the young chit were working with the thieves, and that's why her room wasn't search. And now Lady Anne is selling off the pilfered goods. It sounds fanciful, I know, but—"

"Not to me. But she was carrying nothing except a small reticule."

"She couldn't bring it all, could she? Arrangements need to be made to dispose of large amounts."

The pawnshop door opened, and Lady Anne exited. She set out at an unladylike, hasty pace, taking her back in the direction she had come.

Lucien stepped into the open. "Let's see what the pawnbroker has to say."

"How are you going to approach this?" Sherry asked as they crossed the street.

"Just follow along." Lucien opened the door, the bell jangled, and the pawnbroker's eyes gleamed with interest at the two well-dressed men. "Good afternoon, sir," Lucien said as he approached the counter. "I am here on a matter of some delicacy. I was surprised to see my younger sister leave your shop moments ago disguised as her maid. May I ask why she was here?"

The man pulled on his beard, debating what to say. No doubt he was calculating what profit he might gain from the situation. Coming to a decision, he said, "She wished to dispose of a few baubles."

"Not again." Lucien sighed heavily, shaking his head at Sherry in mild exasperation. "She has such terrible luck at the roulette wheel."

"I told you she had been playing deep," Sherry said, picking up his cue.

"So you did." Lucien turned back to the shop owner. "What was it this time? I will, of course, buy them back. Everything."

"Four pieces, my lord. No more than one hundred pounds." He produced the jewelry still wrapped in the silk scarf and gave an ingratiating smile. "Enough coin to pay off a lost bet or two and enough left for a new bonnet, mayhap."

"Something she *had* to have, I dare say." Lucien studied the items. A broach, a necklace, a set of small diamond earrings, and a jeweled comb. Nothing he recognized from the short list of stolen property, but he wanted to compare them with Sherry's complete notes of the other things taken. "How much did you give her? " When the man hesitated, Lucien added, "Come, my good man. I will ask her, you know."

"Seventy-two pounds," the man mumbled.

Lucien lifted a brow. Disgracefully below their value. "Was she happy with that?"

"Uh, erm, we bargained a bit. They always want more."

So Lady Anne had *not* been satisfied, and yet she completed the sale. A sign of desperation perhaps…not a bonnet. Having seen the few pieces of jewelry, he was doubtful these were stolen goods, but what else could have inspired such a risky venture?

"I will give you eighty-two. Ten is a tidy profit for your trouble." Lucien's tone said the deal was done. He placed his coins on the counter, wrapped the gem pieces in the silk scarf again, and stowed it in his pocket.

The pawnbroker sighed. "Very well, my lord."

• • •

Lucien and Sherry's inquiries into Weatherby and Notley began to yield results later in the day as the gambling dens filled. By the time they returned to the viscount's Hays Mews lodgings near midnight, they had a fair idea of the two men's finances, friends, and reputations within London's underbelly. Weatherby's downward spiral was well-known, and many establishments now excluded him from their gaming tables. Perhaps that was why he had befriended Notley, who still had entrance everywhere. The question was what was in it for Notley?

Despite dissolute reputations, neither man openly advocated any kind of radical politics or reformist ideas, nothing adverse to England or the Crown. Lucien had not heard the slightest hint the men would be entangled in a French plot.

Having shed their winter garments, Lucien and Sherry retired to the warmth of the study to discuss what they'd learned that day over brandy.

Sherry took a sip from his glass, relaxed against the back of the burgundy wing-back chair, and stretched his boots toward the hearth. "What a sordid pair they are. To spend every day in such places, well, it is just bad form. Only in my calf years did I find such establishments of even passing interest. Not counting Paris and Vienna, of course."

Lucien flicked him a look. Their spy work on the Continent had not always taken them to ballrooms and perfumed bed chambers. "Don't despair, Sherry. This day's work may serve us well in the end." Lucien stretched his own chilled feet toward the fire. "Our failure to find a link to the theft or cipher does not acquit them. Not yet."

Sherry snorted. "You think so? Weatherby is a pathetic, drunken dolt. Too unreliable to plan anything, too risky even for the French."

"Alone, yes, but we must consider Notley's influence. He may have lured Weatherby into trouble worse than the gambling hells... even treason."

"We have no proof."

"No, but Notley's reputation is of a man who would take advantage of his own mother. Weatherby would be easy pickings. And look at Notley's own mounting debt. Unpaid creditors to rival Prinny—although Notley has mysteriously made good on most of his gambling IOUs."

"I suppose you're going to say they were paid with blackmail money?"

"It would answer."

Sherry shifted to peer at Lucien. "He may be a thief, even a blackmailer, but treason is still stretching it. He fought for England in the Indies."

"As have other traitors. We cannot exclude him on that alone." Lucien took a drink of brand and tightened his lips. "Did you catch Stanford's remark?"

"About the young girls? It was hard to miss. He wanted us to know."

"Yes, my impression too. Out of mean-spiritedness or something else?"

"Disgust, I dare say. If Notley is preying on young girls, as Stanford implied, procuring them for himself and his friends... Good lord. He is a blackguard."

Lucien sighed. "Yes. If we cannot prove espionage, we must inform Bow Street of his other activities."

"It will be my pleasure," Sherry said with satisfaction. He poured another finger of brandy from the bottle on the table between them. "What do we do about Lady Anne?"

Lucien's brows shot up, and he reached into his pocket for the silk scarf. "I had almost forgotten." He spread the jewelry on the table and retrieved Sherry's notes from his desk drawer. "Let's see if our lady is more devious than we thought."

While Lucien read off the list of stolen property, Sherry studied the jewelry, looking for matches, and finding none. He leaned forward with a frown. "You may have more experience than I with ladies' trappings, Lucien, but something is amiss. I had thought the jewelry belonged to Lady Anne, but she would not wear most of these." He separated out the broach, the matching earrings, and the small necklace.

Lucien peered at the chosen pieces. "Discerning of you, my friend. I should have seen it myself. The broach and earrings are something my grandmother might favor, and the delicate necklace is more suited to a young girl." The disparity made Lady Anne's activities more confusing. The pieces might be family heirlooms, but what lady would travel with jewelry she didn't intend to wear? "I cannot explain it, but unless you think this proof she has taken up as a pickpocket, I see nothing to implicate Lady Anne or her relatives in anything unlawful."

"Exactly my thoughts." Sherry settled back and finished his brandy. "Might I add I'm relieved?"

"Have a partiality for the lady, do you? I thought you were looking in a different direction."

"You think too much," Sherry said. "Annie is an old friend. And she is much too pretty to set foot inside a jail." He gave an exaggerated shudder. "The very image appalls me."

Lucien smiled at his friend's deflection. "Then turn your imagination to something useful. How are we to return these trinkets to the lady in question?"

"Send them with no name," Sherry offered offhandedly as though his attention had already wandered elsewhere.

"And alarm her unduly? Consider the anxiety their mysterious arrival would cause." Lucien scooped the jewelry into the silk cloth. "I shall think of something else."

Sherry straightened and slapped his thigh. "That explains it. The jewelry pieces belong to different women."

"Are you now favoring the pickpocket theory?" Lucien asked dryly.

Sherry ignored his remark. "The aunt and her nieces combined their spare jewelry for some kind of female enterprise. Something caught their eye, and they didn't have the ready. New bonnets, silk stockings, whatever. Yes, that must be it." He smiled with a satisfied wave of one hand.

"So-o, mystery solved," Lucien agreed, emptying his glass. Yet, he wondered what purchase or other need for funds was critical enough to send Lady Anne to a pawnbroker? A domestic problem, no doubt. A lost wager, or a trivial matter he would never know. Willing to accept this reasonable theory, Lucien set his mind to the task of how to reunite Lady Anne and the jewels without embarrassment on either side.

• • •

By Wednesday night, Lucien and Sherry had completed interviews with the last of the house party guests. Albeit they had learned nothing even remotely helpful, Lucien was grateful the tiresome job was behind them. They'd also followed up with other names garnered from social gossip, suggested by Sophy, or passed on by Rothe. Not one solid suspect came of it all.

Nor had Lucien returned Lady Anne's jewelry or come up with a feasible plan for doing so. For some reason, this small problem nagged at him. He had no wish to embarrass her, nor did he relish explaining she'd been suspected of theft.

An urgent note from Rothe the following morning, requesting his prompt attendance, put everything else out of Lucien's mind. Without taking time to find Sherry, he hurried to Whitehall and found Rothe in a meeting with his clerks, under-ministers, and two members of Parliament.

"Very well, I shall wait." Lucien removed his hat and pulled at the fingers of his gloves.

"Oh, no, my lord." Mr. Sloane, Rothe's private secretary, shook his head. "He said to interrupt him the moment you arrived." Sloane tapped on the Rothe's closed door and opened it to announce, "Viscount Ware to see you, my lord."

Eleven men looked up, and Rothe rose. "Ware, a timely arrival. Do come in."

The marquess's face projected surprise as though he had not sent for Lucien. Strange, considering Sloane had confirmed Lucien was expected.

"Gentlemen," Rothe continued. "I believe we are done for today. Keep Sloane informed of any new developments."

Lucien stood to one side as the participants filed out. Their behavior was casual. Whatever had prompted Rothe's urgent message had not been under discussion in this group.

Sloane followed the last man out, and when the door closed behind him, Rothe gestured for Lucien to be seated. The marquess remained standing, taking an ornate snuffbox from his pocket, putting a pinch to his nose, and taking a delicate sniff. Still silent, he remained still, scowling down at his boots.

"I hope I didn't interrupt an important meeting," Lucien said.

Rothe looked up, as though he had forgotten the viscount's presence. "You didn't. Just a nuisance bill to send French prisoners to America. Do they think they wouldn't come back? Or fight us over there? But enough of that nonsense." The marquess shook his head. "I won't make a long tale of it. I have evidence the Whitehall traitor is here in this office...under my direct command."

Lucien's gaze shot to Rothe's face. "Who is it?"

Rothe made an audible sound suspiciously like a growl. "That, I do not know." He turned and began to pace. "A false order was sent to Wellington from this office, using my seal and without my knowledge. I can't pass the blame to the War Secretary or another department. It happened here. But which of them betrayed me, I cannot say." His eyes flashed. "My God, I have a permanent staff of twenty-one—Sloane, six clerks, five sub-ministers, and nine code breakers. It could be any of them. Except Sloane, never Sloane." Rothe raked a hand through his hair, the most agitated Lucien had ever seen him, and then turned, giving Lucien a piercing look. "I don't know who to trust. This treasonous devil isn't working alone. He'd have help to move information back and forth to France. What if some of these other spies are inside Whitehall or the palace? How can I even be sure of the agents under my command?"

Lucien lifted a brow, his voice level. "I fear you exaggerate, sir. You know you can count on me. And Sherbourne."

"Yes, of course." Rothe's voice was bitter. "But then again, that is what the conspirator *would* say. No, do not take umbrage. If I had doubts about you, we would not be talking. I am merely venting my spleen." He sighed and took a seat behind his desk. "What progress on your end?"

"We finished interviews from the house party. Sherbourne and I need to verify a couple of facts to be thorough, but no real suspects among them. Unless…"

"Yes?" Rothe's voice sharpened. "Unless what?"

"Have you considered Skefton himself?"

Rothe exhaled slowly. "He is the easy choice, is he not? Yet I have known his family for many years. It is hard to believe he has sympathy for Napoleon's cause. I have no proof against him. Do you?"

Lucien shook his head. "None, except he was in the best position to pull off the theft. But if not him, we are back to a nearly hopeless search for the gang of thieves. The names we had are now dead men, so Sherbourne and I are concentrating on the ringleader, the alleged member of the Quality."

"Anyone you suspect?"

"Charles Cade is my first choice, but it could be any gentleman or lady with an urgent need for funds and links to the criminal world. We have discovered a handful who might serve, and two are worthy of greater scrutiny. Stephan Weatherby and Bertram Notley. They appear to have formed an odd friendship." He related what he knew of the past duel challenge and the men's recent activities.

"Strange, indeed. Weatherby I know. But Notley…who is he?"

"Second son of Baron Belmont. By all accounts, a reckless gambler and a rakehell."

"Belmont. Ah, yes. I place him now. Dandified fellow with yellow curls. What brought him to your attention?"

"Several sordid tales, rumors of blackmail, and his frequent presence in the seediest of London's establishments. He rubs shoulders with lawbreakers of all kinds most nights. He is also deep in debt."

Rothe nodded. "His politics? Connections to Whitehall or the palace?"

"Unknown."

"Then let us find out. I shall make what inquiries I can without tipping anyone off to the reason for our interest. As far as I know, neither family is active in government affairs. Of course, the sons may have their own political views or a lack of patriotism that makes them vulnerable, particularly to someone willing to pay their debts."

They discussed the potential suspects Rothe's efforts had unearthed, and Lucien left a half hour later with the names of three opposition leaders in parliament and a separate list of everyone at Whitehall under Rothe's command. He and Sherry would have their hands full sorting through the names, searching for thieves by day, and gathering the latest gossip at political and social functions each night.

• • •

Friday morning, December 20, London was rocked by news of a brutal, multiple murder overnight that was eerily similar to the slaughter by the Ratcliffe Highway Killer twelve days earlier. The Prince Regent at once ordered all of Whitehall, including Rothe's unit and the Horse Guards, to suspend other inquiries until the madman was caught.

"I regret this as much as you do," Rothe said when he met with Lucien and Sherbourne to discuss Prinny's edict. "I agree it is shortsighted. The timing could not be worse, and I told him so. But he is worried the people will revolt against the Crown if this killer isn't caught soon. And he could be right. What a coil. Since you two are outside the official line of command, this order need not extend to you. You will be on your own, however, until this is over. Let us pray the lunatic is swiftly apprehended."

Despite the equal or greater peril of a traitor on the loose, Lucien nodded, knowing they had little choice. He too had felt the deep stirrings of fear and rebellion in the streets.

• • •

Lucien strode back and forth, his boots rapping on the bare portions of the study floor, as he waited for Sherry. His friend was late this morning, leaving too much time for Lucien to contemplate yesterday's meeting with Rothe and the temporary loss of the War Office's assistance. He needed more men on the streets, asking questions, running down the possibilities, not less. Two weeks had passed since the cipher vanished. The hope of locating the thieves or tracing the code key grew dimmer each day.

"M'lord! M'lord!"

Lucien turned at the sound of Finn's voice and the clatter of his footsteps on the stairs. The groom arrived breathing hard, his face flushed.

"Take a breath, Finn. What is it this time?"

"Me cousin Ewan wants to meet, m'lord." Finn's eager face stared up at him. "He has news, somethin' important."

"He did not say what?"

Finn shook his head. "Jist to come to Tattersall's. But why ask ye to come if not somethin' big?"

"Why, indeed."

Another set of larger boots on the stairs heralded Sherry's arrival, and as soon as he was apprised of the situation, the three of them set out on foot, notwithstanding the brisk wind. Tattersall's horse auction should provide excellent cover for such a meeting. Masters and servants mingled in the courtyard, buying, selling, and handling horses.

Ewan had specified half eleven, but as they reached Grosvenor Place, they had to circle around a disabled dray blocking the narrow lane next to St. George's Hospital that led to Tattersall's. The delay made them ten minutes late.

"I hope he dint leave," Finn muttered, craning his neck around men and horses.

"Surely he would wait a few minutes." Lucien searched for Ewan's red hair. Tattersall's was typically crowded. The most popular horse auction in London was also noted for its dog kennels—the source of Salcott's original pair of breeding hounds—and its subscription rooms kept both drinking and betting close at hand.

"There! I sees 'im." Finn pointed to his cousin near the horse entrance from the stables. They started toward him, but Tattersall's was such a fashionable place to gather that Lucien and Sherry were stopped repeatedly by acquaintances eager to discuss the latest Ratcliffe Highway murder.

When they finally reached Ewan, he was mauling a woolen cap with nervous hands. "'Bout time," he hissed at Finn. "I need ta be gone 'for they be noticin' me."

"No worries. Jist act like me." Finn grinned, always at home anywhere horses were found. And indeed, there were as many stable boys in the grounds as well-dressed buyers.

Ewan frowned, his gaze flitting from Finn to Lucien. "'Cain't stay long, m'lord. Not after wot happen t' Billy. But I seen a fancy gent with Billy's mates—the ones not kilt—three nights past. In a dark alley, they be. Out of sight, ye ken?"

"Yes," Lucien said. "To avoid being seen together. Could you hear what they were saying?"

"Naw, too far, but seen the nob when 'e left."

"Good enough to describe him?"

Ewan's face broke into a grin, a look so similar to Finn's that the relationship was clear despite the disparity in size between the six foot dockworker and his small cousin. "Better than that, yer lordship. Askt 'round 'an got me a name, I did. Notley."

Lucien shot a grim look at his partner.

"Bloody devil," Sherry said. "We got him."

Keen to question him, Lucien and Sherbourne set out at once, visiting his residence, the regular gentlemen's clubs, and perusing his preferred haunts that evening. But Bertram Notley proved elusive.

It was well after midnight when they returned a second time to Notley's lodgings, a set of shabby-genteel rooms on the near eastside. No one answered to their pounding until the landlord's door on the first floor opened with a bang. Lucien and Sherry hurried down the stairs. A thin, balding man stood in the doorway with a threadbare robe over his night shirt. He was scowling.

"Stop the racket. He's out of town," the man snapped.

He started to close the door, but Lucien stopped him with a question. "When do you expect him?"

"I don't. He's none of my business 'cept for the rent. Now go away, and let me get back to sleep, or I shall call the watch."

Knowing they'd get nothing more, Lucien nodded his thanks, and the door slammed shut.

"Genial fellow," Sherry said, as they returned to Lucien's carriage. "Now what?"

"We find Notley's good friend Weatherby."

"How much do you think he knows of Notley's activities?"

Lucien gave a careless flick of one hand. "Maybe not everything, but some of it, and I'll wager he knows where Notley is or when he'll return."

"What makes you think he'll tell us?"

Lucien cocked his head and calculated. "It is going on two o'clock. Weatherby has been drinking for hours and will be deep in his cups."

Sherry gave a crooked grin. "And his tongue well-loosened."

• • •

They found Stephan, Lord Weatherby at White's gentlemen's club. He was slouched in a chair by the fireplace, his cravat askew, his eyelids heavy from indulgence. He might not be welcome at the gaming tables, but his family name was good enough to get him admitted to drink and dine. He was a friendly drunkard, and he gave them a lopsided smile when Lucien and Sherry approached.

"May we join you?" Lucien asked.

"Absolu-utely. Not my chairs." Weatherby waved his glass at nearby seating and squinted up at them. "Ware and Sherbourne, right? I am Weatherby."

With introductions over, Lucien ordered a round of drinks, and they chatted about the club's food, the best whiskey and brandy, and then mutual friends.

Sherry brought up Bertram Notley. "Friend of yours, is he not? I haven't seen him around this evening."

"Gone to the country." Weatherby frowned in thought, the simple action appearing to take great effort. "Can't say why. Not sure he told me."

Lucien pretended surprise. "You cannot mean he will miss all of London's holiday season."

"What? Uh, no. He hasn't gone far. Back for the Barbary ball. Not to be missed. Everyone goes, and I got to do the nice for the ladies in my family." He leaned drunkenly forward, attempted to wink, but owlishly blinked both eyes instead. "Later we're engaged for a *private* party at Cade's."

Lucien ignored the obvious hint to ask for details. Nothing could be further from his interest. Nor did he want to rouse Weatherby's suspicions by further inquiry about Notley. He had what he came for. He signaled the waiter to bring Weatherby another drink, and then he and Sherbourne excused themselves.

Exiting to the street, Sherry remarked, "I guess we shall be attending the Christmastide Ball this year."

Lucien sent him a wry look. "Not that you would have missed it with Miss Emily Selkirk in town."

Chapter Twelve

Nodding politely to lords and ladies, young and not so young, Lucien made his way around the glittering ballroom. The Barbarys' Christmastide Eve extravaganza was in full swing. A thousand candles reflected off the boughs of holly, mistletoe, and evergreen tied with bows of satin and silk ribbons. Tables on the west end overflowed with delicacies and wassail bowls, giving off enticing aromas of sweet smelling spices, oranges, and apples.

The polished floors were barely visible beneath the crowd of dancers. Gentlemen were resplendent in dark-colored tailcoats, intricately-tied cravats, and fashionable long trousers or pantaloons, while the ladies displayed an array of colors as the newest entrees to society swirled in flowing gowns of pastels among the richer shades worn by married and older women and the sheer silks and bright brocades of the more daring.

Lucien spotted Sherbourne across the room, chatting with Miss Emily—no surprise there—and then located the other four of Rothe's men mingling in the crowd. A suspect in the Ratcliffe Highway killings had been arrested that day—lifting the mood of every London resident—and Lucien had immediately requested assistance in apprehending Notley. Not that he planned to cause a public spectacle at the ball, but he hoped to follow and seize him somewhere between the ball and the party at Cade's Club.

So far Notley had not put in an appearance, but it was early, just going on half ten. New arrivals were still crowding into the ballroom.

Pursuing his normal habit, Lucien danced with several ladies, steering clear of those with matchmaking mothers. With more than half his attention on the crowd, married women and widows

126

made safer partners as he didn't have to be quite so careful of what
he said and did. Mamas would use anything to snare a suitable
prospect—and an earl's heir was always suitable, even with a
tarnished reputation.

Sophia Stine arrived, looking exotic in a dark red, low-cut
gown and her black hair piled high on her head. She was never
short of partners, but he cut in on her first dance and enlisted her
help in watching for Notley.

Four dances later, Sophy caught his eye across the ballroom and
nodded toward a man with guinea-gold curls striding along the
back wall of the ballroom. Notley disappeared through a doorway
that went to the rear of the house. Lucien signaled to Sherry and
then followed, slipping into a dimly lit hallway.

It was empty and quiet, except for footsteps on the back stairs
going down to the first floor. *What the devil?* Had something
warned Notley, and he was leaving?

Lucien followed, his soft dancing shoes nearly soundless. He
paused at the bottom of the stairs to listen. The footsteps had
stopped. Lucien could see enough of this hallway to know he was
alone.

Where had Notley gone? This wasn't the way out. Was he
meeting someone in one of the rooms? Or did he know he was
being followed and had slipped inside to hide or even ambush his
pursuer?

Staying close to the wall, Lucien crept forward, pausing at the
open doors of the study and drawing room to peer inside. Both
were unoccupied. The next door—sure to be a parlor or library—
was closed. He put his ear to it. Nothing at first, then he heard a
faint rustle on the other side. Fearing someone was coming out,
he stepped back, flattening against the wall. From this position, he
readied himself to fight or duck into the drawing room. But the
door didn't open.

After several heartbeats, he eased forward again, reaching out
to rest a hand on the door. He silently turned the latch, swung the
door open, and stepped inside in one swift motion.

He froze in place. A man's body sprawled face down in front of the fireplace. A young woman in a fancy ball gown stood over it. Startled blue eyes turned to stare at him.

But Lucien brushed past her to get a better look at the body, already suspecting who it was. "Good Lord, madam, what happened here?"

"I...I do not know." Her soft voice strengthened as she spoke. "I found him like this."

The bottle-green superfine coat, stained with blood spreading outward from a protruding knife handle, and the gleaming Hessians might have belonged to any London gentleman. The guinea gold curls were unmistakably those of Bertram Notley.

Lucien crouched, pulled off a glove, and slipped two fingers under the man's cravat, not expecting to find a pulse, and he did not. He patted down his pockets, hoping to find the missing code key. It wasn't there.

Bloody hell. This was not supposed to happen. Not again. Was everyone in this mad business going to die? Lucien swallowed a rush of disappointment. He had been so close.

Waltz music from the ballroom drifted in from the hall, the contrast making the atmosphere in the library all the more grotesque. He straightened and shut the door, cutting off the sounds of revelry. Notley wouldn't be attending the ball. The dissolute second son of Baron Belmont had danced his last dance.

Returning his gaze to the dead man, he noted Notley's shiny black boots and corrected his assumption. The man had not come to dance, not in top boots. He'd intended to visit its library for an assignation. For what purpose? To pass on the cipher? Collect blackmail money? Had his killer come to steal the cipher, or had one of Notley's marks taken revenge?

"Is he...?"

The question brought his gaze to the woman, and he took a good look at her for the first time. With a flicker of surprise, he realized it was Lady Anne Ashburn. She looked different, even more beautiful, in her elegant ballroom finery. Extraordinary...to find her here. Or was it? Did this somehow explain her cousin's nervous behavior and the trip to the pawnshop?

Lady Anne met his scrutiny with a steady gaze. She appeared discomforted, even wary, but not to the extent he would expect of a gentlewoman finding herself alone with a man she barely knew—and with a corpse. What the devil was she about? Might she have done this?

He broke eye contact to study her long white gloves, the stylish ivory gown trimmed in dark green silk, and the pale green shawl around her shoulders. No visible bloodstains.

"Yes, he is dead," he finally responded.

A swiftly indrawn breath was her only visible reaction. Not the behavior one would expect of a lady. Shrieking, fainting, maybe, but not this. Was she was always coolheaded or trying hard to hide something that might betray her? His interest piqued, and it was not entirely professional.

"Do not look to me for answers." When she spoke, he realized he had been staring at her too long. She waved a gloved hand toward the still figure. "I entered the library only moments ago... when I heard someone cry out."

Lucien suppressed a snort of skepticism. What lady would rush headlong into an unknown, precarious situation? She was doing it too brown. But he encouraged her to go on. "Did you see what happened?"

She shook her head, stirring the pale tendrils artfully arranged to brush her cheekbones. "I just saw *him*, lying there."

"No one else? In the hall or on the stairs?"

"No. But..." When she hesitated, he shot her a sharp look. "I heard someone. I had been, um, looking for a quiet spot...well, no mind. It does not matter why, but I was about to enter the library when I heard muffled voices from within. Having no wish to intrude, I was leaving—when I heard the cry."

"Could you identify the voices? Or what was being said?"

"No. They were talking very low. It made the single sharp sound all the more startling."

From the corner of his eye, Lucien saw the drapes flutter near the exterior French doors. He leapt toward them, cursing under his breath for failing to search the room. He knew better than to get distracted by a lovely face. He swept the curtains aside. No one jumped out, and he released a tense breath as he realized the movement was due to a gust of wind from an open French door. He stepped outside into a cold but barren courtyard.

The U-shaped area of cobblestones was open on the far end leading to the stables. The other three sides had entrances to the side wings of the house. If Lady Anne had been standing outside the hall door as she claimed, then this had been the murderer's exit…and possible entrance. He scrutinized the immediate area. No place where footprints would show, and nothing dropped or discarded. The killer had slipped away—either returning to the house or exiting through the stables. Someone would need to question the stable hands.

Unless *she* was lying. Who knew better than Lucien that beauty could hide a devious heart? But those pristine gloves… Had she come prepared with a second pair to hide her crime? That kind of planning would take a clever mind and a cold heart.

Intelligent blue eyes silently questioned him as he stepped inside and closed the door.

Lucien shook his head. "No one there." It struck him again how composed she was. Many ladies of his acquaintance would have run from the room in hysterics. He felt a renewed flicker of interest…and suspicion. His eyes narrowed on her reticule. It was large enough to hide a pair of bloody gloves…or a stolen cipher.

"Should you not go after him, my lord?"

And allow you to get away? He gave her a direct look. "He is long gone. Just who *are* you, madam? And while you're coming up with an answer, allow me to look inside your reticule."

Her eyes widened at his curt tone. She pulled her shawl around her, as though to shield herself, and raised her chin. "We have already met, sir. I am surprised your memory serves you so poorly. I am Lady Anne Ashburn."

"Yes, I recall your name. The Earl of Chadley's daughter from Warwickshire. I should have been more precise. Who are you to this man? Why were you meeting with him?"

"I have *never* met him. Well, not alive."

Lucien scowled and held out his hand. "Your bag."

She shoved it at him. "Look all you want. I cannot grasp what you expect to find. If it is a weapon, you must have overlooked the dagger in his back."

He ignored her scathing tone. The reticule was heavier than expected. He opened it and examined the contents: no cipher, no extra gloves, nothing smeared with blood. He pushed aside a lace handkerchief that smelled like lilacs, and his fingers closed around a roll of banknotes. Twenty to thirty coins jingled in the bottom. He thumbed through the large denomination notes—an astounding four or five hundred pounds all total—and lifted his eyes to hers. "Why would you bring these funds to a ball?"

"I scarce see how that concerns you. If you are finished..." She held out her hand.

Considering the murder, everything was his concern, but he had no grounds to press her. Not yet, he thought. Lucien dropped the cash in her reticule and returned it. "Thank you, my lady."

The money still raised new questions about her presence. Had Notley given her the funds? A payoff? For what? Or was she being fleeced in one of his blackmail schemes?

"I had nothing to do with the man's death," she said interrupting his thoughts.

"Have I accused you?"

"Your eyes have."

Her directness was off-putting. But she was wary now... and annoyed. He must soften his approach if he hoped to learn anything further. "I would never take such liberty, my lady," he protested with a small conciliatory bow. "If I have offended you, I beg pardon. Such was not my intent, although you must admit the circumstances are unusual."

"Yes, I will give you that."

He glanced toward the dead man. "Did he say anything before he died?"

"To me?" She gave him a look of disbelief. "No. I thought I made it plain that Lord Notley was beyond any form of communication when I entered the room."

Lucien leaped on the name. "So you *do* know him?"

"We were not acquainted—as I said before—but he does keep the tongues wagging and has been pointed out to me."

The shade of distaste that flashed across her face appeared more personal than she implied, but he had no time to pursue it now. Another guest or one of the servants was apt to discover them soon. "Did you see anything he may have dropped or attempted to hide?"

"Such as?" She frowned and took a step sideways, peering behind him for another look at where the body lay. "I saw nothing. Are you now accusing me of theft? Really, your lordship. Pray where would I hide anything? You already inspected my reticule."

"No accusation, a mere question." Lucien shifted his stance to cut off her view of the corpse. It was time for her to go. "This is not a fit sight for a lady. Nor should we be found here, particularly together, my lady."

At this reminder of the gravity and impropriety of the situation, she nodded, averting her gaze. "Of course, you are right. What happens now? Should we inform our host or contact a constable…?" Her voice faded.

"Leave it to me. You should return to the ballroom and say nothing. No one need know you were here."

She cocked her head and eyed him. "Just like that? You would allow me to walk away?"

"For now, yes." He gave her a sardonic smile. "Unless you have changed your mind and wish to confess, a gentleman should always accept a lady's declaration of innocence."

"Is that what you are, Viscount? A gentleman?"

His sense of humor fled, and he arched a brow. "My grandmother still hopes for my redemption." *Devil it.* For her to say that, his reputation after his years on the Continent must indeed be in tatters. It had been necessary to promote false and exaggerated rumors in order to make certain contacts within French society, and now they were being thrown in his face. "You surprise me, Lady Anne. I thought a lady who failed to shrink at the sight of a corpse would not rely on the prattle of scandalmongers."

The corners of her mouth tightened. "I rarely do, but upon occasion, they get it right."

Lucien began to fear she would continue to quibble with him, delaying her departure, and he swept a hand toward the door, reminding her that discovery and ruin could walk in at any moment. They'd be the *on-dit* for days or weeks, an uncomfortable, if not disastrous, situation.

"Very well, my lord. I shall leave you in charge of this dreadful scene, but do not fool yourself that I will forget."

His brows shot up. What did that mean? Was she implying *he* might be the murderer? What story had she concocted in her beautiful head to explain why the killer would return to the scene?

Actually, he could think of a few.

Lady Anne moved to leave and paused with one hand on the door. "Thank you for your discretion, my lord. Although I suspect your concern is as much for your sake as to protect my reputation." She slipped into the hallway, and the latch clicked softly.

Shrugging off lingering tension, Lucien set to work. Despite their tacit agreement, Lady Anne might have second thoughts and raise an alarm. He searched the dead man's pockets again, and then the library tabletop and its drawers. The floors under and behind furniture yielded nothing except proof of the house maid's diligence. He straightened and studied the room. If Notley had any warning he was in trouble, where might he have hidden the code key in a hurry?

The bookshelves were stuffed with dozens of leather-bound volumes. Lucien pulled out the closest, most accessible, looked behind them, flipped the pages, and finding nothing, returned them to their original locations.

If the cipher had been there, the killer must have carried it away.

He paused, as a less sinister possibility for the rendezvous occurred to him. A romantic dalliance with Lady Anne. But how would that have ended in Notley's death? A lovers' quarrel?

The idea did not sit well with Lucien, and he finally shook his head. A lady with a *tendre* for the dead man could not have remained so calm in view of his corpse. Nor was there time for such a violent argument to develop in the minute or two Notley was out of sight. And there was the dagger. Not a weapon found laying around a library. The killer had brought it. Notley's death had been planned or anticipated in advance. Something more nefarious than a lover's spat was behind this.

Taking a last look around, Lucien blew out the candles and left to arrange for disposal of the body. It would not do for a corpse to be found at the ball.

Slipping back into the ballroom, he found Sherbourne and Rothe's men waiting just inside the door.

"Where did you go?" Sherry demanded. "Did you locate Notley?"

"I did. He is dead. Stabbed in the back." Lucien kept a smile on his face as he nodded to a friend of his grandmother.

"Stabbed?" Sherry hissed the whispered word. "You killed him?"

"Not I. He is no good to us dead."

"Then who did?"

"Excellent question to which I do not have an answer." Lucien surveyed the room. "Have you seen Lady Anne Ashburn?"

"You are looking for a woman? At this moment?" Sherry asked, his voice incredulous. "I agree she is lovely, but I question your timing."

"Don't be daft." Lucien continued to survey the room while relating the events in the library.

"Ah. That explains her quick departure."

Lucien swung his gaze to stare at him. "She left? Why did you not say so? Did she appear agitated?"

"Not that I noticed. Will she alert the authorities?"

"I hope not, but we must act with haste. It will not do for Notley's body to be found here. A Bow Street investigation of the haute ton would hamper our own inquiries."

"Egad, yes. No reason to interrupt the ball and upset the ladies with such unpleasantness."

An awkward scene, best avoided. Not everyone had the composure of Lady Anne.

By half past the hour of midnight, the stable staff had been questioned about early departures from the ball and the body removed through a rear entrance. Lucien cautioned Rothe's men to place it where ruffians and footpads would be the obvious suspects.

"Wait two hours before you do so," he added. "Sherbourne and I need time to visit Notley's residence."

Chapter Thirteen

Desperate to distance herself from the ghastly scene in the library, Anne ran down the hall, heart pounding, her green slippers brushing the smooth surface, and she hurried up the staircase. As reaction set in, her thoughts reeled, unable to take in the unthinkable. The Honorable Bertram Notley—not so honorable since he'd been a blackmailer—was murdered while she was only steps away…while he waited for *her*. What if she had arrived seconds earlier? Anne swallowed hard, raising a gloved hand to the beating pulse in her throat.

What must Viscount Ware think of her? That she was a murderess?

Reaching the ballroom doors, she paused to compose herself, drawing in a ragged breath. Lord Ware had allowed her to go, but he hadn't believed her. Well, who would believe the poor excuse she gave? What lady would wander the halls at a ball looking for a place to be alone? She sighed, her brows slipping into a frown. What would he say if he discovered the blackmail and realized she had a good reason for wanting Notley dead?

Clasping her hands to keep them from trembling, Anne slipped into the ballroom. When no one appeared to notice she'd been absent, she breathed a little easier. She forced a smile and started across the room, flinching when Georgina suddenly linked her arm with hers. Aunt Meg stood behind her, looking worried.

"Did you get it?" Georgina whispered. "Do you have my letter?"

Anne avoided looking at her, but met Aunt Meg's gaze. She shook her head. "Walk me back to our bedchambers, Georgina. I am afraid I have developed the headache."

"Oh, you poor dear," Aunt Meg said, responding to the plea in Anne's eyes. "I shall find Lady Barbary and let her know we are retiring. Georgina, go with your cousin. Can you not see she is unwell?"

Georgina faltered. "I, uh, yes, of course, Auntie."

Their aunt moved off into the crowd. Georgina frowned at Anne, her expression unhappy, but dutifully escorted her from the ballroom. Once in the hallway, they turned toward the residential wings.

"Are you not going to tell me anything?" Georgina muttered.

"I will. But not here." Anne placed a finger against her lips, and when Aunt Meg joined them, they continued in silence until they were inside Aunt Meg's bedchamber.

"What has happened?" Georgina demanded the instant the door was shut.

"It was dreadful. Bertram Notley is, was, the blackmailer," Anne said in a faint voice.

"But I don't even know him," Georgina broke in. "Why would he do this?"

"It doesn't matter any longer. I could not get your letter because…Notley is dead."

"Dead?" Georgina and Aunt Meg echoed together.

She nodded. "I found him in the library. Stabbed with a knife."

Georgina gasped and stifled a shriek. "Murdered?"

"Good Heavens." Aunt Meg grabbed Anne's hand. "Oh, my dear, how terrible. That wretched man. Could he not have died elsewhere? It must have been terrifying for you."

"It was." Anne sank onto the edge of the bed as numbness set in. Georgina sat beside her, and her aunt pulled up a chair. They continued to ask questions, and Anne vaguely paid attention, making an effort to answer them. But nothing felt real. Or maybe she did not want it to be.

"Did you search his pockets for my letter?"

Georgina's breathless question, her face equal parts horror and avid curiosity, snapped Anne out of her lethargy, and she stared at her. Maybe her cousin's total self-absorption should not have surprised her, but it did.

"Search him!" Aunt Meg put a hand to her forehead and let out a small squeak. "Georgina, you cannot expect her to touch a man's body."

"No, I guess not," the girl conceded. "Not even a dead one." She turned to Anne with a startled look. "On, Anne, you could have been murdered too. Did you see the killer?"

"No, thank goodness. When I opened the library door, the room was empty...except for the body...until Viscount Ware arrived."

"He saw you?" Georgina's eyes grew big. "With the body? Oh, no, no, no. You should not have let him find you like that."

"It was not intentional," Anne said softly.

"Yes, but it will all come out now. We shall be given the cut direct everywhere we go." Georgina fell back against the seat, then rallied to lean forward. "Will you be arrested?"

"For what? I did not kill him," Anne snapped, losing her patience. No longer numb, she cut off an angry retort. "I admit it looked bad, very bad, and in the beginning, his lordship was suspicious I might have done it. He, um, might still think so."

Aunt Meg's face drained of color. "You cannot mean that."

"Perhaps not." Anne patted her aunt's hand and gave a shortened version of what had transpired in the library. "He *did* tell me to leave before someone found us."

"There," her aunt said, her cheeks recovering a little pinkness. "See, he *is* a gentleman. I am convinced he will not allow your good name to be sullied."

Anne bit her lip. She was not so certain of Lord Ware's good will. She had said some things she wished she had not, and her denials had fallen on skeptical ears—particularly when he found the money. But she could not waste time worrying over what he thought, not with Georgina's future still at risk. Where was the dratted letter?

Anne stood and wandered across the room, still thinking. The viscount had searched the body—an interesting fact in itself. What had he hoped to find? Was he too being blackmailed? She briefly wondered what kind of secrets he might wish to hide. A natural child? An affair with the wife of a prominent figure? A fatal duel? Gossip from the Continent portrayed him as a dangerous man, prone to illicit affairs with other men's wives that often ended in duels. How much of it was true? But she was allowing herself to get distracted again. Lord Ware's past was not her concern. Nothing mattered except Freddie's missing letter. And Lord Ware's search had turned up nothing. Notley had failed to bring the letter as promised.

Unless the killer took it.

"What are we going to do?" Georgina moaned. "Where is the letter now?"

Aunt Meg shook her head. "Georgina, dear, not now. Poor Anne has had an awful fright."

"I am fine now," Anne said, returning to stand beside them. "Georgina has posed a very good question. Lord Ware searched the body, so Notley didn't bring the letter. I suppose he wanted more money." She cocked her head. "He must have left it at his lodgings."

"Yes! Oh, yes." Georgina nearly bounced on the bed. "Let us go there without delay and get it."

"To a gentleman's lodgings?" Aunt Meg asked, astonished. "Georgina, how can you make such an outrageous suggestion? It would be the height of impropriety."

"*I* do not care," Georgina declared. "Poor Lord John shall not be subjected to scandal because I was afraid to do what must be done."

Anne sighed. God help us. How swiftly Georgina's heart had gone from undying love for poor Freddie to saving poor Lord John. Nevertheless, it was a good omen for her future marriage plans.

"I applaud your worthy feelings, Georgina, but Aunt Meg is right. It will not do for you to enter a bachelor residence." Anne stood, picking up a candle, and gave a loud, weary sigh. "A good night's sleep will make us feel better. We shall think of a plan tomorrow."

Aunt Meg nodded with a look of gratitude. "A sensible thought. I heartily agree. It will all become clear in the light of day."

"I suppose." Georgina stifled a yawn. "May I return to the ball now?"

"Positively not," Aunt Meg declared. "A man has been murdered. Your cousin is exhausted, and so am I. Even you look tired, my dear."

"I am not *that* tired."

"Come, Georgina. No more dancing tonight." Anne linked arms with her cousin. "Let's let Auntie get her rest."

Anne escorted her cousin to her room across the hall before dropping her feigned weariness and hurrying to her own bedchamber. She allowed her maid to prepare her for bed, then sent the girl away. Going to her writing desk, she jotted a message and put her ear to the door to be sure her relatives were not about. Hearing nothing, she stepped out, tiptoed down the hall, and gave the note to the first maid she saw, instructing her to deliver it promptly to Joseph, her aunt's footman. Then she returned to her bedchamber, shifted the boxes in the back of her wardrobe, and after finding what she wanted, she began to change clothes again.

Anne put on the drab clothing she had worn to the pawnshop, then she sat on the edge of her bed and waited. Having regained her serenity enough to form a hasty but practical plan, she was impatient to get on with it. The hall clock chimed. One o'clock. It had been a half hour since she'd sent the note. She rose and paced to the window and turned with a jerk when a small sound drew her attention. A white, folded paper was pushed under the door.

At last. She snatched it up, glanced at the address written inside, and slipped out the door, taking the servants' stairs to the lowest level. Music from the upstairs ballroom reached her, but the festivity would go on most of the night, and her errand could not wait.

Tip-toeing to the rear door, she was outside the mansion and headed down the back lane within seconds. Away from the bright lights of the ball, it was darker than she expected…and eerily quiet.

Anne threw a wary glance at the shadows and tugged her cloak around her. She didn't breathe easy until she spotted the waiting hired hackney. *Thank you, Joseph.* How fortunate her aunt had insisted on bringing her indispensable footman to town.

Anne directed the driver to the street listed on the note, and little time passed before they came to a halt at the intersection she'd designated. "Where to now, my lady?" the coachman asked.

"I shall walk from here. Turn the coach around and wait for me down the street. I shan't be too long." At least, she hoped not.

"Very well, Miss." The man shook his head, his scrutiny making Anne blush. He must be thinking this was a lovers' assignation. Well, she couldn't help what he thought, and it was unlikely she would see him again after tonight.

As she descended from the coach, she pulled her hat low to hide her face and studied her surroundings. Anne was dismayed to find it was an area of small, three-story establishments converted into rented rooms. Multiple tenants in his building would make her intrusion more risky. Taking a deep breath, she circled behind the carriage and darted into a narrow passageway leading to the rear of the row houses. She walked quickly, counting each house until she reached the back gate of what had to be Notley's residence.

Again, she hesitated, assessing the building. Four or six tenants were possible. She frowned, fleetingly unsure of herself. She had thought to pry the outer door with the knife she had brought, hoping to get in and out unheard and unnoticed, but now…

What choice did she have?

Anne entered the garden, tried the back door latch, and drew back in surprise. Why was it unlocked? Had someone forgotten to secure it for the night? She wasn't familiar with rented lodgings, so perhaps they didn't lock the exterior doors with so many tenants going in and out. She opened it and slipped inside.

The hall was lit by a single candle lantern near the front. Joseph's note had said first floor, so there must be a staircase. She eased past two closed doors, one on each side, found the steps at the front, and climbed upward. Another lantern lit this hall. Just as below, one set of rooms on each side. Right or left door? If she chose wrong, she would face an angry sleeper who might call the watch.

She stopped beside the right hand door and tested the latch. It was locked. Before resorting to the knife to pry it, she tried the left door, snatching back her hand when it swung open at her mere touch. What did that mean? Could two unlocked doors truly be a coincidence? Had someone been there before her? Or was it just an unrented room?

She held her breath and listened. No snoring, no heavy breathing, no rustling of bed linens. It appeared empty. Feeling exposed in the hallway, Anne moved inside while she considered what to do, easing the door closed behind her. She fumbled in the eerie dark. The shutters must be closed. She had thought the light from the street lanterns would be sufficient to get around until she could find and light a candle.

She put a hand against the wall, turning toward the front of the house in order to make her way over to the shutters. A small creak of movement warned her she was not alone as an arm snaked around her and a firm hand clamped over her mouth.

Anne's startled scream never left her throat. Her heart seemed to stop, but fear gave her courage, and she lashed out, kicking her assailant's shinbone. Encouraged by a muffled "ouch," she attempted to bite the hand covering her mouth. A spark from flint being struck resulted in a lambent light revealing Andrew Sherbourne's shocked face.

"Egad, it is a woman!"

"Shh. Yes, I had noticed," said a soft voice behind her ear. A voice she recognized all too well. "If you promise to keep quiet, my lady, I will let you go."

She nodded, too angry and mortified to do anything else.

When Viscount Ware relaxed his hold, she pulled away and whirled, knocking back her bonnet.

"Lady Anne." Sherbourne gaped at her.

"What are you two doing here?" she snapped, struggling to keep her voice low.

Lord Ware lifted a brow. "Exactly my question."

"I asked first," she said defiantly.

He studied her face. "Finding you here rather belies your protestations as an innocent bystander to Notley's death, my lady. I assume we are here on the same errand—to search his lodgings. Regrettably, someone was here before us." He swept a hand as Sherbourne lifted the candle to reveal a jumble of clothes and papers scattered around the room. The mattress was pulled halfway off the bed. "So tell me, what is so important that a lady would break into a gentleman's lodgings?" When she only glared at him, he asked, "Are you being blackmailed, Lady Anne?"

Anne sucked in a sharp breath and shot back. "Are you?"

"Can this discussion wait?" Sherry asked in a stage whisper. "While watching you spar is entertaining, we need to get on with it before we're discovered."

"Very true." Lucien turned back to Anne. "I would escort you to your carriage, but it is too dangerous to make an extra trip. Stand over there, please, and remain quiet while we finish."

Anne bristled, wanting to defy him, to resist his high-handed *orders,* but it wasn't sensible under the circumstances. She scowled and moved aside, watching their activities intently, hoping to spot Freddie's letter. The two men worked well together and were very efficient. They searched the desk, the wardrobe, in and under the bed, examined the floorboards and walls, and even ran their hands over the drapes. She concluded they had done this sort of thing before.

When they were done with the desk, she stepped forward and searched it herself. Lord Ware glanced at her and said nothing. She interpreted that as implied permission and continued sorting through Notley's papers. She ran her fingers over and under the desk's surface and each drawer for hidden compartments they might have missed, but, of course, they had not.

She turned and surveyed the rest of the room for obscure niches or cubbyholes. Spying the cannon ball bedposts, she climbed on the bed and tested the top knobs. The men continued to ignore her. The decorative tops were tight and secure…until she reached the third one.

"Ah." Her quiet exclamation drew Sherbourne's attention.

"Find something?" he whispered.

"Maybe." The ball top twisted off with ease, and she dipped her fingers into the hollow interior, feeling a length of twine. She pulled on it, and out popped a lock key.

"Thank you. I will take that," the viscount said, taking it from her fingers and lifting her down from her precarious perch on the wobbling mattress.

"Give it back. I found it," she protested, attempting to grab it as he set her on her feet.

A sudden clattering—as though something had been dropped or knocked over across the hall—silenced the argument, freezing them in place. A man's curse carried to them. Sherbourne doused the candle, and then it grew quiet again.

Anne's heart raced, and she found Lord Ware's presence beside her strangely comforting. "We should go," he whispered. He took her arm, urging her in the general direction of the door. "There is nothing else here. Sherry, a little light, if you please."

Lord Sherbourne stumbled into something in the dark, the candle fell to the floor and rolled across the barren wood. He swore softly, and Anne heard him patting the boards with his hands. "Lost it," he muttered.

At last, something she could do. Concentrating hard, Anne pictured the room as she'd last seen it. She ran through the clutter in her head, searching for what had to be there. She smiled. "You'll find a candle on the table by the bed."

"Which side? I don't remember it," Sherbourne said. "And I'm all turned around."

"I will get it," she whispered. "Just stay where you are."

Early in her childhood, Anne's family had recognized her gift to recall almost anything she had seen. She became used to requests for her to remember or find things, from misplaced sewing baskets to the last guests to leave a party. Locating the candle was simple.

Within moments, she returned, holding it in one hand. Her fingers brushed against Lord Ware's as he attempted to light it, using a pocket tinderbox. How odd he should carry such a unique thing.

The room flared into view again. Anne quickly pulled back from the intimate contact and stepped away. She took a last wistful look around the room but conceded it was time to go. Sherbourne eased the door open; they slipped into the hall and then light-footed it down the stairs, not speaking again until they reached the rear alley.

"What made you look in the bedpost?" Lord Ware asked, breaking the silence.

"I kept all my childhood treasures there." She glanced up at him as they reached the connecting road and stood under the glow of a street lantern. Her coach waited just short of the next corner. "Are you going to give back the key?"

"No, but you have our gratitude for finding it."

She swung around to confront him. "That is not satisfactory, sir. I found it."

"We should keep moving until we're out of the area. We can discuss this later."

"I need to settle it now. My coach is waiting."

His gray eyes shadowed. "Very well. If I gave you the key, what would you do with it?"

"I...I should discover what it opens."

"How?"

"I...well..." *Drat the man.* "I'm not sure. Do you?"

"Do I what?"

Anne gave an unladylike huff of impatience. "You are insufferable. Do you know what it opens?" She emphasized every word.

"Not yet, but I daresay Sherbourne and I have a better chance of discovering that than you do."

That was hard to deny, since she had no thought where to start. But it must open a locked room, a trunk, or a wardrobe where

Notley kept important things, such as Freddie's letter. "It belongs to me," she insisted.

"In fact, it is Notley's, but I have it in my pocket now."

"Because you stole it." Anne knew Lord Sherbourne was watching them, his hands in his pockets, a grin on his face, but she was not finding this the least bit funny.

"I took it into my protective care," Lucien said, maddeningly. He nodded to the street. "Is that your hackney down there?"

"It is. As soon as you hand over my key, I shall be on my way."

"Sherry, would you oblige by paying off her jarvey? I believe we should see Lady Anne safely home."

"Wait. No…" Anne broke off as Lord Sherbourne walked toward the waiting coach.

"I shall only be a moment," he said over his shoulder.

Anne stared at the man beside her. "My lord, you cannot…of all the high-handed—"

"My carriage is not far," he said tucking her arm in his. "You cannot imagine we would allow a lady to travel on her own at this time of night."

"I got here on my own."

"All the more reason not to tempt fate twice." He made it sound so reasonable.

In spite of herself, Anne forced back a smile as the absurdity of the last half hour struck her. "Do you have an answer for everything?"

He pretended to ponder that. "Not always, but when I do, I am rarely wrong."

A sharp set-down was on the tip of her tongue until she noticed the smile on his lips. Odious man. He was provoking her into behavior unbecoming a lady. She sighed and refused to be drawn.

As the viscount handed her into his carriage, Sherbourne arrived. "Did I miss anything?" he asked, climbing inside.

Knowing he referred to her quarrel with Lord Ware, Anne sniffed and turned her head away. She heard the viscount's low chuckle. *Very funny.*

As the carriage made its way toward the mansion, the two men discussed Lord Notley's death—who might have killed him, why, and why at the ball. Anne couldn't add anything without compromising Georgina—and making herself a greater suspect than she already was. She tuned them out and debated what to do about the key. She could scarcely wrestle it away from Viscount Ware, and she doubted if pleading or female tears would move him.

Anne bit her lip in thought. There was one option. She could take a chance and tell them the truth or part of it. Was it possible they could help one another? He had already mentioned blackmail, so he must know something of Notley's activities. Maybe more than she did.

As though reading her thoughts, the viscount broke off his conversation with Sherbourne and turned to her. "You failed to answer when I asked before, Lady Anne. Was Notley blackmailing you?"

She made an impulsive decision and hoped she would not regret it. "No, not me, but…a friend. A letter that would ruin her reputation. I was to meet the blackmailer at the ball to buy it back." She tried to make out the viscount's expression in the dark shadows of the coach. Did he believe her? Would he be sympathetic?

"Hence the money in your bag."

"Yes. Now I need the key to complete my task. Why else would he have hidden it so well unless it opened something that safeguards items of particular value? Secret items. The letter, for one."

"A possibility, if he is in the regular business of blackmail. But your letter may be gone. If Notley brought it to sell, the killer must have it now."

Dear Lord, I hope not. "Why would the killer want it? It would mean nothing to him. Is it not more likely Lord Notley left it at home because he was holding out for more money?" She frowned, still thinking it through. "I wonder if the killer was also being blackmailed. After all, his lodgings were searched for something before we got there, and who else would know he was dead?"

Sherbourne shrugged. "She may be right."

"All the more reason for the key to remain with me."

"Why is that?" she asked.

"You don't want a killer stalking you, or your aunt and cousin, do you? Then again, we may have been too late. He could have found what he wanted and taken everything," Lord Ware added, dampening her spirits. "In truth, this is all speculation. Until we learn more, the key does none of us any good."

Anne gave an audible sigh.

"We will keep looking," Lord Sherbourne assured her. "If we find his secret stash, we can look for your letter and return it without anyone else knowing. Is that not fair?"

The viscount eyed Anne. "I assume this is a love letter?"

She nodded. "Yes, just a bit of foolishness but a worry nonetheless."

"I find it curious your friend asked *you* to do this. Are you sure the letter is not your own?"

Anne bristled. "Do I seem that green to you?" How could he think she would be so naive or indiscreet? Or perhaps he was angling for the friend's name. He wouldn't be getting it. She would protect Georgina, no matter what. "My friend is not in a position to retrieve it herself. Please, do not expect me to betray her."

The viscount shrugged. "It matters little, but if we are to look for the letter, you must describe it."

She told them, confessing it was written by a young gentleman. She stopped as she realized Georgina's name was on the outside and asked, "Can I rely on your complete discretion?"

"You may. Certainly," Sherbourne said.

Lord Ware's eyes lit with amusement. "A little late to be asking, is it not? But yes, if the letter is as you say, I have no interest in exposing ill-fated lovers."

"They are not exactly that, but—what do you mean 'if it is as I say'?" Her voice sharpened. "Do you doubt me?"

"No, but I do enjoy watching your eyes flash with annoyance."

Lord Sherbourne laughed, and Anne was momentarily speechless. How could he even see her eyes in the dim coach light?

Was he indulging in a moment of flirtation? She sat back and dropped her gaze. Had she given him cause to think she would welcome such attention? She flashed through their conversations and found nothing the least bit romantic.

Anne smoothed the creases in her skirt. "You are trying to provoke me…again, your lordship, and it will not do. I regret I am not a man who could take back the key by force and be done with you."

"A regret I do not share," he murmured.

"Despite my reservations," she said, pretending she had not heard, "I see I must trust your discretion and your promise to retrieve the letter on my behalf. I urge you to act swiftly."

"Rest assured… Ah, we are here," Lucien said as the carriage halted. "I had my coachman stop at the corner. To move further amongst the waiting coaches from the ball would be bound to draw unwanted attention. You are not dressed for a social event. Perhaps there is an accessible back entrance?"

"There is." She nodded, giving him a grateful smile. Other than stealing the key from her, the two lords had treated her with consideration. "Thank you for seeing me hone."

Lucien stepped out first and helped her descend. "May I escort you to the door?"

"No need. It is better if I slip through the rear gardens alone." She looked up at him, her gaze seeking his. "I am counting on you to find it, sir."

He bowed before releasing her hand, his eyes grave, yet a faint smile playing across his lips. "Goodnight, my lady. I shall endeavor not to disappoint you."

Chapter Fourteen

Lucien waited until Lady Anne disappeared into the gardens before swinging into the carriage. As the coachman cracked the whip over the top of his showy team of chestnuts, he sat back and gave in to a reluctant grin. The lady boded trouble…and then some. A most unusual woman. He admired her spirit, the clear-eyed intelligence that considered every thought, every move, and yet he feared she would interfere again when least expected. In fact, she had not *said* she would leave it to them to recover the letter.

He raised a hand to flip back an unruly lock of hair. *Drat the woman.* The last thing he needed was to be distracted by concern for her safety. Working undetected was hard enough for experienced agents without Lady Anne's kind of complication.

"She is a tempting armful," Sherry said shooting him an astute look. "And rather plucky. I cannot think of another female who would dare such risks. Uh, Lucien, are you listening?"

"Sorry. I was woolgathering. Were you speaking of Lady Anne?"

Sherry gave a bark of laughter. "You know I was. The lady has caught your interest."

"She has me worried that she won't stay out of this."

"You have the key. What can she do?"

"I have no inkling. That is the problem. She isn't a good liar, and it was plain she fibbed about the letter's owner. My bet is on Georgina, affianced to Lord Bennington. Lady Anne would feel responsible for a young cousin in trouble. I suppose the chit or a youthful swain put their feelings into prose or poetry."

Sherry raised a brow. "Bennington wouldn't care for that, the gossip and all. Clarifies the trip to the pawnshop, though. An attempt to raise the blackmail funds on the sly."

"I'll grant you, they are enterprising. But far too unpredictable. Confound it, Sherry. Why are we even talking about it? We have no control over what they'll do next." Lucien exhaled a frustrated breath. "Let us make our own plans. Perhaps we can recover their letter before they entangle themselves in deeper trouble."

"No argument from me. While you were bidding goodnight to the fair Lady Anne, I was thinking about Notley's recent absence from town, where he might have gone in such a short time, and why. And Weatherby's denial is odd upon reflection. Why wouldn't he know where Notley was?"

"Why would he?"

"They've been in each other's pockets for months. He'd know. And yet he lied. I've tried to sort it out. I wonder if they have a hideout, a place where they store the stolen goods. Wouldn't that also be where Notley hid the documents and letters that supported his blackmail?"

"You have made some rather wild assumptions," Lucien said. "But they make a certain kind of sense. Let's ask Weatherby and not take 'no' for an answer this time."

"Now? At three or four in the morning?"

Lucien pursed his lips. "I suppose not. He is likely passed out drunk by now, and we need him coherent. We'll also need the means to pressure him. Without a compelling reason, he isn't going to admit his part in or even his knowledge of Notley's nefarious schemes."

"What if we tell him the truth about Notley's death, just enough of it to know it wasn't footpads, and imply it was someone seeking revenge for *their* illegal activities..."

"And that he could be, no, that he is next on the killer's list," Lucien finished. "Yes. I think we can work with that." He gave a humorless smile. "Surely we would be remiss in our duty if we did not warn him of his peril."

Sherry grinned. "We shall be his only friends and supporters in a time of need?"

"Something like that."

• • •

Having slept late themselves, it was half eleven by the time Lucien and Sherry met up to roust Weatherby from his bed. The Weatherby townhouse was understaffed during the cold months with the rest of the family wintering in the country, and Lucien and Sherry had no trouble brushing past the footman on the door and gaining access to his lordship's bedchamber. Weatherby was grumpy and bewildered by the abrupt awakening and mumbled at them to go away. Sherry responded by dousing him with a pitcher of water.

"What the bloody hell?" Weatherby sputtered, rearing up in bed. "Who? What? I say, this is outrageous!"

"Get up," Lucien ordered, wrinkling his nose against the strong smell of alcohol. "We are here to save your skin."

Weatherby scrubbed his face with both hands and peered at them with red-rimmed, watery eyes. "Is that you, Ware? And Sherbourne? What time is it?"

Sherry threw him a towel and a robe. "It is time to get out of bed. We need to talk."

Lucien opened the door to find the footman who had followed them up the stairs. "Your master is in dire want of tea and toast or coffee if you have it."

"But, my lord—"

"Now," Lucien said implacably and shut the door.

By the time Weatherby was dry, wrapped in his robe, and seated in a chair before the fire, the footman arrived with a laden breakfast tray. The ravages of a long night of indulgence had the half-drunk lord downing the hot chocolate before attending to tea and toast. He gave the eggs a sour look and pushed them away.

"Ready to talk?" Lucien inquired.

Weatherby sighed in resignation. "What is this about, Ware? I object to this high-handed intrusion."

"Object all you wish, but first you will listen." Lucien pulled up a chair and sat facing the gradually sobering man. Sherbourne leaned against the fireplace mantel.

Weatherby shifted his gaze from one man to the other, settling on Ware as the viscount began to talk.

"Your friend Notley has been murdered and his lodgings searched by the killer. He didn't find what he was looking for and will soon be on your doorstep. Do you know what he wants?"

"No. You've got it wrong. Notley was killed by footpads," Weatherby said. "What has that to do with me?"

"You cannot believe that Banbury tale. Would Notley walk through Hyde Park alone at that time of night? Of course not. His corpse was dumped there after he was stabbed in the back. A single blow by a skilled cutthroat. Think about it. Who wanted Notley dead? French agents? An assassin hired by those bedeviled by blackmail?" Seeing the man's befuddled look, Lucien wondered if Notley had kept most of his activities—and profits—to himself. He tried again. "Of course, it's most likely Notley's gang of thieves turned against him to keep anyone from informing against them. Three or four associates are already dead."

Weatherby's face paled. Lucien's gaze flicked to Sherry. Weatherby *did* know about the thievery.

Rallying, Weatherby shook his head. "More likely an angry husband. Notley had a taste for other men's wives. As I already said, his death had nothing to do with me." He stuck out a stubborn chin, but his voice quavered with uncertainty.

"If it had been a duel, maybe I'd agree," Lucien said. "But this was murder, not a matter of honor."

As they continued to talk, Lucien revealed more of what they knew, and Sherbourne moved to hover behind Weatherby, boxing him in and adding to his discomfort. Weatherby began to sweat.

"Were you not, in fact, his partner?" Lucien demanded, tired of playing subtle.

"I... Dash it, Ware. All right, I knew of a few shady deals."

"And the housebreakings."

"Uh, yes. Those too."

"How deeply were you involved? Equal partners?"

"No. It was all Notley."

"Well, fine," Sherry said. "If he wants to deny the truth, Ware, then let's go. I have better things to do."

Lucien frowned at Weatherby. "We came here to save your life, but if you can't be honest..." He shrugged. "If we leave, you'll have to face these killers on your own."

Doubt and confusion flashed across Weatherby's face, showing just how befuddled his brain still was. "I suppose we were partners in a way. I was desperate for funds, and Notley offered a way to get them." Weatherby went on to describe a year-long enterprise between the two men and a band of thieves working for Notley. He passed on information on homes to be plundered, mostly in and near London, and Notley fenced the stolen goods, giving Weatherby a share of the profit.

"Just a moment," Sherry interrupted. "If you two were in this together, what about the challenge to a duel?"

Weatherby's face darkened. "I wanted to run him through for what he said. But he threatened to talk about the thefts, putting the blame on me, if I did not withdraw." He looked at Lucien. "I wish I had known about the other stuff you mentioned, the blackmail and whatever he was doing with the French agents. Upon my word, I am not that kind of man and no traitor," he said, then brightened with a hopeful look. "If Notley had dealings with the French, maybe it was the Frogs that killed him."

"And if it was the thieves instead?"

"Then I...uh, well, yes, they argued with Notley about their share, but I had no part in cheating them."

"He cheated them?" Lucien shook his head. "No wonder they came after him. I understand you feel it was his doings and not yours, but I doubt if the gang sees the difference."

Weatherby's face grew slack. "You honestly believe I'm in danger?"

"I do."

"Get your head together," Sherry said feigning annoyance. "Why do you think we came to warn you?"

"What do I do? Demme, how did I get in this deep? I just needed the funds so badly. It was that or debtors' prison." He sunk his head into his hands.

"Can you repay the thieves what they were cheated?"

"Of course not. Even if I knew how much it was, everything I had went to hold off creditors—and to repay Notley." At Lucien raised brows, he explained. "He was holding my gambling IOUs."

Lucien shook his head at Weatherby's gullibility. "Perhaps the gang would be satisfied if you turned over the remaining stolen goods. Sherbourne and I could explain the *irregularities* were Notley's, not yours."

"Might it work?"

Weatherby's expression was so hopeful that Lucien felt a twinge of pity for a vulnerable drunk who'd been poorly used by life. The man looked closer to forty than approaching his mid-twenties, his thin face lined, his eyes puffy from years of indulgence. Unless he mended his ways, he was headed for an early grave.

"We could negotiate for you," Lucien said. "How do we get in touch with the thieves?"

Weatherby shrugged. "Notley had a man on the docks. I cannot recall the name. Young, rough-looking rascal with red hair."

"Billy Tate," Sherry said. "Sound familiar?"

"I'm not sure."

Lucien flicked a casual hand. "No matter. He is dead too."

"Lord a mercy." Weatherby licked his dry lips.

"Just so." Lucien waited a moment. "We'll worry about them once we know what we have to offer. Where are the goods?"

"Sold. At least everything from the first six months. The rest is in a cottage Notley bought outside of town. He sold a little at a time to avoid suspicion."

"Won't the gang have cleared it out?" Sherry asked.

"They don't know about it. They loaded a wagon each time and never knew where he took it. He was clever that way." Weatherby gave Lucien a baffled look. "Why would you do this? Help me, I mean? I scarce know you."

"It was the proper thing to do," Lucien said. "But you're right in thinking there is more to it than that. We hope to return a blackmail letter or two to their rightful owners. Nothing of use to you or the gang. Where is this house?"

Weatherby balked again. "How do I know you'll do what you say? And get the gang to leave me alone?" As he regained his wits, he required more reassurance.

"You have a gentleman's word," Lucien said. "We will do our best to keep the gang away from you."

Weatherby stared at him. "I think you mean it, and I have little choice. Saw the cottage just once, but it's easy to find. And less than an hour ride by carriage."

After getting the directions, Lucien stood, picking up his hat. "You should leave London while we handle this. Go now, today, to someplace safe, and send word where we can reach you. While you're gone, you might give some thought to the kind of living that brought you to this point."

As Lucien and Sherry descended the stairs, they heard Weatherby calling for his valet to pack for a journey. Lucien hoped the man took the rest of his advice as readily but knew the odds were poor.

"Are we going straight to the country? Shouldn't we take some of Rothe's men with us?" Sherry asked. "In the event of resistance?"

Lucien shrugged. "By whom? If Weatherby's right, the gang doesn't know about the cottage."

"What about one or more guards?"

"That's why I intend to take my pistols."

"When I change clothes, I'll get mine too." Sherry lifted a leg to admire his new top boots. "I would never hear the end of it if I wore these John Bulls into the country."

Minutes later the coach delivered Sherbourne to his townhouse, and Lucien shouted a reminder as he pulled away. "One hour, Sherry. Be ready if we're to keep the daylight."

He leaned back, still thinking about Weatherby. The man was an easy mark, and Lucien felt a twinge of discomfort over how hard they'd leaned on him. Regardless, Weatherby had chosen his own path, and, indeed, they *may* have saved his life. The disarray at Notley's lodgings proved the killer was looking for...*something*. Whoever he was, he might start looking at Notley's close associates, and since he'd already committed one murder, what was to prevent another?

Enough of Weatherby and Notley. The question now was how did all of this impinge his pursuit of the cipher? The killer was following a similar path. If he got there first—whether he was after the cipher or something else—the code key might disappear forever.

He flicked a speck of dust off his jacket—and was nearly thrown to the floor when the carriage rocked to a sudden halt. He threw out his hands to regain his balance, the door banged open, and a pistol was thrust in his face.

"You'll be comin' with us, m'lord."

Lucien lunged sideways and grabbed the man's wrist, his fingers tightening in a death grip. A loud explosion, burning pain. *Bloody hell* was his final thought.

Chapter Fifteen

The day after the ball, Anne seated herself for a late breakfast and smoothed the skirt of her favorite winter walking gown, an ivory confection trimmed with green embroidery on the sleeves and hem. It also showed well with her deep green pelisse edged in white fur, the matching fur hat and muff. Although Christmas Day was celebrated in the countryside and by most servants, Anne had discovered it was just another day among most of the town Quality. A special dinner perhaps but otherwise the usual social routine.

Accordingly, she had dressed for the anticipated morning calls—those misnamed social visits made in the afternoon. She was anxious to hear the latest gossip. What were they saying about Lord Notley's death? Had anyone seen her near the library or at the dead lord's lodgings? Was her name even now on everyone's lips? She could not help but worry.

"Annie," Georgina called as she hurried into the breakfast room. "Have you heard?"

Fearing the worst from those ominous words, Anne forced a smile. "I'm right here. Please lower your voice. What has excited you so?"

Georgina plopped in the chair next to her and whispered, "Someone moved the body."

Anne stared at her. "Whatever do you mean? Moved it where?"

"Hyde Park. They say he was set upon by footpads." Having delivered this prime piece of gossip, Georgina scooted back in her chair and eyed her cousin. "What do you think of that?"

"Frankly, I am speechless." Questions spun in her head—who and why? Neither Lord Ware nor Lord Sherbourne had mentioned moving it, but they'd had time to do it. She'd left the ball around midnight and had not reached Lord Notley's lodgings until sometime after one o'clock. "Who told you this?"

"My abigail. Oh, you know how it goes. The delivery man told the scullery maid and such juicy news was swiftly passed around."

Anne's appetite fled, and she pushed her plate away. "What precisely was she told?"

"Well…a couple of gentlemen leaving the ball about half two cut through the park and stumbled across it. Right in the path." Georgina gave an exaggerated shiver. "Imagine, finding a body like that."

Anne didn't have to imagine. "It's horridly unpleasant," she murmured. She picked up her cup of chocolate and took a fortifying sip.

"Oh, right. Sorry. For one moment, I forgot." Georgina gave her a sympathetic look. "Do you think the viscount moved him?"

"I hope so. I am loath to think someone else did it." A cold chill settled between her shoulder blades. What if it was the killer? Had he watched and waited for her and Lord Ware to leave the library? But why would he carry the body away? Why would anybody?

As Georgina jumped up to fill her plate from the sideboard, the loud scrape of her chair broke Anne's fretful train of thought. Merciful heavens, she had to quit thinking like that and scaring herself. Viscount Ware must have moved the body with Lord Sherbourne's help, and they had not told her because Lord Ware was annoyed—and suspicious—to find her at the dead man's lodgings, and Lord Sherbourne was too amused. Neither had taken her seriously, so, of course, they had not seen fit to share their activities. She huffed in exasperation.

Still, she couldn't help but wonder why. The obvious answer was to shift the blame to footpads, but why was that necessary? To avoid social embarrassment for the Barbarys? To avoid suspicion falling on the ton? Why would they choose to interfere with the constables' investigation? She tightened her lips. There was so much she did not know.

Such as, how in Heavens' name had they pulled it off? The viscount was alone when she left. Wouldn't he need help? She tapped a finger against her cup of chocolate, and a smile spread across her lips as she pictured the elegant viscount running through a crowded ballroom with a corpse slung over his shoulder. She cut off a giggle. Oh, dear. What a terrible sense of humor she had.

"What is so funny?" Georgina asked, setting her plate down.

"Oh, nothing. Just nerves, I suppose."

Georgina shot her a curious look, but Aunt Meg entered the room just then, and her inquisitive cousin let it drop.

"I assume Georgina told you," Aunt Meg said, joining them with a plate of toast.

"She did," Anne said. "Is that all you are eating?"

"I breakfasted earlier with Bridget and Laurence and have been waiting for you, hoping we could discuss our *situation*." She gave a heavy sigh. "You are very late, my dear, and now we have no time, not till much later."

Anne was relieved. She did not want to lie to her relatives, but she'd decided not to mention her late night excursion. Aunt Meg would be appalled and might even send her home. "I guess I needed the extra rest after…well, you know." She smiled brightly. "I feel ever so much better now. Are we making morning calls or receiving today?"

"Receiving," her aunt said promptly. "Bridget and I are certain a half dozen or more young men will be paying their respects."

Georgina's eyes shone. "Lord John said he would be calling."

"No doubt very early." Aunt Meg gave her a knowing look. "He will have noticed all the attention you received last night and want to remind other admirers of his prior claim."

"Do you think so?" Georgina pressed her palms together and clapped lightly. "That is splendid." She turned to Anne. "I know you shall have callers too. A number of gentleman cast admiring glances in your direction."

"Very gratifying." Anne smiled as expected, but she wasn't thinking about admirers. She lay awake for what felt like hours last night thinking of a hundred questions she should have asked Viscount Ware. At the very least, she should have extracted a promise that he would report his progress...or lack of progress. She had eventually gotten out of bed and composed a letter asking him to call as soon as there were developments.

Her courage had failed this morning, knowing Aunt Meg and Lady Barbary would never approve. For an unmarried lady to send a note to an eligible bachelor was improper, some might even say fast. So the letter remained in her pocket instead of on the hallway table for posting.

But Georgina's news raised a dozen more questions. She *had* to talk with him soon.

Anne sipped her tea. Would it truly be so very bad if she sent the note? Who would know besides the viscount? Somehow, she doubted it would astonish him, nor would he betray such a minor social indiscretion when he knew much worse things she'd done.

But what of the servants? They would talk if she left the letter on the hall table. Maybe it was a bad idea after all. Unless...the corners of her mouth curled up...unless Joseph would deliver it and keep one more secret, just a small one in comparison to last night.

● ● ●

Over the next few hours, Anne kept an eye out for Joseph and bided her time. When the last morning visitors were gone—most of them indeed were gentlemen callers—her patience was rewarded. She was approaching the staircase to run up and change her shoes when Joseph came out of the drawing room.

She turned back and said quietly, "I was hoping to catch you alone."

"My lady?"

She tilted her head, uncertain whether he sounded wary or amused. His expression told her nothing. She retrieved the note from her pocket and pressed it into his hand. "I would like this delivered with as much haste as possible. No one is to know, unless *she* asks you directly." Which had been his only condition last night, that he wouldn't lie to Aunt Meg.

"Understood, my lady." He slipped it into his own pocket. "Should I wait for a response?"

"No. None is expected today."

"Very good. I was leaving on another errand, so no one should wonder at my absence."

Anne hurried up the stairs before she grew faint-hearted and changed her mind. She paused on the top step when she heard the front door close as Joseph left the house. Too late to retrieve it now, and she truly did not want to call him back. She was most anxious to know what Lord Ware was about.

She could not, however, rely entirely on the viscount's efforts. She had her own information gathering to do. Most afternoons about this time two gregarious older matrons, Lady Bell and Dowager Lady Spencer met at Hatchards Booksellers on Piccadilly to exchange the latest gossip. They were certain to be talking about the murder. Maybe they would say something that would point to the killer—the person most likely in possession of Georgina's letter. At all events, she would learn how much the ton knew about the sordid affair.

After telling Aunt Meg of her need for a new book and accepting Lady Barbary's offer of her carriage—for no proper lady would walk down Piccadilly without a gentleman escort—Anne changed her boots, donned her fur-lined winter garments, and set out with Jenny, her new maid. The seventeen-year-old girl with soft brown hair and a merry, forthright disposition had been hired by the Barbarys to help out during ball week. Anne and Jenny had taken a liking to one another, and just that morning, Anne had offered her a permanent position when she returned to Warwickshire. Jenny had readily accepted.

When the carriage stopped and the footman opened the door, Anne and Jenny hurried through the biting cold. It smelled of snow, and Anne was grateful to reach the warmth of the book shop.

Hatchards was crowded, but Anne found the town gossips holding court on the second floor with four other fashionable ladies. Anne positioned herself where she could hear yet remain inconspicuous. As she had hoped, the topic was Lord Notley's murder.

"I knew he would come to a bad end." Dowager Lady Spence, her elegantly coiffed hair almost white, pursed her lips. "Poor breeding. His mother's cousin was in trade. But murder...how terribly scandalous."

Pretending to look at books, Anne inched closer over the next few minutes. So far the only point the ladies agreed on was getting murdered was bad ton.

Anne ran her fingertips over the latest books, looking for the Jane Austen novel a friend had recommended, but kept her attention on the circle of women. To her disgust, the discussion changed to Hyde Park and whether it was safe with murdering footpads on the loose.

"I shall not be taking afternoon walks in the park, not any time soon," Lady Bell declared. "I trust we are still safe in our carriages. Nonetheless, I shall insist my footman carries a pistol."

As the talk continued to center on Hyde Park, Anne was losing hope she'd learn anything of value. Then an exquisitely-attired woman with raven hair arrived.

"Good afternoon, ladies."

Anne recognized her immediately. After Viscount Ware had visited her theatre box, Anne had made the effort to find out who she was—Mrs. Sophia Stine, the Widow Stine.

After the predictable chit-chat, Mrs. Stine smiled sweetly and asked, "Who do you think *really* killed Lord Notley?"

Anne started, almost dropping the book she was holding. Why would she ask that? In just that way, as though she knew the truth? Had the viscount told her? If so, had he told her Anne was there? Stifling her concern, she shifted to hear better. The widow just might raise the very questions Anne longed to ask.

"I hear he frequented all kinds of seedy places," Mrs. Stine continued in an audible whisper. "And had *criminal associates*. A sure way to get yourself killed, I would think."

"Oh, my." The ladies crowded closer, visibly enthralled by this titillating information.

A woman in a yellow hat leaned forward. "My cousin's nephew said his lordship frequents the most lurid establishments in town... even those in Whitechapel."

Hushed gasps were followed by more rumors and rampant speculation regarding alleged visits to various gaming hells including Cade's Club, flash houses, drug dens, and even molly haunts. Places ladies were not supposed to know about, but of course they did. Some of the conjecture sounded doubtful to Anne, even outlandish, yet she took in every word, hoping there would be some tiny piece that would matter.

"All a hum over nothing. Idle gossip," Dowager Lady Spence declared in a somewhat strident voice, swinging the attention away from Widow Stine and back to herself. "I dare say the constables have the right of it. Lord Notley was killed by robbers. Foolish man to be in the park that late. Foxed, I suppose."

"O-oh, perhaps." Mrs. Stine drawled, making her doubts plain, as she smoothed a wrinkle from her gloves. "But a man of Notley's habits is sure to have enemies. His death may not be as it appears."

"What a devious mind you have." The lady in the yellow hat tittered.

The rest of the ladies laughed until Lady Bell said thoughtfully, "But he did have enemies. Lord Langley warned him away from his daughter, and Lord Weatherby was angry enough to challenge him to a duel."

"You cannot mean to suggest that Weatherby..."

"Why not? He is not without faults."

Lord Weatherby's excessive drinking and gambling were discussed at length. But in the end, the group concluded he was still a gentleman and unlikely to stab someone in the back.

A hired cutthroat might, Anne added to herself. Lord Weatherby was a possibility to consider.

Three additional names—involving a high stakes horse race, an alleged cheating incident at a poker game, and a squabble at a cockfight—were bandied about but discarded. One man was thought to be too old, another had fled to the Continent, and the third had recently married and was on his wedding trip.

The ladies dispersed soon after to prepare for evening engagements. Anne paid for Austen's book, *Sense and Sensibility*, and she and Jenny returned to the waiting carriage.

"My lady," Jenny asked when they were seated, "who do you think killed Lord Notley?"

"I wish I knew," Anne said absently. Her head whirled with plans to find and ask Lord Weatherby that exact question.

Chapter Sixteen

Lucien woke to throbbing pain. His right temple burned, his head pounded, made worse by angry voices. He opened his eyes and squinted at Charles Cade shouting at two very large men.

"I said to bring him to me, not shoot him."

"It was an accident, Mr. Cade. I swear. He jumped me an' m' pistol went off."

"So you keep saying. I pay you well not to have *accidents*!"

Memory came flooding back. Lucien looked down at himself. He was slumped in a chair in Cade's office but no blood was evident except a few drops on his chest. He shifted upright and gave an involuntary grunt at the new stab of pain.

Cade broke off his tirade and swung around. "Awake, huh?" He looked over his shoulder. "The rest of you, get out, and close the door. You appear to have fallen short of killing him." As Lucien's abductors beat a hasty retreat, Cade crossed to the sideboard. "Port or something stronger?"

"Brandy," Lucien muttered. He put a hand to the side of his head, and it came away sticky with blood.

Cade brought the brandy glass but offered him a handkerchief first. As Lucien wiped his hand and dabbed at the head injury, the club owner leaned forward to inspect it. "A scrape. The fool was a bad shot." He handed him the brandy. "This should help."

Lucien downed a large swallow and met Cade's gaze. "What am I doing here this time?"

Cade returned to his desk and picked up his own drink. "You've been meddling."

"Wouldn't be the first time, but what particular offense do you have in mind?"

Cade lifted a brow. "Bertram Notley."

"What about him?"

"Don't be coy. I know you killed him."

"As it happens, I did not." Lucien narrowed his eyes. "But why is his death important enough to risk a daylight kidnapping?"

"I wouldn't say important." Cade took a sip of brandy. "A minor annoyance, but I take offense at the murder of those who work for me."

"Notley worked for you?" Lucien straightened, ignoring his pounding head, his attention caught.

Cade shrugged. "From time to time. Shall we say I have a vested interest in one of his enterprises."

"That could cover a multitude of sins, but I repeat, the deed is not mine. I might have shot him purely on principle, but someone was before me with a knife."

"Who?" Cade's voice betrayed nothing.

"You tell me." Lucien touched the handkerchief to his head again. It was still wet, and he held it there for a moment. "I'm told he had several enemies. Did they include you?"

Cade just looked at him. Lucien had no idea what the man was thinking, but he decided not to volunteer anything. He dropped the bloody handkerchief on the table and finished his brandy.

"I had assumed you were a man of integrity, Ware." Cade set down his own empty glass. "But alas, the evidence appears to contradict me. You were observed removing Notley's body from the Barbary mansion."

And they'd been so careful. "How does that impugn my integrity? I found the body and had my own reasons for wanting it elsewhere."

Cade's gaze sharpened. Lucien could almost feel those icy-blue eyes peering inside his head for the answers he wanted. Cade finally asked, "Did he say anything before he died?"

"Not to me. He was already dead. I would have liked nothing better than to question him."

"Regarding what?" The club owner pursed his lips in thought. "Oh, I see, you're searching for something Notley had. That's why you went to his lodgings."

"And *your* ruffians were before us," Lucien countered. "How?"

Cade frowned. "Not mine. My man followed you."

Then it was the killer, as they'd thought. But bloody hell, how long had Lucien been pursued by Cade's man? Hours, days? Despite his dismay, Lucien had spent too many years in the spy game to get rattled now. "I'm flattered you have such avid interest in my affairs."

"Only where they conflict with mine." Cade reached into a drawer, extracted a slender cigar, and lit it, inhaling deeply. "Shall we speak plainly? Notley had property I paid good money for, and I want it back. Perhaps we can both get what we want. What did Weatherby tell you?"

Lucien thought rapidly. What did Cade already know? Too much, if he'd had someone following him around. And Lucien could only blame himself. He should have heeded the uneasiness that had nagged him for days. Instead, he'd acted as though London was different than the spy-ridden Continent.

He reviewed his recent activities, searching for a face he'd seen more than once, and finally it came to mind: weathered features, brown hair, brown jacket, ordinary tradesman. Yes, and again, same features, now a coachman driving a hackney—confound it.

Returning to Cade's question, he felt a jolt of concern. "Why didn't you question Weatherby yourself? Is he dead?"

"Not to my knowledge. Before we could locate him, he left town. Your doing, I understand."

"I encouraged it…for his safety. But you cannot expect one given to inebriety to know much of importance. If that is all you wanted to ask me, I have other appointments." Lucien stood, gave Cade a short nod, and strode toward the hallway.

"I hope you don't expect my men to stand aside as you walk out."

"They will if you allow it." Lucien turned to face Cade short of the door. The ruffians outside would react with violence if he was too hasty. "You don't want me dead, Mr. Cade, or you could have already done it. Whatever you're after—maybe this property you mentioned or something else—you assume I have it or am likely to find it. I'm safe enough for now." He shrugged. "Oh, and next time you wish for a chat, send a note instead of your cutthroats."

Cade released an audible sigh. "My dear viscount, you presume too much." He paused to puff on his cigar. "I could change my mind about you without a moment of regret."

Lucien didn't doubt it. "Good day, sir."

"A carriage is waiting in the alley."

"I prefer to find my own way."

Cade smiled and gave a dismissive wave. "Go then."

When Lucien opened the door to the hall, Cade's men confronted him, but at a nod from their boss, they stepped aside. Lucien turned toward the front staircase, and one of the men blocked his path. "Rear exit."

Lucien was not looking for another fight. Not today. He turned on his heels and took the backstairs to the alley. Prepared to dismiss Cade's coachman, he stepped outside and halted at the sight of his own carriage flanked by Finn and Sherbourne. Their worried faces were a welcome sight.

Hastily climbing into the coach, Lucien was fending off Sherry who was peering at his head wound, when the coach lurched forward. They managed to drop into opposite seats as Finn settled the team.

"How is Gregory, my coachman?" Lucien demanded. "Is he alive?"

"He is. A couple of hard raps to the back of the head, but he has a thick skull. Takes after his master."

"Thank God. So, how did you find me?"

"Your Gregory is an observant man. He'd noted a carriage following yours just before you were waylaid. When I arrived at your townhouse after you failed to appear at mine, your servants were leaving to go to Rothe for help. Gregory described the coach and his assailant, and the whole thing sounded familiar to me—like your earlier encounter with Cade's thugs."

"Rather a big leap," Lucien said.

"Not really. He saw that distinctive crest." Sherry shrugged. "And it paid off, did it not? We handled it without alerting Whitehall. Rothe would have turned out the Horse Guards, exposing us and our inquiry to public scrutiny."

"He might at that," Lucien mused, "if he thought Cade was the traitor. The Prince Regent is pressing Rothe hard to find the spy, no matter what it takes."

"And I have to agree. By Jove, Ware, this affair has gone beyond war tactics. A traitor with access to high levels of our government might strike anywhere, crippling Parliament or the monarchy."

"All true, yet it is best to keep our own counsel. Cade's up to no good, but I doubt it has anything to do with Boney." Lucien shifted to look at Sherbourne. "I'm curious how you planned to rescue me. Did you charge the club's front door?"

"Not quite. Well, we went there first, but three large thugs dressed like gentlemen met us at the entrance and suggested we take our business to the rear door."

Lucien chuckled. "And you agreed to their suggestion?"

"Did I fail to mention the three flintlock pistols? Regardless, they said you were speaking with Cade and should be out soon." He snorted, dispensing with what Lucien assumed had been a heated confrontation. "We agreed to wait ten minutes."

"Then it is fortunate I made a timely departure. It doesn't turn out well when only one side of a conflict has firearms."

"I never said we didn't have them. They were left in the carriage." Sherry's lips curled, hinting at what he had not said…that they had been prepared to shoot their way inside if necessary. "What did Cade want this time?"

"Not entirely sure. He started by accusing me of killing Notley—we were seen moving the body—but I think he wanted to know where Weatherby is. He wants to recover what he referred to as *his property*. Other than that, I can't say. One thing I learned... he has had us watched for days."

"The devil you say. How could we miss that?"

Lucien shook his head. "We let our guard down. I doubt if we were followed all the time. Cade pays shopkeepers and street vendors all over town to spy for him. But thinking back, I can pick out one man I saw more than once. Medium height, brown hair, skin roughened by the elements. He disguised himself as a middle class shopkeeper on High Street and as a coachman near Clerkenwell."

"Oh Lord, yes," Sherry said with a start. "I remember the coachman."

"From now on, we watch our backs like we did in Paris."

"If it's not too late. Did Cade know of Notley's cottage?"

"No mention of it, but the man knows how thievery works. He must suspect such a storage place exists. Ironic, is it not, that by having his thugs pick me up, Cade himself stopped us from leading his hireling straight to it?" Lucien rested his throbbing head against the back of the seat and reported the salient parts of his conversation with the club owner.

"He knows we work for Whitehall?" Sherry groaned. "Are you going to tell Rothe?"

"Not until this is over. Although Cade appears to be more of a side issue to the cipher's theft than a threat to England, Rothe might pull us off the inquiry. And right now, every agent is needed."

Sherry cocked his head. "When confession day comes, are we going to pretend we forgot to mention it?"

Lucien smiled wryly. "Perhaps we should make an effort to think of a better excuse."

"Yes, much better." Sherry rubbed his chin. "Why did Cade let you walk out? Did he think we got nothing from Weatherby?"

"I doubt it. He'll double his efforts to observe everything we do, who we talk to, were we go."

"Ah, that makes sense. We'll have to throw a spoke in that wheel."

The afternoon was passing too quickly to make the country trip before dark. Instead, they discussed methods to shake Cade's surveillance, agreed on a plan, and arranged to meet the following morning.

Upon reaching home just before dusk, Lucien stepped from the coach, and the door to his townhouse flew open. He was nearly dragged into the front hall by his worried butler, valet, and footman.

"My lord," Talbot exclaimed, "you are covered in blood. Shall I send for the doctor?"

"Not necessary. *Covered* is a gross exaggeration, but I will allow I have ruined another shirt and waistcoat."

Talbot sighed. "I suppose it could not be helped."

While everyone wanted to hear the details of his kidnapping, Hughes insisted they'd have to wait until Lucien's injury was properly tended. Consequently Robert left to arrangement for a light supper tray, Talbot went off to see if Lucien's clothes might be salvaged, and Hughes climbed the stairs to set out the required medicine and bandages.

Lucien lingered in the front entry long enough for a cursory look at the stack of letters and invitations on the hall table. He might have taken them with him had he not noticed the top letter was penned in his father's distinctive writing. No, not tonight. He was in no mood to receive another dressing down for whatever had displeased Salcott this time. He turned away and climbed the stairs empty-handed.

• • •

Despite protests from Talbot and Hughes, Lucien left home with Finn at the unusual hour of eight the next morning and drove his curricle to Whitehall. The graze on his head had been smeared with Hughes' secret remedy, covered with a dark bandage, and hidden under Lucien's hat. Sleep had taken care of the headache.

As he descended to the street in front of the Horse Guards, he nodded at Sherry waiting near the Whitehall entrance. Lucien turned to remind Finn, "Wait here for one hour."

"Aye, m'lord. I got it. After a bit, I'll stomp around, actin' impatient." Finn grinned. He was plainly enjoying his part in the subterfuge.

Lucien entered the building with Sherry, cut through and out the other side. They made one more cut through and turned east, watching for anyone who tried to follow. They found Lucien's unmarked travel coach four streets away as arranged. His coachman stood at the head of the team and gestured wildly as they approached.

"Gregory, my good man, whatever is amiss? Were you followed?" Lucien asked, looking carefully around and seeing nothing to disturb his normally stoic driver.

"No, sir. It's not that. I was careful. But…beg pardon, I couldn't stop her. She come up just as I was leaving and was *most* insistent."

"She?" Sherry asked. "What are you talking about?"

But Lucien had already followed Gregory's disapproving gaze and thrown open the coach door. "My lady."

Lady Anne Ashburn and a young woman he assumed by her modest dress was a maid stared back at him. The servant girl had the good grace to drop her gaze, but her mistress showed no such discomfort.

"My lady," he repeated, "how may I be of service to you?"

Lady Anne smiled, although he thought it was a bit tentative. "Since you failed to respond to my letter asking for word of your progress, I came to speak with you in person."

"I have nothing to tell." Nor had he seen or read her letter. It must have been in yesterday's pile…beneath the latest lecture from his father.

"Oh? I was sure you must." She tipped her head fetchingly. "I am eager to hear what you discovered from Lord Weatherby."

What the devil? Was everyone in town privy to his daily itinerary? Seeing that this would not be resolved soon, Lucien leapt into the coach rather than stand outside where he might be seen by one of Cade's spies. He took the seat opposite the ladies, and when Sherry joined him, he tapped on the roof to signal Gregory to get under way. The longer the coach stayed parked on the street, the greater the chance of discovery.

"What do you know of Weatherby? You've been following us too?" Sherry demand.

"Of course not, but people talk." Lady Anne smiled demurely. "Weatherby is often the subject of much gossip."

"Granted, but gossip cannot be how you heard of our visit." Lucien eyed her suspiciously.

"Well, no. After we discovered his lordship was away from home, we asked around and one of his neighbors mentioned it."

"Confound it, madam." Lucien stared at her. "Have you no sense of what befits your rank? You cannot visit a bachelor's residence or question his neighbors."

"Told you," the maid murmured.

"Hush, Jenny." Lady Anne stiffened. "Sir, I have given you no right or cause to chastise me. My behavior is my own concern."

Lucien's irritation had faded, replaced by grudging humor at the maid's remark. The girl shared her mistress's outspoken tongue, making them remarkably well suited. "Pardon my concern for your reputation, my lady. I shall attempt not to repeat such an egregious mistake."

She flushed at his response. "Well, um, yes, see that you do."

"Why did you call upon his lordship?"

"That is where the gossip came into it," she said. "He is thought by some to be Lord Notley's killer."

"By Jove, madam," Sherry interjected. "Why would you go calling on a killer?"

"For the letter, of course."

Lucien sighed. "Fortunately, madam, he is not the killer. But he was Notley's partner in other illegal activities, and you might have been sorely mistreated."

"I did not go alone, and as you can see, I am fine. Now, please share what you learned."

Lucien smiled at her single-mindedness. "Notley owns a cottage not too far from town where they stored the stolen goods. We're going to search it for the lock that matches the key you found. Our efforts may yield nothing, but whatever we find or do not find, I promise to send word."

"I can help—"

"No. We shall escort you home before we go."

Lady Anne's lips firmed, her chin came up, and she clutched her reticule with rigid fingers. "There is no reason I should not assist you. I cannot stop you from driving to the Barbarys, but I shall not get out of the carriage. Nor shall Jenny. I may…no, I shall scream if you attempt to remove us by force."

Lucien might have laughed except he knew she would do it. He persisted in attempts to change her mind with Sherbourne supporting his efforts, but as they approached the Barbary mansion, she only grew more resolute, crossing her arms and staring out the window.

Lucien studied her averted face. They might outwait her, sitting there until someone in the Barbary household grew concerned and made inquiries, but that would result in further delay and embarrassment for everyone. He tapped on the roof and ordered Gregory to drive on. Lady Anne's gaze shot to meet his.

"I have neither time nor taste for a scene, my lady. As we've told you more than once, who or what we will find at the cottage is unpredictable, potentially dangerous. You and your maid shall remain in the coach until we determine it is safe. If you won't agree, I shall have my coachman set you down as soon as we reach the countryside, and you may scream all you wish."

Lady Anne held his gaze several moments until her maid broke the tension.

"Sounds fair to me, your lordship," Jenny piped up. Her mistress gave her a swift look of reproach, but the girl went on. "I agree, and I'm sure my lady will see it is the right and proper thing to do."

Lucien swallowed a laugh and settled back in his seat, accepting Lady Anne's silence as acceptance. Events of the last few days caught up with him, and he closed his eyes, listening as Sherry struck up a conversation with the lively maid. When Lady Anne remained silent, he peeked at her through lowered lashes. She was still turned toward the window but was following the conversation about Jenny's life in the country, which she'd left behind to come to London.

Startled by Jenny's comments, Lady Anne turned to her. "I didn't know you disliked the country? You should have told me."

"Oh, no, ma'am. It wasn't that way. I only came to town looking for work. I love the country. That's why I'm excited we'll soon be leaving for Warwickshire."

"Well, thank goodness. You had me worried."

Sherry looked at them both in surprise. "You're leaving soon? I thought you would stay for the coming season."

"This was just a holiday," Lady Anne said. "We leave for Chadley Hall in a week. Lovely as London and visiting with Aunt Meg are, I have missed my parents."

So…there would soon be an end to the lady's interference, Lucien thought. He discovered he had mixed feelings about that. Something about her was inexplicably appealing. He closed his eyes again as drowsiness took over. The last he heard was Sherry say, "I have never seen Chadley. What's it like?"

For some time after that, Lucien was only vaguely aware of distant voices and the rolling motion of the coach. From the numerous turns they were taking, he was sure the coachman was following his instructions to meander about town, watching for anyone following them and staying away from areas of commerce where Cade might have spies. When Gregory and the footman thought it was safe, they would leave town, making two more loops on country lanes to throw off any lingering pursuer.

Sherry nudged him awake. Lucien sat up and checked his pocket watch. Due to the roundabout path they had decided to take, nearly two hours had passed. He stretched his shoulders and had just smoothed his clothes before they came in view of Notley's cottage.

"That's not good," Sherry said, pointing out the window. Smoke curled upward from the cottage's chimney, indicating someone was inside.

Lady Anne leaned forward to peer out the window, but Lucien gently urged her back. "Careful, my lady. Someone will see you." He signaled the coachman to drive past and pull over on the down side of the next hill.

"Who could be in there?" she asked as he prepared to depart the coach.

Lucien shrugged. "Perhaps a servant. Stay here while we look."

The coachman joined Lucien and Sherry outside, and the three walked up to stand behind a large, spreading tree at the top of the hill. They had a clear view of the cottage's front door and watched in silence for a quarter of an hour without seeing movement.

"Ye think it be trouble?" the coachman asked.

"A complication, at least. A caretaker?" Sherry ventured. "The house is too small for more than a servant or two."

"I suggest we go find out," Lucien said.

"Hard or soft approach?"

Lucien thought about it. "Let's go in easy but cover the back door. If you take it, I'll knock on the front, while Gregory stays with the ladies. Keep your pistols handy in case someone comes out shooting."

Sherry frowned. "You're Salcott's heir. Shouldn't a lowly second son take the front?"

"No."

"Why don't we flip for it?"

"Because I outrank you." Lucien flashed his partner a smile and took a pistol from his coat pocket. "You have two minutes before I start walking toward the door."

Sherry ran across the road, cutting around the sparse trees, with his own pistol in one hand.

Lucien watched Sherbourne's progress while giving final instructions to his coachman. "No matter what happens, don't leave the coach. If shooting or other trouble starts, take the ladies to safety, and then send help."

Gregory nodded, but his eyes clouded with worry.

Chapter Seventeen

When Sherry disappeared behind the cottage, Lucien counted to fifty, giving his friend time to get into place. He swept his gaze over the scene again. It remained quiet, and he stepped into the open, approaching the front door. He held the pistol at his right side, hidden in the folds of his greatcoat and carried a fashionable walking stick in the other hand. He rapped twice on the cottage door with the cane's silver top.

Lucien waited, holding himself in readiness for anything… except the buxom girl of no more than sixteen who swung the door open with a bright smile. "And who be you, sir?" she asked cheerfully. "We don't get many visitors out here." She peered down the road. "Carriage broke down?"

"Yes, Miss, just over the hill. I am Viscount Ware. To whom do I have the pleasure of speaking?"

She dropped an awkward curtsey. "Oh, don't you talk nice. I be Matilda Miller, m'lord. Are you just passin' or are you a friend of Bertie?"

"If Bertie is Bertram Notley," Lucien said, making it up as he went, "I came to evaluate property he is offering for sale and to collect certain documents for him."

"Oh, no! He wouldn't!" she cried. "He's selling my cottage?"

"No, no. Pardon me for not being precise. I was referring to jewelry, silks, silver, and the like."

"Oh." Obvious relief then turned to uncertainty. "I don't know nothin' 'bout the stuff in the back room, and Bertie keeps it locked."

At that moment, Sherbourne came around the corner of the house. "I heard voices. Oh, hello, ma'am. I presume you're the lady of the house?"

Matilda hastily stepped back. "Who's that? I thought you was alone."

"A friend of mine. We thought you might be around back, so he went to look. Please don't be alarmed, Miss Miller. May we step inside?" He kept his voice gentle, hoping to soothe her sudden fright.

She looked doubtful and gripped the door. "I don't know. Maybe you should come back when Bertie is here."

"Hello," a feminine voice called. "Did you find someone to help with the carriage?"

Lady Anne. Lucien clinched his teeth. Could the lady never do as told? He was ready to escort her back to the coach and reprimand Gregory for not stopping her until he saw the transformation on Matilda's face.

"Oh, you have your lady with you." The welcoming smile returned; the door opened wide. "Why didn't you say so? 'Course you can all come in. Please do."

"Thank you, ma'am." Sherry bowed and smiled. "Andrew Sherbourne at your service." He glanced at the approaching women. "May I present my sister, Lady Anne, and her maid."

"Ladies, this is Miss Matilda Miller," Lucien added.

"Just Matilda or Tilly," she corrected, curtseying again. "Pleased to meet you, m'lady. I ain't had other females to talk with in a long time."

"Then we shall have a nice chat." Lady Anne pulled her maid forward. "This is Jenny. Thank you so much for taking us in until our coachman can fix the loose wheel."

Lucien gave Lady Anne the lead. She was giving a superb performance, and Matilda was drinking in every word.

"Fancy all of you knowin' my Bertie," Matilda said, as they entered the cottage's main room. She turned to Lady Anne. "Did you know him well?"

"Not well, but I saw him at a ball just the other night."

Lucien nearly choked, and Sherry gave a brief startled look. Did she have to be quite so forthcoming? But Lady Anne remained composed, and Matilda saw nothing amiss.

"Did he say when he be comin' to see me? He shoulda been here two days ago."

Lady Anne hesitated, "No, he did not mention it."

Lucien intervened before one of them burst into inappropriate laughter. "An unexpected delay, I am sure. You will hear something soon. He is a *close* friend of yours?"

"If by that you be asking if I'm his mistress, then aye, we be *very* close. I hope that don't offend you, m'lady."

"No, not at all," Lady Anne murmured.

"He done good by me, my Bertie. Took me outta the Pink Pig tavern and give me this lovely house. It be mine, you know."

Lucien feared she would suffer a rude awakening soon. As neither funds nor generosity were a likely part of Notley's past, the cottage was probably rented. Nonetheless, it had been set it up as more than a warehouse for stolen spoils. Sturdy furniture, a cozy fire; lemon yellow curtains at the windows. "Do you have servants?"

She shook her head. "I do for meself."

"I asked because I thought Lady Anne might appreciate a cup of tea."

"Oh, dear, where be me manners? Of course, m'lord. I be gettin' it right away, while you do your lookin'."

"I can help you," Jenny offered. "I know just how my lady likes it."

Matilda looked cheered by the prospect but suddenly turned to Lucien. "I forgot. The room you be wantin' is locked, and I don't got the key."

"I do," Lucien said, taking the key they'd found from his pocket. He hoped it was the right key. If not, it would be hard to explain why they were kicking down the door.

Her face cleared. "Oh, good. We be fixin' that tea right away." Bubbling happily, she disappeared into the kitchen with Jenny.

"And I shall help you search," Lady Anne said firmly.

"Don't see why not." Sherry swept a hand indicating she should go before him.

Lucien turned the key in the storage room lock—and the door opened. The thieves' spoils were piled everywhere: small, easy-to-carry pieces of ornate furniture and a wide variety of gold and silver candlesticks, silk shawls, satin pelisses, furry muffs, elegant canes, and parasols with carved and engraved handles, boxes and bags of every shape and size.

Swiftly setting to work, they opened each container and drawer, finding ladies' jewelry, elegant snuff boxes, watches, silverware, cufflinks, bottles of expensive perfume, even liquor and wine. Considering the amount and quality of what was here, Notley had run a large and lucrative operation. Lucien and Sherry unearthed two travel writing desks in the back, but neither matched the description of Skefton's rosewood box. They searched them anyway.

Lucien kept an eye on Lady Anne. She ignored everything except letters and other papers. Since she was reviewing every document he'd rejected, he started handing them to her as soon as he'd taken a look. One drawer contained old business ledgers and a few perfumed letters tied with ribbons—these intrigued Lady Anne for a while—but nothing he found resembled a cipher. Lady Anne had no better luck in finding her letter.

"No room for tea in here." Matilda stood in the doorway. "We set up in the sitting room."

"Excellent. Very kind of you." Lucien gave her smile and set down a small box before following Sherry and Lady Anne into the main part of the cottage. Matilda and Jenny had prepared a more than adequate tea tray complete with biscuits and cream. Lucien ate sparingly of the fancy biscuits, noting his partner and Lady Anne did the same. With Matilda's benefactor dead, such luxuries might be her last.

"Somethin' special you be lookin' for in there?" Matilda asked, jerking her head toward the storage room. "Maybe I could help. I sometimes seen things he brung in."

"There was one item, but it is large enough we couldn't have missed it." Lucien set down his tea cup. "Thank you for the offer, but I'm afraid it's not here. Notley must have—" He broke off. "Unless you recall what he did with a very nice rosewood writing desk."

Her head came up with a big grin. "But I do. If'n you mean a fancy little box for letters. It be in my room."

Lucien stayed calm. "May we see it?"

"Sure. Just take me a minute." Matilda jumped up, her full skirts swishing as she hurried into the bedroom.

"Upon my word. Could it be?" Sherry whispered.

Before Lucien or Lady Anne could comment, Matilda reappeared, carrying a small but elaborate travel desk—rosewood, with distinctive scrolling across the top. Skefton's box, no question. Lucien forced himself not to snatch it from the girl's arms.

"Pretty, ain't it?" She set it next to the tea tray on the table between them.

"It is," Lucien agreed, opening the top and looking inside. He pulled out the contents, two pieces of blank writing paper.

"Bertie gave me those, but I cain't write," Matilda said with a sigh.

Lucien picked up the writing desk and gently shook it, hoping to hear something rattle in a secret compartment. Not a sound. He ran his fingers over every surface in search of a tiny latch or groove that might indicate a drawer. Nothing.

"May I see it?" Lady Anne asked.

He set it in front of her. She might as well try.

"It's what you was lookin' for, ain't it? Are you goin' to take it away?" Matilda asked anxiously.

Lady Anne smiled at her. "Did Bertie give it to you?"

The girl nodded, laying a possessive hand on the box. "He did."

"So it's special to you. Was anything inside? Maybe letters?"

The girl shook her head. "Naw, but there used to be. Bertie kept a bunch of stuff in there. Then one day he took them all out and put the box with other stuff to be sold. Later he picked it up and ask ifn I wanted it, said it were too risky to sell."

"We're not going to take it, Matilda. It's yours. But can you tell us what happened to the contents?"

Lucien heard the underlying eagerness in Lady Anne's voice. He felt it himself.

Matilda shrugged. "Maybe in the back room?"

"We didn't find them. Think back, Matilda," Lucien prodded. "It's important. Where else might he have put them? Did he take them another day?"

She shrugged again. "Not that I seen, but I don't know all he be doing. Did Bertie say they was here? Best ask him agin."

That would be rather difficult. But Lucien was encouraged the letters might still be in the cottage. "Would you mind if we looked around the rest of the house? It is a long ride there and back, and we need those papers. I'm certain Bertram just forgot he moved them."

"Look all you like, m'lord. I seen one bundle all tied up in twine. But don't know what he done with it. I'll help ye look." She jumped up, darted into the bedroom, and set to work opening drawers, looking behind furniture.

Jenny began clearing away the remnants of their tea, and Lady Anne followed Matilda to backup the girl's haphazard search. Sherry took the back of the house, the scullery, kitchen and pantry, while Lucien stayed in the sitting room, inspecting hanging pictures, lifting the rug, moving the sofa. Finding nothing, he stopped in the bedroom doorway, watching the women.

"Does he own a lock box or safe?" he asked.

"Never seen one." Matilda kept going, bending to look under the bed.

Was it not likely Notley had one? Maybe he'd kept it hidden, even from her. Lucien walked through the cottage again, looking for loose boards or a trap door in the floor, hidden doors or cupboards. He helped Sherbourne finished up the back of the house, and they were ready to concede defeat when Lady Anne let out a triumphant shout. "We found something!"

As they arrived at the bedroom door, the women pull a small but sturdy wooden box from the back of the wardrobe and set it between them on the floor. It was padlocked.

Matilda looked up. "Do ye have another key?"

"No such luck." Lucien hunkered beside them to examine it.

"A mallet or bar might open it," Sherry said. "I'll get something from the back room."

"No! You cain't do that." Matilda put her arms protectively around the box. "It belongs to Bertie. What wud he say?" She shook her head vigorously. "Ye best wait for him. He'll have the key."

"Matilda, we've come all this way," Lucien coaxed.

"Sorry, but no."

They discussed it for several minutes with Lucien and Sherry emphasizing the importance of certain papers they believed were inside. The longer it went on the more obstinate and guarded Matilda became. Her lower lip came out in a pout, her eyes narrowed. Lucien considered his options. If he suggested using the pick locks in his carriage, would it make her even more suspicious?

Without warning, Matilda jumped up, reached under the bed mattress and pulled out a pistol. She cocked and pointed it toward the two men. "You should leave now."

Bloody hell. He hoped she knew how to use it and wouldn't shoot anyone by mistake.

"Now, Matilda. No need for this. Put the pistol down." He took a step toward her.

"Don't come no closer." She glanced at Lady Anne. "I be real sorry, m'lady. I don't mean to make ye afeared, but I'm thinking I done wrong letting ye in when Bertie weren't here. That carriage wheel of yorn should be fixed by now. Ifn ye want what's inside the box, come back with Bertie or the key."

Lucien shifted sideways, putting himself between the firearm and Lady Anne. "You are absolutely correct, Matilda, Lord Notley *should* open the box. Since he has been delayed, why don't we take it to London where he can open it for us?"

"Sorry, yer lordship, but don't think I can trust ye. Find Bertie. It be waitin' here." She waved the gun, and Lucien grimaced, half expecting an accidental discharge.

He tried again. "Our errand is urgent. The papers are needed—"

She cut him off. "Then ye best go now so Bertie can come and get them."

Lucien sighed. He and Sherbourne could overpower her, but she was a spunky girl, and would resist. As long as she had that pistol, Lady Anne and her maid were at risk of being injured in the resulting tussle. "Very well. We shall do that. Sherbourne, please escort Lady Anne and Jenny to the carriage. I am right behind you."

"I *am* sorry, m'lord," the girl said, growing more conciliatory now he had agreed to her demand. She followed them to the front door. "But something just ain't feelin' right. Find my Bertie. He'll say what to do."

"Good day, Miss Miller." Lucien smiled, picked up his hat and cane, and tipped his head to her. "Thank you for tea. I hope to see you soon." Sooner than you would wish, he added to himself.

• • •

"What's the plan?" Sherry asked as he and Sherry helped the ladies into the coach. "Now that the ladies are safe, we're going back and take it from her. Right?"

"You cannot," Lady Anne protested. "Matilda has done nothing to deserve rough handling. You know how badly I want my friend's letter, but not if a blameless girl might be harmed. The box could even be empty. Taking it by violence would be so very wrong."

Sherry threw her a frustrated look. "You have no idea what is at stake…"

"Then tell me. What is worth terrifying that poor child?"

"England's security," Sherry snapped.

"Sherbourne," Lucien warned, but it came too late. In the shocked silence, Lady Anne stared at them, her eyes wide and alive with questions.

"Curse my big mouth," Sherry muttered. He blew out an irritated breath and stalked around the back of the coach.

Lucien frowned. How should he handle this? He could almost hear Lady Anne's inner thoughts assessing what Sherry had said—and not said—and leaping to conclusions, whether right or wrong.

She turned a pointed look on Lucien. "Are you going to explain?"

"No, I am not."

"You can't just say nothing. Was Notley blackmailing someone in government? Were secret documents stolen?" Her expressive eyes rounded. "Merciful heavens. Was Lord Notley a French spy?"

Good Lord. The lady was far too clever. Lucien forced an offhand smile. "Such an imagination you have. Sherbourne exaggerated the situation to support his argument."

Her gaze grew skeptical. Lucien regretted deceiving her, but he would not disclose the Crown's secrets. He reached past her and opened the coach door. She didn't move.

"Enough of this, my lady. Get in, or I shall be compelled to put you in."

Her eyes flashed, but she gathered her skirts and boarded the coach in silence, followed by her maid. Lucien closed the door and went to find Sherry. They couldn't leave without knowing the contents of that box. Somehow they had to accomplish that without harming Matilda or allowing Lady Anne to put them all at risk in a foolish attempt to defend the girl.

He found Sherry brooding and fiddling with the horses' harness. His partner shot a look toward the carriage door then gestured for them to walk further away. They stopped beside a tree. "Is Lady Anne going to be difficult?" he asked.

"If given the opportunity. We must act quickly, so let us keep it simple. I'll go in the front again, you the back. No knocking this time." Sherry agreed, crossed the road, and once again took off through the woods. Lucien returned to the coach, asked Gregory to join him, and opened the carriage door. He met Lady Anne's look of inquiry.

"You have decided to go back," she said.

"That was never in question."

"Then I shall come with you." She started to rise, but his stern look stopped her.

"No, you will not."

Lady Anne blinked in surprise, and even Jenny drew back.

"If either of you attempt to set foot outside this carriage,

Gregory has orders to stop you, even if that requires physical restraint. I hope you will not make that necessary."

"He would not dare put hands on me."

Gregory spoke up. "I wouldn't want to, m'lady, but if the master orders it, I would."

She stared at Lucien, but he stared back, unrelenting.

"I see I am allowed no say in this." She sat back, her lips pressed in a thin line.

"No harm will come to Matilda."

"I hope not."

He heard the "or else" in her voice and wondered what she had in mind.

• • •

Less than five minutes later, Lucien kicked in the front door, and Sherry came in the back, finding Matilda in the kitchen. Sherbourne grabbed her around the waist as she ran toward the front room where the pistol lay on a table.

"Unhand me, ye sneaksby, filthy cur, Jack nasty-face." She kicked and scratched, shrieking a string of vulgar names left over from her tavern days. While Lucien pocketed her pistol, Sherbourne wrestled the girl into the front room, well away from the kitchen knives.

"You can let her go now," Lucien said, patting his pocket.

"With pleasure," Sherry grumbled, turning her loose and rubbing his scratched hands.

Silence fell, and Matilda backed away until she reached the wall. Her gaze swung warily between the two men. Gradually realizing no one was coming after her, she straightened, took a fortifying breath, and then crossed her arms in a show of defiance. "Ye won't find it. It be hidden," she said smugly.

"Given the short time you had, there are only so many places to look," Lucien said. In fact, it took Sherbourne less than four minutes to retrieve the lock box from under a pile of bags in the storage room.

"I'm telling Bertie how ye treated me. He won't like it. Not one bit," Matilda threatened, her eyes turning stormy again. She started to grab Sherry as he carried the small chest toward the front door.

"Oh, no, you don't." Lucien stepped between them, and she backed out of his reach. "That's enough, my lass." He took her pistol from his pocket, unloaded the bullets, and juggled them in his hand. "You might need these in case some genuinely bad men come around, so I shall leave them outside. I apologize it had to go this way, Matilda."

He stepped outside, pulled the door closed, and tossed the pistol and bullets onto the ground. He heard her yell, "Bloody varlet," and he grinned as he ran to catch Sherry. As they leaped into the coach, Lucien shouted to his coachman, "Get us out of here, Gregory, before the wench chases us down."

"Is she all right?" Lady Anne demanded.

"She's fine. Better than I am." Sherry set the box on his lap and dabbed at the back of his hand with a handkerchief.

"Did Matilda raise an objection?" she asked sweetly, eyeing Sherbourne's hand with a satisfied air.

Jenny let out a giggle.

Sherry recovered his good humor and chuckled. "She was none too pleased."

"Tell me truly, is she unharmed?"

"Not a scratch. On her," Lucien said.

"And she wasn't much terrified either. That gal's got some mouth on her." Sherry put the handkerchief away, took a slender instrument from a carriage pocket, and set to work on the padlock. "Let us hope this box was worth all the trouble."

Sherry popped the lid open, and Lucien pulled out a roll of banknotes. He whistled but dropped them back inside upon spotting a bundle of papers tied with twine. Lifting out the bundle, he left a stack of loose documents and letters in the bottom for Sherry to sort.

Lucien flipped through the bundle. "Not here," he said.

"Nor here," Sherry responded, sifting the remaining documents.

Devil it. All this for nothing?

"How can you tell so soon? What about my letter?" Lady Anne asked, leaning forward. "May I look?"

"My lady, you astonish me," Lucien said, feigning surprise. "I would not wish to involve you in something *so very wrong*. Were those not your words? I assumed you wanted no part of this."

"You assumed no such thing. Besides, the deed is done." She softened her voice. "I very much wish to find the letter."

"I know," he said, relenting. "You shall have your chance." While the cipher was not in the stack, they might find other evidence, and he began reading each paper and letter in his bundle. Sherry did the same with the rest. As they finished each one, they laid it on the seat between them, and Lady Anne snatched them up. "Notley's personal papers so far," he remarked after they read in silence for a while. "A will. Property deed. IOUs. We shall return those, and Matilda will need the bank notes."

"Ah, take a look at this," Sherry said moments later, handing him a letter.

Lucien ran his gaze down the page, flipped it over to see the name on the other side, and handed it to Lady Anne. "This should ease your mind." As he'd suspected, the love letter had been sent to Georgina St. Clair. It was signed by someone named Freddie.

"Oh, thank heavens." Lady Anne read it through, placed it in her reticule, and sank back onto the seat with a deep sigh. "That foolish, foolish boy. I hope you understand how grateful I am to you both. Georgina will be too, and Auntie," she added, no longer denying what they'd seen with their own eyes.

"Our pleasure," Sherbourne said. "As you know, my lady, we have our own reasons for searching Notley's documents."

"All the same, I was…ungracious before, and I do regret it."

Lucien looked up from his reading and found her gaze on him. "Do not trouble yourself. We all say things that we later wish we had not."

After a moment, she asked, "What you hoped to find is not here?"

"No. We shall keep looking."

"Is there some way I can assist you?"

"Thank you, but no," he said decisively.

She sighed. "Very well, but I shall find a way to express my family's gratitude."

"You already have, very nicely."

"You are kind. Still, I do not feel it is sufficient."

Lucien smiled. Without a doubt he would receive a beautifully written note from Miss Hodges-Jones and her nieces in the next few days. He returned to his task and picked up the next paper.

Three documents later, a letter in French and sent from Paris caught his interest. He read it through twice before allowing himself a grim smile. Armand Paquet. Notley's contact in France. Not a name Lucien had heard before, but Boney recruited new spies every day.

He slipped it into his pocket, away from Lady Anne's sharp eyes. He and Sherry would discuss that one in private.

• • •

After leaving Lady Anne and her maid at the Barbary mansion, Lucien brought out the letter from France. "We may not have the cipher, but today's journey was not wasted. We have proof of Notley's treason…and the name of his Paris contact."

Sherry read in silence. "This Paquet may know the name of our Whitehall traitor. Should I go to Paris? Traveling alone, I might get through."

"Lord, no. It's far too dangerous. You'd be recognized. Supposing you got there, what are the chances Paquet would talk, even under prolonged interrogation? Every hour, every minute you spent in France would make discovery more certain. No, the letter goes to Rothe. He can have one of our spies embedded in France pursue this." Lucien picked up the unread papers. "Let's finish these, on the chance we'll discover something else."

"Yes, all right, but it's hard to feel we accomplished much. I hoped we'd find…" Sherry broke off with a growl. "I suppose the cipher is already in the hands of their London spy."

"Perhaps, but cheer up, my friend. If true, we shall have it the moment we capture the bloody traitor."

Sherry produced a reluctant smile. "Just so. Simple as that."

They stopped at Sherbourne's lodgings to sustain themselves with brandy while looking though Notley's correspondence. The various papers gave Lucien and Sherbourne a fair idea of the man's dissolute life and his blackmail schemes—the latter documents were tossed in the fire—but they found no mention of the Whitehall spy.

Lucien read Paquet's letter again. Most of it was easily understood, but one section appeared to be rather nonsensical chit-chat. Its very lack of substance fit a pattern Lucien recognized. He and Sherry identified several suspicious references and oddly placed words and phrases, just as one agent might transfer vital information to another. Lucien was eager to see what Rothe's codebreakers made of it.

Arriving home tired and cold in the early hours of the morning, Lucien found the townhouse quiet and dark except for one lantern, just as he had expected, having sent word earlier for the servants to go to bed. Inside the front entrance, he discarded his coat and hat and reached for the mail on the hall table, quite a collection after two days. He left the obvious invitations to respond to later and took the letters upstairs.

His faithful Talbot had replenished the fire before retiring, and the bedchamber was warm. Lucien tossed the letters and his cravat on the bed, shrugged out of his coat, and tugged off his boots. Retrieving the messages, he settled before the fire, extending his feet toward its warmth.

The first letter was from his man of business, nothing that couldn't wait. The same with the estate report of the manager at Waring Hall. He pursed his lips and studied the bold handwriting on the unopened letter from the earl. If it was urgent, Salcott would have come in person. Lucien tossed it in the fire.

Finally, the letter he sought. He smiled at Lady Anne's precise but feminine writing.

My Lord Ware,

I hope your inquiries are progressing. As our interests appear mutual, I assume you will inform me of developments, no matter how small. I shall anticipate with pleasure hearing from you soonest.

He chuckled. Only Lady Anne could sound imperative while making a request. The matter was moot now, and he had no reason to see her again. She had what she wanted and was leaving town in a week. It occurred to him he might miss her quick wit…but not the meddling.

Lucien stared into the fire, his thoughts of catching a traitor intruded upon from time to time by a lady's blue eyes.

Chapter Eighteen

Anne arrived home late in the afternoon with the precious letter in her reticule. Impatient to share her news, she asked for Aunt Meg's location and was told she was in the drawing room with Lady Barbary. Anne hesitated upon entering when she saw they had visitors—two ladies she was sure she had met but could not recall their names—and took a deep breath to stem her excitement. Now would be a dreadful time to give their secret away when they were at the end of their troubles. She assumed a benign smile and crossed the room. The ladies looked up.

"Anne, my dear, where have you been?" Aunt Meg exclaimed. "We were getting worried."

"I'm very sorry, Auntie. I was shopping. You know how it is. It's so difficult to decide which fabric is the right one. And then the color, of course. After all that, I ran into Lords Ware and Sherbourne. We got to talking about the ball, and I guess time got away from me. Where is Georgina?"

"Resting before tonight's soiree."

Which meant her cousin was bored with drawing room talk. The girl could chat forever about fashion or almost anything when gentlemen were around. Otherwise she quickly lost interest.

"Then I shall find her there. I wanted to discuss what we are wearing tonight." She gave her aunt a pointed smile. "We would love your opinion, Aunt Meg."

"Oh? Well, yes, of course, my dear. And I would like to lie down myself. I am not used to so many late nights." She excused herself from their hostess and the visitors, and they climbed the stairs together. When they reached the landing, Anne gripped her aunt's arm and whispered, "I shall get Georgina and meet you in your room. I have wonderful news."

A short time later, Aunt Meg's bedchamber erupted in delighted laughter and tears of relief. As Anne finished her tale of the days' events, Georgina was dancing around the room waving Freddie's letter in the air.

"Oh, thank you, thank you, thank you, my darling cousin." She ripped the letter in half and threw it into the fire. "There! It is finally over. My betrothal is saved." She threw her arms around Anne for a tight hug. Her eyes were shining as she ran off to dress for the soirée she was attending with her betrothed.

Aunt Meg sank into a nearby chair, her breast heaving with a prolonged sigh. "What a godsend you are to us, Anne. You have more than saved her marriage, you've saved the family from a dreadful scandal."

"Not me. It was Lords Sherbourne and Ware. I fear I was not very helpful to them." As she had recounted her day to Aunt Meg and Georgina, she'd begun to view her criticism of Viscount Ware with regret. Her own behavior had not been without fault. The man set her on edge sometimes, but now, she realized that Matilda had given him no choice. He had done what was necessary, and the very actions she had railed against had recovered Georgina's letter. Social disaster had been averted. She should have had more faith in him.

Aunt Meg dismissed Anne's concerns with a wave of her handkerchief. "Nonsense. I am sure you contributed more than you realize. Without your courage and persistence we would be objects of scorn and pity. You may rest easy that I shall write to both lords expressing my gratitude for their gallantry and discretion."

Anne nodded pensively. Yes, a note would be nice but poor compensation for the missing document they had been so desperate to find. It must be terribly important. They had tried to conceal their dismay, but she had felt the tension. And no wonder... England's security! Lord Sherbourne's hasty remark had come as a shock, making Georgina's indiscretion pale in comparison.

How frivolous, even selfish, Anne had must have appeared to them. In the circumstances, they had been most gracious. She swallowed a lump of guilt, wondering if she should or could do anything to help them. Would Matilda have revealed something useful if Anne had been more cooperative with Ware's search and talked to her privately, woman to woman, about another letter, another hiding place? Why didn't she try?

• • •

Bright sunshine glinted off the frosty windows when the maid opened Anne's curtains the next morning. Slipping out of the covers, she sat by the fire sipping the hot chocolate Jenny had brought and went over the decision she'd made last night. Was her reasoning sound?

While Notley wouldn't have talked about his spy activities with a young barmaid like Matilda, she must have seen or heard things…names, locations, maybe even plans. She might have met other spies without knowing what they were. Why hadn't Lord Ware and Sherbourne questioned her with more intensity? Had they been too respectful of a young girl, knowing she didn't trust them and wouldn't talk willingly, or had they under-estimated what a female might know just from listening?

Anne pursed her lips in a smug smile. She could do better than that. Matilda might even recall official-looking documents or papers written in a foreign language. It was surely worth another trip to inquire.

"Jenny, we shall need a hackney today."

While getting dressed, Anne confided her plan and was not surprised her maid raised several objections, most of them regarding how angry Matilda might be.

"You cannot think of going back, my lady. She has a pistol." Jenny firmed her lips. "Are you wanting to get shot dead?"

"Oh, Jenny, she didn't shoot anyone, and she even apologized for using it," Anne said with a half laugh. "In truth, she was very sweet and helpful until they disagreed over the box. I don't want anything from her except to talk." She briefly considered taking the bank notes they'd found— that would doubtless improve Matilda's mood—but she'd have to get them from Lord Ware. Naturally, he'd object to her venture. And Anne had made up her mind.

"Well, ma'am." Jenny sighed. "I s'pose I can't let you go by yourself."

Soon after one o'clock, Anne and Jenny left town in a hired carriage. Between the two of them, they were able to give the driver the correct directions with just one wrong turn, and they arrived at the cottage a little over an hour later. Jenny knocked on the door, they waited, and knocked a second time.

Matilda yanked the door open. "I don't see Bertie, so what do ye want? Back to steal somethin' else?"

"We only wish to talk. And apologize," Anne said.

"Oh?" The girl looked taken aback. "Are ye alone?"

"Just the two of us."

Matilda looked toward the coach. "Are ye sure yer alone?"

"Well, there is the coachman. No one else. Look for yourself if you want."

"No, no. Ye just best go. It's not a good time."

Anne was puzzled. Other than her first bitter words, Matilda acted more nervous than angry.

"If you're busy or expecting someone, I promise we shan't stay long," Anne coaxed.

"Really, you should..." Matilda looked fretfully over her shoulder, started to close the door, then sighed. "I guess ye can come in...if ye must."

Anne and Jenny stepped inside, and the door slammed shut behind them. "What...?" Anne whirled, sensing something was wrong, and gasped at the sight of two large brutes blocking the way. She jerked back, but a third man seized her from behind. Jenny screamed as she too was roughly grabbed.

"Let go of me. How dare you." Anne kicked backward, catching her attacker on the shins, beating at him with her muff. Her hat fell off, and he yanked her hair, half-dragging and shoving her to the front door.

When he opened it, Anne screamed a warning at the hackney driver an instant before her attacker fired a pistol.

The coach horses plunged, rearing in fright, lurching the coach, and probably saving the jarvey's life. He yelled, "Whoa," sawing on the reins to control the terrified team.

"Send help," Anne shouted. Her captor fired again, and the horses bolted, the hackney careening down the rutted road. Anne couldn't tell if the driver had been shot, whether he was alive or dead. Or if he'd heard her plea.

She stomped on her assailant's boots. "Take your filthy hands off me, you vile brute." He cuffed her across the face and tossed her on the sofa. "You have no right to keep us here," she snapped, holding a hand over her reddening cheek but straightening and tucking her skirt back in place.

"Shut yer yap. And no more trouble," he snarled. "Otherwise...y' might be of some value to us, but her..." He tipped his head toward Jenny.

Anne stifled a rush of fear for her maid, swallowed hard, and glared at him in silence.

"There, that's better." A sneer turned his ordinary, blunt features into a frightening mask. "Y'll stay that way if y' know what's good fer y' both."

The brawny, younger man shoved Jenny beside Anne on the sofa, and the girl rubbed at the angry red finger marks on her wrists. Anne twisted to look for Matilda and found her huddled against the wall, her eyes rimmed with fear. Good heavens, she wasn't one of *them*. Her odd behavior at the door had been an attempt to warn Anne and Jenny away.

Anne turned back to study their captors. Not local farmers. These rough fellows—dirty, unshaven, with shabby town clothes that smelled of fish—were likely from the London docks. Notley's thieves? What did they want with Matilda?

For the first time, she noticed the condition of the house. Matilda's tidy cottage had been ransacked; they were looking for something. Oh, no. Did they know about the bank notes?

The men began arguing among themselves, and Anne swiftly grasped that Matilda had told them of her previous visit with Lords Ware and Sherbourne, and she'd repeated what she had been told—that Lady Anne was Sherbourne's sister and engaged to Lord Ware. The ruffians were certain their lordships would rush to Anne's rescue, and they couldn't decide what to do.

"Why didn't ya finish the coachman?" the youngest of the three men demanded, scowling at the bearded one Anne had presumed was the leader. Now, she wasn't so sure. "If he's alive, he'll have the runners down on our heads."

"You think I missed him on purpose?" The man rubbed his beard. "It might not be so bad if he does tell someone." He turned to the third man. "Think about it, Judd. Her ladyship should be worth a few quid. We can exchange her and get all the money back them lords took...if Tilly tol' us the truth."

Anne glanced at Matilda. So, the girl had known about the bank notes. How many other secrets had she kept to herself?

"Aye, ransom," the youngest partner grinned. "I could use me some extra coin."

"Yer both fools," Judd said. "The money's gone. Let's get loaded and get out of here. I know that coachman, and he aint gonna go near Bow Street. But her ladyship will be missed." He jerked his head at the younger man. "Bo, get the wagon out front, then come back and watch the women. I'd guess we got two hours before anyone from London comes lookin'. I'd rather be long gone by then, and it'll take us most of that time to load."

"If we ain't gonna get any money, why keep 'em?" Bo groused, scratching his head. "Why not kill 'em now?"

"'Cause, you tarnal fool, we might need hostages—if somebody gets here before we're done."

Anne's heart sank. She wouldn't be missed for hours, and if Judd knew the driver, well, help wouldn't be coming from there, even if he had survived. As for Lord Ware, he'd probably never hear about it. In any event, he was under no obligation to make a long ride to rescue two troublesome women.

Jenny leaned toward her mistress and whispered, "Will their lordships come?"

Anne sighed and answered truthfully, "If they knew we were in trouble, I suspect they would." Despite her remarks at the ball, the viscount was a gentleman. To rescue women in distress was in his breeding. But Jenny had to know it was unlikely any help would arrive in time. As soon as the wagon was loaded, the thieves would have no further need of hostages.

Anne looked at Matilda and whispered, "Do you know them?"

The barmaid shook her head and glanced at Judd, the only ruffian presently in the room. He was watching for Bo to bring the wagon and ignoring the women. As though heartened by this, Matilda slid into a nearby chair. "They come in bold as you please 'bout a hour ago. Said they was *associates* of Bertie." She sniffed. "He'd nothin' to do with the like of them."

Anne grimaced. Matilda knew little of Notley's true character.

As they continued to whisper among themselves, Judd finally glanced at them but turned away with a snigger. Anne suppressed a shiver. Such indifference didn't bode well.

When Bo tromped in a few minutes later, he threw himself into a chair near the women, and Judd and the bearded man started loading the cottage's best furniture onto the wagon.

"That's not yorn," Matilda yelled. When they ignored her, she threw them dirty looks with every trip they made.

"I thought this cottage was a secret. How did they find it?" Anne asked her.

"Me big mouth employer at the Pink Pig. Tol' him all 'bout me new home. Never thought he'd be a leaky one."

Anne nodded. When the gang heard their employer was dead, they must have decided to track down his mistress and reclaim any stolen spoils and money they could find. So did Matilda now know…?

"They tol' me 'bout Bertie." Matilda's lower lip trembled. "Ye shoulda said somethin'."

Anne's voice softened. "I am sorry you had to learn this way."

A tear slid down Matilda's cheek, and she swiped it away. "I knew Bertie did stuff he shouldn't, but he were good to me."

Anne glanced at Jenny. Her maid had grown quiet, and her lips trembled as though she might start crying with Matilda. Time to change the subject. She lowered her voice even further. "I guess you knew about the bank notes in the box, but the documents we need weren't there. Nor at his London lodgings. Is there another place they could be?"

Matilda frowned at her. "I *didn't* know what was in the box. But they kept tearin' up the house, lookin' fer money, so I tol' 'em Lord Ware stole the box. But documents? Naw, nothing."

"They might have been in French," Anne persisted.

The girl's head jerked. "Ye sayin' he's mates with Frogs?" she hissed, then sighed. "I cain't read, so, aint sure I'd know."

Discouraged, Anne sat back, watching the men going back and forth from the back room to the wagon. Each trip letting in a rush of cold air. She turned and looked out when the door opened again, her chest tightening at how swiftly the wagon was filling. They'd been at it more than an hour now. So the jarvey hadn't contacted locals constables. No one was coming to rescue them.

She'd just have to do something herself, find a way to escape—and soon.

Taking a furtive look around for anything to use as a weapon, Anne noted the candlestick on a nearby side table. A possibility, but she'd rather have Matilda's pistol and a handful of bullets. She cleared her throat, caught the girl's eye, and gave her a pointed look. "Were you able to recover *the locket* his lordship tossed out front?"

"Locket?" Matilda's blank expression suddenly cleared. "Oh, um, aye, but, uh, I don't have it no more."

Anne bit her lip. Judd or his men must have taken it. She looked at the candlestick again. If she struck Bo hard enough while the other men were outside, maybe she and the girls could run out the rear door. With luck, one of them might get away and go for help.

Or they could all be shot. But wasn't that what Judd already had in mind?

She nudged Jenny and whispered, "We have to get away. I'm going to hit Bo with the candlestick. As soon as I pick it up, take Matilda and run as fast as you can out the back door. And keep running. Don't stop or look back."

"I'll not leave you."

"I shall be right behind. I promise."

"Hey," Bo's sharp voice made Anne jump. "What's all the whisperin' about?"

"I told her I have the headache," she said more calmly than she felt.

"Aint that too bad. Now shut up. All the *ssp, ssp, ssp* is damned irritating."

When he looked away again, Anne waved her fingers to draw Matilda's attention and mouthed, "We're going to run. Be ready."

The girl's face paled, but she gave a single nod.

Five tense minutes passed before Anne saw her chance. Judd and the bearded man came out of the bedroom carrying a bulky chest between them. Bo stood to hold the door. As soon as he closed it again, Anne snatched the candlestick and whacked him over the head. Jenny and Matilda ran toward the back door.

The young ruffian staggered from the blow but did not go down. "Crikey!" he yelled as Anne swung and hit him again, knocking him to the floor this time. She dropped the candlestick and ran, bursting out the back door.

Oh, no. Anne was dismayed to find Matilda and Jenny waiting for her.

"Run. Split up and run," she yelled. "Jenny, do as I say." Anne lifted her skirts and darted toward the trees on the north. Matilda had already scampered to the south. Jenny finally headed west, but their captors burst from the house, and Anne saw the bearded man tackle her maid.

She nearly turned back to protect Jenny, but what could she do? She was no match for the men. If she kept running, perhaps Judd and Bo would chase her, and Matilda could still get away.

Anne sprinted through the trees. Brush and giant weeds caught at her clothes, scratching her hands and face. The sound of twigs and brush breaking behind her spurred her on.

"Y' might as well stop, yer ladyship. Y'ain't goin' to outrun ol' Judd."

She ran harder, but her skirt snagged as she leaped over a log, and she fell, skinning her chin on the hard bark. Rough hands grabbed her arm and yanked her to her feet.

"Well, ain't y' a feisty one for being such a lady." Judd crowded her up against a tree and leered. "I bet y'd be a good lay, all righty."

Chapter Nineteen

Anne twisted and turned, beating at his face and shoulders, horrified of what he had in mind. Judd suddenly stepped back. "We're short of time, and blackguard that I am, I likes me whores willin'. 'Course if you don't start cooperatin', I could change me mind." He shoved her toward the cottage.

Wiping her sweaty palms on her skirt, Anne did as she was told, her heart pounding. Shock—and yes, near terror—kept her speechless. No one had ever before treated or spoken to her in that vulgar manner. She picked her way through the brush...until the sight of the cottage reminded her what was at stake. In a moment of pure panic, she yanked her arm free and scrambled away. Judd dove, snagging her right leg and slamming her on her back, sitting on top of her and grabbing her wrists.

He leaned his face into hers. "Maybe y' want some from Judd, hey?"

"Get off me, you...you wicked, villainous man." She was surprised her voice sounded strong, because she felt ill, nearly gagging from his sour breath and his body heavy against hers. Despite his tight grip on her wrists, she flexed her fingers. If he gave her the slightest chance, she'd scratch his eyes out.

"Wicked, you say? Aye, I guess that's true." Judd laughed, but he got up when he spotted Bo dragging Matilda by her hair. The barmaid was cussing him out in very unladylike language. "Now there's a lass who knows what she wants to say." Judd continued to laugh, but his fingers bit into Anne's arm, and he jerked her up beside him. Pain shot from elbow to shoulder.

"Yo, Judd. This would go faster with three of us loadin'. How 'bout stashing 'em in that there cave?" Without breaking stride, Bo yanked his human cargo toward a grassy mound.

"What cave? Oh, y' mean the root cellar. Not a bad idea, me lad." Judd gave Anne a malicious grin. "Like them spiders, my lady?"

As a matter of fact, she loathed spiders. They held an unreasonable fear for her since a neighbor boy had dropped one down her dress when she was nine, but anything was better than being pawed by Judd. She shrugged. "They are not a particular bother to me."

He laughed. "We'll see how y' like 'em crawlin' over y'." He marched her toward a battered wooden door in the side of the mound. "You run again," he said, giving her arm a shake, "and I'll kill you this time."

Anne felt she had nothing to lose, but he gave her no opportunity. Pulling the cellar door open with one hand, he shoved her onto the broken and rotting steps inside.

Breaking her fall with her hands, Anne climbed down to the bottom and wiped the cobwebs off her face. She shivered at the sticky feel, imagining spiders all around her, and bit her lip to keep from screaming. She *would not* betray herself to this wretched man.

The open hatch dimly lit the damp enclosure. Empty, sagging, and splintered wood shelves lined both sides. Pieces of torn canvas bags, a broken pot, dried herbs scattered on the dirt floor, and a hook for hanging game indicated it had once been used for food storage. Now it was filthy, freezing cold, and home to a variety of insects, mice, and who knew what else. The bugs she could see were dead, but Anne suspected they had relatives lurking close by.

Jenny was the next down the steps and then Matilda.

As they huddled together, Judd's face appeared at the top of the stairs. "Nice meetin' y' ladies. I reckon y' be wishin' we'd come back to keep you warm before mornin'." He laughed and slammed the door, leaving them in dusky gloom. Tiny streams of light seeped in the cracks in the door and around the ill-fitting frame. Anne sucked in a breath. It was bad, but total darkness would have been much worse.

"Do you think there are snakes?" Jenny asked in a shaky voice.

Anne closed her eyes. Merciful heavens, she had not thought of that. But her country upbringing stifled the instinctual flash of fear. "If there are, they should be sleeping in the cold. Let us be careful not to wake them."

They crowded into the center of the cellar, away from the dark corners that held unknown terrors.

A rustle in the corner made Matilda squeak. "Rats?"

"Mice from the fields, I'd guess," Anne said. Even gently bred ladies in Warwickshire knew something about vermin. Rats preferred the comfort of houses and stables.

"What's gonna happen to us?" Matilda asked in a small voice. For the first time, she sounded like the sixteen-year-old she was. "Do they mean to leave us to starve?"

"We'll freeze to death before that," Jenny said, her teeth already chattering.

"I hope that is their plan," Anne said sturdily to bolster flagging spirits. "It means they'll leave us alone, and maybe someone will find us."

Jenny rubbed her arms. "But who? Nobody knows we're here."

"Maybe Lord Ware and his friend will come," Matilda said.

How was he to know they were in trouble? A very small chance still existed the driver would notify Bow Street. She had thought him a nice man. Of course, if he was a friend of Judd...

"Someone will come," she said. "But it could take a while, and if we could get out of here, we would have a much warmer wait in the cottage as soon as Judd and his men leave." Unless Judd decided to finish them off, but she mustn't think about that. She peered up at the weathered door. "This is our only way out, and the wood doesn't look very sturdy."

"Is it bolted on the outside?" Matilda asked, her spirits reviving. She scrambled up the steps and pushed on it, but the door failed to budge. "I see a crossbar," she said peeking through the cracks. "They've blocked it."

Not unexpected—but a setback nonetheless.

"Can you see anything else?" Anne asked.

"The back of the house. They must be inside or 'round front."

"We need to break the door slates, but it will make a lot of noise. We'll have to wait until they are gone," Anne said reluctantly. "If they should catch us trying to escape again…"

The women looked at one another. They all knew what would happen.

• • •

By Anne's reckoning, they had been in the cellar a half hour or more. They'd heard nothing from Judd and his men, but the bitter cold had become a deadly enemy. Anne was walking back and forth to keep her toes from freezing; Matilda and Jenny were huddled together, shivering uncontrollably. Was this to be the end of them?

Anne blamed herself. If she hadn't insisted on coming, Jenny would be safe at home, and Matilda might have kept herself in the ruffians' good graces. Why had she interfered in Lord Ware's affairs again, thinking *she* could make a difference?

With her mother so frail, she had grown up in charge of the household and making decisions far beyond her years. Had she grown too self-confident, assuming she could prevail outside her own small world? She knew nothing of London, spies, or gangs of thieves. Judd's treatment had made her woefully aware of how sheltered her life had been.

Bringing her pacing to a sudden halt, Anne said, "I've had enough of this." Speaking as much to herself as the others, she went on. "We cannot just wait for…whatever. It's past time we got out of here, and keeping busy will also keep us warm. Let us push on the door again. All together this time."

The women scrambled up the narrow steps, braced themselves, and shoved as hard as they could. They tried again, even standing and kicking at the boards. The door creaked, a few weathered boards split on the edges, but the outside brace held.

"I guess we dig then," Anne said. "I saw something we might use." She slid down the steps, felt around in awkward pats with her nearly numb fingers, and returned with the largest pieces of broken pottery she could find. "Not the best tools, but better than our bare hands."

They set to work with renewed purpose, clawing and scraping at the frozen dirt next to the door's wooden frame. They worked in silence until Matilda cried out, "Ow. crikey, that hurts." She pulled out a large splinter and sucked on her bleeding finger.

Anne had removed her gloves long ago as the torn shreds had gotten in her way, and they all had cuts and broken fingernails. Taking a moment to inspect their progress, they stared at the small pile of frozen chunks of earth and wood and then at the door.

Matilda broke the silence. "Not much, is it?"

"I'm not as cold as I was," Jenny offered.

"That is worth something." Annie gave them an encouraging smile. "We can do this. Shall we get back to work?"

"Why not?" Matilda managed a faint grin. "I ain't got nothin' else to do."

Time passed slowly, but Anne was making progress at the left edge. She was so intent on her work that she jumped when gunshots rang out.

"God save us. They're still here," Jenny squeaked. She squeezed her mistress's hand. "Are they coming to kill us now?"

"Shh, be quiet and listen."

"Sounds like fightin'," Matilda whispered.

Someone yelled, but the words were indistinct, then more shots. When a loud thud hit the door, the women fled down the stairs. A man cursed loudly and grunted as he clawed at the door's crossbar.

Judd. Anne was sure of it. She shoved the younger women into a dark corner and faced the door, gripping the broken pot chard, the only weapon she had. Whatever the man wanted with them, it would not be good.

The door flew open with a crash, and Judd loomed over them, a knife in one hand, the other dripping blood. Jenny whimpered and threw her arms around her mistress. Matilda broke away from them and crouched in the opposite corner. But Judd was looking at Anne.

"Yer comin' with me." He leapt down the steps, ripped Jenny away, flinging her to the floor, and grabbed Anne's arm, squeezing it until she dropped the chard.

"What's happening?" she asked, as he dragged her toward the cellar's steps. "Who's doing the shooting?"

He didn't answer but pushed her up the stairs ahead of him. Near the top he gripped her wrists behind her back in one hand and held the knife at her throat with the other. "Behave yerself, and we might both git outta here," he snarled in her ear, his foul breath and sweat swarming around her. He forced her up the last step.

Anne's heart hammered as she tried not to stumble. She was thrust into blinding sunlight, and for a moment she could only hear and feel. A loud thump, then Judd grunted. The knife fell away, and her wrists were free. She tripped, nearly falling.

"Good Lord, Anne. Did he harm you?" Lord Ware's strong arms pulled her close, and she clung to him, steadying herself. Neither moved for a long moment.

"I am fine. Truly I am." She stepped back ending the highly improper embrace, and she didn't realize she was crying until he dabbed her cheek with a handkerchief. "I am most pleased to see you, my lord.

"And I you. Was anyone harmed?" he asked, taking in her dirty and disheveled appearance.

She knew what he was asking. "No, my lord. Greed and fear of discovery kept them busy with the stolen goods."

"Thank God." He clasped her hands, staring at them, "Your poor fingers. What did they do to you?"

"Self-inflicted, digging our way out. It is a trifle. Believe me, sir, we are well, considering what might have been."

"Everything under control?" Lord Sherbourne called. He walked toward them and behind him two men Anne didn't know dragged Judd around the cottage, headed for the road. She couldn't see Bo or the bearded man.

"There were three. Did you get them all?" she asked anxiously.

Sherbourne flashed a grin. "Caught and trussed like the animals they are."

We are truly safe. Anne sighed and pulled her hands free from Lord Ware's hold. Bending over the opening into the root cellar, she called down, "You can come out now, ladies. We've been found."

• • •

While Sherbourne and four men they'd brought from Whitehall took the thieves to the nearest constable, Anne, Matilda, and Jenny warmed up inside, washing their hands and brushing off their clothes as best they could. Afterward, they packed Matilda's meager belongings. Lord Ware boarded up the root cellar, loaded a few extra items for Matilda in his coach— small pieces of furniture, dishes and food from the pantry—and secured the cottage.

Matilda made a final trip into the bedchamber and returned carrying a letter. She handed it to Lady Anne. "This came earlier today. I can't read it, but the writing looks funny. Is this what you came back for?"

"No. The letter I wanted was in the box."

Matilda frowned in confusion. "Then why'd you come, m'lady?"

"An excellent question," the viscount said, striding in the front door.

Anne was too tired to dissemble. "If you must know, my lord, I was attempting to help you. In a way, to thank you. I thought Matilda might know something we had not thought to ask about Bertie's *friends* or other documents she may have seen." Instead of meeting the stern look he must be giving her right now, she glanced down at the letter. It was written in French! Her gaze flew up to his. "My lord, this letter..."

"What is it?" His frown gave way to a smile as he unfolded the letter and began to read. "Bless you, Matilda. This holds very helpful information."

Not what you were searching for, Anne thought, studying his face and quelling her own disappointment, but nonetheless, worth something.

He stuffed it in a pocket, patted the outside of his jacket in apparent satisfaction, and picked up the last of Matilda's bags. "Are we ready?"

"More than ready," Anne said. "I have seen all I want of this place."

His lordship's coachman loaded Matilda's bags on top of the coach with the other pieces already there. A short, red-haired man held the reins on the thieves' rackety wagon that overflowed with stolen goods.

"What are you going to do with it?" Anne asked.

"Take it to London, return what we can."

"Surely you won't find all the owners," she said, as he helped her into the coach.

"Probably not." He followed the last of the women inside and settled into the facing seat. The ladies were a bit crowded with this arrangement but Matilda was not traveling far. "Someone has laid claim to the whole," he added, "but we shall worry about that in due course." He tapped on the roof, and the coach started forward. "It will be dark before we reach London, my lady. Your aunt and cousin may grow anxious at our lateness."

Her hand flew up to cover her mouth. She had not given them a moment's thought,. "Oh, dear me. I have been gone for many hours, much of the day. Auntie will be frantic."

"Not quite frantic. Not yet. When the message of your plight reached me, I sent word you were delayed but that I would have you home for dinner." He smiled gently. "I had counted on finding you so you could provide whatever detailed explanation you saw fit."

"How thoughtful." Anne breathed a sigh of relief. "I am grateful to you. For everything. I must think how much to tell them. They know nothing of our previous trip."

"You *have* been keeping secrets. Next time we meet, you must tell me what you said so that I do not unwittingly contradict you.

As for being grateful, you have more than repaid us." He tapped the pocket with the French letter again.

Anne wondered if she would ever learn what they'd been looking for and why the letter was so important. She tilted her head to see Matilda in the other corner. The girl had been subdued throughout most of their departure. "Are you all right, Matilda? You're very quiet."

"Just thinkin' how I won't see Bertie again. I reckon no one else has reason to miss him, but he treated me right. Gave me pretty things." She fingered a blue necklace she had put on while they were packing.

Glass gems, Anne thought, but no less important to the girl. "I am sure he cared for you. Hold on to your pleasant memories."

Matilda sighed. "I'll try."

A few minutes later, the coach stopped outside the Pink Pig tavern. As Matilda climbed down to the road, a dozen people poured out of the pub to see what was happening. Upon realizing Matilda had returned, they carried her inside on a wave of rousing laughter.

When Matilda's belongings and furniture were unloaded from the coach and wagon, she stuck her head in the coach door for a last good-bye. Anne pressed several coins in her hand.

"But, my lady, his lordship—"

"It is all right, Matilda. Take them," the viscount said. He grinned at Anne. "I returned the bank notes from the box."

"And a few extra quid." The barmaid leaned toward them and whispered, "I be rich."

Anne laughed. "All the better. You had best get it into a safe."

"All done. That's what I was doin' inside just now."

"I wish you a good life, Matilda. If you ever make it to Warwickshire, come see us."

"Yes, do," Jenny echoed.

"I will, ifn I goes so far." The girl stepped back from the carriage and waved, her natural vivacity restored by the welcome of old friends—and a pile of money. "Good wishes, m'lady. And to all of you." She smiled at Lord Ware. "Thank ye for savin' us."

"My pleasure." He swung the door closed.

As the coach started rolling again, Anne leaned back resting her head against the soft padding of the coach seat. The hours of emotional stress had left her exhausted. Jenny too, as her maid was soon fast asleep. Viscount Ware was lost in his own thoughts.

• • •

Anne opened her eyes to discover it was dark outside. She had been asleep for quite a while. Stifling a yawn, she sat up and looked at Lord Ware. "Where are we?" she asked softly so as not to disturb her sleeping maid.

"About a mile from London, another quarter hour after that to the Barbarys."

"I am sorry to be such poor company."

"You had a trying day. If you wish, I can wake you when we are nearly there."

"A kind offer, sir, but I am somewhat refreshed." She smoothed the wrinkles from her skirt and straightened her hat. She had found it in the cottage, where it had fallen undamaged. "I have been wondering…I mean, before I fell asleep I was…how did you learn of our capture? How would the hackney driver know about you?"

"He didn't, not exactly. He must have lived a colorful life for he recognized Judd from his days of working for London's notorious Mr. Cade."

"My goodness, sir. Are you referring to the Gentleman Thief?"

"The very one. While the driver wanted to help you, he also wanted to stay on the right side of Cade. He went straight to his former employer upon reaching London, who put the pieces of the story together, and sent a note to me. In it, he was most definite he had no part in your abduction and that Judd had not been in his employ for some eighteen months."

"But I do not know this man. Why did he help me?" She added hesitantly, "Is he a friend of yours?"

"Scarcely that, although we have met. Twice now. Cade is a… shall we say a unique individual who lives by an ethical code of his own." His lips twitched. "And he wants something from me."

Anne thought about it. "The stolen goods."

The viscount shot her a wry look. "Exactly."

"I assume he is the person who made a claim to the goods." She frowned."If that is all he wanted, why tell you? He could have gone to the cottage and taken it all."

The viscount grew silent for a moment. "I suspect he was concerned what he might find…and was reluctant to deal with it."

"I still do not understand."

Lord Ware cleared his throat. "Servants and cutthroats may disappear without too much official fuss, but it is hard even for a man such as Cade to explain the body of a titled lady."

"Oh." Anne drew in a deep breath, unable to think of a proper response. His lordship ended the uncomfortable moment by asking what happened at the cottage before he arrived.

He let out a laugh over the candlestick, but his face darkened at other points in her story. She left out the details of Judd's threats and her capture in the woods, but she had not fooled him. The viscount swore under his breath, and she thought it best that she could not distinguish his words. She had barely finished when the coach stopped in front of the Barbary mansion.

Lord Ware leapt down and escorted her to the front steps.

"Where is the wagon?" She asked, looking behind the coach.

"I sent it ahead. It would not do to have your relatives and the Barbarys asking questions."

Before she could say anything else, the butler opened the front door, and Aunt Meg and cousin Georgina spilled into the freezing night air. Lord and Lady Barbary stood behind them in the doorway.

"Good-night, my lady," he said softly.

Anne was swept into hugs by her relatives. When she freed herself and turned to thank him again, the coach had pulled away. *Botheration!* She had not even said good-bye. Anne sighed. Instead of returning his kindness, the day's activities had left her more indebted to the enigmatic lord than before.

Chapter Twenty

After seeing Lady Anne safely home, Lucien instructed Gregory to cut over by way of Grosvenor Square to meet Finn and the thieves' wagon behind the Salcott mansion. He planned to hide the wagon on his father's town estate until he could deal with the stolen goods.

The mansion's cream-colored walls with dark gold trim stood in solitary splendor, surrounded by rail fencing that enclosed several gardens, a small stand of woods in back, a coach house and stables. They drove past the main gate, curved around to the coach entrance, and found the heavily loaded wagon. Lucien waved at Finn to follow them inside.

As he had expected, the earl's servants, many known to him since childhood, were eager to accommodate the heir's requests, and they waved him into the cobblestone yard, scarcely blinking at the rickety wagon. Leaving the load onboard, Lucien secured the wagon in a rear section of the coach house. Within minutes of arrival, his carriage left by the back gate, and Lucien heaved a sigh of satisfaction.

An eventful, sometimes harrowing day. It could easily have gone so wrong. If Lady Anne's hired coachman had been less conscientious or if Cade had chosen to ignore her plight... Well, it was over now. The audacious, incredibly brave, Lady Anne was home, three members of Notley's gang of thieves were under arrest, and the stolen goods were secured for the night. In the next day or two, he and Sherbourne would disperse the thieves' loot, and with luck, the earl would never know it had been there.

A good day's work, yet it wasn't over. Within minutes, Lucien was admitted to Sherbourne's residence and made his way to the library. Sherry was already pouring two glasses of brandy. "Heard you arrive," he said, holding out a glass. "Judd and his friends are tucked away all right and tight. I assume the ladies are home without incident?" At Lucien's nod, he continued. "I am a bit surprised to see you again tonight."

"I'm not staying long, but I wanted to show you this." Lucien took the letter from his pocket. "A second communiqué to Notley from the agent in Paris. Matilda gave it to Lady Anne just as we were leaving."

"What's in it?"

"Confirmation of Notley's treason." He exchanged the letter for the glass of brandy. "Tell me what you think. As before, parts of it are in code, but it mentions two meetings with an unnamed person from Whitehall."

Sherry whistled under his breath when he finished reading. "Pretty damning. The dates of the two meetings may help Rothe get his staff sorted. Some of them are bound to have an alibi for one meeting or the other."

"I thought I'd send it to him tonight along with a request for a property list from recent housebreakings. The faster we get the stolen goods off my father's estate, the better."

• • •

Lucien was still at breakfast near noon the following day when a message arrived from Rothe. With his usual efficiency, the marquess must have lit a fire under Bow Street and surrounding jurisdictions, resulting in the inventory list Lucien held in his hands and a promise of additional information by tomorrow.

Two hours later, Lucien and Sherbourne arrived at Salcott's London estate and entered unobtrusively by the back gate. The initial list from Rothe was limited on such short notice, and they made fast work of sorting through the wagon's contents. Since Whitehall would be making the returns to owners in hopes of keeping Lucien's and Sherry's names out of it, they dispatched a dozen items to Rothe by late afternoon.

"Tomorrow should be easy," Lucien said as they climbed down from the wagon and dusted off their clothes. He nodded at Finn to bring the curricle around. "Now that we have similar items laid out together, we can quickly see what we have."

"There's a lot here. What about the pieces we can't return?"

"I have a thought—" He broke off as the side door opened.

"What is it this time, Lucien?" a familiar voice asked in a mildly sardonic tone. "Are you taking up trade, or gone on the high toby?"

Devil it. Lucien turned to face his father. The earl's gray eyes—so like his son's—held more curiosity than warmth. His usual composure and neat attire made Lucien conscious of how disheveled he must look. "Just so, my lord."

"You cannot mean they are stolen?" The earl waited for further explanation. When it did not come, his face clouded. "Is that not a bit much, even for you? You would involve the estate in your irregular activities?"

"Sir, you have the wrong of it," Sherry began, but both men acted as though he were not present.

Lucien held the earl's gaze. "I beg pardon, sir. I was under the mistaken belief I was free to come and go on Salcott property as I pleased."

"And so you are," the earl interrupted, his brows lowering even further as they often did when frustrated by his sole surviving son, "whenever you come to your senses and start acting as the rightful heir should act."

Meaning, as you wish me to act, Lucien amended. A time-worn argument, and he was not taking it up today. Instead, he said, "As it happens, I had no part in the theft, and everything will be gone by tomorrow evening. Take no further heed of it…or me. If you will excuse me, sir, I have a pressing engagement." He picked up his greatcoat from the corner of the wagon and strode toward the door. Finn should be waiting with the curricle by now.

"Lucien."

The sharp, demanding word held a mixture of the earl's irritation and something like an appeal that Lucien had no interest in hearing. They had never been close. That honor had been reserved to Arthur, the older son and intended heir. Lucien had not begrudged his brother, not for a moment. They had been great friends as brothers should be. Art had even tried to make peace between the earl and Lucien, but Salcott had little interest in his spare, resenting his very existence. Lucien saw no reason to change that now.

"Good day, my lord."

He kept walking and Sherry caught up with him. "Why not tell him the truth?" After a long moment of silence, he persisted. "Not just about this, but about your work for the Crown. I swear you act like you *want* him to think the worst of you."

Lucien leapt into the curricle and waited until Sherry was beside him, Finn on the back. "He always does, always has, so why confuse him with the truth? He is comfortable in his beliefs." In fact, Lucien had tried, once, four years ago, but Salcott had refused to listen.

Sherry snorted. "You must wrong him. No father wants to think ill of his son and heir. Allow me to talk with him, if you will not."

"No, absolutely not. You mean well, Sherry, but this is between Salcott and me. It is what it is."

• • •

The following day Lucien and Sherry returned to finish matching the stolen belongings with owners' names on an expanded list from Whitehall. The earl failed to make a second appearance, and although Sherry muttered something about people being too obstinate for their own good, he refrained from repeating his well-intentioned but unwelcome advice. They finished their task by early afternoon, and Lucien dispatched a servant to Whitehall with a small coach load of identified goods.

"Now for the rest." Lucien sent one of Salcott's footmen to the house for writing materials and set about composing a note upon his return.

"Are you sure about this?" Sherry asked. "Cade's a criminal. To reward him like this...it just doesn't sit right." When Lucien kept writing with no response, Sherry sighed, glancing at the earl's footman waiting by the gate. "You could at least be discreet. You know that fellow will report to your father…and what Salcott will think."

"Let him." Lucien gave an indifferent lift of one shoulder. "I owe Cade for sending word that Lady Anne was in trouble. And he tells me he paid good coin for the thieves' spoils. I have no reason to doubt him. What else would we do with this stuff?"

"All right, I guess I'm fine with that part, but this?" He glanced at the footman again.

"Finn's driving the wagon, so who else would you suggest?" He clapped a companionable hand on Sherry's shoulder. "Don't make too much of it, my friend. An association with Cade cannot possibly lower Salcott's opinion of me." He stepped away, folded the note, and handed it to the servant. "No need to wait for a response."

Lucien took one last look around the coach house. It would not do to leave anything behind to annoy Salcott. Satisfied, he joined Sherry in the curricle and flicked the reins. Within twenty minutes they had left the wagon in the alley behind Cade's Club, collected Finn, and not long afterwards they pulled up in front of the Sherbourne residence.

Sherry jumped down, hunching his shoulders against a bitter gust of wind, and looked up. "We still have real work to do."

"It appears so. I'd hoped to hear of progress from Rothe, but I presume Paquet's letter failed to provide alibis to enough staff members for the traitor to stand out."

"In that event, he'll reach out to us soon." Sherry pulled his scarf higher against the penetrating cold. "Look, I am freezing. Let me know if you hear anything." He hesitated with a self-conscious grin. "Not right away, if you please. I'm promised to Miss Emily and her friends for a trip to the bookstore this afternoon. I'll see you tonight, I presume. Lady St. Martin's rout party?"

"Who would dare miss it? She serves an excellent champagne, and Sophy is certain to attend."

"Lady Anne is still in town."

"Is she?" Lucien laughed and loosened the reins on his impatient team.

Sherry quickly stepped away from the carriage and shouted after him, "You know damn well she is."

• • •

Lucien strolled into the St. Martins' drawing room in full evening dress, breeches of pale champagne, waistcoat of champagne and white under a deep blue Weston coat, and a cravat tied with precision. His progress was slowed by the size of the crowd. The gossips would declare the rout-party a *crush*, a high compliment indeed.

Affecting the fashionable, rather bored arrogance he had perfected in the Continent's ballrooms, he worked his way around the room. He soon wearied of hearing the gruesome news on everyone's lips—that the Ratcliffe Killer had hanged himself in his prison cell. An untidy end to a terrible story.

His mood lightened to see Miss Marjorie Hodges-Jones seated with the older matrons on padded benches along the wall. Although neither niece was attending her, they were sure to be close by.

His lips curved into a rakish grin at the sight of Sophy in a very low-cut gown of primrose yellow that set off her dark curls to advantage. Gentlemen vying for her favor and young ladies wishing to share in her popularity hung on her every word. She exchanged a smile with Lucien over the crowd, but he kept moving, intending to catch up with her later.

At present, he was looking for Sherry and keeping an eye out in the event Rothe put in an appearance. He'd had no word from the marquess and was keen to hear the latest on the hunt for the French agent.

Noticing the Earl of Salcott in a group near the refreshment tables, Lucien veered to the right. He had known his father would be present—after all, rout-parties were primarily for conversation, much of it political, and Salcott was an active voice in the House of Lords—but Lucien thought to avoid their usual meaningless conversation.

While passing one of the small tables scattered around the room, Lucien paused to glance over its contents: a variety of the latest pamphlets, political cartoons, and print articles intended to stimulate discussion and make for a rousing evening. A successful effort, judging by the mixture of intense exchanges and hearty laughter that threatened to drown out the harp music.

He snagged a glass of champagne and spied Lady Anne and her cousin not far away. Several young bucks were in attendance. Georgina was modestly attired in a pale green gown with Lord John at her side. Lady Anne's elegant gown was a soft shade of blue-green trimmed in silver. Her fair curls where drawn high on her head with a few longer locks almost touching her shoulders. By all appearance, she had recovered from yesterday's ordeal. She truly was charming, he thought. Yet she acted unaware of the effect on her admirers, returning their avid attention with light-hearted responses.

She caught his eye and smiled. "My Lord Ware," she said as he approached.

He nodded at Lord John and the other gentlemen. "Lady Anne, Miss St. Clair, how lovely you both look."

"You are too kind. A pleasure to see you, my lord." For a moment, Lady Anne's gaze held the warmth of shared secrets.

"Oh, la, sir." Miss St. Clair broke in with a lively grin. "We were just talking about you, wondering if you would attend."

Lucien hid a twinge of alarm. Had she spoken of the events at Notley's cottage? It would not do. Lady Anne's reputation would be in tatters. Then he caught the mischief in Miss St. Clair's eyes. She was playing the tease. He should have known she would never mention it in front of Lord John. "Most gratifying to claim even a moment of your attention, my lady, but I make a rather poor subject of conversation." He turned to Lady Anne. "As I recall, you leave London soon."

She sighed with a nod. "Yes, on Thursday. I go home to Warwickshire, Aunt Meg and Georgina to Calney. My parents have written that they have not seen me in nearly a month, and in truth, I miss them very much."

"Well, I am sad to leave," Miss St. Clair chimed in. "London has so many exciting things to do. We are to attend one final event, the New Year's concert at the Banqueting Hall. Will you be there, sir?" she asked demurely, glancing at her cousin.

"Perhaps. I have other obligations…" *Such as unmasking a traitor.*

"Oh, surely they will wait. Please come. I know Lady Anne agrees we would love to see you one last time."

The minx. Was he mistaken or had she made Lady Anne blush?

"Georgina," her great-aunt admonished.

"You should not press him," Lord John added, but his chuckle outweighed the mild reproof.

Lucien gave a laugh. "I shall make a special effort just for you, Miss St. Clair. It should be quite the thing." The Banqueting Hall was rarely used for such concerts, but the Prince Regent had expressed a desire to hear the symphony group that fled Paris, and the hall had been made available. With Prinny attending, it would be another crush, but Lucien was loathe to miss the opportunity to bid Lady Anne good-bye. "I shall look for you."

"It will be my first opportunity to view Rubens' paintings on the ceiling," Lady Anne said. "Perhaps you will point out their finer points."

"With pleasure."

"Until next Wednesday then."

"My Lady." He gave a small bow, their eyes met for an instant, then Lucien excused himself and continued his search for Sherbourne. What was it about this woman that intrigued him so? Nonetheless, she would be gone after Thursday, and it was a lengthy ride from London to Warwickshire.

He surveyed the drawing room again, failing to spot his partner or Miss Emily Selkirk. He stepped into the small parlor, where five tables accommodated the inevitable card players. Aha. Sherry was among them, frowning at his cards, and Lucien stopped to watch.

"About time you showed," Sherry said. "My luck is not in tonight." He threw down his cards as the game ended and stood with a rueful laugh. "Pardon me, gentlemen. I am gracefully bowing out before I lose the family silver." Friendly laughter followed them as they returned to the main party room. To Lucien it looked even more packed than before.

"Miss Emily is not here tonight?"

"I believe they are coming later."

"Ah, yes. Hence the cards."

"Have you heard from Rothe?" Sherry asked, refusing to be drawn. "Oh, pardon me," he exclaimed, side-stepping after bumping into a well-dressed gentleman. "My fault entirely."

The gentleman, Lord Darby, and his companions turned, all well-known politicians and government officials, including War Secretary Robert Jenkinson, and Lucien found himself face to face with Salcott.

"Forgive our intrusion, my lords," Lucien said inclining his head to the group. "We were making our way to the exit and finding it a hazardous task."

"Nothing to forgive," Lord Darby chuckled. "You interrupted a disagreement that your father and I will not resolve tonight."

"Very true," Salcott said, matter-of-factly. "We may never agree on enclosures."

Although Salcott exhibited no concern over his son's abrupt intrusion, Lucien was wondering if it was too soon to excuse himself and move on when loud voices from the entrance interrupted the party.

"Eh, what is that?" Darby asked.

Flanked by two uniformed members of the Horse Guards, Colonel Skefton forged a path toward the War Secretary. The crowd moved out of his way. Lucien was astonished when Skefton halted in front of him, the colonel's expression harsh, the veins bulging on his throat.

"Where were you an hour ago?" Skefton demanded.

Lucien lifted a brow, outwardly calm. "Where do you think I was?"

Skefton clenched his fists, not liking this response, but got himself in hand before actually striking out. "Whitehall. Lord Rothe was attacked, stabbed in his office."

Bloody hell. Lucien froze in shock.

Over the gasps and exclamations of the crowd, Secretary Jenkinson's clear voice demanded, "Does he live?"

Skefton's gaze flicked to him. "For now, my lord, no thanks to this man." He turned to point a finger at Lucien.

Lucien took a step toward him. "See here, Skefton. Am I to understand you are accusing me? On what grounds?"

"Rothe's own words." The colonel's face turned smug. "When his secretary found him close to unconsciousness, he stated the name of his assassin. Your name, Viscount Ware."

Lucien shook his head. "No, Colonel. You are mistaken." What the devil had happened? Why would Skefton say such a thing?

"Ware was here," Sherry snapped. "He joined me in the card room half an hour ago. He could not have done this and gotten here in that time."

The colonel gave a derisive snort. "You would say anything to defend him."

Lucien took another quick step toward Skefton, his voice low and taut. "Careful, Colonel. I might allow you some latitude in insulting me, but you may not disparage my friends with impunity."

Sherry gripped Lucien's arm. "Not here," he muttered. "We shall deal with this—"

"Colonel, Gentlemen," Secretary Jenkinson interrupted sharply. "I agree with Sherbourne. Let us settle this in private."

"Does the colonel also think I would lie?" asked a familiar feminine voice. Lucien turned to see Sophia Stine move gracefully out of the crowd. "I observed Lord Ware arrive an hour ago, just before ten o'clock."

"Our party spoke with him only minutes later," Lady Anne added from the crowd. "You accuse the wrong man, Colonel."

Lord John verified what she'd said, and then others spoke up.

"I have heard enough of this nonsense," Secretary Jenkinson said, his words clipped. "You have made a grave mistake, Skefton.

Take your men and go." The Secretary eyed Lucien. "I shall go to Whitehall immediately. If Rothe indeed said your name, I assume he wished to speak with you."

Yes, finally something made sense. Lucien turned to Skefton. "Where is he?"

"His residence, but I doubt they will allow you near him."

Jenkinson eyed Skefton sternly. "I thought you were leaving." The Colonel spun on his heels and walked away, and Jenkinson's gaze turned to Lucien.

"Well, Ware, don't keep Rothe waiting."

"Yes, sir. I shall speak with his lordship directly and then report to Whitehall."

"Very good." Jenkinson excused himself, and the crowd cleared a path to the doorway.

Lucien turned to follow, but Salcott stopped him with a hand on his arm. "Why would Lord Rothe ask to see you? Why are you going to Whitehall?"

Lucien met his gaze. "Does it matter, sir? I really must go." He stepped away from him and hurried across the drawing room, Sherbourne matching his stride. Lucien's gaze swept the crowd, looking for Sophy and Lady Anne. He gave a nod of thanks to each woman for bringing an ugly, awkward scene to an end.

• • •

Jeremy, Marquess of Rothe, gave a weak wave of his hand. "Get that away from me. I will not take it. Not until I speak with Viscount Ware." His voice was growing faint and those around him took little notice of what he said. They were working desperately to stem the blood pouring out a jagged hole in his side. It burned like the devil. Damnation, he must be getting old for an assailant to get the better of him like that.

"We cannot wait, my lord." The doctor held a glass of brandy liberally dosed with laudanum to his lips. "The wound must be stitched with all haste."

"Then do it without the drug."

"I won't do that," Doctor Long stated firmly. "My lord, just a sip or two."

Bordering on unconsciousness from blood loss, pain, or both, Rothe's lips parted, allowing the liquid to slip down his throat.

"You can talk with Lord Ware later," Doctor Long said.

"No, tell him…tell h—" Rothe was too drowsy to finish.

Chapter Twenty One

Rothe's spacious townhouse was hushed, and a somber-faced butler showed Lucien and Sherbourne into the main hall. It felt like death already hovered. Lucien shook off the thought, confident Rothe's strong will would not let go without a fight.

Mr. Sloane, Rothe's personal secretary, met them at the bottom of the staircase. "He is alive, " he said promptly. "The doctor was able to stop the bleeding. His lordship is barely conscious but still asking for you, Lord Ware. If you would follow me." Sloane showed them to the family's private rooms on the second floor. A dozen family members and close associates stood outside the master bedchamber, and Sherbourne joined them. The viscount was ushered inside.

Despite the drapes pulled across two of the three windows to darken the room, Lucien could see Rothe lying in a large canopied bed. Frightfully pale, but his chest moved with each breath. Two medical men stood next to Lady Rothe as she sat by the bedside. Lucien walked toward them; the doctors turned to meet him.

"Viscount Ware?"

"Yes, I am Ware," Lucien acknowledged. He turned to speak with Rothe's wife first. "My Lady, we are all praying for his swift recovery."

"Thank you. I am relieved you are here. Perhaps you can settle his mind. He wanted to delay treatment to speak with you, but the doctors overruled him. I am not sure he is yet able to hold a sensible conversation, but I shall leave you to try." The marchioness lifted a handkerchief to her quivering lips. Although she and Rothe were in their fifties, she normally mirrored her husband's youthful appearance. Today that illusion was gone.

"I shall not keep you long from his side."

She attempted a smile. "Thank you, but it will be good to take tea while you visit."

As she exited the room, the physician introduced himself. "I'm Doctor Long, and this is the surgeon, Mr. Michael Ramsey. His lordship is weak and still drowsy from the laudanum. All normal, I assure you, but you must keep it brief. What he needs now is rest."

"I understand. His prognosis?"

Doctor Long frowned. "I'd like to say good, but frankly, it's too soon."

Lucien moved past him and looked down at Rothe's pale face. My Lord," he said quietly. "It is Ware. You wished to see me?"

The marquess's eyes opened. "Ah, at last." His voice was slurred. "Come close. For your ears only." When Lucien crouched to his level, Rothe whispered. "It was him, the spy, going through my desk. Cloak, hood, but…familiar. It…it almost came to me… before, but now…. Confound it, I cannot think." He brought one hand up to grip Lucien's arm. "I was leaving Whitehall. Went back up…and found him. No one passed me."

"He came from upstairs." Proof the traitor was someone who belonged in the building…who worked in the War Offices. He could even now be standing outside in the waiting crowd or back at Whitehall doing further damage—or fleeing to France.

"Yes. Knew you would understand." Rothe's voice faded, his head sank into the pillow, and his hand dropped to the blanket.

The marquess appeared too tired to go on, and Lucien rose, but Rothe opened his eyes again. Lucien tried another question. "If you were leaving Whitehall, sir, what made you go back to your office? Did you see or hear something suspicious?"

Rothe sighed, and his eyes flickered shut. He appeared asleep… and then he muttered, "Forgot my gloves."

As simple as that…poor timing.

"I must insist you leave now," Doctor Long interrupted, coming up behind him. "Perhaps you can talk again tomorrow."

Lucien nodded. "One last question." He turned to Rothe. "Did he get away with anything critical?"

"No, not possible," Rothe murmured. "I locked the reports away."

"Excellent." Wellington's latest notes and any troop maneuvers were safe. "A swift recovery, sir."

Rothe's eyes opened again. "Find him…end it, Ware." He let out a long sigh this time; his eyes fluttered and closed. Lucien shot a look at the doctor, who put a reassuring hand on his shoulder and walked him to the door.

"He just dozed off. It's natural. The laudanum has a strong hold on him. We have done what we can, and his lordship is a healthy man. Now, the rest is up to him."

"Thank you. Good day, doctor." Lucien opened the bedchamber door and searched the waiting faces. There was one man from Whitehall he thought he could still trust. "Where is Mr. Sloane?"

"He had to leave," Sherbourne said. "Secretary Jenkinson summoned him to Whitehall."

"Actually, that is convenient. We can question him and talk to Jenkinson while we're there."

"How is Rothe?" Sherry asked as they hurried down the stairs.

"Groggy, weak, but talking some," Lucien said. "His recovery is not yet certain, although I was encouraged." In the carriage on the way to Whitehall, Lucien repeated his brief conversation with the marquess.

"Not much to go on," Sherry said with a frown. "Even his reference to 'familiar.' We already knew it was someone inside Whitehall…and probably his own staff. Had he cleared any of them?"

"I did not think to ask, and he's in no shape to tell us for a day or two."

"Surely he kept notes. We can look through his desk."

"They will not be there," Lucien said with certainty. "Rothe is too careful. If he put anything in writing, it is in that locked box of his, and not even Sloane has a key."

"Wouldn't Rothe give it to him or you in this situation?"

Lucien lifted his brows. "England's deepest secrets are kept in there. Most known only to Rothe. He has refused a key to the War Secretary and to Prinny. So, what do you think the chances are?"

Sherry frowned. "I see your point."

• • •

Whitehall was lit from top to bottom, wall sconces and lanterns in every room and hall. War Secretary Jenkinson had indeed rallied the Horse Guards and Whitehall staff to secure the building and called upon Bow Street to assist the hunt for the would-be assassin.

But the War Offices were in utter chaos. Far too many soldiers and civilians were packed into the area, most of them talking in raised voices to be heard over the din, speculating wildly, and achieving nothing except worrying and waiting for something more to happen, something that might reveal Rothe's attacker. Secretary Jenkinson had already left. Whether he had retired to his home for the night or was out chasing a tip depended on whom you asked.

Mr. Terrell, Jenkinson's highest ranking under-minister, stood in the middle of Rothe's private office surrounded by a dozen men arguing over a dark, pressed-metal chest with brass detail and sturdy double locks. Terrell's face was pinched with uncertainty… and annoyance. "Please, gentlemen. I am certain we can reach agreement."

Nobody appeared to be listening.

Rothe's private secretary, Benjamin Sloane, a small man with wire-rimmed glasses who had been with Rothe long before the marquess took this office, was red in the face. "It is *private*, I tell you. Lord Rothe would not want this."

"What is going on in here?" Lucien's voice of authority brought swift silence as everyone turned to look at him and Sherbourne.

Terrell's face lit with hope. "Oh, Viscount Ware, perhaps you can settle this. Secretary Jenkinson asked us to search his lordship's office for anything that might point to the assassin, and we found this unusual box inside a locked cabinet. We can find no keys and were discussing if the locks should be broken."

"By no means." Lucien strode forward and placed a firm hand on the chest. "I know the nature of its contents. They are highly sensitive, and it should only be accessed by the Marquess of Rothe himself." Lucien used Rothe's full title as a reminder of the power the man exerted well-beyond Whitehall and of the danger in rousing his displeasure. When everyone relaxed, some even stepping back, Lucien knew he'd made himself understood. "Carry on with whatever else you were doing." He turned to Sloane and lowered his voice, "Lord Rothe has charged us with investigating the attack, and I need to hear everything you can recall. When we are finished here, Sherbourne and I will transport the chest to the marquess's home, where it will be safest in his possession."

"Very good, sir. An excellent suggestion." Sloane's relief was palpable. "I will assist you in any way I can."

As Lucien and Sherry had discussed on their way up the stairs, Sherry was talking with Terrell, urging him to clear the office of unnecessary people. Indeed, the entire floor. Anyone without a specific task was just adding to the confusion. Terrell's quick nod indicated he was of a like mind. While he and Sherry set out to thin the crowd, Lucien drew Sloane to one side.

"Tell me every detail, no matter how small."

"Yes, of course, sir." Sloane wrinkled his nose in thought. "Where to begin...Lord Rothe and I were the last two in the office. We had finished for the day, and his lordship was running late for an evening engagement. I went into the Code Room—as I do every night—to see that papers and ciphers had been put away. I heard his lordship leave and go down the stairs, then two or three minutes later, I heard his footsteps return."

"You are positive sure it was Rothe?"

"Oh, yes. I stepped into the hall as he passed and asked if he needed me. He said no, that he had forgotten his gloves and had come back for them. I then returned to the Code Room. If I had known..." Sloane shook his head. "I believe I was locking the door when I heard a loud noise, a thump—like a chair falling over—

then his lordship yelled, and I ran toward his office. A man all in black rushed out, knocking me to the floor before fleeing down the stairs."

"Did you see his face?" Lucien interrupted. "Hair? Anything?

"No, sir. He wore a dark cloak and the hood was pulled forward. The best I can say is he was quite agile."

So, young or very fit. "Did he say anything?"

"Not a sound beyond a grunt when we collided. He ran down the stairs two or three steps at a time, and I rushed into his lordship's office, calling his name. He failed to answer, and I found him on the floor bleeding... So much blood. It frightened me, sir, that he might die right then. I yanked a window open and shouted for a doctor. When a guard answered me, I told him Rothe had been attacked, and I went back to sit with his lordship. Then, everyone came running."

"Was anyone still in the offices prior to the attack? Say, within twenty minutes?"

"It was late," he said thoughtfully. "Most of the staff had been gone an hour or more. The last of the codebreakers left about eight." He paused. "Under-ministers Storr and Oberon had just left, maybe ten minutes earlier. And the clerks—they often stay until his lordship is ready to leave—I believe Coatley, Sanborn, and maybe Justin Wynn—yes, Wynn was with them—walked out together next, and Joshia Hatcher was hurrying to catch them just as I entered the Code Room. That makes seven, counting me."

Which of the other six had failed to leave the building? Each man's movements would have to be accounted for. Could someone else had hidden himself earlier in the day and waited without being spotted? Lucien didn't think it was possible.

"Do any of them own dark cloaks?"

Sloane's gaze sharpened. "You suspect one of us attacked him?"

"Not necessarily," Lucien hedged. "And not you, Sloane, but it is good to gather all the facts we can."

"I see, yes, I suppose so," the secretary said, but Lucien could tell Sloane was now considering everyone in a different light. "No, no dark cloaks. Coats, scarves, and winter hats. The one frequent visitor with such a cloak is Colonel Skefton."

Devil it. Had they taken the colonel off the list too soon? "Was he in the office today?"

"Not that I saw. No. I didn't mean to imply—"

"Of course not, but what about his secretary, Horace Simms?"

"Well, yes. He brought several final reports, but that was well before noon."

Not likely then. The fact that Sloane even thought of Skefton might say more about the colonel's sour personality than his guilt.

Returning his attention to other possibilities, Lucien pictured the scene as Sloane described it moments before the stabbing. Had one of the six men slipped into a nearby room, retrieved a cloak hidden at some earlier time, and waited for Rothe to leave? They'd have to interview each man about his movements. If the traitor's goal was to steal information or documents, why hadn't he waited a little longer until Sloane was gone? He couldn't have anticipated Rothe's return, but he must have known Sloane was there, following his normal routine.

Of course, during his final round, Sloane would have turned out the lights and locked all the doors, making the traitor's task harder, if not impossible, and broken doors or latches would have alerted Rothe to alter existing plans, making the stolen intelligence useless.

The intruder, a probable French agent, had known going into this that his time would be limited, so whatever he was after, he knew exactly what he wanted and where it should be.

"Has Lord Rothe received a highly secret report or message in the last day or two? Something unusual that a French agent might take risks to obtain?"

Sloane did not hesitate. "Yes, yesterday morning." They had been talking quietly, but now he lowered his voice even further. "Wellington's plan for an advance through Spain. Naturally, I do not know the details, but if obtained by the enemy, well, I daresay it would be a disaster."

Lucien nodded. A risk well worth taking.

"When you found Lord Rothe, what did he say?"

"He asked for you, and he cursed his gloves. There was something strange…about citron. I assumed he was not thinking clearly."

"What about citron?"

"I just heard the word, my lord."

Strange, indeed. But it had to mean something. "Could it have been a color, a fragrance?"

"I cannot say, my lord. I may have heard him wrong. In truth, what I remember most was him telling me to get help…that he needed help." Sloane pressed his lips together for a moment, regaining composure. "It was not like him to seek help, you see, so I knew his injury was severe."

"You have done well, Mr. Sloane. After we deliver the chest to Lord Rothe, you should go home. Tomorrow will be another challenge for all of us."

The noise in Whitehall had dropped to a purposeful hum by the time Rothe's box was loaded in the carriage. Under-minister Terrell was meeting behind closed doors with five government officials, a representative from Bow Street was on the scene, a handful of select clerks were searching and sorting through relevant files, and guards stood at the doors. The rest of the crowd had dispersed.

At the Rothe mansion, Lucien and Sherry carried the box past the Horse Guards at the entrance and up the stairs to be met by two more guards. Lucien knocked on the bedchamber and insisted on setting the chest inside Rothe's room. His bedchamber was presently one of the most secure locations in London.

Chapter Twenty Two

By morning, word of the attack on Lord Rothe had spread throughout London. Security was tightened at the palace and all government buildings. If not for the severe cold weather, the streets might have filled with frightened and angry citizens protesting the Crown's failure to curb violence in the city. The situation was aggravated by following so closely in the wake of the brutal killings by the Ratcliffe Highway Killer. Small bands of those dissatisfied with living conditions and the long war had latched on to these latest incidents, braved the icy cold, and gathered around Whitehall and the palace, shouting a variety of demands.

Last night's sweep of London's environs had turned up a dark green cloak abandoned outside Whitehall in St. James Park. The traitor himself had eluded pursuit. Lucien and Sherry joined the scores of officers and constables scouring the town, tramping through dark alleys and dens of criminal activity. Dozens of street thugs and cutthroats were rounded up and taken in for questioning.

The weather—extreme enough to create ice floats on the Thames—made the searchers increasingly uncomfortable, numbing fingers and toes. The snow that began to fall around two o'clock that afternoon added to the misery. Roads became rutted and slippery.

Lucien finally traded his curricle for the heavier, enclosed coach. He and Sherry were headed back to rejoin the search when they heard the coachman shout, "Watch out!" and they came to a lurching halt in the middle of the road.

"A message for Viscount Ware," a young boy's voice called.

Lucien popped open the carriage door and leaned out. "I am Ware."

A lad of ten or twelve, wearing tattered clothes and clutching a thin blanket that offered little protection from the harsh weather, waved a note.

"Just a moment." Lucien dug two quid from his pocket and unwound the woolen scarf from his neck. He handed them to the boy in exchange for the message. "Get out of this deadly cold, lad."

"Yes, *sir*! Thank ye, sir."

The boy ran off with a huge grin, and the carriage drove on.

"An enterprising lad to find you in this weather," Sherry said, peering curiously at the note.

"Bow Street could use his skills. Now, let us see who sent him and why." Lucien broke the seal and unfolded the paper. He jerked upright. "How did he learn that?" Lucien thrust the note at Sherry, opened the door to stick his head out, and shouted to his coachman. "Gregory, all haste to Whitehall."

He sank back into his seat as Sherry read aloud, "*A visit with Notley's cousin, Dorothea Mead, could be most enlightening. Cade.*"

Had the Gentleman Thief felt indebted by the wagonload of goods? Or was he, indeed, the patriot he professed to be?

"Is this *Mr.* Cade?"

"The very one."

"You two are becoming quite sociable. Honestly, Lucien, why would he tell you this? What does it mean? Is he suggesting Rothe was struck down by a woman?"

"Why not me? Confound it, Sherry, I cannot fathom the workings of Cade's mind. Nor am I going to waste time thinking about it. He must believe this woman can tell us something we need to know." The carriage stopped in front of Whitehall, and Lucien leaped out. "Gregory, keep the team ready to go. We shouldn't be long."

Within minutes they set Whitehall scrambling with their news of a reliable citizen tip. Clerks dug for information on Dorothea Mead, her residence, her relation to Bertram Notley, her friends, her activities, and in particular any connection to Lord Rothe or Whitehall. Rothe's staff worked with fixed determination, and forty-five minutes later they'd verified Miss Mead was a third cousin to Notley, having a great-great-grandmother in common, and that she lived as a paid companion in the Walford residence on Piccadilly.

Lucien and Sherry had all they needed for now. While others continued to identify possible associates and looked for a government connection, they set out for Piccadilly in the heavy snow. The viscount retrieved his pistols from a hidden compartment in the coach and offered one of them to Sherry. "Hard to say what we will find when we get there."

"Appreciated." Sherry gave the pistol a once over. "You keep them loaded?"

"Not very useful if they aren't. Gregory takes care of it every time the coach goes out."

Sherbourne slipped it into his coat pocket. "I doubt this woman was Rothe's attacker. I wonder who she is to the French spy? Friend, lover, accomplice?"

"My first thought was that her employer, Miles Walford, might be the spy, but he is a banker with no association with Whitehall."

"Unless he is living under an alias."

"Devil it, Sherry. The War Office makes mistakes, but surely they haven't shared any secrets with a banker, and his employment was verified." Regardless, he sighed heavily. "We should know soon."

• • •

The Walford residence was a modest townhouse, and a young maid answered the door in place of a butler. Lucien gave their names, and they stepped inside, where she offered to take their coats. "Thank you, but no," Lucien said. "We will not stay long." Nor was he willing to be separated from the pistol in his coat pocket.

The maid tapped on a door down the hall, disappeared inside, and emerged with a tall, thin man about Lucien's age. "Viscount Ware, Lord Sherbourne," he greeted, coming forward with an inquiring smile. "I am Miles Walford. How may I be of service?"

"I apologize for the unexpected intrusion, sir, but we urgently wish to speak with Miss Dorothea Mead. "

"My wife's companion? May I ask why?"

"I prefer to explain only once," Lucien said. "It concerns a relative of hers."

Walford frowned, uncomfortable with the situation, but in deference to Lucien's rank, he waved them across the hall. "She is sitting with my wife." He showed them into a warm, snug parlor. Two women sat sewing by the fire, the more fashionable one in a noticeably delicate condition. They looked up when the men entered.

"We have visitors, my dear. Viscount Ware, Lord Sherbourne, may I present my wife, Mary, and Miss Dorothea Mead." He waited while the introductions were acknowledged, then added, "Dorothea, they came to talk with you."

"With me? I do not understand." She turned a bewildered look on the visitors.

"May my wife and I remain?" Mr. Walford made it a question, but it was plain from the set of his chin that he would not leave his wife's companion unprotected.

"By all means." Lucien looked at Miss Mead again. A small woman, dainty but rather plain. She set her sewing in her lap and waited quietly. "You are related to Bertram Notley, is that not so?"

"Why, yes," she said in a shy voice. "He is a distant cousin. Is something amiss?"

"Then you have not heard. I am sorry to bear sad tidings. Your cousin died the night before Christmastide. He was attacked by footpads in Hyde Park."

She looked surprised but not unduly grieved. "Oh, I did not know. We were out of town for most of a week. He and I were not close, having met only a year ago, but I am sorry to hear it."

"Why would Joshia not tell us this?" Mr. Walford asked, looking at his wife and Miss Mead, clearly taken aback.

"It is odd." Mrs. Walford looked at her paid companion.

Miss Mead frowned and echoed the sentiment. "Yes, very odd."

Lucien suck in a breath. Was the name a coincidence? He kept his tone casual. "If I may ask, who is Joshia?"

"Pardon us." Walford gave a rueful smile. "We were rather speaking in riddles, were we not? Mr. Joshia Hatcher is Dorothea's betrothed. Her cousin introduced them."

"He is…was a particular friend of Cousin Bertram," Miss Mead added. "Oh, my. Perhaps he does not know. He will be vastly saddened by the news."

Oh, yes, Hatcher knew all right. Satisfaction surged through Lucien, but he was careful not to let it show. A wrong word or action now might result in Hatcher being warned in time to flee the country.

"In that case, he should hear it from you. Will you see him this evening?"

"No. I mean, it was not planned. He said he would come midweek, and that was before the storm." She looked at Mr. Walford. "Perhaps I might send word for him to call tomorrow… if the storm is over?"

"By all means, Miss Mead. I shall do it for you," Walford offered.

After expressing their condolences again, Lucien and Sherbourne excused themselves and returned through the snow to the waiting carriage.

They knew the traitor now: Joshia Hatcher, clerk to Lord Rothe.

As they made their way to Whitehall as swiftly as the bad roads would allow, Lucien pictured Hatcher. Medium stature, wiry, narrow face. An unassuming man in his late thirties, diligent, even enthusiastic, in his duties—yet always *about*, always watching. *A sly boots.* Lucien recalled those probing eyes looking into Rothe's office while they were discussing the stolen cipher that first day. Lucien had been uneasy at the time, but he hadn't followed up.

Not that Hatcher had been overlooked. As part of the staff, his name had come up once or twice in discussions with Rothe, but nothing they knew had made him a suspect. His fiancée's connection to Notley was so distant it hadn't been noticed, and his only apparent fault had been his close proximity when things happened.

Now they knew why. And once they had the traitor in custody, they would force him to turn over the cipher.

Sherry nudged him with his boot. "Have you heard a word I said?"

Lucien blinked his eyes, belatedly realizing his friend had been talking most of the coach ride. "Sorry, I was woolgathering. It is surprising Hatcher did not become a suspect before now."

"I was saying much the same," Sherry said dryly. "He is so...so self-effacing."

"Yes, an excellent disguise. It allowed him to operate freely."

"No longer," Sherry said. "We can finally put a stop to it."

"Not unless we catch him."

• • •

Despite the efforts of Whitehall, the militia, the constables, and Bow Street, Hatcher remained on the run throughout the night. His lodgings were searched, his relatives and friends rousted from bed and questioned. Lucien suspected he'd had a plan already in place in the event he needed to make a hasty departure.

Whitehall dug into its secret files and searched the lodgings of dozens of known French sympathizers. Although the War Office was quite certain Hatcher had not made it out of town, fast riders were dispatched to alert the border towns.

When Lucien and Sherbourne ran out of places to look, they rode out to Notley's cottage. It was empty and in disarray. The few pieces of larger furniture they'd left behind were toppled, the curtains pulled down. Perhaps others from Billy's former gang had broken in hoping to find overlooked spoils, or it had been pillaged by local vandals. A spy fleeing pursuit would not have made his trail so obvious.

Dawn was breaking as they returned to London. Lucien's servants were up and about their daily chores when he fell into bed.

• • •

By late morning, Lucien and Sherbourne were back in the viscount's closed carriage being jostled by mounds of snow and uneven streets. Lucien had not slept much, but a hot bath, clean clothes, and dry boots had pushed back the effects of fatigue.

Despite their keenness to get on with the hunt, their first stop was the Rothe mansion. The household was heavy-eyed from exhaustion, but a sense of relief was pervasive. His lordship had made it through the night and was awake and talkative. Doctor Long met them in the hallway. The dark circles under his eyes spoke of his long night, but his expression was lighter, optimistic.

"May we speak with him?"

Long frowned with a reluctant nod. "If it's necessary in order to find his assailant or for the running of government, I suppose we must allow it." He eyed them both. "Yes, you may go in, but the Prime Minister is expected soon. Five minutes, no more," he warned. "He is not as strong as he thinks."

Lucien suppressed a smile. "I'm not surprised, doctor. We will not linger."

Inside the dimly lit room, Lucien studied the still figure as they approached the canopied bed. For a moment, he thought Rothe was asleep, then the marquess opened his eyes and gave a crooked smile.

"No, I am not dead yet. Although I have felt better. I heard it was Hatcher. Is that true?"

"Afraid so, sir."

"Is he in custody?"

"Not yet. He—"

"Why not?" Rothe demanded.

"He has slipped through every net. But hundreds of people, including the Horse Guards and Bow Street, are out there looking."

"Yes, of course they are," Rothe conceded. "I just feel so useless lying in this bed. I should have suspected Hatcher. Despite his outstanding office skills, I never warmed to him. His manner was so indecisive, so weak spirited. All an act, I suppose. Damn his eyes. And that terrible cologne he used did not endear him." Rothe's mouth dropped open. "That's it, by Jove. I tried to tell Sloane... right after the attack, and then it slipped my mind."

"The citron," Lucien said, catching on.

"Yes, that's it. Did Sloane tell you?"

"He did, but it meant nothing to us."

"Yes, well, not much good for me to recall it now." Rothe snorted softly. "He was a cunning, treasonous scoundrel…and now proving to be slippery as well."

"Not to worry, my lord. With searchers in every part of the city, he cannot evade us for long. I wager he will he sighted before the day is out."

Rothe gave a weak laugh. "You should better guard your money, Ware. That could be a losing bet."

"Not this time." Lucien spoke with more confidence than he felt.

The bedchamber door opened, saving Lucien from confessing his belief was based on nothing more than a sense that events were rushing headlong toward an obscure end. He turned at the sound of the Prime Minister's voice, his smile stiffening as he realized the PM had brought two members of the House of Lords with him. One of them was Salcott.

Lucien's gaze returned to Rothe. "Our time is up, my lord. We'll send word when Hatcher is in custody."

"Tarry a moment, Ware. I see your father is here." The marquess frowned. "Jenkinson told me…well, it appears Salcott does not understand how much you have done for your country. I wish to clear up the misunderstanding."

"I did nothing out of the ordinary, sir. Sherbourne and I are in a hurry—"

"Nonsense. A few moments won't matter." Rothe greeted the new arrivals and launched into praise for Ware and Sherbourne's fine efforts on behalf of the Crown.

"I am naturally pleased, Lord Rothe, that my son has recognized his duty to country," Salcott said. "But the traitor is not yet caught, is he?"

"You must excuse me," Lucien inserted, offering Rothe a swift bow and turning away. "I truly cannot delay further." By the time he finished talking, he had reached the door and was then outside in the hallway. He paused, waiting for Sherry to join him, but heard Rothe call his partner back. *What now?*

Lucien rocked impatiently on his heels. After a minute or two, he started to pace, anxious to be on his way before Salcott came out. He wanted his father's false praise even less than his criticism. Rothe meant well, but his ill-timed tribute had created an awkward situation for everyone.

He turned when the door open and Sherry walked out.

"Bloody hell," his partner muttered as he brushed past and headed for the stairs.

Lucien kept pace with him. "What happened in there?"

"You are not going to like it. I certainly did not."

"Devil it, Sherry. Quit stalling. Just tell me."

Sherbourne's eyes flicked to those around them. "Outside."

The moment the coach door closed, Lucien eyed his friend with misgiving. "What I am not going to like?"

"Blast it, Lucien. Rothe confronted Salcott. He demanded to know what he meant by his remark. Your father bristled, and let me tell you, I would have gotten out of there if Rothe had allowed it. He told your father everything and kept dragging me in to confirm or give details." Sherry tugged at his cravat as though still feeling discomfited.

Lucien's eyes narrowed. "What do you mean by *everything*?"

"All of it," Sherry said ruefully. "The four years on the Continent. The missions, the injuries, the close escapes, the months under Wellington's command." Sherry frowned at Lucien's lack of response. "Salcott knows it all, even our continuing efforts through the War Offices and the current assignment."

Lucien turned his head to stare at the falling snow outside the carriage window. "He should not have said anything. Salcott will find a way to dismiss it."

"Not so easy this time. Even the Prime Minister retold two of our missions he'd heard from Prinny himself."

"Which ones?" Lucien asked, curious despite his disapproval of the whole business.

"The chase through the French forest, and the intercepted courier outside Vienna."

Lucien nearly smiled recalling his scant attire during the first incident, then shrugged. "The earl hears what he wants."

"I don't know about that. Honestly, he looked dumbfounded. And he wanted to know why you had not told him."

Lucien turned to meet Sherry's gaze. "And you said?"

"I asked if he would have listened."

Lucien gave a short bark of laughter. "I hope he said no. The one time I tried, he walked away. What did he tell you?"

"The truth, I guess. He said 'Probably not.' By Jove, Lucien, the whole thing was bloody awkward. I fled at the first opportunity."

Silence hung in the carriage until Lucien cleared his throat. "Rothe should not have interfered. I regret he embarrassed the earl in front of his friends. It changes nothing...not for Salcott, not for me."

• • •

A unit of the Horse Guards nearly caught Joshia Hatcher that night. He escaped out a back window of the Pheasant Inn just moments before they broke down the door to his rented room. They followed his tracks in the snow, entering an area of old warehouses and ending outside an abandoned building. Despite calling in reinforcements for a floor by floor search, they found nothing beyond a few wet footprints next to the window he'd first entered. The pursuit was extended to the surrounding buildings, but somehow Hatcher slipped away from them in the dark, their own footprints making further tracking impossible.

Lucien heard the news from his valet. Amazing how gossip flew from servant to servant, house to house, so early in the morning. Over breakfast, he pondered the possible ways Hatcher had made his escape, concluding the rooftops were most likely. He avoided dwelling on the family issues Rothe had stirred the day before. Lucien had heard nothing from Salcott...no more than he'd expected.

During his second cup of coffee, he turned his mind to what role he and Sherbourne should take in the ongoing manhunt. The street and neighborhood searches throughout London and the surrounding territory were best left to organized search parties. Frustration would be running high at Whitehall, and he would prefer to stay away, but it was unavoidable. Those in charge of the investigation, including Lucien and Sherry at Rothe's behest, needed to stop frequently at the War Offices to smooth disputes among agencies and direct responses to evolving information.

One question kept nagging him. Why no reports of Hatcher outside London? What kept him here? His days spying for Napoleon were over, and the English punishment for treason was a swift visit from the hangman's noose. Was he not safer in France—or anywhere other than England? Soldiers might be watching the roads to the borders, but no one knew better than Lucien there were always holes to slip through.

"Anything else I can get you, my lord?"

Lucien looked up at his footman's gentle reminder his staff was waiting to clear, and he pushed his partially eaten breakfast away. "No, thank you, Robert. I have little appetite this morning." He finished his coffee in one long swallow, hoping it would clear his head.

So, where *did* he and Sherbourne go from here? They needed a tip, a chance sighting. Or to sort out Hatcher's reason for lingering. Was he hoping for rescue? Was there a task yet undone?

Expelling a deep sigh, Lucien rose and crossed to the breakfast room window. The snow had stopped, leaving behind a coating of three inches or more on streets and roofs. The town wore a clean, fresh look, but street traffic would soon leave deep ruts and chunks of frozen snow and ice. Carriage travel would be nigh impossible, and those who tried would block the way for others. He debated whether to ride or walk. But thinking of his favorite Arabian stallion standing in the cold wind made up his mind.

He changed his boots, added a warm scarf to his normal winter attire, dispatched a message to Sherbourne, and set off for

Whitehall on foot, still mulling over Hatcher's behavior. Arriving at the War Offices and noting the anticipated tension, he headed straight to Rothe's office. Mr. Sloane was alone, straightening up the room.

"Did you stop to see his lordship this morning?" Lucien asked.

"I did, sir." Sloane's smile was broad. "He was drinking tea and chaffing to get back to work."

"Excellent. Feeling more himself, I dare say."

"Yes, indeed, and he sent you a note," Mr. Sloane continued.

It held one line, a question: *Why has Hatcher not left town?*

Lucien threw back his head and laughed.

At Sloane's startled look, Lucien showed him the note. "I just spent a twenty minute walk turning over the possibilities in my head, attempting to answer this very question."

"Ah, I understand, sir. I am confident you shall find one soon." With a nod, he stepped away and returned to his work in the outer room.

Lucien seated himself at Rothe's desk, turning the chair to one side to stretch out his long legs while he waited for Sherbourne. He went over the question again, looking for different answers, new possibilities, and hoping for *the* answer.

Hatcher was waiting for something—for the hunt to die down? Surely not, it would be a lengthy wait. And he couldn't expect a rescue. With the country on alert and watching the borders, it was doubtful word of the agent's peril had reached France. Nor would Boney risk French lives in a lost cause. So, what did that leave—an unfulfilled mission? It wouldn't be those Wellington reports this time. The war moved quickly, making the general's location and strategies already out of date. No, it had to be something else.

What the devil was worth this kind of risk?

Lucien straightened in his chair, pulling his feet back. Only one thing would hold him here: the bloody cipher. Was it not in Hatcher's possession? Could he still be awaiting delivery?

Surely not. He *must* have received it by now. Was he afraid he'd be caught with it in his possession? Then why not destroy it?

The obvious answer…he didn't have it. He'd hidden it. And now—due to the manhunt perhaps—he couldn't get to it. So where was it? In his lodgings? It was worth another search. A bank box would be too inconvenient for regular use. Friends, relatives would all be too risky—then where?

Whitehall.

He leapt from his chair, nearly colliding with Sherbourne as he exited into the outer office. "Pardon me, my friend, but we may have missed the obvious. Hatcher's desk needs to be turned inside out." Brushing past, he pulled out the main drawer on the desk and dumped the contents on top.

Sherry stared at the disordered pile of papers. "Might I ask what you're doing?"

"If I am correct, looking for the cipher." Lucien turned over the drawer, inspecting each side, then sorted through the papers one at a time.

"A bit of wishful thinking, is it not? The desk has been searched half a dozen times by now."

"I don't care. For if not the desk, then somewhere."

"Well, of course, it's bloody som—"

Lucien cut him off to explain his cryptic remark, beginning with Rothe's question. Sherry got it immediately, and they gave the desk a thorough going over, looking for secret compartments or papers stuffed under or behind the drawers. While Sloane and other bewildered staff gathered to watch, the two men turned the desk upside down and shook it.

"Did we miss something, my lords?" Sloane finally inquired. "Might we be of assistance?"

Lucien looked up. "You could go through those books." He pointed to a pile on the table behind Hatcher's desk. "Every page. Bring me any letters, papers, or anything else you find stuck inside or between them."

They located a handful of research notes and scraps of paper marking passages for future reference, but after a thorough inspection of Hatcher's desk area and those nearby tables, files, and shelves used in common, Sherbourne looked at Lucien and shrugged. "Where now?"

"My premise is good. I just know it."

"His lodgings then. Hatcher hasn't been there. It's under constant surveillance."

• • •

A three hour, painstaking rummage of Hatcher's residence—including taking off the tops of the bedposts—had come up empty. Sherry dusted off his hands. "Next? Might he have a hideout in the country like Notley did?"

Lucien shook his head, reining in his frustration. "He had no use for one. More to the point, Hatcher is *here*. Maybe it's not the cipher after all, but there is something in London he wants or feels compelled to do. Or have I totally misread the situation?"

"Don't question yourself so readily. Your instincts have always been good."

Lucien snorted. "With what we know or think we know, maybe. But the code key could be tucked in his pocket and his delay about any number of things." Lucien ran a hand over the back of his neck. "I just cannot think of anything else that important."

"Nor can I."

Lucien glanced at his pocket watch. "It's late. I shall stop by the Walford house again on my way home. They have disavowed him after his attack on Rothe, but maybe he left something with Miss Mead that she had forgotten. Or he said something she now recalls. Doubtful, I know, but I want to ask. Then I am off to change clothes for the symphony concert. I promised Miss St. Clair I would be there to say good-bye. Their party leaves London tomorrow."

"Miss St. Clair? I beg pardon, Lucien, but is it not Lady Anne who is on your mind?"

Shrugging, Lucien said, "Since you assume you know the answer, I wonder that you bother to ask."

"I do not belittle your interest, my friend, only your denial," Sherry said with a sly grin. "If she had given me the least bit of encouragement…" He broke off and laughed at Lucien's quick frown. "Since I have tickets with my brother-in-law's party, I shall no doubt see you there."

Chapter Twenty Three

The symphony concert was sold out, every available seat spoken for by ladies and gentlemen in elegant evening attire of glittering gowns and well-fitted tailcoats. Quality entertainment was scarce in mid-winter, and the gaiety-driven haute ton had turned out to see and be seen. The Prince Regent and his party held many of the seats in front, and as usual, they were a primary piece of the evening's attraction. Prinny's huge personality, matched as it was by his substantial size and ostentatious attire, drew every eye.

When Lucien entered the hall, it was early yet, and few had taken their seats. He spotted Lady Anne, her aunt, and cousin among the throng of small groups passing the time in conversation. When the crowd parted, he smiled to see Sherbourne was also among their company with Miss Emily Selkirk on his arm. Sherry gave every sign of being smitten, and Lucien had to admit Miss Emily looked lovely in the latest fashion, a paloma green gown trimmed with darker green and ivory ribbons.

As he made his way toward them, a better view of Lady Anne nearly brought him to a halt. She was stunning. Her elegant gown was a snug fit across its white bodice trimmed in blue, and the azure blue satin skirt swirled gently as she turned to greet him. Her gaze met his for a fleeting moment, sparkling with laughter at something Sherry had said, and he drew in a quick breath.

Curse it, Lucien, get a hold of yourself. She is not the first beautiful woman you've seen.

Maintaining outward poise, he nodded to everyone in the party and smiled at Miss St. Clair. "My lady, I am dutifully presenting myself as requested."

"As well you should," she said with a mischievous grin. "Anne and Aunt Meg are in need of a gentleman escort. Lord John and I will be joining his cousin's party—and here he is now." She linked her arm through that of her betrothed.

"It will be my pleasure to escort them, Miss St. Clair." Lucien watched in amusement as the couple strolled away. The impetuous girl had grown into a young woman since the incident with the letter, but she was still seventeen. Lord John would have to keep a watchful eye on his future bride.

When the symphony began tuning their instruments, Sherry and Emily left to find his older sister's party, and Lucien seated Miss Hodges-Jones and Lady Anne. Over the next hour, the stuffy air heated by so many bodies and the soothing music created a general languor among the audience. Lucien noticed Prinny's chin had fallen forward on his chest, and he appeared to be asleep.

When the orchestra broke for intermission, Lucien stood and shrugged into his winter dress cloak. "I feel a need to take the air. May I escort you ladies on a short walk?"

"Oh, yes." Lady Anne rose. "I would be ever so grateful."

"Not me." Aunt Meg shook her head. "You two enjoy yourselves. Nothing could compel me to set foot outside in this horrid weather no more than I must. I see friends over there and will have a nice chat while you are gone. Mind you stay with the other young people."

"Yes, Auntie."

Lucien helped Lady Anne with her coat and offered his arm. They followed others similarly inclined out onto Whitehall Street, just opposite the War Offices and Horse Guards building.

Lucien drew in a deep breath of crisp air. "A few minutes more and I might have emulated our prince."

Lady Anne's lips curved, her eyes twinkling. "I saw that, but who can blame him? I hope the second half will include more lively pieces."

As they wandered among the small crowd braving the cold, they picked up snatches of conversation. One gentleman's voice in particular was distinct. "You missed seeing the body?" he asked the lady on his arm. "The details are gruesome, but if you insist…"

Lady Anne increased her pace, pulling on Lucien's arm until they were out of earshot. "I do not wish to hear further of that sad event," she whispered.

"No more do I." Lucien regretted the Crown's decision to parade the dead body of John Williams, the Ratcliffe Killer, through the streets. He understood why they allowed it, an attempt to calm public fear by giving them an object for their rage, but he found it distasteful.

Once they were clear of the other couples, they strolled in companionable quiet until she asked, "How is Lord Rothe? I heard he is recovering very nicely."

Lucien hesitated. Her question intimated he had more than passing knowledge of the marquess's condition, but after all that had happened, he was not surprised she'd figured out there was a connection. "Yes, improving by the hour. I expect him to defy his doctors soon and return to work."

"And the coward who stabbed him? Have you knowledge of him?"

"To my belief, he has not been captured."

She eyed him. "Honestly, my lord, you need not pretend with me. Are you and Lord Sherbourne not in pursuit of this attacker?"

He gave her a sidelong look. "Not officially. Not publicly."

"Oh. I see." Her charming smile appeared. "Then just between us, are you getting close? Or must I continue to guess?"

A smile tugged at the corners of Lucien's mouth. "You are incorrigible, my lady. I will tell you this…which you are not free to share." He waited until she nodded. "His name is known to us, but he is not yet in custody."

"Good Gracious." She turned to stare at him. "Who is it? Why did he want to harm the marquess?"

Lucien shook his head with a laugh. "No more. Your curiosity must be content for now. Let us talk of something else. I believe you leave for Warwickshire tomorrow. Is your home a large estate?"

"I should not talk to you at all if you're going to keep secrets," she said, "but yes, Father's lands are wide-spread." She sighed, accepting the change of subject, and went on to describe the mansion, its gardens, and the fields filled with wildflowers in the summer. She was talking about a small waterfall when Lucien was distracted by the sight of someone in a dark cloak furtively skirting the left wall of the Horse Guards courtyard. The figure disappeared through the door that led up to the War Office.

Lucien halted, pulling Lady Anne to a standstill beside him. His eyes narrowed. Was it possible? The height and build were right. *Bloody hell.* Had Hatcher the audacity to return to Whitehall?

"Is something wrong?" Lady Anne asked.

"I cannot be sure." He released her arm. "Pardon me, Anne. Wait here, no, better yet, go back to the concert." He took off at a run toward the Whitehall entrance.

• • •

Anne stared after him. Well of all the… How could he just leave her standing there? And when had she given him permission to call her by her Christian name? How infuriating he could be.

She glanced around to see if anyone had witnessed the odd incident and was surprised to find others had returned to the concert, except one couple so engrossed in each other they were paying no attention. If she could slip back inside unnoticed, Lord Ware's peculiar behavior might not become the latest *on-dit*.

Yet, she hesitated. What had he seen? Or had he remembered something urgent? Her annoyance faded as curiosity and then concern took over. Did he need help? Perhaps she could catch him and ask. Anne started to follow and then stopped.

What could *she* do? Would it not be better if she told Lord Sherbourne? Yet, what if it was a matter of little consequence? Then both lords would be annoyed with her…again.

Anne shivered in the cold wind. One thing for certain, she had to get inside somewhere. Her gloved hands were stiffening inside her fur muff. She glanced back at the Banqueting Hall. She *should* return to the concert, but she could already hear the music. Intermission was over, and her late return—alone—would draw avid gossip.

Turning to face the War Office building, Anne lifted her wet hem above the worst of the snow and hurried across the frozen courtyard. She could at least wait for him inside.

Slipping into the building, she stomped the snow from her boots and hugged herself, relieved to be out of the wind. She dispensed with her muff and rubbed her gloved hands together to warm them. Her shivering gradually stopped, and as she looked around, she realized how quiet it was…how dark and empty.

The government offices were closed, and anyone who might have come in for work that day would have gone home hours ago. In the dim light coming in the windows, she could make out a staircase in front of her ascending to the next floor and a dark hallway to her right. Where had Lord Ware gone? Should she stay where she was or try to find him?

Growing uneasy in the prolonged silence, she lit one of several lanterns from a tinderbox she found at the bottom of the stairs. The light made her feel better until it occurred to her that Viscount Ware might have left the building by another door. Was she all alone—in a building where she had no right to be?

A board creaked, then distinct footsteps overhead. Ah, there he was. She clutched the lantern in relief and climbed the steps to meet him, pausing at the top to listen again. She studied the maze of corridors and rooms; most of the doors were closed. Should she call out to him?

Anne let out an exasperated sigh. She felt rather foolish prowling around a government building like this. And it would be comforting to blame Lord Ware, but he hadn't ask for her company or her help. In truth, he had told her to go back. Once again, her innate curiosity had put her in an untenable position…where no lady should be. How absurd for her to have worried when he was fully capable of fending for himself.

Anne started back down the stairs, already making plans in her head to hail a passing hackney and go home before her folly was discovered. She would send a footman to inform Aunt Meg she had left suffering with the headache and then use the extra time to pack for the journey home.

A sharp yell stopped her in mid-step. *Good heavens.* Was he injured or overcome by sudden illness? She ran up the steps, calling, "Lord Ware, where are you?" But the building had grown silent again, and she asked more tentatively, "Is anyone there?"

After a moment, she heard a loud thump...and another. What was happening? Had he dropped something...or fallen? She ran toward the sounds, turned a corner, and dashed through an open door into a workroom filled with desks and shelves.

"Oh mercy!" She clapped a gloved hand against her mouth. Lord Ware and an unknown man were fighting, punching and wrestling, banging against desks, knocking over chairs. "Stop. Stop right now," she shouted. Belatedly realizing the futility of her demand, Anne was astonished when both men looked at her, still clutching one another.

Lord Ware recovered first. "Anne, what are— Take the code letter and run. There, on the floor. Get it to Sherry."

"No!" the stranger snarled. "I shall kill you." He twisted to break free, landing a hard blow on the side of the viscount's head. Ware shook it off and connected with one of his own.

Anne tore her gaze away. *What letter?* Her eyes frantically searched the floor littered with books, papers, and ink wells knocked from the desktops. She shoved aside two chairs and spotted an unfolded letter with columns of symbols, numbers and letters. She picked it up and brought it closer to the lantern. She studied it a moment, but it made little sense. A code, he had said. This must be it.

She held it tight in one hand, grasped the lantern, and took a last glance at the grappling men. Much as she hated to leave the viscount like this, it was what he'd asked of her. *Get Sherry.* She could do that. She spun around, her skirt swirling as she ran toward the door.

Two pistol shots banged in rapid succession. Anne screamed as one thudded into the desk beside her. She jumped back, tripped over a broken chair, and dropped her lantern, plunging the room into shadows.

"Anne, watch out!"

For what? She reached out to break her fall, but a hard body—reeking of sweat and fear—bowled into her, ripping the paper from her hand and spinning her off her feet.

She hit the floor with a hard thud, and the viscount leaped over her to tackle the fleeing man. They went down amongst the shattered furniture. Anne scrambled to a sitting position and gasped in horror at a new danger. Fire flared among the scattered papers and books under the broken lantern. Moving swiftly from paper to paper the flames edged close to the struggling men.

"Fire!" she shouted as they rolled about. "Watch the fire!" Lord Ware sprang into a crouch, clutching the other man's boot to drag him back to safety. The intruder kicked upward with his free boot, catching the viscount on the chin and breaking his hold. The man scuttled backward into the burning debris. His left sleeve caught fire.

At last perceiving his peril, the man yelled—whether in pain or terror, Anne could not say—but he leaped to his feet, swatting at the flames. He shot a wild-eyed look toward Lord Ware, now standing between him and the only exit door, before turning and bolting into the connected office with large windows overlooking the archway's courtyard.

Lord Ware started after him. "Hatcher! Halt, you fool, and let me help you. There is no way out."

But the man kept running, each step fanning the flames. Without breaking stride, he crashed through the large windows. Glass shattered like exploding ice. An eternity passed before his screams abruptly cut off.

Anne covered her face with both hands. "Oh, no, no, no. God help him!" She was vaguely aware Lord Ware had taken off his coat and was beating at the burning papers, but she was too stunned to move until he pulled her up, turning her away from the sight of the gaping window and into his arms.

"Do not look…or think about him," he whispered into her hair. "Are you all right?"

Anne murmured some nonsense that appeared to satisfy him, and he held her until they heard pounding footsteps on the stairs. Lord Ware stepped back, yanking her hood up to shield her face. Lord Sherbourne and several other men carrying lanterns and hats filled with snow burst into the room.

"Where's the fire?" someone asked.

Lucien pointed at the smoldering books and papers, the snow was dumped over them, and the rest was stomped out.

"We heard shots," Sherbourne said. "Is anyone hurt?"

She peered at her gloved hand that had clutched the viscount's arm. It was wet…and red. "My Lord, you are bleeding," she said unsteadily. "He shot you."

"Nothing to speak of."

"I don't agree," Sherry interrupted, shining a lantern over them. "Blood is dripping onto the floor."

They looked down at a red pool forming at their feet. The front of her gown was streaked with a dark stain.

"I have ruined your beautiful gown." Lucien gave her a rueful smile.

She stared at him—disheveled, bruised, and bleeding—and gave a nervous laugh at his remark. "It is of no importance, my lord. Your arm…let me see it."

Then someone said, "Let the doctor through," and the viscount was pulled away.

"Sherry, see to her," Lord Ware said, looking back over the crowd.

Anne started to follow him, but Lord Sherbourne took her arm.

"You need not worry, my lady. I have seen him with far worse injuries. Now, we must get you out of the building. An inquisitive crowd waits below, and Lucien would not want you exposed to gossip. We shall find another way."

She glanced at the office where Ware was half-perched on the corner of the desk, but she nodded at Sherbourne, acknowledging the truth. "Yes, thank you. I would be most grateful for your assistance."

As Lord Sherbourne hurried her through the dark corridors and down a rear staircase, Anne recovered her flagging composure. "What happened to that man? Is he…is he dead?"

"No. Unfortunately for him."

"You need not spare my sensibilities. Tell me the worst."

Lord Sherbourne was still hesitant. "The snow put out the fire and may have softened his fall a bit, but he still suffered a broken leg. I believe he will survive long enough to hang."

"Oh, dear. I am quite sure he deserves it, I know he does, but…" She glanced at Lord Sherbourne. "Who is he?"

"I suppose I can tell you. It will be all over London by morning. His name is Joshia Hatcher, one of Lord Rothe's clerks. He's a French spy, the traitor who stabbed Rothe." Lord Sherbourne unlocked a servants' and delivery door, and they exited into the freezing night. When he stopped and scrutinized her appearance with a frown, she shook out her gown and pushed a straggling lock of hair under her hood. "That's better," he said. "The blood stain is not noticeable on your dark skirt. If you hold your cloak closed over that stained white top, I think we can get you away without notice. Do not acknowledge anyone. We cannot stop to talk." He led her into the courtyard, turning away from the noisy gawkers huddled below the broken windows, and crossed the street. "Ah, I see your aunt and cousin now."

Sherbourne hurried her toward them.

"Anne, where have you been?" Georgina exclaimed, grabbing to hug her, her hand catching Anne's cloak and flipping it open for a brief moment. "Oh, your poor gown. What happened? Did you spill something? Or…" Her eyes went to the scene in front of the archway.

"Hush, my lady." Lord Sherbourne shot a pleading look at Lord John, who quieted Georgina with a hand on her arm. "Miss Hodges-Jones, where is your carriage? Lady Anne needs to go home, and it would be best to save your questions until you are alone."

Aunt Meg appeared confused for a moment. "Are you all right, Anne dear?"

"Yes, Auntie. Truly, I am, but Lord Sherbourne is right. We must go."

"Oh, yes, indeed. Then we shall...all else can wait. The carriage was already ordered and should be waiting."

Lord John stepped forward, having grasped a general idea of the situation. "I shall see them home, Sherbourne. No doubt you need to get back."

"I do. My gratitude, sir." Lord Sherbourne nodded to the ladies, spun on his heels, and moved rapidly toward Whitehall.

Anne drooped with sudden fatigue, allowing herself to be hustled into the carriage and whisked away from the scene. Wishing for nothing but to forget that frightful leap through the windows, she leaned back and closed her eyes.

Georgina's curiosity would not wait. "Annie," she wheedled. "Tell us what happened. Is that blood on your gown?"

Anne opened her eyes. "Yes, not mine but Viscount Ware's." Choosing her words and facts with care, making no mention of the code key, she kept it as short as possible. "And then he just ran through the windows."

Georgina stifled a cry, and Aunt Meg put the back of her hand to her forehead as though she might faint. Even Lord John was taken aback. "He jumped?"

She nodded wearily.

"How frightening. Are you sure you're all right?" Aunt Meg leaned forward and anxiously peered at her.

"Yes, Auntie," she repeated for the third or fourth time.

"But my dear, what possessed you to follow Lord Ware into that building?"

Anne waved a helpless hand, not knowing what to say.

"Do not scold her, Auntie. I think it was brave, exceedingly brave...and thrilling." Georgina's eyes gleamed with fervor. "I wish I had been there."

"You cannot mean that," Aunt Meg protested.

Lord John took Georgina's hand. "Nor can you expect Lady Anne to share your youthful sentiments. I am sure she regrets the impulse—no matter how well intentioned—that put her in danger."

Anne said nothing for she did *not* regret it. She would never say aloud the unladylike thoughts that were sure to scandalize Aunt Meg and maybe Lord John. Nor did she wish to encourage Georgina's reckless tendencies. Regardless, the last few weeks Anne had felt *alive* as never before. Even tonight had been, well, yes, terrifying and horrid, but also…exciting. All of it—the gang of ruffians, the spies, code letters…and, yes, to be perfectly honest, Viscount Ware. She gave a deep sigh. It was an intriguing world that she was leaving behind her. Warwickshire would seem very dull indeed.

Chapter Twenty Four

Lucien sat on the corner of Rothe's desk and frowned at the sting of whiskey poured on the bullet wound. He peered over the heads of the men crowded in the room to confirm Sherry had gotten Lady Anne away. He nodded to himself at their absence. *Good man, his partner.*

"Well, doctor... sorry, I don't recall your name," Lucien said to the well-dressed surgeon tending his arm. He had heard someone say two medical men attending the concert had responded to shouts for assistance. He presumed the other man was with Hatcher.

"Pettigrew. Noah Pettigrew."

"Ah, yes, Pettigrew. I remember now. We met recently in a dark alley."

The doctor gave a brief chuckle, his focus still on Lucien's injury. "Twice, if I'm not mistaken."

"So it was. Nothing so serious this time."

"You are fortunate he was a poor shot," the surgeon remarked. "Another inch, and it would have shattered the bone."

"He had little opportunity to aim," Lucien said dryly. "I was attempting to break his wrist at the moment the gun went off."

The doctor grunted something and set to work bandaging the injury. As he was fastening the last strip in place, they heard loud voices in the outer office. Lucien glanced toward the door and found Rothe pushing his way into the room.

"Ware, how bad is it? I heard you were shot."

"'Twas nothing, my lord. You should not have come."

"And miss this? Not on your life. Where the bloody hell is Hatcher?"

Lucien resisted bringing up the marquess's health. Wise or

not, Rothe had abandoned his sickbed and come to Whitehall to take command.

Which is what he did; a series of firm orders soon cleared most of the building, and even the bystanders in the courtyard were hustled on their way. Joshia Hatcher was located in a ground floor room where another surgeon and two assistants were tending his wounds.

After a glass of whiskey and the surgeon had finished with him, Lucien accompanied Rothe and Sherry downstairs. Rothe brought them to a halt outside Hatcher's make-shift sickroom. "The doctor wants to move him to his surgery," Rothe growled, his eyes steely. "But Hatcher is not leaving Whitehall until I am through questioning him. If the treasonous fellow dies, so be it. It will save us the trouble of hanging him." He threw the door open.

Hatcher was in visible pain. While the snow had put out the flames before he was engulfed, his arm and half his chest were burned and blistered. He was greased with liniment and wrapped in loose bandages. His left leg had shattered under the weight of the fall, and the surgeon had just finished setting the break and bracing it with splints. Hatcher's face was deathly pale and sweaty, his breathing labored. Quite an ordeal, Lucien observed, but he felt little sympathy. The man had shot a pistol at Lady Anne.

Two hours of interrogation later, Rothe was not yet finished. Lucien, Sherbourne, two of the Horse Guards, and the medical people had stayed throughout. Lucien had interjected questions now and then, but Rothe was furious over his clerk's betrayal and insisted on doing most of it.

Hatcher initially refused to talk about his associates, even those already known. As the night wore on, perhaps he realized it no longer mattered, or his tongue was loosened by the small sips of laudanum that Rothe permitted now and then. In any event, he started talking about Notley, describing him as a greedy rotter rather than an agent of France. Hatcher knew of Notley's gambling debts and his contacts with London's underworld. When the cipher was intercepted, and he heard about the house party theft, he paid Notley to obtain the key code by any means he could.

"How did you know Skefton had the cipher?" Lucien demanded. "Even Whitehall didn't know for sure until the colonel arrived in London."

"There was a message slipped under Rothe's door—"

"So it was you! How did you get it?" Rothe interrupted. "Sloane has the only duplicate key."

Hatcher's gave a sly smile. "Saw the messenger near your door. After he left, I looked under it and snagged the letter with the end of a quill pen. It said the cipher was being taken to Colonel Skefton. Then there was the uproar over the housebreaking at that country house, and it wasn't hard to put it together."

"So Notley brought it to you," Rothe said.

"Not right away. He kept it for days, saying he didn't have it yet and needed more blunt to pay off informers. But he was lying all along."

"That's why you killed him."

"Sorted it out, did you?" Hatcher laughed, grimacing at the pain it cost him. The surgeon gave him a sip of water. "Would you not have done the same, Lord Rothe? Betrayal and all that rot?"

Notley had fooled everyone for a while, Lucien mused. The French agents had continued to follow Lucien because they believed the code key was still out there.

"Why kill him at the ball?" Lucien asked. "There are more discreet places."

"His choice, not mine. Once I confronted him with his lies, he avoided me. With good cause, as I could no longer trust him. He even sent the cipher to me by a street boy and then left town. When he returned the night of the ball, I was watching the house and followed him. I found him alone in the library. Someone almost caught me, you know."

"How so?" Lucien tensed, waiting for the answer.

"Never saw him, but he opened the library door just as I slipped into the courtyard."

Lucien relaxed. Hatcher didn't even know it was a woman. Lady Anne's secret was safe.

A sudden knock on the door brought a curse from Rothe. Under-minister Terrell stuck his head inside. "Lord Rothe, when you have a minute…"

"Later," Rothe snapped, but the doctor interceded, pleading that his patient needed a break. Rothe shoved back his chair and stood. "Ten minutes, doctor. That is all you get. And go easy on the medicine. I aim to know everything he knows before the night is over."

Rothe, Lucien and Sherry stepped into the hall.

"What was so important you had to interrupt?" Rothe demanded of Terrell.

"The code paper you had everyone searching for in the snow—"

"Yes, yes. Do you have it?" Rothe asked eagerly.

The under-minister held out a wet scrap of paper. "I'm afraid this is all they found."

A one inch corner, blackened on the edges. The ink on the small piece had been blurred by wet snow. One letter was readable, a G.

Lucien lowered his chin, staring thoughtfully at his boots. So it was gone. Hard to hear the truth, but what else could he expect? The man holding it had been on fire.

"What? This cannot be all." Unable or unwilling to accept it, Rothe frowned. "Are you positive? They searched everywhere?"

"Yes, sir. We went over the area twice."

"Damnation." Rothe stalked off, disappeared up the stairs, and they heard the distant slam of his office door. No one followed him, and the marquess did not return until the ten minute break had lapsed twice over.

The doctor drew Rothe's immediate ire when Hatcher appeared sluggish from additional medicine, but the prisoner was still coherent, and the interrogation resumed. Nor did Hatcher's attitude change, made worse by an irritating drug-induced drawl. He remained unrepentant, even boastful at times.

"I kept it in my desk for a week," Hatcher said smugly. "And worked late at night decoding messages and sending coded reports right under your nose. It was very easy."

"Bollocks! You are a bloody liar." Rothe hit the table with his fist, and Lucien feared he might burst a blood vessel or beat the clerk senseless. "You think we didn't search your desk? It was not there."

"Of course not. I could tell you were suspicious of something, and I moved it."

"To where?"

Hatcher grinned as though he couldn't resist provoking Rothe. "The old file drawer next to Sloane's desk. It was taped to the bottom."

"The devil it was." The marquess slumped in his chair and stared at him.

"You returned tonight to retrieve it," Lucien said flatly.

"Naturally. I could not leave the country and risk its discovery."

"Why not take it the night you stabbed me?" Rothe asked. "You must have had a few minutes alone."

"How was I do know it would be my last opportunity? I came for Wellington's report, and when you returned unexpectedly... well, the rest just happened. I heard Sloane's footsteps in the hall, and I got out of there. If I *had* known, I would have killed you both, taken the cipher, and left for France that night."

Cold but efficient, Lucien thought.

Rothe had heard enough by dawn, and everyone went home. Lucien trudged up the stairs of his townhouse. His arm ached, and his eyes were gritty. Dragging off his boots and clothes, he fell across the bed, hoping to get a few hours of sleep and still call on Lady Anne before she left London. Now that the traitor was caught, she deserved to hear the rest of the story. Of course, he thought before drifting off, it would also be good to know she had suffered no harm from the evening's events.

• • •

Sherbourne swept in and woke Lucien at noon. Talbot was one step behind him, scolding and protesting mightily. "An injured man needs his rest, Lord Sherbourne."

"Never mind, Talbot." Lucien groaned and rolled over, pushing up to sit on the edge of the bed. "You will never change him."

"Change *me*? When did you ever show me the least bit of deference?" Sherry countered, crossing the room, grabbing a pair of clean breeches, and tossing them at Lucien. "Get dressed. Rothe wants us."

"See here, sir." Talbot snatched up the breeches and put them back in the wardrobe, selecting the clothes he preferred and laying them on the end of the bed.

"Now? Today?" Lucien threw off the covers. "Does the man never sleep? What does he want? We caught the traitor, and the cipher is in ashes."

"I am sure he will enlighten us," Sherry said, plopping into a chair before the fire and dangling one leg negligently over the arm. "If we ever get there."

"The viscount is not leaving until his wound is tended, and he has had a proper breakfast." Talbot gave them a black look that brooked no opposition.

Lucien looked at Sherry and shrugged. "Have you eaten?"

It was an hour and a half before they reached Lord Rothe's mansion and learned he had suffered a setback from last night's activities. His wife and doctors had managed to keep him at home but not in bed, and they found him in his study wrapped in a heavy robe. His face was grayer than yesterday, and he scowled when his butler announced them.

"About time. I want a copy of that code, gentlemen. The last name we have left to follow is the French fellow who wrote to Notley. Pagli or Paquet, whatever it was. Find him. Bring me the damn code…or bring me the Frenchman." He stood abruptly, swayed, and caught himself. "Well, what do you say? Yes, it is a risky trip, but I cannot abide the loss of that cipher."

"My lord," Sherry said doubtfully. "We agreed it was not safe to return to France. And now, with Ware injured…"

Rothe looked Lucien over, an unusual glint in his eyes. "He

looks fine to me. Are you refusing my orders?" he asked in a querulous voice.

Lucien and Sherry exchange a quick look. Orders? Rothe was overstepping. They were no longer under official obligations. More to the point, Wellington had pulled them from the Continent because it had become impossibly dangerous. During their final assignment, they had been exposed as British agents and would be shot or captured on sight. At all events, there was little assurance they'd find Paquet or he would have a copy of the cipher. It would be a fool's trip at best.

Hoping for time to sort this out, Lucien told Rothe what he wanted to hear. "Without question, we shall follow orders, sir, but I have urgent business to settle if I am to make such a trip. We could return, in say two hours, to discuss the particulars."

Rothe's scowl returned as though he might object, then he relented. "Very well. Two hours. But you leave for the border by nightfall. I shall send word for Monsieur LePonte to meet you at the usual crossing."

Lucien's misgivings deepened. What was wrong with Rothe?

The moment they were outside the mansion, Sherry blurted, "What the devil, Lucien? Something is off the beam with him. Don't tell me you didn't notice."

"If you mean sending us on a death mission and assigning a dead agent to assist us, then yes, I noticed." Lucien pulled on his gloves and turned toward the carriage. LePonte had been their French connection until he was killed during that final mission.

Sherry looked worried. "LePonte's name could have been a slip of the tongue, I suppose. But the rest…he was unsteady on his feet, his eyes nearly black."

"Yes, the pupils enlarged," Lucien said, thinking how Rothe had looked during those few minutes. "The medicine, I'd say. Opium does that."

"I knew I'd seen it before. We have to talk with his doctors. Rothe is in no condition to be making decisions, not about my life or yours."

"I agree. Doctor Long may offer us the easiest way out of this." Lucien glanced at his watch. "I shall meet you at his house in an hour."

Sherry frowned. "Are you due somewhere? Can it not wait? We must resolve this quickly. Long will need time to do whatever he has to before we see Rothe again."

Lucien sighed, acknowledging the truth of it. Unless Rothe withdrew his order—binding or not—they were bound by loyalty to go to France or appeal to the Prince Regent to intercede. Lucien would not put Rothe in such a position. Nor was he thrilled with the possibility of losing his head to Napoleon's guillotine.

"Of course, Sherry. Doctor Long comes first." After all, the visit to Lady Anne was a mere formality, a courtesy of no great import. If he missed her departure, so be it.

• • •

They found the good doctor spending Sunday afternoon at home with his family. He nodded often as he stood in the hallway and listened to their account of Rothe's behavior. "I think you have the right of it," he said. "A lesser dose is needed. I will confer with the surgeon and apothecary right away." The doctor grabbed his hat and coat and walked out with them.

"I apologize for taking you away from your family," Lucien said, securing his hat against a fierce gust of wind. For a minute all three men were occupied with their hats and scarves.

"Blast this weather," Long muttered. "Don't worry about the family, my lord. It isn't the first time I have been called away, nor will it be the last. A doctor's family has to adapt to such interruptions." He gave a quick smile. "And this shouldn't take long. I intend to be back in time for a roast duck dinner."

Outside Rothe's mansion, Long turned and waved. "Give us a couple of hours. You should find a changed man."

As the coach lurched forward on the uneven pavement, Sherry tilted his head toward Lucien and drawled, "So, what is this pressing business you have?"

"A mere fabrication for Rothe's benefit. However, I do have a stop to make. Can I drop you somewhere?" In truth, Lucien had little hope of getting rid of him. His partner could be far too perceptive—and given to meddling.

"I think I shall tag along. If you've no objection."

Lucien sighed. "As you like."

"Superb." Sherry's eyes lit with an unholy glee. "You may need me to keep her aunt and cousin busy while you say a proper good-bye."

Lucien readjusted his wool scarf and stared outside at the snowy landscape. If Sherry thought he was going to get a response from him, he was sadly mistaken.

• • •

The Barbarys' butler gave a deferential nod and took their coats and hats. "Lord Ware, Lord Sherbourne. Lady Barbary is in the drawing room."

"And Lady Anne?" Lucien asked.

The butler shook his head. "I am sorry, my lord. She is not here."

Ah, well, he was too late. She must be on her way to Warwickshire, not unexpected, considering the hour. He was sorry, nonetheless. It felt as though he had left something unfinished.

"I see. I had hoped to say good-bye."

"Oh, but—" The butler's words were cut off by the outer door opening behind them, letting in a rush of frigid air. "Ah, here they are now."

Lucien turned and smiled at the sight of Lady Anne. Her cheeks were rosy from the cold, and the dark blue pelisse brought out the blue in her eyes.

"Well met, Lord Ware."

"Indeed. I feared we had missed you, my lady. Have you extended your stay?"

Lucien and Sherry stepped aside to allow Lady Anne and Miss St. Clair to divest themselves of their winter garments.

"Only a day. After such a frightful night, and a late morning to recover, we put off our departure until tomorrow. Georgina and I have been making a few final visits."

"Leaving is so hard," Miss St. Clair lamented. "I shall miss our new friends and, well, *everything*."

As the ladies shed their coats, Lucien complimented Lady Anne on her light blue visiting gown and took her arm, leaving Sherry to escort Miss St. Clair. Lady Barbary and Miss Hodges-Jones were deep in conversation and looked up in surprise.

"Gentlemen, how delightful." Lady Barbary turned her smile on Lady Anne. "Thank you for bringing us company to brighten such a cold day."

"I cannot take credit for a happy coincidence. We met in the hallway."

"No less fortunate either way. Please, all of you, sit by the fire and warm yourselves," Lady Barbary urged. "It is dreadfully cold."

Over a fresh tea tray, Lady Anne and Miss St. Clair related the latest gossip they had picked up on their visits. They talked about the concert but said nothing of the extraordinary events at Whitehall. After several minutes, Sherry kept his unsolicited promise by engaging Miss St. Clair and the older ladies in a discussion of Mrs. Radcliffe's latest novel.

Seizing the opportunity, Lucien turned to Lady Anne. "I gather last night is a forbidden topic?"

"Not entirely, but they have decided the less said, the wiser." She gave him a mischievous smile that produced a tiny dimple he had not noticed before. "Aunt Meg is happy I will have a chance to rusticate for a while until the talk dies down."

"Your name is being bandied about?" he asked sharply.

"No, not yet, at least. Aunt Meg believes it will stay that way if we refrain from talking or even thinking about it."

Lucien chuckled. "Are you looking forward to your journey?"

"Seeing my family, of course, but getting there will be a cold and dreary two days. We await reports of the northern roads but plan to leave at dawn."

"Then I am glad for a moment to speak freely before you go. Are you recovered from last night?"

"It was not I who was shot, my lord. I am well. And you, I am amazed to say, look much the same."

"Nearly mended," he said, belying the sharp pain if he moved without caution. "But I did want to talk about last night, to explain what happened and what we've learned since." He gave her a wry smile. "I thought you might be interested."

"Oh, la. Surely you jest. I am keen to hear every detail."

Knowing even Sherry's charm would not keep the other ladies diverted for long, Lucien kept it succinct. Anne's face indicated she understood more than was said.

"I had guessed some of it," she said when he finished. "Fancy, this Hatcher fellow working right in Whitehall." She sighed. "I *am* sorry I did not get the cipher to safety."

"You are not at fault, my lady. Indeed, I beg your pardon for asking you to try. I almost got you shot."

"Oh, no. The blame is not yours. I followed you into the building…unbidden. I very much wanted to help, and…I may have been a bit curious. It is one of my abiding faults." She smiled, showing that dimple again. "I confess it had not occurred to me I might be shot. Regardless, it is a shame the code was destroyed."

"A serious loss to the war effort. Rothe is determined to have it, one way or another. Sherbourne and I may be sent to find another."

"Oh, heavens. To the Continent? Is that not dangerous with the war and all?" She frowned and leaned closer. "I…well, I might be able to help. I had thought to write to you this afternoon." She hesitated, glancing toward her aunt.

"Yes?" he prompted. "I hope you're not suggesting going with us."

"No, nothing like that. You see, I have an ability for recalling things."

"I remember. It was helpful in locating a certain candle," he said with a provocative glance at her relatives. To his knowledge, they were still unaware of her visit to Notley's lodgings.

"Exactly so, but I am certain you will not refer to the incident again," she said. "Not when I am about to do you a great favor." She arched a brow. "Unless you are going to refuse my assistance…again?"

"What are you offering?"

"Last night, I held the cipher, and I inspected it just for a moment—to verify what it was—before it was snatched away by that dreadful man. I recall parts of it. The columns, some sections of symbols, letters, and numbers. Not all, by any means, but perhaps enough to aid your code experts."

"Good heavens, Anne!" In his excitement, he captured her hands in his, drawing the astonished disapproval of everyone in the room—everyone except Sherry, that is, who turned a snicker into a cough.

"My lord, restrain yourself," Aunt Meg admonished. "Your behavior is close to being unseemly."

"No, Auntie." Lady Anne was laughing. "It is all right. You must forgive his lordship. He is just very pleased with your eldest niece."

"Pleased is too mild a word," he said holding her gaze a moment before releasing her hands and turning toward Miss Hodges-Jones. "I beg pardon, ma'am, but Lady Anne has offered to do her country a great service." He nodded at Sherry. "She looked at it. Enough to describe it."

"What? The, uh…the letter?" Sherry asked, searching for the right word to use in the situation.

"Yes. Come along, Sherbourne. We have to see Lord Rothe." Lucien rose and urged Anne toward the door, already calling for their coats. "I promise to have her back before dinner," he called over his shoulder.

"Well, my heavens," Aunt Meg said.

• • •

Lucien took one look at Rothe and knew the doctors had done their work. The marquess's eyes were clear and full of intelligence, his movements purposeful. That was not to say he was yet himself.

As soon as he saw them, he rose and launched into a rambling explanation of why they could not make the proposed trip to France. It was indicative of his inattention that he did not question Lady Anne's presence.

"Returning to France would be a needless risk," he concluded. "I cannot imagine why I suggested it, except the doctors said something about an improper dose of medicine. We shall find someone else to—"

Fearing his new verbosity would go on until curbed, Lucien interrupted. "Pardon me, my lord, but it may not be necessary for anyone to take that risk. Lady Anne Ashburn has come with us to provide some assistance." He introduced them to each other and described her exceptional memory. "She saw the cipher last night, sir. Briefly, I admit, but she believes she can draw parts of it."

Rothe lifted a skeptical brow. "The devil, you say. Uh, pardon the language, my lady, but it does sound unusual."

"Perhaps if I showed you?" she suggested.

Someone produced paper and pen. As Anne drew the dividing columns and cross lines to establish the structure of the key, Rothe moved closer to watch, his eyes widening when she filled in the first letters and symbols. She continued adding marks and characters, and the marquess shouted for someone to send for his best code breakers.

Having no part to play in this, Lucien and Sherbourne stood by the fireplace and watched the scene unfold.

"Lady Anne is something all right." Sherry's voice held admiration.

"Indeed," Lucien agreed. Her ability *was* uncommon. She had held the cipher for mere seconds under terrifying circumstances, and yet she recalled all this with such precision. He must remember never to bet against her at the card table.

"Rothe thinks so too. Look at him. He will want to keep her," Sherry predicted.

Lucien lowered his brows. Sherbourne was right. Rothe would try to recruit her, but Lucien rather hoped she would decline.

He could not wish for her to spend her days confined to a code room, or worse yet, facing the daily challenges and dangers of an intelligence agent.

Shortly after the code breakers arrived, Anne handed her drawing to Lord Rothe. She had filled in a third of the grid. "This is all I can do," she said with regret. "The paper was crumpled and time was short…and, well, truthfully, I am better at recalling people and scenes, such as dancers at a ball, flowers in a garden."

"No apology needed," one of the code breakers interrupted, seizing the drawing from the marquess's hands in his enthusiasm. "Unbelievable! My lady, you may have shortened years of work into one or two, maybe less."

Rothe's smile was all too benevolent. "My dear Lady Anne, you have done a splendid thing for your country today. I could make use of someone with your talent. Shall we meet in my office in the morning, say eleven o'clock?"

Lady Anne gave him a sweet smile as she drew on her gloves. "I am flattered, my lord, and deeply honored, but what you ask is not possible. I leave for home in Warwickshire at dawn. And this," she pointed her chin toward the men working on the cipher, "is just a pastime, I suppose you might say."

"But, Lady Anne," Rothe said.

"No, my lord, you must not protest for I do not like to disoblige you. I am pleased if I was useful today, but my family would surely disown me if I were to take any kind of employment." Her eyes twinkled as she looked up at Lucien. "Are we ready?"

Suppressing a laugh at the expression on Lord Rothe's face, he took her arm. It must have been a long time since anyone had denied the marquess with such grace.

When they stepped out of the Rothe mansion into the crisp, fresh air, the sun had come out, and the sparkling snow turned London into a wonderland, covering all its defects under a blanket of white. Lucien handed Lady Anne into his carriage.

"A fine day it has turned out to be," she said, settling into the cushioned leather seat while he draped a blanket over her lap.

"With such sunshine, my journey home shall not be as gloomy as I feared."

He murmured a polite agreement but not without regret at the thought of her leaving. He had gotten rather used to seeing her. At the Barbary mansion, Sherry discreetly stayed in the carriage while Lucien walked Lady Anne to the front steps.

She turned at the doorway and offered him her hand. "Thank you, Viscount Ware. I am so grateful for all you have done."

"I should be thanking you. You made Rothe a very happy man. At least until you refused to join his staff." He chuckled. "I do have a small token of gratitude." He reached into his pocket and pulled out the silk cloth containing the jewelry she had pawned. "I believe these belong to you and your relatives."

"My lord," she looked at him in astonishment. "Where did you get these?"

"From the pawnshop owner. By happenstance, you were observed, and it aroused my curiosity."

"Oh, dear. I thought I was so careful." Her cheeks flushed prettily. "I am sorry I cannot redeem them at present, my lord."

"There can be no thought of payment. Your country is much in your debt."

"All the same…"

He closed her hands around the small bundle and smiled into her eyes. "It is done, my lady." As she murmured "thank you," he stepped back and bowed over her hand, continuing to hold her frank gaze. "I have enjoyed making your acquaintance and regret we had so little time to talk of much beyond murder, thievery, and secret codes." He surprised himself by adding, "If I find myself in Warwickshire in the future, may I call upon you?"

"Oh, please do." Her smile took on added warmth, the dimple appearing yet again. "But did I not tell you? London has not seen the last of me. I shall return to town in the spring. April, I believe. Aunt Meg has offered to bring my cousin Georgina and me into fashionable society this year. We shall no doubt meet again."

"Splendid. I shall look forward to it." Lucien's smile broadened as he doffed his hat and returned to the carriage. He laughed at Sherry's inquiring look. "It is going to be an interesting Spring, my friend." Yes, indeed, a quite promising London season.

ABOUT THE AUTHOR

After retiring from a legal career with the Juvenile Court System, J.L. Buck published sixteen urban fantasy/paranormal novels. In 2019 she decided to write in the mystery genre she was currently reading and began work on the Viscount Ware Mystery series.

She lives in the Midwest with Latte, a mischievous Siamese cat, who often attempts to co-author her writing by taking over the keyboard. When not writing or running two blogs, Ms Buck enjoys her eight grandchildren and great-grandson, reading (preferably on a sunny deck), travel (USA and abroad from Africa to Europe to the British Isles to Disney World in Florida), and binge-watching any sub-genre of mystery shows.

Ms Buck loves to hear from readers and can be contacted through her website or social media (twitter: @janetlbuck or her fantasy pen name account: @ShieldsAlly)

CPSIA information can be obtained
at www.ICGtesting.com
Printed in the USA
LVHW091508110722
723210LV00021B/170